The Wind in the Willows and Other Stories

The Wind in the Willows and Other Stories

KENNETH GRAHAME

Illustrations by Arthur Rackham

Word Cloud Classics

San Diego

Canterbury Classics
An imprint of Printers Row Publishing Group
10350 Barnes Canyon Road, Suite 100, San Diego, CA 92121
www.canterburyclassicsbooks.com

Printers Row Publishing Group is a division of Readerlink Distribution Services, LLC. The Canterbury Classics and Word Cloud Classics names and logos are registered trademarks of Readerlink Distribution Services, LLC.

All correspondence concerning the content of this book should be addressed to Canterbury Classics, Editorial Department, at the above address.

Publisher: Peter Norton
Associate Publisher: Ana Parker
Publishing/Editorial Team: April Farr, Kelly Larsen, Kathryn C. Dalby
Editorial Team: JoAnn Padgett, Melinda Allman, Dan Mansfield, Traci Douglas
Production Team: Jonathan Lopes, Rusty von Dyl
Cover and endpaper design: Ray Caramanna

Interior illustrations used with permission from the Stapleton Collection/Bridgeman Images.

Library of Congress Cataloging-in-Publication Data

Names: Grahame, Kenneth, 1859-1932, author. | Rackham, Arthur, 1867-1939, illustrator. | Container of (work): Grahame, Kenneth, 1859-1932. Short stories Selections.
Title: The wind in the willows and other stories / Kenneth Grahame ; illustrations by Arthur Rackham.
Description: San Diego, California : Canterbury Classics, [2019] | Series: Word cloud classics | Summary: The escapades of four animal friends who live along a river in the English countryside--Toad, Mole, Rat, and Badger, plus more than two dozen short stories from Grahame's collections The Golden Age (1895) and Dream Days (1898).
Identifiers: LCCN 2018031287 | ISBN 9781684126613 (paperback)
Subjects: | CYAC: Animals--Fiction. | Brothers and sisters--Fiction. | Orphans--Fiction. | Adventure and adventurers--Fiction. | BISAC: FICTION / Classics. | FICTION / Literary. | FICTION / Action & Adventure.
Classification: LCC PZ7.G759 Win 2019 | DDC [Fic]--dc23
LC record available at https://lccn.loc.gov/2018031287

Printed in China

23 22 21 20 19 1 2 3 4 5

CONTENTS

Dream Days

List of Illustrations

The Wind in the Willows

Chapter 1. The River Bank

The Mole had been working very hard all the morning, spring-cleaning his little home. First with brooms, then with dusters; then on ladders and steps and chairs, with a brush and a pail of whitewash; till he had dust in his throat and eyes, and splashes of whitewash all over his black fur, and an aching back and weary arms. Spring was moving in the air above and in the earth below and around him, penetrating even his dark and lowly little house with its spirit of divine discontent and longing. It was small wonder, then, that he suddenly flung down his brush on the floor, said "Bother!" and "O blow!" and also "Hang spring-cleaning!" and bolted out of the house without even waiting to put on his coat. Something up above was calling him imperiously, and he made for the steep little tunnel which answered in his case to the gravelled carriage-drive owned by animals whose residences are nearer to the sun and air. So he scraped and scratched and scrabbled and scrooged and then he scrooged again and scrabbled and scratched and scraped, working busily with his little paws and muttering to himself, "Up we go! Up we go!" till at last, pop! his snout came out into the sunlight, and he found himself rolling in the warm grass of a great meadow.

"This is fine!" he said to himself. "This is better than whitewashing!" The sunshine struck hot on his fur, soft breezes caressed his heated brow, and after the seclusion of the cellarage he had lived in so long the carol of happy birds fell on his dulled hearing almost like a shout. Jumping off all his four legs at once, in the joy of living and the delight of spring without its cleaning, he pursued his way across the meadow till he reached the hedge on the further side.

"Hold up!" said an elderly rabbit at the gap. "Sixpence for the privilege of passing by the private road!" He was bowled over in an instant by the impatient and contemptuous Mole, who trotted along the side of the hedge chaffing the other rabbits as they peeped hurriedly from their holes to see what the row was about. "Onion-sauce! Onion-sauce!" he remarked jeeringly, and was gone before they could think of a thoroughly satisfactory reply. Then they all

"Onion-sauce! Onion-sauce!" he remarked jeeringly, and was gone before they could think of a thoroughly satisfactory reply.

started grumbling at each other. "How *stupid* you are! Why didn't you tell him——" "Well, why didn't *you* say——" "You might have reminded him——" and so on, in the usual way; but, of course, it was then much too late, as is always the case.

It all seemed too good to be true. Hither and thither through the meadows he rambled busily, along the hedgerows, across the copses, finding everywhere birds building, flowers budding, leaves thrusting—everything happy, and progressive, and occupied. And instead of having an uneasy conscience pricking him and whispering "whitewash!" he somehow could only feel how jolly it was to be the only idle dog among all these busy citizens. After all, the best part of a holiday is perhaps not so much to be resting yourself, as to see all the other fellows busy working.

He thought his happiness was complete when, as he meandered aimlessly along, suddenly he stood by the edge of a full-fed river. Never in his life had he seen a river before—this sleek, sinuous, full-bodied animal, chasing and chuckling, gripping things with a gurgle and leaving them with a laugh, to fling itself on fresh playmates that shook themselves free, and were caught and held again. All was a-shake and a-shiver—glints and gleams and sparkles, rustle and swirl, chatter and bubble. The Mole was bewitched, entranced, fascinated. By the side of the river he trotted as one trots, when very small, by the side of a man who holds one spell-bound by exciting stories; and when tired at last, he sat on the bank, while the river still chattered on to him, a babbling procession of the best stories in the world, sent from the heart of the earth to be told at last to the insatiable sea.

As he sat on the grass and looked across the river, a dark hole in the bank opposite, just above the water's edge, caught his eye, and dreamily he fell to considering what a nice snug dwelling-place it would make for an animal with few wants and fond of a bijou riverside residence, above flood level and remote from noise and dust. As he gazed, something bright and small seemed to twinkle down in the heart of it, vanished, then twinkled once more like a tiny star. But it could hardly be a star in such an unlikely situation; and it was too glittering and small for a glow-worm. Then, as he looked, it winked at him, and so declared itself to be an eye; and a small face began gradually to grow up round it, like a frame round a picture.

A brown little face, with whiskers.

A grave round face, with the same twinkle in its eye that had first attracted his notice.

Small neat ears and thick silky hair.

It was the Water Rat!

Then the two animals stood and regarded each other cautiously.

"Hullo, Mole!" said the Water Rat.

"Hullo, Rat!" said the Mole.

"Would you like to come over?" enquired the Rat presently.

"Oh, it's all very well to *talk*," said the Mole, rather pettishly, he being new to a river and riverside life and its ways.

The Rat said nothing, but stooped and unfastened a rope and hauled on it; then lightly stepped into a little boat which the Mole had not observed. It was painted blue outside and white within, and was just the size for two animals; and the Mole's whole heart went out to it at once, even though he did not yet fully understand its uses.

The Rat sculled smartly across and made fast. Then he held up his fore-paw as the Mole stepped gingerly down. "Lean on that!" he said. "Now then, step lively!" and the Mole to his surprise and rapture found himself actually seated in the stern of a real boat.

"This has been a wonderful day!" said he, as the Rat shoved off and took to the sculls again. "Do you know, I've never been in a boat before in all my life."

"What?" cried the Rat, open-mouthed: "Never been in a—you never—well I—what have you been doing, then?"

"Is it so nice as all that?" asked the Mole shyly, though he was quite prepared to believe it as he leant back in his seat and surveyed the cushions, the oars, the rowlocks, and all the fascinating fittings, and felt the boat sway lightly under him.

"Nice? It's the *only* thing," said the Water Rat solemnly, as he leant forward for his stroke. "Believe me, my young friend, there is *nothing*—absolute nothing—half so much worth doing as simply messing about in boats. Simply messing," he went on dreamily: "messing—about—in—boats; messing—"

"Look ahead, Rat!" cried the Mole suddenly.

It was too late. The boat struck the bank full tilt. The dreamer, the joyous oarsman, lay on his back at the bottom of the boat, his heels in the air.

"—about in boats—or *with* boats," the Rat went on composedly, picking himself up with a pleasant laugh. "In or out of 'em, it doesn't matter. Nothing seems really to matter, that's the charm of it. Whether you get away, or whether you don't; whether you arrive at your destination or whether you reach somewhere else, or whether you never get anywhere at all, you're always busy, and you never do anything in particular; and when you've done it there's always something else to do, and you can do it if you like, but you'd much better not. Look here! If you've really nothing else on hand this morning, supposing we drop down the river together, and have a long day of it?"

The Mole waggled his toes from sheer happiness, spread his chest with a sigh of full contentment, and leaned back blissfully into the soft cushions. "*What* a day I'm having!" he said. "Let us start at once!"

"Hold hard a minute, then!" said the Rat. He looped the painter through a ring in his landing-stage, climbed up into his hole above, and after a short interval reappeared staggering under a fat wicker luncheon-basket.

"Shove that under your feet," he observed to the Mole, as he passed it down into the boat. Then he untied the painter and took the sculls again.

"What's inside it?" asked the Mole, wriggling with curiosity.

"There's cold chicken inside it," replied the Rat briefly; "coldtonguecoldhamcoldbeefpickledgherkinssaladfrenchrolls-cresssandwichespottedmeatgingerbeerlemonadesodawater—"

"O stop, stop," cried the Mole in ecstacies: "This is too much!"

"Do you really think so?" enquired the Rat seriously. "It's only what I always take on these little excursions; and the other animals are always telling me that I'm a mean beast and cut it *very* fine!"

The Mole never heard a word he was saying. Absorbed in the new life he was entering upon, intoxicated with the sparkle, the ripple, the scents and the sounds and the sunlight, he trailed a paw in the water and dreamed long waking dreams. The Water Rat, like the good little fellow he was, sculled steadily on and forebore to disturb him.

"I like your clothes awfully, old chap," he remarked after some half an hour or so had passed. "I'm going to get a black velvet smoking-suit myself someday, as soon as I can afford it."

"Shove that under your feet," he observed to the Mole, as he passed it
down into the boat.

"I beg your pardon," said the Mole, pulling himself together with an effort. "You must think me very rude; but all this is so new to me. So—this—is—a—River!"

"*The* River," corrected the Rat.

"And you really live by the river? What a jolly life!"

"By it and with it and on it and in it," said the Rat. "It's brother and sister to me, and aunts, and company, and food and drink, and (naturally) washing. It's my world, and I don't want any other. What it hasn't got is not worth having, and what it doesn't know is not worth knowing. Lord! the times we've had together! Whether in winter or summer, spring or autumn, it's always got its fun and its excitements. When the floods are on in February, and my cellars and basement are brimming with drink that's no good to me, and the brown water runs by my best bedroom window; or again when it all drops away and shows patches of mud that smells like plum-cake, and the rushes and weed clog the channels, and I can potter about dry shod over most of the bed of it and find fresh food to eat, and things careless people have dropped out of boats!"

"But isn't it a bit dull at times?" the Mole ventured to ask. "Just you and the river, and no one else to pass a word with?"

"No one else to—well, I mustn't be hard on you," said the Rat with forbearance. "You're new to it, and of course you don't know. The bank is so crowded nowadays that many people are moving away altogether: O no, it isn't what it used to be, at all. Otters, kingfishers, dabchicks, moorhens, all of them about all day long and always wanting you to *do* something—as if a fellow had no business of his own to attend to!"

"What lies over *there*?" asked the Mole, waving a paw towards a background of woodland that darkly framed the water-meadows on one side of the river.

"That? O, that's just the Wild Wood," said the Rat shortly. "We don't go there very much, we river-bankers."

"Aren't they—aren't they very *nice* people in there?" said the Mole, a trifle nervously.

"W-e-ll," replied the Rat, "let me see. The squirrels are all right. *And* the rabbits—some of 'em, but rabbits are a mixed lot. And then there's Badger, of course. He lives right in the heart of it; wouldn't live anywhere else, either, if you paid him to do it. Dear old Badger! Nobody interferes with *him*. They'd better not," he added significantly.

"Why, who *should* interfere with him?" asked the Mole.

"Well, of course—there—are others," explained the Rat in a hesitating sort of way. "Weasels—and stoats—and foxes—and so on. They're all right in a way—I'm very good friends with them— pass the time of day when we meet, and all that—but they break out sometimes, there's no denying it, and then—well, you can't really trust them, and that's the fact."

The Mole knew well that it is quite against animal-etiquette to dwell on possible trouble ahead, or even to allude to it; so he dropped the subject.

"And beyond the Wild Wood again?" he asked: "Where it's all blue and dim, and one sees what may be hills or perhaps they mayn't, and something like the smoke of towns, or is it only cloud-drift?"

"Beyond the Wild Wood comes the Wide World," said the Rat. "And that's something that doesn't matter, either to you or me. I've never been there, and I'm never going, nor you either, if you've got any sense at all. Don't ever refer to it again, please. Now then! Here's our backwater at last, where we're going to lunch."

Leaving the main stream, they now passed into what seemed at first sight like a little land-locked lake. Green turf sloped down to either edge, brown snaky tree-roots gleamed below the surface of the quiet water, while ahead of them the silvery shoulder and foamy tumble of a weir, arm-in-arm with a restless dripping mill-wheel, that held up in its turn a grey-gabled mill-house, filled the air with a soothing murmur of sound, dull and smothery, yet with little clear voices speaking up cheerfully out of it at intervals. It was so very beautiful that the Mole could only hold up both forepaws and gasp, "O my! O my! O my!"

The Rat brought the boat alongside the bank, made her fast, helped the still awkward Mole safely ashore, and swung out the luncheon-basket. The Mole begged as a favour to be allowed to unpack it all by himself; and the Rat was very pleased to indulge him, and to sprawl at full length on the grass and rest, while his excited friend shook out the table-cloth and spread it, took out all the mysterious packets one by one and arranged their contents in due order, still gasping, "O my! O my!" at each fresh revelation.

*The Mole begged as a favour to be allowed to
unpack it all by himself.*

When all was ready, the Rat said, "Now, pitch in, old fellow!" and the Mole was indeed very glad to obey, for he had started his spring-cleaning at a very early hour that morning, as people *will* do, and had not paused for bite or sup; and he had been through a very great deal since that distant time which now seemed so many days ago.

"What are you looking at?" said the Rat presently, when the edge of their hunger was somewhat dulled, and the Mole's eyes were able to wander off the table-cloth a little.

"I am looking," said the Mole, "at a streak of bubbles that I see travelling along the surface of the water. That is a thing that strikes me as funny."

"Bubbles? Oho!" said the Rat, and chirruped cheerily in an inviting sort of way.

A broad glistening muzzle showed itself above the edge of the bank, and the Otter hauled himself out and shook the water from his coat.

"Greedy beggars!" he observed, making for the provender. "Why didn't you invite me, Ratty?"

"This was an impromptu affair," explained the Rat. "By the way—my friend Mr. Mole."

"Proud, I'm sure," said the Otter, and the two animals were friends forthwith.

"Such a rumpus everywhere!" continued the Otter. "All the world seems out on the river today. I came up this backwater to try and get a moment's peace, and then stumble upon you fellows!—At least—I beg pardon—I don't exactly mean that, you know."

There was a rustle behind them, proceeding from a hedge wherein last year's leaves still clung thick, and a stripy head, with high shoulders behind it, peered forth on them.

"Come on, old Badger!" shouted the Rat.

The Badger trotted forward a pace or two; then grunted, "H'm! Company," and turned his back and disappeared from view.

"That's *just* the sort of fellow he is!" observed the disappointed Rat. "Simply hates Society! Now we shan't see any more of him today. Well, tell us, *who*'s out on the river?"

"Toad's out, for one," replied the Otter. "In his brand-new wager-boat; new togs, new everything!"

The two animals looked at each other and laughed.

"Once, it was nothing but sailing," said the Rat, "Then he tired of that and took to punting. Nothing would please him but to punt all day and every day, and a nice mess he made of it. Last year it was house-boating, and we all had to go and stay with him in his house-boat, and pretend we liked it. He was going to spend the rest of his life in a house-boat. It's all the same, whatever he takes up; he gets tired of it, and starts on something fresh."

"Such a good fellow, too," remarked the Otter reflectively: "But no stability—especially in a boat!"

From where they sat they could get a glimpse of the main stream across the island that separated them; and just then a wager-boat flashed into view, the rower—a short, stout figure—splashing badly and rolling a good deal, but working his hardest. The Rat stood up and hailed him, but Toad—for it was he—shook his head and settled sternly to his work.

"He'll be out of the boat in a minute if he rolls like that," said the Rat, sitting down again.

"Of course he will," chuckled the Otter. "Did I ever tell you that good story about Toad and the lock-keeper? It happened this way. Toad . . ."

An errant May-fly swerved unsteadily athwart the current in the intoxicated fashion affected by young bloods of May-flies seeing life. A swirl of water and a "cloop!" and the May-fly was visible no more.

Neither was the Otter.

The Mole looked down. The voice was still in his ears, but the turf whereon he had sprawled was clearly vacant. Not an Otter to be seen, as far as the distant horizon.

But again there was a streak of bubbles on the surface of the river.

The Rat hummed a tune, and the Mole recollected that animal-etiquette forbade any sort of comment on the sudden disappearance of one's friends at any moment, for any reason or no reason whatever.

"Well, well," said the Rat, "I suppose we ought to be moving. I wonder which of us had better pack the luncheon-basket?" He did not speak as if he was frightfully eager for the treat.

"O, please let me," said the Mole. So, of course, the Rat let him.

Packing the basket was not quite such pleasant work as unpacking the basket. It never is. But the Mole was bent on enjoying everything, and although just when he had got the basket packed and strapped up tightly he saw a plate staring up at him from the grass, and when the job had been done again the Rat pointed out a fork which anybody ought to have seen, and last of all, behold! the mustard pot, which he had been sitting on without knowing it—still, somehow, the thing got finished at last, without much loss of temper.

The afternoon sun was getting low as the Rat sculled gently homewards in a dreamy mood, murmuring poetry-things over to himself, and not paying much attention to Mole. But the Mole was very full of lunch, and self-satisfaction, and pride, and already quite at home in a boat (so he thought) and was getting a bit restless besides: and presently he said, "Ratty! Please, *I* want to row, now!"

The Rat shook his head with a smile. "Not yet, my young friend," he said; "wait till you've had a few lessons. It's not so easy as it looks."

The Mole was quiet for a minute or two. But he began to feel more and more jealous of Rat, sculling so strongly and so easily along, and his pride began to whisper that he could do it every bit as well. He jumped up and seized the sculls, so suddenly, that the Rat, who was gazing out over the water and saying more poetry-things to himself, was taken by surprise and fell backwards off his seat with his legs in the air for the second time, while the triumphant Mole took his place and grabbed the sculls with entire confidence.

"Stop it, you *silly* ass!" cried the Rat, from the bottom of the boat. "You can't do it! You'll have us over!"

The Mole flung his sculls back with a flourish, and made a great dig at the water. He missed the surface altogether, his legs flew up above his head, and he found himself lying on the top of the prostrate Rat. Greatly alarmed, he made a grab at the side of the boat, and the next moment—Sploosh!

Over went the boat, and he found himself struggling in the river.

O my, how cold the water was, and O, how *very* wet it felt. How it sang in his ears as he went down, down, down! How bright and welcome the sun looked as he rose to the surface coughing and spluttering! How black was his despair when he felt himself sinking again! Then a firm paw gripped him by the back of his neck. It was the Rat, and he was evidently laughing—the Mole could *feel* him laughing, right down his arm and through his paw, and so into his—the Mole's—neck.

The Rat got hold of a scull and shoved it under the Mole's arm; then he did the same by the other side of him and, swimming behind, propelled the helpless animal to shore, hauled him out, and set him down on the bank, a squashy, pulpy lump of misery.

When the Rat had rubbed him down a bit, and wrung some of the wet out of him, he said, "Now, then, old fellow! Trot up and down the towing-path as hard as you can, till you're warm and dry again, while I dive for the luncheon-basket."

So the dismal Mole, wet without and ashamed within, trotted about till he was fairly dry, while the Rat plunged into the water again, recovered the boat, righted her and made her fast, fetched his floating property to shore by degrees, and finally dived successfully for the luncheon-basket and struggled to land with it.

When all was ready for a start once more, the Mole, limp and dejected, took his seat in the stern of the boat; and as they set off, he said in a low voice, broken with emotion, "Ratty, my generous friend! I am very sorry indeed for my foolish and ungrateful conduct. My heart quite fails me when I think how I might have lost that beautiful luncheon-basket. Indeed, I have been a complete ass, and I know it. Will you overlook it this once and forgive me, and let things go on as before?"

"That's all right, bless you!" responded the Rat cheerily. "What's a little wet to a Water Rat? I'm more in the water than out of it most days. Don't you think any more about it; and, look here! I really think you had better come and stop with me for a little time. It's very plain and rough, you know—not like Toad's house at all—but you haven't seen that yet; still, I can make you comfortable. And I'll teach you to row, and to swim, and you'll soon be as handy on the water as any of us."

The Mole was so touched by his kind manner of speaking that he could find no voice to answer him; and he had to brush away a tear or two with the back of his paw. But the Rat kindly looked in another direction, and presently the Mole's spirits revived again, and he was even able to give some straight back-talk to a couple of moorhens who were sniggering to each other about his bedraggled appearance.

When they got home, the Rat made a bright fire in the parlour, and planted the Mole in an armchair in front of it, having fetched down a dressing-gown and slippers for him, and told him river stories till supper-time. Very thrilling stories they were, too, to an earth-dwelling animal like Mole. Stories about weirs, and sudden floods, and leaping pike, and steamers that flung hard bottles—at least bottles were certainly flung, and *from* steamers, so presumably *by* them; and about herons, and how particular they were whom they spoke to; and about adventures down drains, and night-fishings with Otter, or excursions far a-field with Badger. Supper was a most cheerful meal; but very shortly afterwards a terribly sleepy Mole had to be escorted upstairs by his considerate host, to the best bedroom, where he soon laid his head on his pillow in great peace and contentment, knowing that his new-found friend the River was lapping the sill of his window.

This day was only the first of many similar ones for the emancipated Mole, each of them longer and full of interest as the ripening summer moved onward. He learnt to swim and to row, and entered into the joy of running water; and with his ear to the reed-stems he caught, at intervals, something of what the wind went whispering so constantly among them.

Chapter 2. The Open Road

Ratty," said the Mole suddenly, one bright summer morning, "if you please, I want to ask you a favour."

The Rat was sitting on the river bank, singing a little song. He had just composed it himself, so he was very taken up with it, and would not pay proper attention to Mole or anything else. Since early morning he had been swimming in the river, in company with his friends the ducks. And when the ducks stood on their heads suddenly, as ducks will, he would dive down and tickle their necks, just under where their chins would be if ducks had chins, till they were forced to come to the surface again in a hurry, spluttering and angry and shaking their feathers at him, for it is impossible to say quite *all* you feel when your head is under water. At last they implored him to go away and attend to his own affairs and leave them to mind theirs. So the Rat went away, and sat on the river bank in the sun, and made up a song about them, which he called

DUCKS' DITTY

All along the backwater,
Through the rushes tall,
Ducks are a-dabbling,
Up tails all!

Ducks' tails, drakes' tails,
Yellow feet a-quiver,
Yellow bills all out of sight
Busy in the river!

Slushy green undergrowth
Where the roach swim—
Here we keep our larder,
Cool and full and dim.

Everyone for what he likes!
We *like to be*
Heads down, tails up,
Dabbling free!

High in the blue above
Swifts whirl and call—
We *are down a-dabbling*
Uptails all!

"I don't know that I think so *very* much of that little song, Rat," observed the Mole cautiously. He was no poet himself and didn't care who knew it; and he had a candid nature.

"Nor don't the ducks neither," replied the Rat cheerfully. "They say, '*Why* can't fellows be allowed to do what they like *when* they like and *as* they like, instead of other fellows sitting on banks and watching them all the time and making remarks and poetry and things about them? What *nonsense* it all is!' That's what the ducks say."

"So it is, so it is," said the Mole, with great heartiness.

"No, it isn't!" cried the Rat indignantly.

"Well then, it isn't, it isn't," replied the Mole soothingly. "But what I wanted to ask you was, won't you take me to call on Mr. Toad? I've heard so much about him, and I do so want to make his acquaintance."

"Why, certainly," said the good-natured Rat, jumping to his feet and dismissing poetry from his mind for the day. "Get the boat out, and we'll paddle up there at once. It's never the wrong time to call on Toad. Early or late he's always the same fellow. Always good-tempered, always glad to see you, always sorry when you go!"

"He must be a very nice animal," observed the Mole, as he got into the boat and took the sculls, while the Rat settled himself comfortably in the stern.

"He is indeed the best of animals," replied Rat. "So simple, so good-natured, and so affectionate. Perhaps he's not very clever—we can't all be geniuses; and it may be that he is both boastful and conceited. But he has got some great qualities, has Toady."

Rounding a bend in the river, they came in sight of a handsome, dignified old house of mellowed red brick, with well-kept lawns reaching down to the water's edge.

"There's Toad Hall," said the Rat; "and that creek on the left, where the notice-board says, 'Private. No landing allowed,' leads to his boat-house, where we'll leave the boat. The stables are over there to the right. That's the banqueting-hall you're looking at now—very old, that is. Toad is rather rich, you know, and this is really one of the nicest houses in these parts, though we never admit as much to Toad."

They glided up the creek, and the Mole shipped his sculls as they passed into the shadow of a large boat-house. Here they saw many handsome boats, slung from the cross beams or hauled up on a slip, but none in the water; and the place had an unused and a deserted air.

The Rat looked around him. "I understand," said he. "Boating is played out. He's tired of it, and done with it. I wonder what new fad he has taken up now? Come along and let's look him up. We shall hear all about it quite soon enough."

They disembarked, and strolled across the gay flower-decked lawns in search of Toad, whom they presently happened upon resting in a wicker garden-chair, with a pre-occupied expression of face, and a large map spread out on his knees.

"Hooray!" he cried, jumping up on seeing them, "this is splendid!" He shook the paws of both of them warmly, never waiting for an introduction to the Mole. "How *kind* of you!" he went on, dancing round them. "I was just going to send a boat down the river for you, Ratty, with strict orders that you were to be fetched up here at once, whatever you were doing. I want you badly—both of you. Now what will you take? Come inside and have something! You don't know how lucky it is, your turning up just now!"

"Let's sit quiet a bit, Toady!" said the Rat, throwing himself into an easy chair, while the Mole took another by the side of him and made some civil remark about Toad's "delightful residence."

"Finest house on the whole river," cried Toad boisterously. "Or anywhere else, for that matter," he could not help adding.

Here the Rat nudged the Mole. Unfortunately the Toad saw him do it, and turned very red. There was a moment's painful silence. Then Toad burst out laughing. "All right, Ratty," he said. "It's only my way, you know. And it's not such a very bad house, is it? You know you rather like it yourself. Now, look here. Let's be sensible. You are the very animals I wanted. You've got to help me. It's most important!"

"It's about your rowing, I suppose," said the Rat, with an innocent air. "You're getting on fairly well, though you splash a good bit still. With a great deal of patience, and any quantity of coaching, you may—"

"O, pooh! boating!" interrupted the Toad, in great disgust. "Silly boyish amusement. I've given that up *long* ago. Sheer waste of time, that's what it is. It makes me downright sorry to see you fellows, who ought to know better, spending all your energies in that aimless manner. No, I've discovered the real thing, the only genuine occupation for a lifetime. I propose to devote the remainder of mine to it, and can only regret the wasted years that lie behind me, squandered in trivialities. Come with me, dear Ratty, and your amiable friend also, if he will be so very good, just as far as the stable-yard, and you shall see what you shall see!"

He led the way to the stable-yard accordingly, the Rat following with a most mistrustful expression; and there, drawn out of the coach-house into the open, they saw a gypsy caravan, shining with newness, painted a canary-yellow picked out with green, and red wheels.

"There you are!" cried the Toad, straddling and expanding himself. "There's real life for you, embodied in that little cart. The open road, the dusty highway, the heath, the common, the hedgerows, the rolling downs! Camps, villages, towns, cities! Here today, up and off to somewhere else tomorrow! Travel, change, interest, excitement! The whole world before you, and a horizon that's always changing! And mind! this is the very finest cart of its sort that was ever built, without any exception. Come inside and look at the arrangements. Planned 'em all myself, I did!"

The Mole was tremendously interested and excited, and followed him eagerly up the steps and into the interior of the caravan. The Rat only snorted and thrust his hands deep into his pockets, remaining where he was.

It was indeed very compact and comfortable. Little sleeping bunks—a little table that folded up against the wall—a cooking-stove, lockers, bookshelves, a bird-cage with a bird in it; and pots, pans, jugs and kettles of every size and variety.

"All complete!" said the Toad triumphantly, pulling open a locker. "You see—biscuits, potted lobster, sardines—everything you can possibly want. Soda-water here—baccy there—letter-paper, bacon, jam, cards and dominoes—you'll find," he continued, as they descended the steps again, "you'll find that nothing whatever has been forgotten, when we make our start this afternoon."

"I beg your pardon," said the Rat slowly, as he chewed a straw, "but did I overhear you say something about '*we*,' and '*start*,' and '*this afternoon*'?"

"Now, you dear good old Ratty," said Toad, imploringly, "don't begin talking in that stiff and sniffy sort of way, because you know you've *got* to come. I can't possibly manage without you, so please consider it settled, and don't argue—it's the one thing I can't stand. You surely don't mean to stick to your dull fusty old river all your life, and just live in a hole in a bank, and *boat*? I want to show you the world! I'm going to make an *animal* of you, my boy!"

"I don't care," said the Rat, doggedly. "I'm not coming, and that's flat. And I *am* going to stick to my old river, *and* live in a hole, *and* boat, as I've always done. And what's more, Mole's going to stick to me and do as I do, aren't you, Mole?"

"Of course I am," said the Mole, loyally. "I'll always stick to you, Rat, and what you say is to be—has got to be. All the same, it sounds as if it might have been—well, rather fun, you know!" he added, wistfully. Poor Mole! The Life Adventurous was so new a thing to him, and so thrilling; and this fresh aspect of it was so tempting; and he had fallen in love at first sight with the canary-coloured cart and all its little fitments.

The Rat saw what was passing in his mind, and wavered. He hated disappointing people, and he was fond of the Mole, and would do almost anything to oblige him. Toad was watching both of them closely.

"Come along in, and have some lunch," he said, diplomatically, "and we'll talk it over. We needn't decide anything in a hurry. Of course, *I* don't really care. I only want to give pleasure to you fellows. 'Live for others!' That's my motto in life."

During luncheon—which was excellent, of course, as everything at

Toad Hall always was—the Toad simply let himself go. Disregarding the Rat, he proceeded to play upon the inexperienced Mole as on a harp. Naturally a voluble animal, and always mastered by his imagination, he painted the prospects of the trip and the joys of the open life and the roadside in such glowing colours that the Mole could hardly sit in his chair for excitement. Somehow, it soon seemed taken for granted by all three of them that the trip was a settled thing; and the Rat, though still unconvinced in his mind, allowed his good-nature to over-ride his personal objections. He could not bear to disappoint his two friends, who were already deep in schemes and anticipations, planning out each day's separate occupation for several weeks ahead.

When they were quite ready, the now triumphant Toad led his companions to the paddock and set them to capture the old grey horse, who, without having been consulted, and to his own extreme annoyance, had been told off by Toad for the dustiest job in this dusty expedition. He frankly preferred the paddock, and took a deal of catching. Meantime Toad packed the lockers still tighter with necessaries, and hung nosebags, nets of onions, bundles of hay, and baskets from the bottom of the cart. At last the horse was caught and harnessed, and they set off, all talking at once, each animal either trudging by the side of the cart or sitting on the shaft, as the humour took him. It was a golden afternoon. The smell of the dust they kicked up was rich and satisfying; out of thick orchards on either side the road, birds called and whistled to them cheerily; good-natured wayfarers, passing them, gave them "Good-day," or stopped to say nice things about their beautiful cart; and rabbits, sitting at their front doors in the hedgerows, held up their fore-paws, and said, "O my! O my! O my!"

Late in the evening, tired and happy and miles from home, they drew up on a remote common far from habitations, turned the horse loose to graze, and ate their simple supper sitting on the grass by the side of the cart. Toad talked big about all he was going to do in the days to come, while stars grew fuller and larger all around them, and a yellow moon, appearing suddenly and silently from nowhere in particular, came to keep them company and listen to their talk. At last they turned in to their little bunks in the cart; and Toad, kicking out his legs, sleepily said, "Well, good-night, you fellows! This is the real life for a gentleman! Talk about your old river!"

It was a golden afternoon. The smell of the dust they kicked up was rich and satisfying.

"I *don't* talk about my river," replied the patient Rat. "You *know* I don't, Toad. But I *think* about it," he added pathetically, in a lower tone: "I think about it—all the time!"

The Mole reached out from under his blanket, felt for the Rat's paw in the darkness, and gave it a squeeze. "I'll do whatever you like, Ratty," he whispered. "Shall we run away tomorrow morning, quite early—*very* early—and go back to our dear old hole on the river?"

"No, no, we'll see it out," whispered back the Rat. "Thanks awfully, but I ought to stick by Toad till this trip is ended. It wouldn't be safe for him to be left to himself. It won't take very long. His fads never do. Good night!"

The end was indeed nearer than even the Rat suspected.

After so much open air and excitement the Toad slept very soundly, and no amount of shaking could rouse him out of bed next morning. So the Mole and Rat turned to, quietly and manfully, and while the Rat saw to the horse, and lit a fire, and cleaned last night's cups and platters, and got things ready for breakfast, the Mole trudged off to the nearest village, a long way off, for milk and eggs and various necessaries the Toad had, of course, forgotten to provide. The hard work had all been done, and the two animals were resting, thoroughly exhausted, by the time Toad appeared on the scene, fresh and gay, remarking what a pleasant easy life it was they were all leading now, after the cares and worries and fatigues of housekeeping at home.

They had a pleasant ramble that day over grassy downs and along narrow by-lanes, and camped as before, on a common, only this time the two guests took care that Toad should do his fair share of work. In consequence, when the time came for starting next morning, Toad was by no means so rapturous about the simplicity of the primitive life, and indeed attempted to resume his place in his bunk, whence he was hauled by force. Their way lay, as before, across country by narrow lanes, and it was not till the afternoon that they came out on the high-road, their first high-road; and there disaster, fleet and unforeseen, sprang out on them—disaster momentous indeed to their expedition, but simply overwhelming in its effect on the after-career of Toad.

They were strolling along the high-road easily, the Mole by the horse's head, talking to him, since the horse had complained that he was being frightfully left out of it, and nobody considered him in the least; the Toad and the Water Rat walking behind the cart talking together—at least Toad was talking, and Rat was saying at intervals, "Yes, precisely; and what did *you* say to *him*?"—and thinking all the time of something very different, when far behind them they heard a faint warning hum; like the drone of a distant bee. Glancing back, they saw a small cloud of dust, with a dark centre of energy, advancing on them at incredible speed, while from out the dust a faint "Poop-poop!" wailed like an uneasy animal in pain. Hardly regarding it, they turned to resume their conversation, when in an instant (as it seemed) the peaceful scene was changed, and with a blast of wind and a whirl of sound that made them jump for the nearest ditch, It was on them! The "Poop-poop" rang with a brazen shout in their ears, they had a moment's glimpse of an interior of glittering plate-glass and rich morocco, and the magnificent motor-car, immense, breath-snatching, passionate, with its pilot tense and hugging his wheel, possessed all earth and air for the fraction of a second, flung an enveloping cloud of dust that blinded and enwrapped them utterly, and then dwindled to a speck in the far distance, changed back into a droning bee once more.

The old grey horse, dreaming, as he plodded along, of his quiet paddock, in a new raw situation such as this simply abandoned himself to his natural emotions. Rearing, plunging, backing steadily, in spite of all the Mole's efforts at his head, and all the Mole's lively language directed at his better feelings, he drove the cart backwards towards the deep ditch at the side of the road. It wavered an instant—then there was a heartrending crash—and the canary-coloured cart, their pride and their joy, lay on its side in the ditch, an irredeemable wreck.

The Rat danced up and down in the road, simply transported with passion. "You villains!" he shouted, shaking both fists, "You scoundrels, you highwaymen, you—you—roadhogs!—I'll have the law of you! I'll report you! I'll take you through all the Courts!" His home-sickness had quite slipped away from him, and for the moment he was the skipper of the canary-coloured vessel driven on a shoal by the reckless jockeying of rival mariners, and he was trying to recollect all the fine and biting things he used to say to masters of steam-launches when their wash, as they drove too near the bank, used to flood his parlour-carpet at home.

Toad sat straight down in the middle of the dusty road, his legs stretched out before him, and stared fixedly in the direction of the disappearing motor-car. He breathed short, his face wore a placid satisfied expression, and at intervals he faintly murmured "Poop-poop!"

The Mole was busy trying to quiet the horse, which he succeeded in doing after a time. Then he went to look at the cart, on its side in the ditch. It was indeed a sorry sight. Panels and windows smashed, axles hopelessly bent, one wheel off, sardine-tins scattered over the wide world, and the bird in the bird-cage sobbing pitifully and calling to be let out.

The Rat came to help him, but their united efforts were not sufficient to right the cart. "Hi! Toad!" they cried. "Come and bear a hand, can't you!"

The Toad never answered a word, or budged from his seat in the road; so they went to see what was the matter with him. They found him in a sort of a trance, a happy smile on his face, his eyes still fixed on the dusty wake of their destroyer. At intervals he was still heard to murmur "Poop-poop!"

The Rat shook him by the shoulder. "Are you coming to help us, Toad?" he demanded sternly.

"Glorious, stirring sight!" murmured Toad, never offering to move. "The poetry of motion! The *real* way to travel! The *only* way to travel! Here today—in next week tomorrow! Villages skipped, towns and cities jumped—always somebody else's horizon! O bliss! O poop-poop! O my! O my!"

"O *stop* being an ass, Toad!" cried the Mole despairingly.

"And to think I never *knew*!" went on the Toad in a dreamy monotone. "All those wasted years that lie behind me, I never knew, never even *dreamt*! But *now*—but now that I know, now that I fully realise! O what a flowery track lies spread before me, henceforth! What dust-clouds shall spring up behind me as I speed on my reckless way! What carts I shall fling carelessly into the ditch in the wake of my magnificent onset! Horrid little carts—common carts— canary-coloured carts!"

"What are we to do with him?" asked the Mole of the Water Rat.

"Nothing at all," replied the Rat firmly. "Because there is really nothing to be done. You see, I know him from of old. He is now possessed. He has got a new craze, and it always takes him that way, in its first stage. He'll continue like that for days now, like an animal walking in a happy dream, quite useless for all practical purposes. Never mind him. Let's go and see what there is to be done about the cart."

A careful inspection showed them that, even if they succeeded in righting it by themselves, the cart would travel no longer. The axles were in a hopeless state, and the missing wheel was shattered into pieces.

The Rat knotted the horse's reins over his back and took him by the head, carrying the bird-cage and its hysterical occupant in the other hand. "Come on!" he said grimly to the Mole. "It's five or six miles to the nearest town, and we shall just have to walk it. The sooner we make a start the better."

"But what about Toad?" asked the Mole anxiously, as they set off together. "We can't leave him here, sitting in the middle of the road by himself, in the distracted state he's in! It's not safe. Supposing another Thing were to come along?"

"O, *bother* Toad," said the Rat savagely; "I've done with him!"

They had not proceeded very far on their way, however, when there was a pattering of feet behind them, and Toad caught them up and thrust a paw inside the elbow of each of them; still breathing short and staring into vacancy.

"Now, look here, Toad!" said the Rat sharply: "as soon as we get to the town, you'll have to go straight to the police-station, and see if they know anything about that motor-car and who it belongs to, and lodge a complaint against it. And then you'll have to go to a blacksmith's or a wheelwright's and arrange for the cart to be fetched and mended and put to rights. It'll take time, but it's not quite a hopeless smash. Meanwhile, the Mole and I will go to an inn and find comfortable rooms where we can stay till the cart's ready, and till your nerves have recovered their shock."

"Police-station! Complaint!" murmured Toad dreamily. "Me *complain* of that beautiful, that heavenly vision that has been vouchsafed me! *Mend the cart*! I've done with carts forever. I never want to see the cart, or to hear of it, again. O, Ratty! You can't think how obliged I am to you for consenting to come on this trip! I wouldn't have gone without you, and then I might never have seen that—that swan, that sunbeam, that thunderbolt! I might never have heard that entrancing sound, or smelt that bewitching smell! I owe it all to you, my best of friends!"

The Rat turned from him in despair. "You see what it is?" he said to the Mole, addressing him across Toad's head: "He's quite hopeless. I give it up—when we get to the town we'll go to the railway station, and with luck we may pick up a train there that'll get us back to river bank tonight. And if ever you catch me going a-pleasuring with this provoking animal again!"—He snorted, and during the rest of that weary trudge addressed his remarks exclusively to Mole.

On reaching the town they went straight to the station and deposited Toad in the second-class waiting-room, giving a porter twopence to keep a strict eye on him. They then left the horse at an inn stable, and gave what directions they could about the cart and its contents. Eventually, a slow train having landed them at a station not very far from Toad Hall, they escorted the spell-bound, sleep-walking Toad to his door, put him inside it, and instructed his housekeeper to feed him, undress him, and put him to bed. Then they got out their boat from the boat-house, sculled down the river home, and at a very late hour sat down to supper in their own cosy riverside parlour, to the Rat's great joy and contentment.

The following evening the Mole, who had risen late and taken things very easy all day, was sitting on the bank fishing, when the Rat, who had been looking up his friends and gossiping, came strolling along to find him. "Heard the news?" he said. "There's nothing else being talked about, all along the river bank. Toad went up to Town by an early train this morning. And he has ordered a large and very expensive motor-car."

Chapter 3. The Wild Wood

The Mole had long wanted to make the acquaintance of the Badger. He seemed, by all accounts, to be such an important personage and, though rarely visible, to make his unseen influence felt by everybody about the place. But whenever the Mole mentioned his wish to the Water Rat he always found himself put off. "It's all right," the Rat would say. "Badger'll turn up some day or other—he's always turning up—and then I'll introduce you. The best of fellows! But you must not only take him *as* you find him, but *when* you find him."

"Couldn't you ask him here—dinner or something?" said the Mole.

"He wouldn't come," replied the Rat simply. "Badger hates Society, and invitations, and dinner, and all that sort of thing."

"Well, then, supposing we go and call on *him*?" suggested the Mole.

"O, I'm sure he wouldn't like that at *all*," said the Rat, quite alarmed. "He's so very shy, he'd be sure to be offended. I've never even ventured to call on him at his own home myself, though I know him so well. Besides, we can't. It's quite out of the question, because he lives in the very middle of the Wild Wood."

"Well, supposing he does," said the Mole. "You told me the Wild Wood was all right, you know."

"O, I know, I know, so it is," replied the Rat evasively. "But I think we won't go there just now. Not *just* yet. It's a long way, and he wouldn't be at home at this time of year anyhow, and he'll be coming along someday, if you'll wait quietly."

The Mole had to be content with this. But the Badger never came along, and every day brought its amusements, and it was not till summer was long over, and cold and frost and miry ways kept them much indoors, and the swollen river raced past outside their windows with a speed that mocked at boating of any sort or kind, that he found his thoughts dwelling again with much persistence on the solitary grey Badger, who lived his own life by himself, in his hole in the middle of the Wild Wood.

In the winter time the Rat slept a great deal, retiring early and rising late. During his short day he sometimes scribbled poetry or did other small domestic jobs about the house; and, of course, there were always animals dropping in for a chat, and consequently there was a good deal of story-telling and comparing notes on the past summer and all its doings.

Such a rich chapter it had been, when one came to look back on it all! With illustrations so numerous and so very highly coloured! The pageant of the river bank had marched steadily along, unfolding itself in scene-pictures that succeeded each other in stately procession. Purple loosestrife arrived early, shaking luxuriant tangled locks along the edge of the mirror whence its own face laughed back at it. Willow-herb, tender and wistful, like a pink sunset cloud, was not slow to follow. Comfrey, the purple hand-in-hand with the white, crept forth to take its place in the line; and at last one morning the diffident and delaying dog-rose stepped delicately on the stage, and one knew, as if string-music had announced it in stately chords that strayed into a gavotte, that June at last was here. One member of the company was still awaited; the shepherd-boy for the nymphs to woo, the knight for whom the ladies waited at the window, the prince that was to kiss the sleeping summer back to life and love. But when meadow-sweet, debonair and odorous in amber jerkin, moved graciously to his place in the group, then the play was ready to begin.

And what a play it had been! Drowsy animals, snug in their holes while wind and rain were battering at their doors, recalled still keen mornings, an hour before sunrise, when the white mist, as yet undispersed, clung closely along the surface of the water; then the shock of the early plunge, the scamper along the bank, and the radiant transformation of earth, air, and water, when suddenly the sun was with them again, and grey was gold and colour was born and sprang out of the earth once more. They recalled the languorous siesta of hot mid-day, deep in green undergrowth, the sun striking through in tiny golden shafts and spots; the boating and bathing of the afternoon, the rambles along dusty lanes and through yellow cornfields; and the long, cool evening at last, when so many threads were gathered up, so many friendships rounded, and so many adventures planned for the morrow. There was plenty to talk about on those short winter days when the animals found themselves round the fire; still, the Mole had a good deal of spare time on his hands, and so one afternoon, when the Rat in his armchair before the blaze was alternately dozing and trying over rhymes that wouldn't fit, he formed the resolution to go out by himself and explore the Wild Wood, and perhaps strike up an acquaintance with Mr. Badger.

It was a cold, still afternoon with a hard, steely sky overhead when he slipped out of the warm parlour into the open air. The country lay bare and entirely leafless around him, and he thought that he had never seen so far and so intimately into the insides of things as on that winter day when Nature was deep in her annual slumber and seemed to have kicked the clothes off. Copses, dells, quarries, and all hidden places, which had been mysterious mines for exploration in leafy summer, now exposed themselves and their secrets pathetically, and seemed to ask him to overlook their shabby poverty for a while, till they could riot in rich masquerade as before, and trick and entice him with the old deceptions. It was pitiful in a way, and yet cheering—even exhilarating. He was glad that he liked the country undecorated, hard, and stripped of its finery. He had got down to the bare bones of it, and they were fine and strong and simple. He did not want the warm clover and the play of seeding grasses; the screens of quickset, the billowy drapery of beech and elm seemed best away; and with great cheerfulness of spirit he pushed on towards the Wild Wood, which lay before him low and threatening, like a black reef in some still southern sea.

There was nothing to alarm him at first entry. Twigs crackled under his feet, logs tripped him, funguses on stumps resembled caricatures, and startled him for the moment by their likeness to something familiar and far away; but that was all fun, and exciting. It led him on, and he penetrated to where the light was less, and trees crouched nearer and nearer, and holes made ugly mouths at him on either side.

Everything was very still now. The dusk advanced on him steadily, rapidly, gathering in behind and before; and the light seemed to be draining away like flood-water.

Then the faces began.

It was over his shoulder, and indistinctly, that he first thought he saw a face; a little evil wedge-shaped face, looking out at him from a hole. When he turned and confronted it, the thing had vanished.

He quickened his pace, telling himself cheerfully not to begin imagining things, or there would be simply no end to it. He passed another hole, and another, and another; and then—yes!—no!—yes! certainly a little narrow face, with hard eyes, had flashed up for an instant from a hole, and was gone. He hesitated—braced himself up for an effort and strode on. Then suddenly, and as if it had been so all the time, every hole, far and near, and there were hundreds of them, seemed to possess its face, coming and going rapidly, all fixing on him glances of malice and hatred: all hard-eyed and evil and sharp.

If he could only get away from the holes in the banks, he thought, there would be no more faces. He swung off the path and plunged into the untrodden places of the wood.

Then the whistling began.

Very faint and shrill it was, and far behind him, when first he heard it; but somehow it made him hurry forward. Then, still very faint and shrill, it sounded far ahead of him, and made him hesitate and want to go back. As he halted in indecision it broke out on either side, and seemed to be caught up and passed on throughout the whole length of the wood to its farthest limit. They were up and alert and ready, evidently, whoever they were! And he—he was alone, and unarmed, and far from any help; and the night was closing in.

Then the pattering began.

He thought it was only falling leaves at first, so slight and delicate was the sound of it. Then as it grew it took a regular rhythm, and he knew it for nothing else but the pat-pat-pat of little feet still a very long way off. Was it in front or behind? It seemed to be first one, and then the other, then both. It grew and it multiplied, till from every quarter as he listened anxiously, leaning this way and that, it seemed to be closing in on him. As he stood still to hearken, a rabbit came running hard towards him through the trees. He waited, expecting it to slacken pace, or to swerve from him into a different course. Instead, the animal almost brushed him as it dashed past, his face set and hard, his eyes staring. "Get out of this, you fool, get out!" the Mole heard him mutter as he swung round a stump and disappeared down a friendly burrow.

The pattering increased till it sounded like sudden hail on the dry leaf-carpet spread around him. The whole wood seemed running now, running hard, hunting, chasing, closing in round something or—somebody? In panic, he began to run too, aimlessly, he knew not whither. He ran up against things, he fell over things and into things, he darted under things and dodged round things. At last he took refuge in the deep, dark hollow of an old beech tree, which offered shelter, concealment—perhaps even safety, but who could tell? Anyhow, he was too tired to run any further, and could only snuggle down into the dry leaves which had drifted into the hollow and hope he was safe for a time. And as he lay there panting and trembling, and listened to the whistlings and the patterings outside, he knew it at last, in all its fullness, that dread thing which other little dwellers in field and hedgerow had encountered here, and known as their darkest moment—that thing which the Rat had vainly tried to shield him from—the Terror of the Wild Wood!

Meantime the Rat, warm and comfortable, dozed by his fireside. His paper of half-finished verses slipped from his knee, his head fell back, his mouth opened, and he wandered by the verdant banks of dream-rivers. Then a coal slipped, the fire crackled and sent up a spurt of flame, and he woke with a start. Remembering what he had been engaged upon, he reached down to the floor for his verses, pored over them for a minute, and then looked round for the Mole to ask him if he knew a good rhyme for something or other.

But the Mole was not there.

He listened for a time. The house seemed very quiet.

Then he called "Moly!" several times, and, receiving no answer, got up and went out into the hall.

The Mole's cap was missing from its accustomed peg. His goloshes, which always lay by the umbrella-stand, were also gone.

The Rat left the house, and carefully examined the muddy surface of the ground outside, hoping to find the Mole's tracks. There they were, sure enough. The goloshes were new, just bought for the winter, and the pimples on their soles were fresh and sharp. He could see the imprints of them in the mud, running along straight and purposeful, leading direct to the Wild Wood.

The Rat looked very grave, and stood in deep thought for a minute or two. Then he re-entered the house, strapped a belt round his waist, shoved a brace of pistols into it, took up a stout cudgel that stood in a corner of the hall, and set off for the Wild Wood at a smart pace.

It was already getting towards dusk when he reached the first fringe of trees and plunged without hesitation into the wood, looking anxiously on either side for any sign of his friend. Here and there wicked little faces popped out of holes, but vanished immediately at sight of the valorous animal, his pistols, and the great ugly cudgel in his grasp; and the whistling and pattering, which he had heard quite plainly on his first entry, died away and ceased, and all was very still. He made his way manfully through the length of the wood, to its furthest edge; then, forsaking all paths, he set himself to traverse it, laboriously working over the whole ground, and all the time calling out cheerfully, "Moly, Moly, Moly! Where are you? It's me—it's old Rat!"

He had patiently hunted through the wood for an hour or more, when at last to his joy he heard a little answering cry. Guiding himself by the sound, he made his way through the gathering darkness to the foot of an old beech tree, with a hole in it, and from out of the hole came a feeble voice, saying "Ratty! Is that really you?"

The Rat crept into the hollow, and there he found the Mole, exhausted and still trembling. "O Rat!" he cried, "I've been so frightened, you can't think!"

"O, I quite understand," said the Rat soothingly. "You shouldn't really have gone and done it, Mole. I did my best to keep you from it. We river-bankers, we hardly ever come here by ourselves. If we have to come, we come in couples, at least; then we're generally all right. Besides, there are a hundred things one has to know, which we understand all about and you don't, as yet. I mean passwords, and signs, and sayings which have power and effect, and plants you carry in your pocket, and verses you repeat, and dodges and tricks you practise; all simple enough when you know them, but they've got to be known if you're small, or you'll find yourself in trouble. Of course if you were Badger or Otter, it would be quite another matter."

"Surely the brave Mr. Toad wouldn't mind coming here by himself, would he?" inquired the Mole.

"Old Toad?" said the Rat, laughing heartily. "He wouldn't show his face here alone, not for a whole hatful of golden guineas, Toad wouldn't."

The Mole was greatly cheered by the sound of the Rat's careless laughter, as well as by the sight of his stick and his gleaming pistols, and he stopped shivering and began to feel bolder and more himself again.

"Now then," said the Rat presently, "we really must pull ourselves together and make a start for home while there's still a little light left. It will never do to spend the night here, you understand. Too cold, for one thing."

"Dear Ratty," said the poor Mole, "I'm dreadfully sorry, but I'm simply dead beat and that's a solid fact. You *must* let me rest here a while longer, and get my strength back, if I'm to get home at all."

"O, all right," said the good-natured Rat, "rest away. It's pretty nearly pitch dark now, anyhow; and there ought to be a bit of a moon later."

So the Mole got well into the dry leaves and stretched himself out, and presently dropped off into sleep, though of a broken and troubled sort; while the Rat covered himself up, too, as best he might, for warmth, and lay patiently waiting, with a pistol in his paw.

When at last the Mole woke up, much refreshed and in his usual spirits, the Rat said, "Now then! I'll just take a look outside and see if everything's quiet, and then we really must be off."

He went to the entrance of their retreat and put his head out. Then the Mole heard him saying quietly to himself, "Hullo! hullo! here—*is*—a—go!"

"What's up, Ratty?" asked the Mole.

"*Snow* is up," replied the Rat briefly; "or rather, *down*. It's snowing hard."

The Mole came and crouched beside him, and, looking out, saw the wood that had been so dreadful to him in quite a changed aspect. Holes, hollows, pools, pitfalls, and other black menaces to the wayfarer were vanishing fast, and a gleaming carpet of faery was springing up everywhere, that looked too delicate to be trodden upon by rough feet. A fine powder filled the air and caressed the cheek with a tingle in its touch, and the black boles of the trees showed up in a light that seemed to come from below.

"Well, well, it can't be helped," said the Rat, after pondering. "We must make a start, and take our chance, I suppose. The worst of it is, I don't exactly know where we are. And now this snow makes everything look so very different."

It did indeed. The Mole would not have known that it was the same wood. However, they set out bravely, and took the line that seemed most promising, holding on to each other and pretending with invincible cheerfulness that they recognized an old friend in every fresh tree that grimly and silently greeted them, or saw openings, gaps, or paths with a familiar turn in them, in the monotony of white space and black tree-trunks that refused to vary.

An hour or two later—they had lost all count of time—they pulled up, dispirited, weary, and hopelessly at sea, and sat down on a fallen tree-trunk to recover their breath and consider what was to be done. They were aching with fatigue and bruised with tumbles; they had fallen into several holes and got wet through; the snow was getting so deep that they could hardly drag their little legs through it, and the trees were thicker and more like each other than ever. There seemed to be no end to this wood, and no beginning, and no difference in it, and, worst of all, no way out.

"We can't sit here very long," said the Rat. "We shall have to make another push for it, and do something or other. The cold is too awful for anything, and the snow will soon be too deep for us to wade through." He peered about him and considered. "Look here," he went on, "this is what occurs to me. There's a sort of dell down here in front of us, where the ground seems all hilly and humpy and hummocky. We'll make our way down into that, and try and find some sort of shelter, a cave or hole with a dry floor to it, out of the snow and the wind, and there we'll have a good rest before we try again, for we're both of us pretty dead beat. Besides, the snow may leave off, or something may turn up."

So once more they got on their feet, and struggled down into the dell, where they hunted about for a cave or some corner that was dry and a protection from the keen wind and the whirling snow. They were investigating one of the hummocky bits the Rat had spoken of, when suddenly the Mole tripped up and fell forward on his face with a squeal.

"O my leg!" he cried. "O my poor shin!" and he sat up on the snow and nursed his leg in both his front paws.

"Poor old Mole!" said the Rat kindly.

"You don't seem to be having much luck today, do you? Let's have a look at the leg. Yes," he went on, going down on his knees to look, "you've cut your shin, sure enough. Wait till I get at my handkerchief, and I'll tie it up for you."

"I must have tripped over a hidden branch or a stump," said the Mole miserably. "O, my! O, my!"

"It's a very clean cut," said the Rat, examining it again attentively. "That was never done by a branch or a stump. Looks as if it was made by a sharp edge of something in metal. Funny!" He pondered awhile, and examined the humps and slopes that surrounded them.

"Well, never mind what done it," said the Mole, forgetting his grammar in his pain. "It hurts just the same, whatever done it."

But the Rat, after carefully tying up the leg with his handkerchief, had left him and was busy scraping in the snow. He scratched and shovelled and explored, all four legs working busily, while the Mole waited impatiently, remarking at intervals, "O, *come* on, Rat!"

Suddenly the Rat cried, "Hooray!" and then, "Hooray-oo-ray-oo-ray-oo-ray!" and fell to executing a feeble jig in the snow.

"What *have* you found, Ratty?" asked the Mole, still nursing his leg.

"Come and see!" said the delighted Rat, as he jigged on.

The Mole hobbled up to the spot and had a good look.

"Well," he said at last, slowly, "I *see* it right enough. Seen the same sort of thing before, lots of times. Familiar object, I call it. A door-scraper! Well, what of it? Why dance jigs around a door-scraper?"

"But don't you see what it *means*, you—you dull-witted animal?" cried the Rat impatiently.

"Of course I see what it means," replied the Mole. "It simply means that some *very* careless and forgetful person has left his door-scraper lying about in the middle of the Wild Wood, *just* where it's *sure* to trip *everybody* up. Very thoughtless of him, I call it. When I get home I shall go and complain about it to—to somebody or other, see if I don't!"

"O, dear! O, dear!" cried the Rat, in despair at his obtuseness. "Here, stop arguing and come and scrape!" And he set to work again and made the snow fly in all directions around him.

After some further toil his efforts were rewarded, and a very shabby door-mat lay exposed to view.

"There, what did I tell you?" exclaimed the Rat in great triumph.

"Absolutely nothing whatever," replied the Mole, with perfect

The Rat pondered awhile, and examined the humps and slopes that surrounded them.

truthfulness. "Well now," he went on, "you seem to have found another piece of domestic litter, done for and thrown away, and I suppose you're perfectly happy. Better go ahead and dance your jig round that if you've got to, and get it over, and then perhaps we can go on and not waste any more time over rubbish-heaps. Can we *eat* a door-mat? Or sleep under a door-mat? Or sit on a door-mat and sledge home over the snow on it, you exasperating rodent?"

"Do—you—mean—to—say," cried the excited Rat, "that this door-mat doesn't *tell* you anything?"

"Really, Rat," said the Mole, quite pettishly, "I think we'd had enough of this folly. Who ever heard of a door-mat *telling* anyone anything? They simply don't do it. They are not that sort at all. Door-mats know their place."

"Now look here, you—you thick-headed beast," replied the Rat, really angry, "this must stop. Not another word, but scrape—scrape and scratch and dig and hunt round, especially on the sides of the hummocks, if you want to sleep dry and warm tonight, for it's our last chance!"

The Rat attacked a snow-bank beside them with ardour, probing with his cudgel everywhere and then digging with fury; and the Mole scraped busily too, more to oblige the Rat than for any other reason, for his opinion was that his friend was getting light-headed.

Some ten minutes' hard work, and the point of the Rat's cudgel struck something that sounded hollow. He worked till he could get a paw through and feel; then called the Mole to come and help him. Hard at it went the two animals, till at last the result of their labours stood full in view of the astonished and hitherto incredulous Mole.

In the side of what had seemed to be a snow-bank stood a solid-looking little door, painted a dark green. An iron bell-pull hung by the side, and below it, on a small brass plate, neatly engraved in square capital letters, they could read by the aid of moonlight MR. BADGER.

The Mole fell backwards on the snow from sheer surprise and delight. "Rat!" he cried in penitence, "you're a wonder! A real wonder, that's what you are. I see it all now! You argued it out, step by step, in that wise head of yours, from the very moment that I fell and cut my shin, and you looked at the cut, and at once your majestic mind said to itself, 'Door-scraper!' And then you turned to and found the very door-scraper that done it! Did you stop there? No. Some people would have been quite satisfied; but not you. Your intellect went on working. 'Let me only just find a door-mat,' says you to yourself, 'and my theory is proved!' And of course you found your door-mat. You're so clever, I believe you could find anything you liked. 'Now,' says you, 'that door exists, as plain as if I saw it. There's nothing else remains to be done but to find it!' Well, I've read about that sort of thing in books, but I've never come across it before in real life. You ought to go where you'll be properly appreciated. You're simply wasted here, among us fellows. If I only had your head, Ratty—"

"But as you haven't," interrupted the Rat, rather unkindly, "I suppose you're going to sit on the snow all night and *talk*? Get up at once and hang on to that bell-pull you see there, and ring hard, as hard as you can, while I hammer!"

While the Rat attacked the door with his stick, the Mole sprang up at the bell-pull, clutched it and swung there, both feet well off the ground, and from quite a long way off they could faintly hear a deep-toned bell respond.

Chapter 4. Mr. Badger

They waited patiently for what seemed a very long time, stamping in the snow to keep their feet warm. At last they heard the sound of slow shuffling footsteps approaching the door from the inside. It seemed, as the Mole remarked to the Rat, like someone walking in carpet slippers that were too large for him and down at heel; which was intelligent of Mole, because that was exactly what it was.

There was the noise of a bolt shot back, and the door opened a few inches, enough to show a long snout and a pair of sleepy blinking eyes.

"Now, the *very* next time this happens," said a gruff and suspicious voice, "I shall be exceedingly angry. Who is it *this* time, disturbing people on such a night? Speak up!"

"Oh, Badger," cried the Rat, "let us in, please. It's me, Rat, and my friend Mole, and we've lost our way in the snow."

"What, Ratty, my dear little man!" exclaimed the Badger, in quite a different voice. "Come along in, both of you, at once. Why, you must be perished. Well I never! Lost in the snow! And in the Wild Wood, too, and at this time of night! But come in with you."

The two animals tumbled over each other in their eagerness to get inside, and heard the door shut behind them with great joy and relief.

The Badger, who wore a long dressing-gown, and whose slippers were indeed very down at heel, carried a flat candlestick in his paw and had probably been on his way to bed when their summons sounded. He looked kindly down on them and patted both their heads. "This is not the sort of night for small animals to be out," he said paternally. "I'm afraid you've been up to some of your pranks again, Ratty. But come along; come into the kitchen. There's a first-rate fire there, and supper and everything."

He shuffled on in front of them, carrying the light, and they followed him, nudging each other in an anticipating sort of way, down a long, gloomy, and, to tell the truth, decidedly shabby passage, into a sort of a central hall, out of which they could dimly see other long tunnel-like passages branching, passages mysterious and without apparent end. But there were doors in the hall as well—stout oaken comfortable-looking doors. One of these the Badger flung open, and at once they found themselves in all the glow and warmth of a large fire-lit kitchen.

The floor was well-worn red brick, and on the wide hearth burnt a fire of logs, between two attractive chimney-corners tucked away in the wall, well out of any suspicion of draught. A couple of high-backed settles, facing each other on either side of the fire, gave further sitting accommodations for the sociably disposed. In the middle of the room stood a long table of plain boards placed on trestles, with benches down each side. At one end of it, where an armchair stood pushed back, were spread the remains of the Badger's plain but ample supper. Rows of spotless plates winked from the shelves of the dresser at the far end of the room, and from the rafters overhead hung hams, bundles of dried herbs, nets of onions, and baskets of eggs. It seemed a place where heroes could fitly feast after victory, where weary harvesters could line up in scores along the table and keep their Harvest Home with mirth and song, or where two or three friends of simple tastes could sit about as they pleased and eat and smoke and talk in comfort and contentment. The ruddy brick floor smiled up at the smoky ceiling; the oaken settles, shiny with long wear, exchanged cheerful glances with each other; plates on the dresser grinned at pots on the shelf, and the merry firelight flickered and played over everything without distinction.

The kindly Badger thrust them down on a settle to toast themselves at the fire, and bade them remove their wet coats and boots. Then he fetched them dressing-gowns and slippers, and himself bathed the Mole's shin with warm water and mended the cut with sticking-plaster till the whole thing was just as good as new, if not better. In the embracing light and warmth, warm and dry at last, with weary legs propped up in front of them, and a suggestive clink of plates being arranged on the table behind, it seemed to the storm-driven animals, now in safe anchorage, that the cold and trackless Wild Wood just left outside was miles and miles away, and all that they had suffered in it a half-forgotten dream.

When at last they were thoroughly toasted, the Badger summoned them to the table, where he had been busy laying a repast. They had felt pretty hungry before, but when they actually saw at last the supper that was spread for them, really it seemed only a question of what they should attack first where all was so attractive, and whether the other things would obligingly wait for them till they had time to give them attention. Conversation was impossible for a long time; and when it was slowly resumed, it was that regrettable sort of conversation that results from talking with your mouth full. The Badger did not mind that sort of thing at all, nor did he take any notice of elbows on the table, or everybody speaking at once. As he did not go into Society himself, he had got an idea that these things belonged to the things that didn't really matter. (We know of course that he was wrong, and took too narrow a view; because they do matter very much, though it would take too long to explain why.) He sat in his armchair at the head of the table, and nodded gravely at intervals as the animals told their story; and he did not seem surprised or shocked at anything, and he never said, "I told you so," or, "Just what I always said," or remarked that they ought to have done so-and-so, or ought not to have done something else. The Mole began to feel very friendly towards him.

When supper was really finished at last, and each animal felt that his skin was now as tight as was decently safe, and that by this time he didn't care a hang for anybody or anything, they gathered round the glowing embers of the great wood fire, and thought how jolly it was to be sitting up *so* late, and *so* independent, and *so* full; and after they had chatted for a time about things in general, the Badger said heartily, "Now then! tell us the news from your part of the world. How's old Toad going on?"

"Oh, from bad to worse," said the Rat gravely, while the Mole, cocked up on a settle and basking in the firelight, his heels higher than his head, tried to look properly mournful. "Another smash-up only last week, and a bad one. You see, he will insist on driving himself, and he's hopelessly incapable. If he'd only employ a decent, steady, well-trained animal, pay him good wages, and leave everything to him, he'd get on all right. But no; he's convinced he's a heaven-born driver, and nobody can teach him anything; and all the rest follows."

"How many has he had?" inquired the Badger gloomily.

"Smashes, or machines?" asked the Rat. "Oh, well, after all, it's the same thing—with Toad. This is the seventh. As for the others—you know that coach-house of his? Well, it's piled up—literally piled up to the roof—with fragments of motor-cars, none of them bigger than your hat! That accounts for the other six—so far as they can be accounted for."

"He's been in hospital three times," put in the Mole; "and as for the fines he's had to pay, it's simply awful to think of."

"Yes, and that's part of the trouble," continued the Rat. "Toad's rich, we all know; but he's not a millionaire. And he's a hopelessly bad driver, and quite regardless of law and order. Killed or ruined—it's got to be one of the two things, sooner or later. Badger! we're his friends—oughtn't we to do something?"

The Badger went through a bit of hard thinking. "Now look here!" he said at last, rather severely; "of course you know I can't do anything *now?*"

His two friends assented, quite understanding his point. No animal, according to the rules of animal-etiquette, is ever expected to do anything strenuous, or heroic, or even moderately active during the off-season of winter. All are sleepy—some actually asleep. All are weather-bound, more or less; and all are resting from arduous days and nights, during which every muscle in them has been severely tested, and every energy kept at full stretch.

"Very well then!" continued the Badger. "*But,* when once the year has really turned, and the nights are shorter, and halfway through them one rouses and feels fidgety and wanting to be up and doing by sunrise, if not before—*you* know!—"

Both animals nodded gravely. *They* knew!

"Well, *then,*" went on the Badger, "we—that is, you and me and our friend the Mole here—we'll take Toad seriously in hand. We'll stand no nonsense whatever. We'll bring him back to reason, by force if need be. We'll *make* him be a sensible Toad. We'll—you're asleep, Rat!"

"Not me!" said the Rat, waking up with a jerk.

"He's been asleep two or three times since supper," said the Mole, laughing. He himself was feeling quite wakeful and even lively, though he didn't know why. The reason was, of course, that he being naturally an underground animal by birth and breeding, the situation of Badger's house exactly suited him and made him feel at home; while the Rat, who slept every night in a bedroom the windows of which opened on a breezy river, naturally felt the atmosphere still and oppressive.

"Well, it's time we were all in bed," said the Badger, getting up and fetching flat candlesticks. "Come along, you two, and I'll show you your quarters. And take your time tomorrow morning—breakfast at any hour you please!"

He conducted the two animals to a long room that seemed half bedchamber and half loft. The Badger's winter stores, which indeed were visible everywhere, took up half the room—piles of apples, turnips, and potatoes, baskets full of nuts, and jars of honey; but the two little white beds on the remainder of the floor looked soft and inviting, and the linen on them, though coarse, was clean and smelt beautifully of lavender; and the Mole and the Water Rat, shaking off their garments in some thirty seconds, tumbled in between the sheets in great joy and contentment.

In accordance with the kindly Badger's injunctions, the two tired animals came down to breakfast very late next morning, and found a bright fire burning in the kitchen, and two young hedgehogs sitting on a bench at the table, eating oatmeal porridge out of wooden bowls. The hedgehogs dropped their spoons, rose to their feet, and ducked their heads respectfully as the two entered.

"There, sit down, sit down," said the Rat pleasantly, "and go on with your porridge. Where have you youngsters come from? Lost your way in the snow, I suppose?"

"Yes, please, sir," said the elder of the two hedgehogs respectfully. "Me and little Billy here, we was trying to find our way to school—mother *would* have us go, was the weather ever so—and of course we lost ourselves, sir, and Billy he got frightened and took and cried, being young and faint-hearted. And at last we happened up against Mr. Badger's back-door, and made so bold as to knock, sir, for Mr. Badger he's a kind-hearted gentleman, as everyone knows—"

"I understand," said the Rat, cutting himself some rashers from a side of bacon, while the Mole dropped some eggs into a saucepan. "And what's the weather like outside? You needn't 'sir' me quite so much," he added.

"O, terrible bad, sir, terrible deep the snow is," said the hedgehog. "No getting out for the likes of you gentlemen today."

The Badger's winter stores, which indeed were visible everywhere, took up half the room.

"Where's Mr. Badger?" inquired the Mole, as he warmed the coffee-pot before the fire.

"The master's gone into his study, sir," replied the hedgehog, "and he said as how he was going to be particular busy this morning, and on no account was he to be disturbed."

This explanation, of course, was thoroughly understood by everyone present. The fact is, as already set forth, when you live a life of intense activity for six months in the year, and of comparative or actual somnolence for the other six, during the latter period you cannot be continually pleading sleepiness when there are people about or things to be done. The excuse gets monotonous. The animals well knew that Badger, having eaten a hearty breakfast, had retired to his study and settled himself in an armchair with his legs up on another and a red cotton handkerchief over his face, and was being "busy" in the usual way at this time of the year.

The front-door bell clanged loudly, and the Rat, who was very greasy with buttered toast, sent Billy, the smaller hedgehog, to see who it might be. There was a sound of much stamping in the hall, and presently Billy returned in front of the Otter, who threw himself on the Rat with an embrace and a shout of affectionate greeting.

"Get off!" spluttered the Rat, with his mouth full.

"Thought I should find you here all right," said the Otter cheerfully. "They were all in a great state of alarm along River Bank when I arrived this morning. Rat never been home all night—nor Mole either—something dreadful must have happened, they said; and the snow had covered up all your tracks, of course. But I knew that when people were in any fix they mostly went to Badger, or else Badger got to know of it somehow, so I came straight off here, through the Wild Wood and the snow! My! it was fine, coming through the snow as the red sun was rising and showing against the black tree-trunks! As you went along in the stillness, every now and then masses of snow slid off the branches suddenly with a flop! making you jump and run for cover. Snow-castles and snow-caverns had sprung up out of nowhere in the night—and snow bridges, terraces, ramparts—I could have stayed and played with them for hours. Here and there great branches had been torn away by the sheer weight of the snow, and robins perched and hopped on them in their perky conceited way, just as if they had done it themselves.

A ragged string of wild geese passed overhead, high on the grey sky, and a few rooks whirled over the trees, inspected, and flapped off homewards with a disgusted expression; but I met no sensible being to ask the news of. About halfway across I came on a rabbit sitting on a stump, cleaning his silly face with his paws. He was a pretty scared animal when I crept up behind him and placed a heavy fore-paw on his shoulder. I had to cuff his head once or twice to get any sense out of it at all. At last I managed to extract from him that Mole had been seen in the Wild Wood last night by one of them. It was the talk of the burrows, he said, how Mole, Mr. Rat's particular friend, was in a bad fix; how he had lost his way, and 'They' were up and out hunting, and were chivvying him round and round. 'Then why didn't any of you *do* something?' I asked. 'You mayn't be blest with brains, but there are hundreds and hundreds of you, big, stout fellows, as fat as butter, and your burrows running in all directions, and you could have taken him in and made him safe and comfortable, or tried to, at all events.'

" 'What, *us*?' he merely said: '*Do* something? us rabbits?' So I cuffed him again and left him. There was nothing else to be done. At any rate, I had learnt something; and if I had had the luck to meet any of 'Them' I'd have learnt something more—or *they* would."

"Weren't you at all—er—nervous?" asked the Mole, some of yesterday's terror coming back to him at the mention of the Wild Wood.

"Nervous?" The Otter showed a gleaming set of strong white teeth as he laughed. "I'd give 'em nerves if any of them tried anything on with me. Here, Mole, fry me some slices of ham, like the good little chap you are. I'm frightfully hungry, and I've got any amount to say to Ratty here. Haven't seen him for an age."

So the good-natured Mole, having cut some slices of ham, set the hedgehogs to fry it, and returned to his own breakfast, while the Otter and the Rat, their heads together, eagerly talked river-shop, which is long shop and talk that is endless, running on like the babbling river itself.

A plate of fried ham had just been cleared and sent back for more, when the Badger entered, yawning and rubbing his eyes, and greeted them all in his quiet, simple way, with kind enquiries for everyone. "It must be getting on for luncheon time," he remarked to the Otter. "Better stop and have it with us. You must be hungry, this cold morning."

"Rather!" replied the Otter, winking at the Mole. "The sight of these greedy young hedgehogs stuffing themselves with fried ham makes me feel positively famished."

The hedgehogs, who were just beginning to feel hungry again after their porridge, and after working so hard at their frying, looked timidly up at Mr. Badger, but were too shy to say anything.

"Here, you two youngsters be off home to your mother," said the Badger kindly. "I'll send someone with you to show you the way. You won't want any dinner today, I'll be bound."

He gave them sixpence apiece and a pat on the head, and they went off with much respectful swinging of caps and touching of forelocks.

Presently they all sat down to luncheon together. The Mole found himself placed next to Mr. Badger, and, as the other two were still deep in river-gossip from which nothing could divert them, he took the opportunity to tell Badger how comfortable and home-like it all felt to him. "Once well underground," he said, "you know exactly where you are. Nothing can happen to you, and nothing can get at you. You're entirely your own master, and you don't have to consult anybody or mind what they say. Things go on all the same overhead, and you let 'em, and don't bother about 'em. When you want to, up you go, and there the things are, waiting for you."

The Badger simply beamed on him. "That's exactly what I say," he replied. "There's no security, or peace and tranquillity, except underground. And then, if your ideas get larger and you want to expand—why, a dig and a scrape, and there you are! If you feel your house is a bit too big, you stop up a hole or two, and there you are again! No builders, no tradesmen, no remarks passed on you by fellows looking over your wall, and, above all, no *weather*. Look at Rat, now. A couple of feet of flood-water, and he's got to move into hired lodgings; uncomfortable, inconveniently situated, and horribly expensive. Take Toad. I say nothing against Toad Hall; quite the best house in these parts, *as* a house. But supposing a fire breaks out—where's Toad? Supposing tiles are blown off, or walls sink or crack, or windows get broken—where's Toad? Supposing the rooms are draughty—I *hate* a draught myself—where's Toad?

No, up and out of doors is good enough to roam about and get one's living in; but underground to come back to at last—that's my idea of *home*."

The Mole assented heartily; and the Badger in consequence got very friendly with him. "When lunch is over," he said, "I'll take you all round this little place of mine. I can see you'll appreciate it. You understand what domestic architecture ought to be, you do."

After luncheon, accordingly, when the other two had settled themselves into the chimney-corner and had started a heated argument on the subject of *eels*, the Badger lighted a lantern and bade the Mole follow him. Crossing the hall, they passed down one of the principal tunnels, and the wavering light of the lantern gave glimpses on either side of rooms both large and small, some mere cupboards, others nearly as broad and imposing as Toad's dining-hall. A narrow passage at right angles led them into another corridor, and here the same thing was repeated. The Mole was staggered at the size, the extent, the ramifications of it all; at the length of the dim passages, the solid vaultings of the crammed store-chambers, the masonry everywhere, the pillars, the arches, the pavements. "How on earth, Badger," he said at last, "did you ever find time and strength to do all this? It's astonishing!"

"It *would* be astonishing indeed," said the Badger simply, "if I *had* done it. But as a matter of fact I did none of it—only cleaned out the passages and chambers, as far as I had need of them. There's lots more of it, all round about. I see you don't understand, and I must explain it to you. Well, very long ago, on the spot where the Wild Wood waves now, before ever it had planted itself and grown up to what it now is, there was a city—a city of people, you know. Here, where we are standing, they lived, and walked, and talked, and slept, and carried on their business. Here they stabled their horses and feasted, from here they rode out to fight or drove out to trade. They were a powerful people, and rich, and great builders. They built to last, for they thought their city would last forever."

"But what has become of them all?" asked the Mole.

"Who can tell?" said the Badger. "People come—they stay for a while, they flourish, they build—and they go. It is their way. But we remain. There were badgers here, I've been told, long before that same city ever came to be. And now there are badgers here again.

*Crossing the hall, they passed down one of the
principal tunnels.*

We are an enduring lot, and we may move out for a time, but we wait, and are patient, and back we come. And so it will ever be."

"Well, and when they went at last, those people?" said the Mole.

"When they went," continued the Badger, "the strong winds and persistent rains took the matter in hand, patiently, ceaselessly, year after year. Perhaps we badgers too, in our small way, helped a little—who knows? It was all down, down, down, gradually—ruin and levelling and disappearance. Then it was all up, up, up, gradually, as seeds grew to saplings, and saplings to forest trees, and bramble and fern came creeping in to help. Leaf-mould rose and obliterated, streams in their winter freshets brought sand and soil to clog and to cover, and in course of time our home was ready for us again, and we moved in. Up above us, on the surface, the same thing happened. Animals arrived, liked the look of the place, took up their quarters, settled down, spread, and flourished. They didn't bother themselves about the past—they never do; they're too busy. The place was a bit humpy and hillocky, naturally, and full of holes; but that was rather an advantage. And they don't bother about the future, either—the future when perhaps the people will move in again—for a time—as may very well be. The Wild Wood is pretty well populated by now; with all the usual lot, good, bad, and indifferent—I name no names. It takes all sorts to make a world. But I fancy you know something about them yourself by this time."

"I do indeed," said the Mole, with a slight shiver.

"Well, well," said the Badger, patting him on the shoulder, "it was your first experience of them, you see. They're not so bad really; and we must all live and let live. But I'll pass the word around tomorrow, and I think you'll have no further trouble. Any friend of *mine* walks where he likes in this country, or I'll know the reason why!"

When they got back to the kitchen again, they found the Rat walking up and down, very restless. The underground atmosphere was oppressing him and getting on his nerves, and he seemed really to be afraid that the river would run away if he wasn't there to look after it. So he had his overcoat on, and his pistols thrust into his belt again. "Come along, Mole," he said anxiously, as soon as he caught sight of them. "We must get off while it's daylight. Don't want to spend another night in the Wild Wood again."

"It'll be all right, my fine fellow," said the Otter. "I'm coming along with you, and I know every path blindfold; and if there's a head that needs to be punched, you can confidently rely upon me to punch it."

"You really needn't fret, Ratty," added the Badger placidly. "My passages run further than you think, and I've bolt-holes to the edge of the wood in several directions, though I don't care for everybody to know about them. When you really have to go, you shall leave by one of my short cuts. Meantime, make yourself easy, and sit down again."

The Rat was nevertheless still anxious to be off and attend to his river, so the Badger, taking up his lantern again, led the way along a damp and airless tunnel that wound and dipped, part vaulted, part hewn through solid rock, for a weary distance that seemed to be miles. At last daylight began to show itself confusedly through tangled growth overhanging the mouth of the passage; and the Badger, bidding them a hasty good-bye, pushed them hurriedly through the opening, made everything look as natural as possible again, with creepers, brushwood, and dead leaves, and retreated.

They found themselves standing on the very edge of the Wild Wood. Rocks and brambles and tree-roots behind them, confusedly heaped and tangled; in front, a great space of quiet fields, hemmed by lines of hedges black on the snow, and, far ahead, a glint of the familiar old river, while the wintry sun hung red and low on the horizon. The Otter, as knowing all the paths, took charge of the party, and they trailed out on a bee-line for a distant stile. Pausing there a moment and looking back, they saw the whole mass of the Wild Wood, dense, menacing, compact, grimly set in vast white surroundings; simultaneously they turned and made swiftly for home, for firelight and the familiar things it played on, for the voice, sounding cheerily outside their window, of the river that they knew and trusted in all its moods, that never made them afraid with any amazement.

As he hurried along, eagerly anticipating the moment when he would be at home again among the things he knew and liked, the Mole saw clearly that he was an animal of tilled field and hedge-row, linked to the ploughed furrow, the frequented pasture, the lane of evening lingerings, the cultivated garden-plot. For others the asperities, the stubborn endurance, or the clash of actual conflict, that went with Nature in the rough; he must be wise, must keep to the pleasant places in which his lines were laid and which held adventure enough, in their way, to last for a lifetime.

Chapter 5. Dulce Domum

The sheep ran huddling together against the hurdles, blowing out thin nostrils and stamping with delicate fore-feet, their heads thrown back and a light steam rising from the crowded sheep-pen into the frosty air, as the two animals hastened by in high spirits, with much chatter and laughter. They were returning across country after a long day's outing with Otter, hunting and exploring on the wide uplands where certain streams tributary to their own River had their first small beginnings; and the shades of the short winter day were closing in on them, and they had still some distance to go. Plodding at random across the plough, they had heard the sheep and had made for them; and now, leading from the sheep-pen, they found a beaten track that made walking a lighter business, and responded, moreover, to that small inquiring something which all animals carry inside them, saying unmistakably, "Yes, quite right; *this* leads home!"

"It looks as if we were coming to a village," said the Mole somewhat dubiously, slackening his pace, as the track, that had in time become a path and then had developed into a lane, now handed them over to the charge of a well-metalled road. The animals did not hold with villages, and their own highways, thickly frequented as they were, took an independent course, regardless of church, post office, or public-house.

"Oh, never mind!" said the Rat. "At this season of the year they're all safe indoors by this time, sitting round the fire; men, women, and children, dogs and cats and all. We shall slip through all right, without any bother or unpleasantness, and we can have a look at them through their windows if you like, and see what they're doing."

The rapid nightfall of mid-December had quite beset the little village as they approached it on soft feet over a first thin fall of powdery snow. Little was visible but squares of a dusky orange-red on either side of the street, where the firelight or lamplight of each cottage overflowed through the casements into the dark world without. Most of the low latticed windows were innocent of blinds, and to the lookers-in from outside, the inmates, gathered round the tea-table, absorbed in handiwork, or talking with laughter and gesture, had each that happy grace which is the last thing the skilled actor shall capture—the natural grace which goes with perfect unconsciousness of observation. Moving at will from one theatre to another, the two spectators, so far from home themselves, had something of wistfulness in their eyes as they watched a cat being stroked, a sleepy child picked up and huddled off to bed, or a tired man stretch and knock out his pipe on the end of a smouldering log.

But it was from one little window, with its blind drawn down, a mere blank transparency on the night, that the sense of home and the little curtained world within walls—the larger stressful world of outside Nature shut out and forgotten—most pulsated. Close against the white blind hung a bird-cage, clearly silhouetted, every wire, perch, and appurtenance distinct and recognisable, even to yesterday's dull-edged lump of sugar. On the middle perch the fluffy occupant, head tucked well into feathers, seemed so near to them as to be easily stroked, had they tried; even the delicate tips of his plumped-out plumage pencilled plainly on the illuminated screen. As they looked, the sleepy little fellow stirred uneasily, woke, shook himself, and raised his head. They could see the gape of his tiny beak as he yawned in a bored sort of way, looked round, and then settled his head into his back again, while the ruffled feathers gradually subsided into perfect stillness. Then a gust of bitter wind took them in the back of the neck, a small sting of frozen sleet on the skin woke them as from a dream, and they knew their toes to be cold and their legs tired, and their own home distant a weary way.

Once beyond the village, where the cottages ceased abruptly, on either side of the road they could smell through the darkness the friendly fields again; and they braced themselves for the last long stretch, the home stretch, the stretch that we know is bound to end, some time, in the rattle of the door-latch, the sudden firelight, and the sight of familiar things greeting us as long-absent travellers from far over-sea. They plodded along steadily and silently, each of them thinking his own thoughts. The Mole's ran a good deal on supper, as it was pitch-dark, and it was all a strange country for him as far as he knew, and he was following obediently in the wake of the Rat, leaving the guidance entirely to him. As for the Rat, he was walking a little way ahead, as his habit was, his shoulders humped, his eyes fixed on the straight grey road in front of him; so he did not notice poor Mole when suddenly the summons reached him, and took him like an electric shock.

We others, who have long lost the more subtle of the physical senses, have not even proper terms to express an animal's inter-communications with his surroundings, living or otherwise, and have only the word "smell," for instance, to include the whole range of delicate thrills which murmur in the nose of the animal night and day, summoning, warning, inciting, repelling. It was one of these mysterious fairy calls from out the void that suddenly reached Mole in the darkness, making him tingle through and through with its very familiar appeal, even while yet he could not clearly remember what it was. He stopped dead in his tracks, his nose searching hither and thither in its efforts to recapture the fine filament, the telegraphic current, that had so strongly moved him. A moment, and he had caught it again; and with it this time came recollection in fullest flood.

Home! That was what they meant, those caressing appeals, those soft touches wafted through the air, those invisible little hands pulling and tugging, all one way! Why, it must be quite close by him at that moment, his old home that he had hurriedly forsaken and never sought again, that day when he first found the river! And now it was sending out its scouts and its messengers to capture him and bring him in. Since his escape on that bright morning he had hardly given it a thought, so absorbed had he been in his new life, in all its pleasures, its surprises, its fresh and captivating experiences. Now, with a rush of old memories, how clearly it stood up before him, in the darkness! Shabby indeed, and small and poorly furnished, and yet his, the home he had made for himself, the home he had been so happy to get back to after his day's work. And the home had been happy with him, too, evidently, and was missing him, and wanted him back, and was telling him so, through his nose, sorrowfully, reproachfully, but with no bitterness or anger; only with plaintive reminder that it was there, and wanted him.

The call was clear, the summons was plain. He must obey it instantly, and go. "Ratty!" he called, full of joyful excitement, "hold on! Come back! I want you, quick!"

"Oh, *come* along, Mole, do!" replied the Rat cheerfully, still plodding along.

"*Please* stop, Ratty!" pleaded the poor Mole, in anguish of heart. "You don't understand! It's my home, my old home! I've just come across the smell of it, and it's close by here, really quite close. And I *must* go to it, I must, I must! Oh, come back, Ratty! Please, please come back!"

The Rat was by this time very far ahead, too far to hear clearly what the Mole was calling, too far to catch the sharp note of painful appeal in his voice. And he was much taken up with the weather, for he too could smell something—something suspiciously like approaching snow.

"Mole, we mustn't stop now, really!" he called back. "We'll come for it tomorrow, whatever it is you've found. But I daren't stop now—it's late, and the snow's coming on again, and I'm not sure of the way! And I want your nose, Mole, so come on quick, there's a good fellow!" And the Rat pressed forward on his way without waiting for an answer.

Poor Mole stood alone in the road, his heart torn asunder, and a big sob gathering, gathering, somewhere low down inside him, to leap up to the surface presently, he knew, in passionate escape. But even under such a test as this his loyalty to his friend stood firm. Never for a moment did he dream of abandoning him. Meanwhile, the wafts from his old home pleaded, whispered, conjured, and finally claimed him imperiously. He dared not tarry longer within their magic circle. With a wrench that tore his very heartstrings he set his face down the road and followed submissively in the track of the Rat, while faint, thin little smells, still dogging his retreating nose, reproached him for his new friendship and his callous forgetfulness.

With an effort he caught up to the unsuspecting Rat, who began chattering cheerfully about what they would do when they got back, and how jolly a fire of logs in the parlour would be, and what a supper he meant to eat; never noticing his companion's silence and distressful state of mind. At last, however, when they had gone some considerable way further, and were passing some tree-stumps at the edge of a copse that bordered the road, he stopped and said kindly, "Look here, Mole old chap, you seem dead tired. No talk left in you, and your feet dragging like lead. We'll sit down here for a minute and rest. The snow has held off so far, and the best part of our journey is over."

The Mole subsided forlornly on a tree-stump and tried to control himself, for he felt it surely coming. The sob he had fought with so long refused to be beaten. Up and up, it forced its way to the air, and then another, and another, and others thick and fast; till poor Mole at last gave up the struggle, and cried freely and helplessly and openly, now that he knew it was all over and he had lost what he could hardly be said to have found.

The Rat, astonished and dismayed at the violence of Mole's paroxysm of grief, did not dare to speak for a while. At last he said, very quietly and sympathetically, "What is it, old fellow? Whatever can be the matter? Tell us your trouble, and let me see what I can do."

Poor Mole found it difficult to get any words out between the upheavals of his chest that followed one upon another so quickly and held back speech and choked it as it came. "I know it's a— shabby, dingy little place," he sobbed forth at last, brokenly: "not like—your cosy quarters—or Toad's beautiful hall—or Badger's great house—but it was my own little home—and I was fond of it—and I went away and forgot all about it—and then I smelt it suddenly—on the road, when I called and you wouldn't listen, Rat—and everything came back to me with a rush—and I *wanted* it!—O dear, O dear!—and when you *wouldn't* turn back, Ratty— and I had to leave it, though I was smelling it all the time—I thought my heart would break.—We might have just gone and had one look at it, Ratty—only one look—it was close by—but you wouldn't turn back, Ratty, you wouldn't turn back! O dear, O dear!"

Recollection brought fresh waves of sorrow, and sobs again took full charge of him, preventing further speech.

The Rat stared straight in front of him, saying nothing, only patting Mole gently on the shoulder. After a time he muttered gloomily, "I see it all now! What a *pig* I have been! A pig—that's me! Just a pig—a plain pig!"

He waited till Mole's sobs became gradually less stormy and more rhythmical; he waited till at last sniffs were frequent and sobs only intermittent. Then he rose from his seat, and, remarking carelessly, "Well, now we'd really better be getting on, old chap!" set off up the road again, over the toilsome way they had come.

"Wherever are you (hic) going to (hic), Ratty?" cried the tearful Mole, looking up in alarm.

"We're going to find that home of yours, old fellow," replied the Rat pleasantly; "so you had better come along, for it will take some finding, and we shall want your nose."

"Oh, come back, Ratty, do!" cried the Mole, getting up and hurrying after him. "It's no good, I tell you! It's too late, and too dark, and the place is too far off, and the snow's coming! And—and I never meant to let you know I was feeling that way about it—it was all an accident and a mistake! And think of River Bank, and your supper!"

"Hang River Bank, and supper too!" said the Rat heartily. "I tell you, I'm going to find this place now, if I stay out all night. So cheer up, old chap, and take my arm, and we'll very soon be back there again."

Still snuffling, pleading, and reluctant, Mole suffered himself to be dragged back along the road by his imperious companion, who by a flow of cheerful talk and anecdote endeavoured to beguile his spirits back and make the weary way seem shorter. When at last it seemed to the Rat that they must be nearing that part of the road where the Mole had been "held up," he said, "Now, no more talking. Business! Use your nose, and give your mind to it."

They moved on in silence for some little way, when suddenly the Rat was conscious, through his arm that was linked in Mole's, of a faint sort of electric thrill that was passing down that animal's body. Instantly he disengaged himself, fell back a pace, and waited, all attention.

The signals were coming through!

Mole stood a moment rigid, while his uplifted nose, quivering slightly, felt the air.

Then a short, quick run forward—a fault—a check—a try back; and then a slow, steady, confident advance.

The Rat, much excited, kept close to his heels as the Mole, with something of the air of a sleep-walker, crossed a dry ditch, scrambled through a hedge, and nosed his way over a field open and trackless and bare in the faint starlight.

Suddenly, without giving warning, he dived; but the Rat was on the alert, and promptly followed him down the tunnel to which his unerring nose had faithfully led him.

It was close and airless, and the earthy smell was strong, and it seemed a long time to Rat ere the passage ended and he could stand erect and stretch and shake himself. The Mole struck a match, and by its light the Rat saw that they were standing in an open space, neatly swept and sanded underfoot, and directly facing them was Mole's little front door, with "Mole End" painted, in Gothic lettering, over the bell-pull at the side.

Mole reached down a lantern from a nail on the wall and lit it . . . and the Rat, looking round him, saw that they were in a sort of fore-court. A garden-seat stood on one side of the door, and on the other a roller; for the Mole, who was a tidy animal when at home, could not stand having his ground kicked up by other animals into little runs that ended in earth-heaps. On the walls hung wire baskets with ferns in them, alternating with brackets carrying plaster statuary—Garibaldi, and the infant Samuel, and Queen Victoria, and other heroes of modern Italy. Down on one side of the forecourt ran a skittle-alley, with benches along it and little wooden tables marked with rings that hinted at beer-mugs. In the middle was a small round pond containing gold-fish and surrounded by a cockle-shell border. Out of the centre of the pond rose a fanciful erection clothed in more cockle-shells and topped by a large silvered glass ball that reflected everything all wrong and had a very pleasing effect.

Mole's face beamed at the sight of all these objects so dear to him, and he hurried Rat through the door, lit a lamp in the hall, and took one glance round his old home. He saw the dust lying thick on everything, saw the cheerless, deserted look of the long-neglected house, and its narrow, meagre dimensions, its worn and shabby contents—and collapsed again on a hall-chair, his nose to his paws. "O Ratty!" he cried dismally, "why ever did I do it? Why did I bring you to this poor, cold little place, on a night like this, when you might have been at River Bank by this time, toasting your toes before a blazing fire, with all your own nice things about you!"

The Rat paid no heed to his doleful self-reproaches. He was running here and there, opening doors, inspecting rooms and cupboards, and lighting lamps and candles and sticking them up everywhere. "What a capital little house this is!" he called out cheerily. "So compact! So well planned! Everything here and everything in its place! We'll make a jolly night of it. The first thing we want is a good fire; I'll see to that—I always know where to find things. So this is the parlour?

Splendid! Your own idea, those little sleeping-bunks in the wall? Capital! Now, I'll fetch the wood and the coals, and you get a duster, Mole—you'll find one in the drawer of the kitchen table—and try and smarten things up a bit. Bustle about, old chap!"

Encouraged by his inspiriting companion, the Mole roused himself and dusted and polished with energy and heartiness, while the Rat, running to and fro with armfuls of fuel, soon had a cheerful blaze roaring up the chimney. He hailed the Mole to come and warm himself; but Mole promptly had another fit of the blues, dropping down on a couch in dark despair and burying his face in his duster. "Rat," he moaned, "how about your supper, you poor, cold, hungry, weary animal? I've nothing to give you—nothing—not a crumb!"

"What a fellow you are for giving in!" said the Rat reproachfully. "Why, only just now I saw a sardine-opener on the kitchen dresser, quite distinctly; and everybody knows that means there are sardines about somewhere in the neighbourhood. Rouse yourself! pull yourself together, and come with me and forage."

They went and foraged accordingly, hunting through every cupboard and turning out every drawer. The result was not so very depressing after all, though of course it might have been better; a tin of sardines—a box of captain's biscuits, nearly full—and a German sausage encased in silver paper.

"There's a banquet for you!" observed the Rat, as he arranged the table. "I know some animals who would give their ears to be sitting down to supper with us tonight!"

"No bread!" groaned the Mole dolorously; "no butter, no—"

"No pate de foie gras, no champagne!" continued the Rat, grinning. "And that reminds me—what's that little door at the end of the passage? Your cellar, of course! Every luxury in this house! Just you wait a minute."

He made for the cellar-door, and presently reappeared, somewhat dusty, with a bottle of beer in each paw and another under each arm. "Self-indulgent beggar you seem to be, Mole," he observed. "Deny yourself nothing. This is really the jolliest little place I ever was in. Now, wherever did you pick up those prints? Make the place look so home-like, they do. No wonder you're so fond of it, Mole. Tell us all about it, and how you came to make it what it is."

Then, while the Rat busied himself fetching plates, and knives

He presently reappeared, somewhat dusty, with a bottle of beer in each paw and another under each arm.

and forks, and mustard which he mixed in an egg-cup, the Mole, his bosom still heaving with the stress of his recent emotion, related— somewhat shyly at first, but with more freedom as he warmed to his subject—how this was planned, and how that was thought out, and how this was got through a windfall from an aunt, and that was a wonderful find and a bargain, and this other thing was bought out of laborious savings and a certain amount of "going without." His spirits finally quite restored, he must needs go and caress his possessions, and take a lamp and show off their points to his visitor and expatiate on them, quite forgetful of the supper they both so much needed; Rat, who was desperately hungry but strove to conceal it, nodding seriously, examining with a puckered brow, and saying, "wonderful," and "most remarkable," at intervals, when the chance for an observation was given him.

At last the Rat succeeded in decoying him to the table, and had just got seriously to work with the sardine-opener when sounds were heard from the fore-court without—sounds like the scuffling of small feet in the gravel and a confused murmur of tiny voices, while broken sentences reached them—"Now, all in a line—hold the lantern up a bit, Tommy—clear your throats first—no coughing after I say one, two, three.—Where's young Bill?—Here, come on, do, we're all a-waiting—"

"What's up?" inquired the Rat, pausing in his labours.

"I think it must be the field-mice," replied the Mole, with a touch of pride in his manner. "They go round carol-singing regularly at this time of the year. They're quite an institution in these parts. And they never pass me over—they come to Mole End last of all; and I used to give them hot drinks, and supper too sometimes, when I could afford it. It will be like old times to hear them again."

"Let's have a look at them!" cried the Rat, jumping up and running to the door.

It was a pretty sight, and a seasonable one, that met their eyes when they flung the door open. In the fore-court, lit by the dim rays of a horn lantern, some eight or ten little field-mice stood in a semicircle, red worsted comforters round their throats, their fore-paws thrust deep into their pockets, their feet jigging for warmth. With bright beady eyes they glanced shyly at each other, sniggering a little, sniffing and applying coat-sleeves a good deal. As the door opened, one of the elder ones that carried the lantern was just saying, "Now then, one, two, three!" and forthwith their shrill little voices uprose on the air, singing one of the old-time carols that their forefathers composed in fields that were fallow and held by frost, or when snow-bound in chimney corners, and handed down to be sung in the miry street to lamp-lit windows at Yule-time.

CAROL

Villagers all, this frosty tide,
Let your doors swing open wide,
Though wind may follow, and snow beside,
Yet draw us in by your fire to bide;
  Joy shall be yours in the morning!

Here we stand in the cold and the sleet,
Blowing fingers and stamping feet,
Come from far away you to greet—
You by the fire and we in the street—
  Bidding you joy in the morning!

For ere one half of the night was gone,
Sudden a star has led us on,
Raining bliss and benison—
Bliss tomorrow and more anon,
  Joy for every morning!

Goodman Joseph toiled through the snow—
Saw the star o'er a stable low;
Mary she might not further go—
Welcome thatch, and litter below!
  Joy was hers in the morning!

And then they heard the angels tell
"Who were the first to cry Nowell*?*
Animals all, as it befell,
In the stable where they did dwell!
  Joy shall be theirs in the morning!"

The voices ceased, the singers, bashful but smiling, exchanged sidelong glances, and silence succeeded—but for a moment only. Then, from up above and far away, down the tunnel they had so lately travelled was borne to their ears in a faint musical hum the sound of distant bells ringing a joyful and clangorous peal.

"Very well sung, boys!" cried the Rat heartily. "And now come along in, all of you, and warm yourselves by the fire, and have something hot!"

"Yes, come along, field-mice," cried the Mole eagerly. "This is quite like old times! Shut the door after you. Pull up that settle to the fire. Now, you just wait a minute, while we—O, Ratty!" he cried in despair, plumping down on a seat, with tears impending. "Whatever are we doing? We've nothing to give them!"

"You leave all that to me," said the masterful Rat. "Here, you with the lantern! Come over this way. I want to talk to you. Now, tell me, are there any shops open at this hour of the night?"

"Why, certainly, sir," replied the field-mouse respectfully. "At this time of the year our shops keep open to all sorts of hours."

"Then look here!" said the Rat. "You go off at once, you and your lantern, and you get me—"

Here much muttered conversation ensued, and the Mole only heard bits of it, such as—"Fresh, mind!—no, a pound of that will do—see you get Buggins's, for I won't have any other—no, only the best—if you can't get it there, try somewhere else—yes, of course, home-made, no tinned stuff—well then, do the best you can!" Finally, there was a chink of coin passing from paw to paw, the field-mouse was provided with an ample basket for his purchases, and off he hurried, he and his lantern.

The rest of the field-mice, perched in a row on the settle, their small legs swinging, gave themselves up to enjoyment of the fire, and toasted their chilblains till they tingled; while the Mole, failing to draw them into easy conversation, plunged into family history and made each of them recite the names of his numerous brothers, who were too young, it appeared, to be allowed to go out a-carolling this year, but looked forward very shortly to winning the parental consent.

The Rat, meanwhile, was busy examining the label on one of the beer-bottles. "I perceive this to be Old Burton," he remarked approvingly. "*Sensible* Mole! The very thing! Now we shall be able to mull some ale! Get the things ready, Mole, while I draw the corks."

It did not take long to prepare the brew and thrust the tin heater well into the red heart of the fire; and soon every field-mouse was sipping and coughing and choking (for a little mulled ale goes a long way) and wiping his eyes and laughing and forgetting he had ever been cold in all his life.

"They act plays too, these fellows," the Mole explained to the Rat. "Make them up all by themselves, and act them afterwards. And very well they do it, too! They gave us a capital one last year, about a field-mouse who was captured at sea by a Barbary corsair, and made to row in a galley; and when he escaped and got home again, his lady-love had gone into a convent. Here, *you*! You were in it, I remember. Get up and recite a bit."

The field-mouse addressed got up on his legs, giggled shyly, looked round the room, and remained absolutely tongue-tied. His comrades cheered him on, Mole coaxed and encouraged him, and the Rat went so far as to take him by the shoulders and shake him; but nothing could overcome his stage-fright. They were all busily engaged on him like watermen applying the Royal Humane Society's regulations to a case of long submersion, when the latch clicked, the door opened, and the field-mouse with the lantern reappeared, staggering under the weight of his basket.

There was no more talk of play-acting once the very real and solid contents of the basket had been tumbled out on the table. Under the generalship of Rat, everybody was set to do something or to fetch something. In a very few minutes supper was ready, and Mole, as he took the head of the table in a sort of a dream, saw a lately barren board set thick with savoury comforts; saw his little friends' faces brighten and beam as they fell to without delay; and then let himself loose—for he was famished indeed—on the provender so magically provided, thinking what a happy home-coming this had turned out, after all. As they ate, they talked of old times, and the field-mice gave him the local gossip up to date, and answered as well as they could the hundred questions he had to ask them. The Rat said little or nothing, only taking care that each guest had what he wanted, and plenty of it, and that Mole had no trouble or anxiety about anything.

They clattered off at last, very grateful and showering wishes of the season, with their jacket pockets stuffed with remembrances for the small brothers and sisters at home. When the door had closed on the last of them and the chink of the lanterns had died away, Mole and Rat kicked the fire up, drew their chairs in, brewed themselves a last nightcap of mulled ale, and discussed the events of the long day. At last the Rat, with a tremendous yawn, said, "Mole, old chap, I'm ready to drop. Sleepy is simply not the word. That your own bunk over on that side? Very well, then, I'll take this. What a ripping little house this is! Everything so handy!"

He clambered into his bunk and rolled himself well up in the blankets, and slumber gathered him forthwith, as a swathe of barley is folded into the arms of the reaping machine.

The weary Mole also was glad to turn in without delay, and soon had his head on his pillow, in great joy and contentment. But ere he closed his eyes he let them wander round his old room, mellow in the glow of the firelight that played or rested on familiar and friendly things which had long been unconsciously a part of him, and now smilingly received him back, without rancour. He was now in just the frame of mind that the tactful Rat had quietly worked to bring about in him. He saw clearly how plain and simple—how narrow, even—it all was; but clearly, too, how much it all meant to him, and the special value of some such anchorage in one's existence. He did not at all want to abandon the new life and its splendid spaces, to turn his back on sun and air and all they offered him and creep home and stay there; the upper world was all too strong, it called to him still, even down there, and he knew he must return to the larger stage. But it was good to think he had this to come back to; this place which was all his own, these things which were so glad to see him again and could always be counted upon for the same simple welcome.

Chapter 6. Mr. Toad

It was a bright morning in the early part of summer; the river had resumed its wonted banks and its accustomed pace, and a hot sun seemed to be pulling everything green and bushy and spiky up out of the earth towards him, as if by strings. The Mole and the Water Rat had been up since dawn, very busy on matters connected with boats and the opening of the boating season; painting and varnishing, mending paddles, repairing cushions, hunting for missing boat-hooks, and so on; and were finishing breakfast in their little parlour and eagerly discussing their plans for the day, when a heavy knock sounded at the door.

"Bother!" said the Rat, all over egg. "See who it is, Mole, like a good chap, since you've finished."

The Mole went to attend the summons, and the Rat heard him utter a cry of surprise. Then he flung the parlour door open, and announced with much importance, "Mr. Badger!"

This was a wonderful thing, indeed, that the Badger should pay a formal call on them, or indeed on anybody. He generally had to be caught, if you wanted him badly, as he slipped quietly along a hedgerow of an early morning or a late evening, or else hunted up in his own house in the middle of the Wood, which was a serious undertaking.

The Badger strode heavily into the room, and stood looking at the two animals with an expression full of seriousness. The Rat let his egg-spoon fall on the table-cloth, and sat open-mouthed.

"The hour has come!" said the Badger at last with great solemnity.

"What hour?" asked the Rat uneasily, glancing at the clock on the mantelpiece.

"*Whose* hour, you should rather say," replied the Badger. "Why, Toad's hour! The hour of Toad! I said I would take him in hand as soon as the winter was well over, and I'm going to take him in hand today!"

"Toad's hour, of course!" cried the Mole delightedly. "Hooray! I remember now! *We*'ll teach him to be a sensible Toad!"

"This very morning," continued the Badger, taking an armchair, "as I learnt last night from a trustworthy source, another new and exceptionally powerful motor-car will arrive at Toad Hall on approval or return. At this very moment, perhaps, Toad is busy arraying himself in those singularly hideous habiliments so dear to him, which transform him from a (comparatively) good-looking Toad into an Object which throws any decent-minded animal that comes across it into a violent fit. We must be up and doing, ere it is too late. You two animals will accompany me instantly to Toad Hall, and the work of rescue shall be accomplished."

"Right you are!" cried the Rat, starting up. "We'll rescue the poor unhappy animal! We'll convert him! He'll be the most converted Toad that ever was before we've done with him!"

They set off up the road on their mission of mercy, Badger leading the way. Animals when in company walk in a proper and sensible manner, in single file, instead of sprawling all across the road and being of no use or support to each other in case of sudden trouble or danger.

They reached the carriage-drive of Toad Hall to find, as the Badger had anticipated, a shiny new motor-car, of great size, painted a bright red (Toad's favourite colour), standing in front of the house. As they neared the door it was flung open, and Mr. Toad, arrayed in goggles, cap, gaiters, and enormous overcoat, came swaggering down the steps, drawing on his gauntleted gloves.

"Hullo! come on, you fellows!" he cried cheerfully on catching sight of them. "You're just in time to come with me for a jolly—to come for a jolly—for a—er—jolly—"

His hearty accents faltered and fell away as he noticed the stern unbending look on the countenances of his silent friends, and his invitation remained unfinished.

The Badger strode up the steps. "Take him inside," he said sternly to his companions. Then, as Toad was hustled through the door, struggling and protesting, he turned to the chauffeur in charge of the new motor-car.

"I'm afraid you won't be wanted today," he said. "Mr. Toad has changed his mind. He will not require the car. Please understand that this is final. You needn't wait." Then he followed the others inside and shut the door.

"Now then!" he said to the Toad, when the four of them stood together in the Hall, "first of all, take those ridiculous things off!"

"Shan't!" replied Toad, with great spirit. "What is the meaning of this gross outrage? I demand an instant explanation."

"Take them off him, then, you two," ordered the Badger briefly.

They had to lay Toad out on the floor, kicking and calling all sorts of names, before they could get to work properly. Then the Rat sat on him, and the Mole got his motor-clothes off him bit by bit, and they stood him up on his legs again. A good deal of his blustering spirit seemed to have evaporated with the removal of his fine panoply. Now that he was merely Toad, and no longer the Terror of the Highway, he giggled feebly and looked from one to the other appealingly, seeming quite to understand the situation.

"You knew it must come to this, sooner or later, Toad," the Badger explained severely. "You've disregarded all the warnings we've given you, you've gone on squandering the money your father left you, and you're getting us animals a bad name in the district by your furious driving and your smashes and your rows with the police. Independence is all very well, but we animals never allow our friends to make fools of themselves beyond a certain limit; and that limit you've reached. Now, you're a good fellow in many respects, and I don't want to be too hard on you. I'll make one more effort to bring you to reason. You will come with me into the smoking-room, and there you will hear some facts about yourself; and we'll see whether you come out of that room the same Toad that you went in."

He took Toad firmly by the arm, led him into the smoking-room, and closed the door behind them.

"*That's* no good!" said the Rat contemptuously. "*Talking* to Toad'll never cure him. He'll *say* anything."

They made themselves comfortable in armchairs and waited patiently. Through the closed door they could just hear the long continuous drone of the Badger's voice, rising and falling in waves of oratory; and presently they noticed that the sermon began to be punctuated at intervals by long-drawn sobs, evidently proceeding from the bosom of Toad, who was a soft-hearted and affectionate fellow, very easily converted—for the time being—to any point of view.

After some three-quarters of an hour the door opened, and the Badger reappeared, solemnly leading by the paw a very limp and dejected Toad. His skin hung baggily about him, his legs wobbled, and his cheeks were furrowed by the tears so plentifully called forth by the Badger's moving discourse.

"Sit down there, Toad," said the Badger kindly, pointing to a chair. "My friends," he went on, "I am pleased to inform you that Toad has at last seen the error of his ways. He is truly sorry for his misguided conduct in the past, and he has undertaken to give up motor-cars entirely and forever. I have his solemn promise to that effect."

"That is very good news," said the Mole gravely.

"Very good news indeed," observed the Rat dubiously, "if only—*if* only—"

He was looking very hard at Toad as he said this, and could not help thinking he perceived something vaguely resembling a twinkle in that animal's still sorrowful eye.

"There's only one thing more to be done," continued the gratified Badger. "Toad, I want you solemnly to repeat, before your friends here, what you fully admitted to me in the smoking-room just now. First, you are sorry for what you've done, and you see the folly of it all?"

There was a long, long pause. Toad looked desperately this way and that, while the other animals waited in grave silence. At last he spoke.

"No!" he said, a little sullenly, but stoutly; "I'm *not* sorry. And it wasn't folly at all! It was simply glorious!"

"What?" cried the Badger, greatly scandalised. "You backsliding animal, didn't you tell me just now, in there—"

"Oh, yes, yes, in *there*," said Toad impatiently. "I'd have said anything in *there*. You're so eloquent, dear Badger, and so moving, and so convincing, and put all your points so frightfully well—you can do what you like with me in *there*, and you know it. But I've been searching my mind since, and going over things in it, and I find that I'm not a bit sorry or repentant really, so it's no earthly good saying I am; now, is it?"

"Then you don't promise," said the Badger, "never to touch a motor-car again?"

"Certainly not!" replied Toad emphatically. "On the contrary, I faithfully promise that the very first motor-car I see, poop-poop! off I go in it!"

"Told you so, didn't I?" observed the Rat to the Mole.

"Very well, then," said the Badger firmly, rising to his feet. "Since you won't yield to persuasion, we'll try what force can do. I feared it would come to this all along. You've often asked us three to come and stay with you, Toad, in this handsome house of yours; well, now we're going to. When we've converted you to a proper point of view we may quit, but not before. Take him upstairs, you two, and lock him up in his bedroom, while we arrange matters between ourselves."

"It's for your own good, Toady, you know," said the Rat kindly, as Toad, kicking and struggling, was hauled up the stairs by his two faithful friends. "Think what fun we shall all have together, just as we used to, when you've quite got over this—this painful attack of yours!"

"We'll take great care of everything for you till you're well, Toad," said the Mole; "and we'll see your money isn't wasted, as it has been."

"No more of those regrettable incidents with the police, Toad," said the Rat, as they thrust him into his bedroom.

"And no more weeks in hospital, being ordered about by female nurses, Toad," added the Mole, turning the key on him.

They descended the stair, Toad shouting abuse at them through the keyhole; and the three friends then met in conference on the situation.

"It's going to be a tedious business," said the Badger, sighing. "I've never seen Toad so determined. However, we will see it out. He must never be left an instant unguarded. We shall have to take it in turns to be with him, till the poison has worked itself out of his system."

They arranged watches accordingly. Each animal took it in turns to sleep in Toad's room at night, and they divided the day up between them. At first Toad was undoubtedly very trying to his careful guardians. When his violent paroxysms possessed him he would arrange bedroom chairs in rude resemblance of a motor-car and would crouch on the foremost of them, bent forward and staring fixedly ahead, making uncouth and ghastly noises, till the climax was reached, when, turning a complete somersault, he would lie prostrate amidst the ruins of the chairs, apparently completely satisfied for the moment. As time passed, however, these painful seizures grew gradually less frequent, and his friends strove to divert his mind into fresh channels. But his interest in other matters did not seem to revive, and he grew apparently languid and depressed.

One fine morning the Rat, whose turn it was to go on duty, went upstairs to relieve Badger, whom he found fidgeting to be off and stretch his legs in a long ramble round his wood and down his earths and burrows. "Toad's still in bed," he told the Rat, outside the door. "Can't get much out of him, except, 'O leave him alone, he wants nothing, perhaps he'll be better presently, it may pass off in time, don't be unduly anxious,' and so on. Now, you look out, Rat! When Toad's quiet and submissive and playing at being the hero of a Sunday-school prize, then he's at his artfullest. There's sure to be something up. I know him. Well, now, I must be off."

"How are you today, old chap?" inquired the Rat cheerfully, as he approached Toad's bedside.

He had to wait some minutes for an answer. At last a feeble voice replied, "Thank you so much, dear Ratty! So good of you to inquire! But first tell me how you are yourself, and the excellent Mole?"

"O, *we're* all right," replied the Rat. "Mole," he added incautiously, "is going out for a run round with Badger. They'll be out till luncheon time, so you and I will spend a pleasant morning together, and I'll do my best to amuse you. Now jump up, there's a good fellow, and don't lie moping there on a fine morning like this!"

"Dear, kind Rat," murmured Toad, "how little you realise my condition, and how very far I am from 'jumping up' now—if ever! But do not trouble about me. I hate being a burden to my friends, and I do not expect to be one much longer. Indeed, I almost hope not."

"Well, I hope not, too," said the Rat heartily. "You've been a fine bother to us all this time, and I'm glad to hear it's going to stop. And in weather like this, and the boating season just beginning! It's too bad of you, Toad! It isn't the trouble we mind, but you're making us miss such an awful lot."

"I'm afraid it *is* the trouble you mind, though," replied the Toad languidly. "I can quite understand it. It's natural enough. You're tired of bothering about me. I mustn't ask you to do anything further. I'm a nuisance, I know."

"You are, indeed," said the Rat. "But I tell you, I'd take any trouble on earth for you, if only you'd be a sensible animal."

"If I thought that, Ratty," murmured Toad, more feebly than ever, "then I would beg you—for the last time, probably—to step round to the village as quickly as possible—even now it may be too late—and fetch the doctor. But don't you bother. It's only a trouble, and perhaps we may as well let things take their course."

"Why, what do you want a doctor for?" inquired the Rat, coming closer and examining him. He certainly lay very still and flat, and his voice was weaker and his manner much changed.

"Surely you have noticed of late—" murmured Toad. "But, no—why should you? Noticing things is only a trouble. Tomorrow, indeed, you may be saying to yourself, 'O, if only I had noticed sooner! If only I had done something!' But no; it's a trouble. Never mind—forget that I asked."

"Look here, old man," said the Rat, beginning to get rather alarmed, "of course I'll fetch a doctor to you, if you really think you want him. But you can hardly be bad enough for that yet. Let's talk about something else."

"I fear, dear friend," said Toad, with a sad smile, "that 'talk' can do little in a case like this—or doctors either, for that matter; still, one must grasp at the slightest straw. And, by the way—while you are about it—I *hate* to give you additional trouble, but I happen to remember that you will pass the door—would you mind at the same time asking the lawyer to step up? It would be a convenience to me, and there are moments—perhaps I should say there is *a* moment—when one must face disagreeable tasks, at whatever cost to exhausted nature!"

"A lawyer! O, he must be really bad!" the affrighted Rat said to himself, as he hurried from the room, not forgetting, however, to lock the door carefully behind him.

Outside, he stopped to consider. The other two were far away, and he had no one to consult.

"It's best to be on the safe side," he said, on reflection. "I've known Toad fancy himself frightfully bad before, without the slightest reason; but I've never heard him ask for a lawyer! If there's nothing really the matter, the doctor will tell him he's an old ass, and cheer him up; and that will be something gained. I'd better humour him and go; it won't take very long." So he ran off to the village on his errand of mercy.

The Toad, who had hopped lightly out of bed as soon as he heard the key turned in the lock, watched him eagerly from the window till he disappeared down the carriage-drive. Then, laughing heartily, he dressed as quickly as possible in the smartest suit he could lay hands on at the moment, filled his pockets with cash which he took from a small drawer in the dressing-table, and next, knotting the sheets from his bed together and tying one end of the improvised rope round the central mullion of the handsome Tudor window which formed such a feature of his bedroom, he scrambled out, slid lightly to the ground, and, taking the opposite direction to the Rat, marched off light-heartedly, whistling a merry tune.

It was a gloomy luncheon for Rat when the Badger and the Mole at length returned, and he had to face them at table with his pitiful and unconvincing story. The Badger's caustic, not to say brutal, remarks may be imagined, and therefore passed over; but it was painful to the Rat that even the Mole, though he took his friend's side as far as possible, could not help saying, "You've been a bit of a duffer this time, Ratty! Toad, too, of all animals!"

"He did it awfully well," said the crestfallen Rat.

"He did *you* awfully well!" rejoined the Badger hotly. "However, talking won't mend matters. He's got clear away for the time, that's certain; and the worst of it is, he'll be so conceited with what he'll think is his cleverness that he may commit any folly. One comfort is, we're free now, and needn't waste any more of our precious time doing sentry-go. But we'd better continue to sleep at Toad Hall for a while longer. Toad may be brought back at any moment—on a stretcher, or between two policemen."

So spoke the Badger, not knowing what the future held in store, or how much water, and of how turbid a character, was to run under bridges before Toad should sit at ease again in his ancestral Hall.

* * * * *

Meanwhile, Toad, gay and irresponsible, was walking briskly along the high-road, some miles from home. At first he had taken by-paths, and crossed many fields, and changed his course several times, in case of pursuit; but now, feeling by this time safe from recapture, and the sun smiling brightly on him, and all Nature joining in a chorus of approval to the song of self-praise that his own heart was singing to him, he almost danced along the road in his satisfaction and conceit.

"Smart piece of work that!" he remarked to himself chuckling. "Brain against brute force—and brain came out on the top—as it's bound to do. Poor old Ratty! My! won't he catch it when the Badger gets back! A worthy fellow, Ratty, with many good qualities, but very little intelligence and absolutely no education. I must take him in hand someday, and see if I can make something of him."

Filled full of conceited thoughts such as these he strode along, his head in the air, till he reached a little town, where the sign of "The Red Lion," swinging across the road halfway down the main street, reminded him that he had not breakfasted that day, and that he was exceedingly hungry after his long walk. He marched into the Inn, ordered the best luncheon that could be provided at so short a notice, and sat down to eat it in the coffee-room.

He was about halfway through his meal when an only too familiar sound, approaching down the street, made him start and fall a-trembling all over. The poop-poop! drew nearer and nearer, the car could be heard to turn into the inn-yard and come to a stop, and Toad had to hold on to the leg of the table to conceal his over-mastering emotion. Presently the party entered the coffee-room, hungry, talkative, and gay, voluble on their experiences of the morning and the merits of the chariot that had brought them along so well. Toad listened eagerly, all ears, for a time; at last he could stand it no longer. He slipped out of the room quietly, paid his bill at the bar, and as soon as he got outside sauntered round quietly to the inn-yard. "There cannot be any harm," he said to himself, "in my only just *looking* at it!"

The car stood in the middle of the yard, quite unattended, the stable-helps and other hangers-on being all at their dinner. Toad walked slowly round it, inspecting, criticising, musing deeply.

"I wonder," he said to himself presently, "I wonder if this sort of car *starts* easily?"

Next moment, hardly knowing how it came about, he found he had hold of the handle and was turning it. As the familiar sound broke forth, the old passion seized on Toad and completely mastered him, body and soul. As if in a dream, he found himself, somehow, seated in the driver's seat; as if in a dream, he pulled the lever and swung the car round the yard and out through the archway; and, as if in a dream, all sense of right and wrong, all fear of obvious consequences, seemed temporarily suspended. He increased his pace, and as the car devoured the street and leapt forth on the high-road through the open country, he was only conscious that he was Toad once more, Toad at his best and highest, Toad the terror, the traffic-queller, the Lord of the lone trail, before whom all must give way or be smitten into nothingness and everlasting night. He chanted as he flew, and the car responded with sonorous drone; the miles were eaten up under him as he sped he knew not whither, fulfilling his instincts, living his hour, reckless of what might come to him.

* * * * *

"To my mind," observed the Chairman of the Bench of Magistrates cheerfully, "the *only* difficulty that presents itself in this otherwise very clear case is, how we can possibly make it sufficiently hot for the incorrigible rogue and hardened ruffian whom we see cowering in the dock before us. Let me see: he has been found guilty, on the clearest evidence, first, of stealing a valuable motor-car; secondly, of driving to the public danger; and, thirdly, of gross impertinence to the rural police. Mr. Clerk, will you tell us, please, what is the very stiffest penalty we can impose for each of these offences? Without, of course, giving the prisoner the benefit of any doubt, because there isn't any."

The Clerk scratched his nose with his pen. "Some people would consider," he observed, "that stealing the motor-car was the worst offence; and so it is. But cheeking the police undoubtedly carries the severest penalty; and so it ought. Supposing you were to say twelve months for the theft, which is mild; and three years for the furious driving, which is lenient; and fifteen years for the cheek, which was pretty bad sort of cheek, judging by what we've heard from the witness-box, even if you only believe one-tenth part of what you heard, and I never believe more myself—those figures, if added together correctly, tot up to nineteen years—"

"First-rate!" said the Chairman.

"—So you had better make it a round twenty years and be on the safe side," concluded the Clerk.

"An excellent suggestion!" said the Chairman approvingly.

THE WIND IN THE WILLOWS

"Prisoner! Pull yourself together and try and stand up straight. It's going to be twenty years for you this time. And mind, if you appear before us again, upon any charge whatever, we shall have to deal with you very seriously!"

Then the brutal minions of the law fell upon the hapless Toad; loaded him with chains, and dragged him from the Court House, shrieking, praying, protesting; across the marketplace, where the playful populace, always as severe upon detected crime as they are sympathetic and helpful when one is merely "wanted," assailed him with jeers, carrots, and popular catch-words; past hooting school children, their innocent faces lit up with the pleasure they ever derive from the sight of a gentleman in difficulties; across the hollow-sounding drawbridge, below the spiky portcullis, under the frowning archway of the grim old castle, whose ancient towers soared high overhead; past guardrooms full of grinning soldiery off duty, past sentries who coughed in a horrid, sarcastic way, because that is as much as a sentry on his post dare do to show his contempt and abhorrence of crime; up time-worn winding stairs, past men-at-arms in casquet and corselet of steel, darting threatening looks through their vizards; across courtyards, where mastiffs strained at their leash and pawed the air to get at him; past ancient warders, their halberds leant against the wall, dozing over a pasty and a flagon of brown ale; on and on, past the rack-chamber and the thumbscrew-room, past the turning that led to the private scaffold, till they reached the door of the grimmest dungeon that lay in the heart of the innermost keep. There at last they paused, where an ancient gaoler sat fingering a bunch of mighty keys.

"Oddsbodikins!" said the sergeant of police, taking off his helmet and wiping his forehead. "Rouse thee, old loon, and take over from us this vile Toad, a criminal of deepest guilt and matchless artfulness and resource. Watch and ward him with all thy skill; and mark thee well, greybeard, should aught untoward befall, thy old head shall answer for his— and a murrain on both of them!"

The gaoler nodded grimly, laying his withered hand on the shoulder of the miserable Toad. The rusty key creaked in the lock, the great door clanged behind them; and Toad was a helpless prisoner in the remotest dungeon of the best-guarded keep of the stoutest castle in all the length and breadth of Merry England.

Chapter 7. The Piper at the Gates of Dawn

The Willow-Wren was twittering his thin little song, hidden himself in the dark selvedge of the river bank. Though it was past ten o'clock at night, the sky still clung to and retained some lingering skirts of light from the departed day; and the sullen heats of the torrid afternoon broke up and rolled away at the dispersing touch of the cool fingers of the short midsummer night. Mole lay stretched on the bank, still panting from the stress of the fierce day that had been cloudless from dawn to late sunset, and waited for his friend to return. He had been on the river with some companions, leaving the Water Rat free to keep an engagement of long standing with Otter; and he had come back to find the house dark and deserted, and no sign of Rat, who was doubtless keeping it up late with his old comrade. It was still too hot to think of staying indoors, so he lay on some cool dock-leaves, and thought over the past day and its doings, and how very good they all had been.

The Rat's light footfall was presently heard approaching over the parched grass. "O, the blessed coolness!" he said, and sat down, gazing thoughtfully into the river, silent and preoccupied.

"You stayed to supper, of course?" said the Mole presently.

"Simply had to," said the Rat. "They wouldn't hear of my going before. You know how kind they always are. And they made things as jolly for me as ever they could, right up to the moment I left. But I felt a brute all the time, as it was clear to me they were very unhappy, though they tried to hide it. Mole, I'm afraid they're in trouble. Little Portly is missing again; and you know what a lot his father thinks of him, though he never says much about it."

"What, that child?" said the Mole lightly. "Well, suppose he is; why worry about it? He's always straying off and getting lost, and turning up again; he's so adventurous. But no harm ever happens to him. Everybody hereabouts knows him and likes him, just as they do old Otter, and you may be sure some animal or other will come across him and bring him back again all right. Why, we've found him ourselves, miles from home, and quite self-possessed and cheerful!"

"Yes; but this time it's more serious," said the Rat gravely. "He's been missing for some days now, and the Otters have hunted everywhere, high and low, without finding the slightest trace. And they've asked every animal, too, for miles around, and no one knows anything about him. Otter's evidently more anxious than he'll admit. I got out of him that young Portly hasn't learnt to swim very well yet, and I can see he's thinking of the weir. There's a lot of water coming down still, considering the time of the year, and the place always had a fascination for the child. And then there are—well, traps and things—*you* know. Otter's not the fellow to be nervous about any son of his before it's time. And now he *is* nervous. When I left, he came out with me—said he wanted some air, and talked about stretching his legs. But I could see it wasn't that, so I drew him out and pumped him, and got it all from him at last. He was going to spend the night watching by the ford. You know the place where the old ford used to be, in by-gone days before they built the bridge?"

"I know it well," said the Mole. "But why should Otter choose to watch there?"

"Well, it seems that it was there he gave Portly his first swimming-lesson," continued the Rat. "From that shallow, gravelly spit near the bank. And it was there he used to teach him fishing, and there young Portly caught his first fish, of which he was so very proud. The child loved the spot, and Otter thinks that if he came wandering back from wherever he is—if he *is* anywhere by this time, poor little chap—he might make for the ford he was so fond of; or if he came across it he'd remember it well, and stop there and play, perhaps. So Otter goes there every night and watches—on the chance, you know, just on the chance!"

They were silent for a time, both thinking of the same thing—the lonely, heart-sore animal, crouched by the ford, watching and waiting, the long night through—on the chance.

"Well, well," said the Rat presently, "I suppose we ought to be thinking about turning in." But he never offered to move.

"Rat," said the Mole, "I simply can't go and turn in, and go to sleep, and *do* nothing, even though there doesn't seem to be anything to be done. We'll get the boat out, and paddle upstream. The moon will be up in an hour or so, and then we will search as well as we can—anyhow, it will be better than going to bed and doing *nothing*."

"Just what I was thinking myself," said the Rat. "It's not the sort of night for bed anyhow; and daybreak is not so very far off, and then we may pick up some news of him from early risers as we go along."

They got the boat out, and the Rat took the sculls, paddling with caution. Out in midstream, there was a clear, narrow track that faintly reflected the sky; but wherever shadows fell on the water from bank, bush, or tree, they were as solid to all appearance as the banks themselves, and the Mole had to steer with judgment accordingly. Dark and deserted as it was, the night was full of small noises, song and chatter and rustling, telling of the busy little population who were up and about, plying their trades and vocations through the night till sunshine should fall on them at last and send them off to their well-earned repose. The water's own noises, too, were more apparent than by day, its gurglings and "cloops" more unexpected and near at hand; and constantly they started at what seemed a sudden clear call from an actual articulate voice.

The line of the horizon was clear and hard against the sky, and in one particular quarter it showed black against a silvery climbing phosphorescence that grew and grew. At last, over the rim of the waiting earth the moon lifted with slow majesty till it swung clear of the horizon and rode off, free of moorings; and once more they began to see surfaces—meadows wide-spread, and quiet gardens, and the river itself from bank to bank, all softly disclosed, all washed clean of mystery and terror, all radiant again as by day, but with a difference that was tremendous. Their old haunts greeted them again in other raiment, as if they had slipped away and put on this pure new apparel and come quietly back, smiling as they shyly waited to see if they would be recognised again under it.

Fastening their boat to a willow, the friends landed in this silent, silver kingdom, and patiently explored the hedges, the hollow trees, the runnels and their little culverts, the ditches and dry water-ways. Embarking again and crossing over, they worked their way up the stream in this manner, while the moon, serene and detached in a cloudless sky, did what she could, though so far off, to help them in their quest; till her hour came and she sank earthwards reluctantly, and left them, and mystery once more held field and river.

Then a change began slowly to declare itself. The horizon became clearer, field and tree came more into sight, and somehow with a different look; the mystery began to drop away from them. A bird piped suddenly, and was still; and a light breeze sprang up and set the reeds and bulrushes rustling. Rat, who was in the stern of the boat, while Mole sculled, sat up suddenly and listened with a passionate intentness. Mole, who with gentle strokes was just keeping the boat moving while he scanned the banks with care, looked at him with curiosity.

"It's gone!" sighed the Rat, sinking back in his seat again. "So beautiful and strange and new. Since it was to end so soon, I almost wish I had never heard it. For it has roused a longing in me that is pain, and nothing seems worth while but just to hear that sound once more and go on listening to it forever. No! There it is again!" he cried, alert once more. Entranced, he was silent for a long space, spellbound.

"Now it passes on and I begin to lose it," he said presently. "O Mole! the beauty of it! The merry bubble and joy, the thin, clear, happy call of the distant piping! Such music I never dreamed of, and the call in it is stronger even than the music is sweet! Row on, Mole, row! For the music and the call must be for us."

The Mole, greatly wondering, obeyed. "I hear nothing myself," he said, "but the wind playing in the reeds and rushes and osiers."

The Rat never answered, if indeed he heard. Rapt, transported, trembling, he was possessed in all his senses by this new divine thing that caught up his helpless soul and swung and dandled it, a powerless but happy infant in a strong sustaining grasp.

In silence Mole rowed steadily, and soon they came to a point where the river divided, a long backwater branching off to one side. With a slight movement of his head Rat, who had long dropped the rudder-lines, directed the rower to take the backwater. The creeping tide of light gained and gained, and now they could see the colour of the flowers that gemmed the water's edge.

"Clearer and nearer still," cried the Rat joyously. "Now you must surely hear it! Ah—at last—I see you do!"

Breathless and transfixed the Mole stopped rowing as the liquid run of that glad piping broke on him like a wave, caught him up, and possessed him utterly. He saw the tears on his comrade's cheeks, and bowed his head and understood. For a space they hung there, brushed by the purple loosestrife that fringed the bank; then the clear imperious summons that marched hand-in-hand with the intoxicating melody imposed its will on Mole, and mechanically he bent to his oars again. And the light grew steadily stronger, but no birds sang as they were wont to do at the approach of dawn; and but for the heavenly music all was marvellously still.

On either side of them, as they glided onwards, the rich meadow-grass seemed that morning of a freshness and a greenness unsurpassable. Never had they noticed the roses so vivid, the willow-herb so riotous, the meadow-sweet so odorous and pervading. Then the murmur of the approaching weir began to hold the air, and they felt a consciousness that they were nearing the end, whatever it might be, that surely awaited their expedition.

A wide half-circle of foam and glinting lights and shining shoulders of green water, the great weir closed the backwater from bank to bank, troubled all the quiet surface with twirling eddies and floating foam-streaks, and deadened all other sounds with its solemn and soothing rumble. In midmost of the stream, embraced in the weir's shimmering arm-spread, a small island lay anchored, fringed close with willow and silver birch and alder. Reserved, shy, but full of significance, it hid whatever it might hold behind a veil, keeping it till the hour should come, and, with the hour, those who were called and chosen.

Slowly, but with no doubt or hesitation whatever, and in something of a solemn expectancy, the two animals passed through the broken tumultuous water and moored their boat at the flowery margin of the island. In silence they landed, and pushed through the blossom and scented herbage and undergrowth that led up to the level ground, till they stood on a little lawn of a marvellous green, set round with Nature's own orchard-trees—crab-apple, wild cherry, and sloe.

"This is the place of my song-dream, the place the music played to me," whispered the Rat, as if in a trance. "Here, in this holy place, here if anywhere, surely we shall find Him!"

Then suddenly the Mole felt a great Awe fall upon him, an awe that turned his muscles to water, bowed his head, and rooted his feet to the ground. It was no panic terror—indeed he felt wonderfully at peace and happy—but it was an awe that smote and held him and, without seeing, he knew it could only mean that some august Presence was very, very near. With difficulty he turned to look for his friend and saw him at his side cowed, stricken, and trembling violently. And still there was utter silence in the populous bird-haunted branches around them; and still the light grew and grew.

Perhaps he would never have dared to raise his eyes, but that, though the piping was now hushed, the call and the summons seemed still dominant and imperious. He might not refuse, were Death himself waiting to strike him instantly, once he had looked with mortal eye on things rightly kept hidden. Trembling he obeyed, and raised his humble head; and then, in that utter clearness of the imminent dawn, while Nature, flushed with fullness of incredible colour, seemed to hold her breath for the event, he looked in the very eyes of the Friend and Helper; saw the backward sweep of the curved horns, gleaming in the growing daylight; saw the stern, hooked nose between the kindly eyes that were looking down on them humourously, while the bearded mouth broke into a half-smile at the corners; saw the rippling muscles on the arm that lay across the broad chest, the long supple hand still holding the pan-pipes only just fallen away from the parted lips; saw the splendid curves of the shaggy limbs disposed in majestic ease on the sward; saw, last of all, nestling between his very hooves, sleeping soundly in entire peace and contentment, the little, round, podgy, childish form of the baby otter. All this he saw, for one moment breathless and intense, vivid on the morning sky; and still, as he looked, he lived; and still, as he lived, he wondered.

"Rat!" he found breath to whisper, shaking. "Are you afraid?"

"Afraid?" murmured the Rat, his eyes shining with unutterable love. "Afraid! Of *him*? O, never, never! And yet—and yet—O, Mole, I am afraid!"

Then the two animals, crouching to the earth, bowed their heads and did worship.

Sudden and magnificent, the sun's broad golden disc showed itself over the horizon facing them; and the first rays, shooting across the level water-meadows, took the animals full in the eyes and dazzled them. When they were able to look once more, the Vision had vanished, and the air was full of the carol of birds that hailed the dawn.

As they stared blankly in dumb misery deepening as they slowly realised all they had seen and all they had lost, a capricious little breeze, dancing up from the surface of the water, tossed the aspens, shook the dewy roses and blew lightly and caressingly in their faces; and with its soft touch came instant oblivion. For this is the last best gift that the kindly demi-god is careful to bestow on those to whom he has revealed himself in their helping: the gift of forgetfulness. Lest the awful remembrance should remain and grow, and overshadow mirth and pleasure, and the great haunting memory should spoil all the after-lives of little animals helped out of difficulties, in order that they should be happy and light-hearted as before.

Mole rubbed his eyes and stared at Rat, who was looking about him in a puzzled sort of way. "I beg your pardon; what did you say, Rat?" he asked.

"I think I was only remarking," said Rat slowly, "that this was the right sort of place, and that here, if anywhere, we should find him. And look! Why, there he is, the little fellow!" And with a cry of delight he ran towards the slumbering Portly.

But Mole stood still a moment, held in thought. As one wakened suddenly from a beautiful dream, who struggles to recall it, and can re-capture nothing but a dim sense of the beauty of it, the beauty! Till that, too, fades away in its turn, and the dreamer bitterly accepts the hard, cold waking and all its penalties; so Mole, after struggling with his memory for a brief space, shook his head sadly and followed the Rat.

Portly woke up with a joyous squeak, and wriggled with pleasure at the sight of his father's friends, who had played with him so often in past days. In a moment, however, his face grew blank, and he fell to hunting round in a circle with pleading whine. As a child that has fallen happily asleep in its nurse's arms, and wakes to find itself alone and laid in a strange place, and searches corners and cupboards, and runs from room to room, despair growing silently in its heart, even so Portly searched the island and searched, dogged and unwearying, till at last the black moment came for giving it up, and sitting down and crying bitterly.

The Mole ran quickly to comfort the little animal; but Rat, lingering, looked long and doubtfully at certain hoof-marks deep in the sward.

"Some—great—animal—has been here," he murmured slowly and thoughtfully; and stood musing, musing; his mind strangely stirred.

"Come along, Rat!" called the Mole. "Think of poor Otter, waiting up there by the ford!"

Portly had soon been comforted by the promise of a treat—a jaunt on the river in Mr. Rat's real boat; and the two animals conducted him to the water's side, placed him securely between them in the bottom of the boat, and paddled off down the backwater. The sun was fully up by now, and hot on them, birds sang lustily and without restraint, and flowers smiled and nodded from either bank, but somehow—so thought the animals—with less of richness and blaze of colour than they seemed to remember seeing quite recently somewhere—they wondered where.

The main river reached again, they turned the boat's head upstream, towards the point where they knew their friend was keeping his lonely vigil. As they drew near the familiar ford, the Mole took the boat in to the bank, and they lifted Portly out and set him on his legs on the tow-path, gave him his marching orders and a friendly farewell pat on the back, and shoved out into mid-stream. They watched the little animal as he waddled along the path contentedly and with importance; watched him till they saw his muzzle suddenly lift and his waddle break into a clumsy amble as he quickened his pace with shrill whines and wriggles of recognition. Looking up the river, they could see Otter start up, tense and rigid, from out of the shallows where he crouched in dumb patience, and could hear his amazed and joyous bark as he bounded up through the osiers on to the path. Then the Mole, with a strong pull on one oar, swung the boat round and let the full stream bear them down again whither it would, their quest now happily ended.

"I feel strangely tired, Rat," said the Mole, leaning wearily over his oars as the boat drifted. "It's being up all night, you'll say, perhaps; but that's nothing. We do as much half the nights of the week, at this time of the year. No; I feel as if I had been through something very exciting and rather terrible, and it was just over; and yet nothing particular has happened."

"Or something very surprising and splendid and beautiful," murmured the Rat, leaning back and closing his eyes. "I feel just as you do, Mole; simply dead tired, though not body tired. It's lucky we've got the stream with us, to take us home. Isn't it jolly to feel the sun again, soaking into one's bones! And hark to the wind playing in the reeds!"

"It's like music—far-away music," said the Mole nodding drowsily.

"So I was thinking," murmured the Rat, dreamful and languid. "Dance-music—the lilting sort that runs on without a stop—but with words in it, too—it passes into words and out of them again—I catch them at intervals—then it is dance-music once more, and then nothing but the reeds' soft thin whispering."

"You hear better than I," said the Mole sadly. "I cannot catch the words."

"Let me try and give you them," said the Rat softly, his eyes still closed. "Now it is turning into words again—faint but clear—*Lest the awe should dwell—And turn your frolic to fret—You shall look on my power at the helping hour—But then you shall forget!* Now the reeds take it up—*forget, forget*, they sigh, and it dies away in a rustle and a whisper. Then the voice returns—

"*Lest limbs be reddened and rent—I spring the trap that is set—As I loose the snare you may glimpse me there—For surely you shall forget!* Row nearer, Mole, nearer to the reeds! It is hard to catch, and grows each minute fainter.

"*Helper and healer, I cheer—Small waifs in the woodland wet—Strays I find in it, wounds I bind in it—Bidding them all forget!* Nearer, Mole, nearer! No, it is no good; the song has died away into reed-talk."

"But what do the words mean?" asked the wondering Mole.

"That I do not know," said the Rat simply. "I passed them on to you as they reached me. Ah! now they return again, and this time full and clear! This time, at last, it is the real, the unmistakable thing, simple—passionate—perfect—"

"Well, let's have it, then," said the Mole, after he had waited patiently for a few minutes, half-dozing in the hot sun.

But no answer came. He looked, and understood the silence. With a smile of much happiness on his face, and something of a listening look still lingering there, the weary Rat was fast asleep.

Chapter 8. Toad's Adventures

When Toad found himself immured in a dank and noisome dungeon, and knew that all the grim darkness of a medieval fortress lay between him and the outer world of sunshine and well-metalled high-roads where he had lately been so happy, disporting himself as if he had bought up every road in England, he flung himself at full length on the floor, and shed bitter tears, and abandoned himself to dark despair. "This is the end of everything" (he said), "at least it is the end of the career of Toad, which is the same thing; the popular and handsome Toad, the rich and hospitable Toad, the Toad so free and careless and debonair! How can I hope to be ever set at large again" (he said), "who have been imprisoned so justly for stealing so handsome a motor-car in such an audacious manner, and for such lurid and imaginative cheek, bestowed upon such a number of fat, red-faced policemen!" (Here his sobs choked him.) "Stupid animal that I was" (he said), "now I must languish in this dungeon, till people who were proud to say they knew me, have forgotten the very name of Toad! O wise old Badger!" (he said), "O clever, intelligent Rat and sensible Mole! What sound judgments, what a knowledge of men and matters you possess! O unhappy and forsaken Toad!" With lamentations such as these he passed his days and nights for several weeks, refusing his meals or intermediate light refreshments, though the grim and ancient gaoler, knowing that Toad's pockets were well lined, frequently pointed out that many comforts, and indeed luxuries, could by arrangement be sent in—at a price—from outside.

Now the gaoler had a daughter, a pleasant wench and good-hearted, who assisted her father in the lighter duties of his post. She was particularly fond of animals, and, besides her canary, whose cage hung on a nail in the massive wall of the keep by day, to the great annoyance of prisoners who relished an after-dinner nap, and was shrouded in an antimacassar on the parlour table at night, she kept several piebald mice and a restless revolving squirrel. This kind-hearted girl, pitying the misery of Toad, said to her father one day, "Father! I can't bear to see that poor beast so unhappy, and getting so thin! You let me have the managing of him. You know how fond of animals I am. I'll make him eat from my hand, and sit up, and do all sorts of things."

Her father replied that she could do what she liked with him. He was tired of Toad, and his sulks and his airs and his meanness. So that day she went on her errand of mercy, and knocked at the door of Toad's cell.

"Now, cheer up, Toad," she said, coaxingly, on entering, "and sit up and dry your eyes and be a sensible animal. And do try and eat a bit of dinner. See, I've brought you some of mine, hot from the oven!"

It was bubble-and-squeak, between two plates, and its fragrance filled the narrow cell. The penetrating smell of cabbage reached the nose of Toad as he lay prostrate in his misery on the floor, and gave him the idea for a moment that perhaps life was not such a blank and desperate thing as he had imagined. But still he wailed, and kicked with his legs, and refused to be comforted. So the wise girl retired for the time, but, of course, a good deal of the smell of hot cabbage remained behind, as it will do, and Toad, between his sobs, sniffed and reflected, and gradually began to think new and inspiring thoughts: of chivalry, and poetry, and deeds still to be done; of broad meadows, and cattle browsing in them, raked by sun and wind; of kitchen-gardens, and straight herb-borders, and warm snap-dragon beset by bees; and of the comforting clink of dishes set down on the table at Toad Hall, and the scrape of chair-legs on the floor as everyone pulled himself close up to his work. The air of the narrow cell took a rosy tinge; he began to think of his friends, and how they would surely be able to do something; of lawyers, and how they would have enjoyed his case, and what an ass he had been not to get in a few; and lastly, he thought of his own great cleverness and resource, and all that he was capable of if he only gave his great mind to it; and the cure was almost complete.

When the girl returned, some hours later, she carried a tray, with a cup of fragrant tea steaming on it; and a plate piled up with very hot buttered toast, cut thick, very brown on both sides, with the butter running through the holes in it in great golden drops, like honey from the honeycomb. The smell of that buttered toast simply talked to Toad, and with no uncertain voice; talked of warm kitchens, of breakfasts on bright frosty mornings, of cosy parlour firesides on winter evenings, when one's ramble was over and slippered feet were propped on the fender; of the purring of contented cats, and the twitter of sleepy canaries. Toad sat up on end once more, dried his eyes, sipped his tea and munched his toast, and soon began talking freely about himself, and the house he lived in, and his doings there, and how important he was, and what a lot his friends thought of him.

The gaoler's daughter saw that the topic was doing him as much good as the tea, as indeed it was, and encouraged him to go on.

"Tell me about Toad Hall," said she. "It sounds beautiful."

"Toad Hall," said the Toad proudly, "is an eligible self-contained gentleman's residence very unique; dating in part from the fourteenth century, but replete with every modern convenience. Up-to-date sanitation. Five minutes from church, post-office, and golf-links, Suitable for—"

"Bless the animal," said the girl, laughing, "I don't want to *take* it. Tell me something *real* about it. But first wait till I fetch you some more tea and toast."

She tripped away, and presently returned with a fresh trayful; and Toad, pitching into the toast with avidity, his spirits quite restored to their usual level, told her about the boat-house, and the fish-pond, and the old walled kitchen-garden; and about the pig-styes, and the stables, and the pigeon-house, and the hen-house; and about the dairy, and the wash-house, and the china-cupboards, and the linen-presses (she liked that bit especially); and about the banqueting-hall, and the fun they had there when the other animals were gathered round the table and Toad was at his best, singing songs, telling stories, carrying on generally. Then she wanted to know about his animal-friends, and was very interested in all he had to tell her about them and how they lived, and what they did to pass their time. Of course, she did not say she was fond of animals as *pets*, because she had the sense to see that Toad would be extremely offended. When she said good night, having filled his water-jug and shaken up his straw for him, Toad was very much the same sanguine, self-satisfied animal that he had been of old. He sang a little song or two, of the sort he used to sing at his dinner-parties, curled himself up in the straw, and had an excellent night's rest and the pleasantest of dreams.

They had many interesting talks together, after that, as the dreary days went on; and the gaoler's daughter grew very sorry for Toad, and thought it a great shame that a poor little animal should be locked up in prison for what seemed to her a very trivial offence. Toad, of course, in his vanity, thought that her interest in him proceeded from a growing tenderness; and he could not help half-regretting that the social gulf between them was so very wide, for she was a comely lass, and evidently admired him very much.

One morning the girl was very thoughtful, and answered at random, and did not seem to Toad to be paying proper attention to his witty sayings and sparkling comments.

"Toad," she said presently, "just listen, please. I have an aunt who is a washerwoman."

"There, there," said Toad, graciously and affably, "never mind; think no more about it. *I* have several aunts who *ought* to be washerwomen."

"Do be quiet a minute, Toad," said the girl. "You talk too much, that's your chief fault, and I'm trying to think, and you hurt my head. As I said, I have an aunt who is a washerwoman; she does the washing for all the prisoners in this castle—we try to keep any paying business of that sort in the family, you understand. She takes out the washing on Monday morning, and brings it in on Friday evening. This is a Thursday. Now, this is what occurs to me: you're very rich—at least you're always telling me so—and she's very poor. A few pounds wouldn't make any difference to you, and it would mean a lot to her. Now, I think if she were properly approached—squared, I believe is the word you animals use—you could come to some arrangement by which she would let you have her dress and bonnet and so on, and you could escape from the castle as the official washerwoman. You're very alike in many respects—particularly about the figure."

"We're *not*," said the Toad in a huff. "I have a very elegant figure—for what I am."

"So has my aunt," replied the girl, "for what *she* is. But have it your own way. You horrid, proud, ungrateful animal, when I'm sorry for you, and trying to help you!"

"Yes, yes, that's all right; thank you very much indeed," said the Toad hurriedly. "But look here! you wouldn't surely have Mr. Toad of Toad Hall, going about the country disguised as a washerwoman!"

"Then you can stop here as a Toad," replied the girl with much spirit. "I suppose you want to go off in a coach-and-four!"

Honest Toad was always ready to admit himself in the wrong. "You are a good, kind, clever girl," he said, "and I am indeed a proud and a stupid toad. Introduce me to your worthy aunt, if you will be so kind, and I have no doubt that the excellent lady and I will be able to arrange terms satisfactory to both parties."

Next evening the girl ushered her aunt into Toad's cell, bearing his week's washing pinned up in a towel. The old lady had been prepared beforehand for the interview, and the sight of certain gold sovereigns that Toad had thoughtfully placed on the table in full view practically completed the matter and left little further to discuss. In return for his cash, Toad received a cotton print gown, an apron, a shawl, and a rusty black bonnet; the only stipulation the old lady made being that she should be gagged and bound and dumped down in a corner. By this not very convincing artifice, she explained, aided by picturesque fiction which she could supply herself, she hoped to retain her situation, in spite of the suspicious appearance of things.

Toad was delighted with the suggestion. It would enable him to leave the prison in some style, and with his reputation for being a desperate and dangerous fellow untarnished; and he readily helped the gaoler's daughter to make her aunt appear as much as possible the victim of circumstances over which she had no control.

"Now it's your turn, Toad," said the girl. "Take off that coat and waistcoat of yours; you're fat enough as it is."

Shaking with laughter, she proceeded to "hook-and-eye" him into the cotton print gown, arranged the shawl with a professional fold, and tied the strings of the rusty bonnet under his chin.

"You're the very image of her," she giggled, "only I'm sure you never looked half so respectable in all your life before. Now, good-bye, Toad, and good luck. Go straight down the way you came up; and if anyone says anything to you, as they probably will, being but men, you can chaff back a bit, of course, but remember you're a widow woman, quite alone in the world, with a character to lose."

With a quaking heart, but as firm a footstep as he could command, Toad set forth cautiously on what seemed to be a most hare-brained and hazardous undertaking; but he was soon agreeably surprised to find how easy everything was made for him, and a little humbled

She arranged the shawl with a professional fold, and tied the strings of the rusty bonnet under his chin.

at the thought that both his popularity, and the sex that seemed to inspire it, were really another's. The washerwoman's squat figure in its familiar cotton print seemed a passport for every barred door and grim gateway; even when he hesitated, uncertain as to the right turning to take, he found himself helped out of his difficulty by the warder at the next gate, anxious to be off to his tea, summoning him to come along sharp and not keep him waiting there all night. The chaff and the humourous sallies to which he was subjected, and to which, of course, he had to provide prompt and effective reply, formed, indeed, his chief danger; for Toad was an animal with a strong sense of his own dignity, and the chaff was mostly (he thought) poor and clumsy, and the humour of the sallies entirely lacking. However, he kept his temper, though with great difficulty, suited his retorts to his company and his supposed character, and did his best not to overstep the limits of good taste.

It seemed hours before he crossed the last courtyard, rejected the pressing invitations from the last guardroom, and dodged the outspread arms of the last warder, pleading with simulated passion for just one farewell embrace. But at last he heard the wicket-gate in the great outer door click behind him, felt the fresh air of the outer world upon his anxious brow, and knew that he was free!

Dizzy with the easy success of his daring exploit, he walked quickly towards the lights of the town, not knowing in the least what he should do next, only quite certain of one thing, that he must remove himself as quickly as possible from the neighbourhood where the lady he was forced to represent was so well-known and so popular a character.

As he walked along, considering, his attention was caught by some red and green lights a little way off, to one side of the town, and the sound of the puffing and snorting of engines and the banging of shunted trucks fell on his ear. "Aha!" he thought, "this is a piece of luck! A railway station is the thing I want most in the whole world at this moment; and what's more, I needn't go through the town to get it, and shan't have to support this humiliating character by repartees which, though thoroughly effective, do not assist one's sense of self-respect."

He made his way to the station accordingly, consulted a time-table, and found that a train, bound more or less in the direction of his home, was due to start in half-an-hour. "More luck!" said Toad, his spirits rising rapidly, and went off to the booking-office to buy his ticket.

He gave the name of the station that he knew to be nearest to the village of which Toad Hall was the principal feature, and mechanically put his fingers, in search of the necessary money, where his waistcoat pocket should have been. But here the cotton gown, which had nobly stood by him so far, and which he had basely forgotten, intervened, and frustrated his efforts. In a sort of nightmare he struggled with the strange uncanny thing that seemed to hold his hands, turn all muscular strivings to water, and laugh at him all the time; while other travellers, forming up in a line behind, waited with impatience, making suggestions of more or less value and comments of more or less stringency and point. At last—somehow—he never rightly understood how—he burst the barriers, attained the goal, arrived at where all waistcoat pockets are eternally situated, and found—not only no money, but no pocket to hold it, and no waistcoat to hold the pocket!

To his horror he recollected that he had left both coat and waistcoat behind him in his cell, and with them his pocket-book, money, keys, watch, matches, pencil-case—all that makes life worth living, all that distinguishes the many-pocketed animal, the lord of creation, from the inferior one-pocketed or no-pocketed productions that hop or trip about permissively, unequipped for the real contest.

In his misery he made one desperate effort to carry the thing off, and, with a return to his fine old manner—a blend of the Squire and the College Don—he said, "Look here! I find I've left my purse behind. Just give me that ticket, will you, and I'll send the money on tomorrow? I'm well-known in these parts."

The clerk stared at him and the rusty black bonnet a moment, and then laughed. "I should think you were pretty well known in these parts," he said, "if you've tried this game on often. Here, stand away from the window, please, madam; you're obstructing the other passengers!"

An old gentleman who had been prodding him in the back for some moments here thrust him away, and, what was worse, addressed him as his good woman, which angered Toad more than anything that had occurred that evening.

Baffled and full of despair, he wandered blindly down the platform where the train was standing, and tears trickled down each side of his nose. It was hard, he thought, to be within sight of safety and almost of home, and to be baulked by the want of a few wretched shillings and by the pettifogging mistrustfulness of paid officials. Very soon his escape would be discovered, the hunt would be up, he would be caught, reviled, loaded with chains, dragged back again to prison and bread-and-water and straw; his guards and penalties would be doubled; and O, what sarcastic remarks the girl would make! What was to be done? He was not swift of foot; his figure was unfortunately recognisable. Could he not squeeze under the seat of a carriage? He had seen this method adopted by schoolboys, when the journey-money provided by thoughtful parents had been diverted to other and better ends. As he pondered, he found himself opposite the engine, which was being oiled, wiped, and generally caressed by its affectionate driver, a burly man with an oil-can in one hand and a lump of cotton-waste in the other.

"Hullo, mother!" said the engine-driver, "what's the trouble? You don't look particularly cheerful."

"O, sir!" said Toad, crying afresh, "I am a poor unhappy washerwoman, and I've lost all my money, and can't pay for a ticket, and I must get home tonight somehow, and whatever I am to do I don't know. O dear, O dear!"

"That's a bad business, indeed," said the engine-driver reflectively. "Lost your money—and can't get home—and got some kids, too, waiting for you, I dare say?"

"Any amount of 'em," sobbed Toad. "And they'll be hungry—and playing with matches—and upsetting lamps, the little innocents!— and quarrelling, and going on generally. O dear, O dear!"

"Well, I'll tell you what I'll do," said the good engine-driver. "You're a washerwoman to your trade, says you. Very well, that's that. And I'm an engine-driver, as you well may see, and there's no denying it's terribly dirty work. Uses up a power of shirts, it does, till my missus is fair tired of washing of 'em. If you'll wash a few shirts for me when you get home, and send 'em along, I'll give you a ride on my engine. It's against the Company's regulations, but we're not so very particular in these out-of-the-way parts."

The Toad's misery turned into rapture as he eagerly scrambled up into the cab of the engine. Of course, he had never washed a shirt in his life, and couldn't if he tried and, anyhow, he wasn't going to begin; but he thought: "When I get safely home to Toad Hall, and have money again, and pockets to put it in, I will send the engine-driver enough to pay for quite a quantity of washing, and that will be the same thing, or better."

The guard waved his welcome flag, the engine-driver whistled in cheerful response, and the train moved out of the station. As the speed increased, and the Toad could see on either side of him real fields, and trees, and hedges, and cows, and horses, all flying past him, and as he thought how every minute was bringing him nearer to Toad Hall, and sympathetic friends, and money to chink in his pocket, and a soft bed to sleep in, and good things to eat, and praise and admiration at the recital of his adventures and his surpassing cleverness, he began to skip up and down and shout and sing snatches of song, to the great astonishment of the engine-driver, who had come across washerwomen before, at long intervals, but never one at all like this.

They had covered many and many a mile, and Toad was already considering what he would have for supper as soon as he got home, when he noticed that the engine-driver, with a puzzled expression on his face, was leaning over the side of the engine and listening hard. Then he saw him climb on to the coals and gaze out over the top of the train; then he returned and said to Toad: "It's very strange; we're the last train running in this direction tonight, yet I could be sworn that I heard another following us!"

Toad ceased his frivolous antics at once. He became grave and depressed, and a dull pain in the lower part of his spine, communicating itself to his legs, made him want to sit down and try desperately not to think of all the possibilities.

By this time the moon was shining brightly, and the engine-driver, steadying himself on the coal, could command a view of the line behind them for a long distance.

Presently he called out, "I can see it clearly now! It is an engine, on our rails, coming along at a great pace! It looks as if we were being pursued!"

The miserable Toad, crouching in the coal-dust, tried hard to think of something to do, with dismal want of success.

"They are gaining on us fast!" cried the engine-driver. "And the engine is crowded with the queerest lot of people! Men like ancient warders, waving halberds; policemen in their helmets, waving truncheons; and shabbily dressed men in pot-hats, obvious and unmistakable plain-clothes detectives even at this distance, waving revolvers and walking-sticks; all waving, and all shouting the same thing—'Stop, stop, stop!'"

Then Toad fell on his knees among the coals and, raising his clasped paws in supplication, cried, "Save me, only save me, dear kind Mr. Engine-driver, and I will confess everything! I am not the simple washerwoman I seem to be! I have no children waiting for me, innocent or otherwise! I am a toad—the well-known and popular Mr. Toad, a landed proprietor; I have just escaped, by my great daring and cleverness, from a loathsome dungeon into which my enemies had flung me; and if those fellows on that engine recapture me, it will be chains and bread-and-water and straw and misery once more for poor, unhappy, innocent Toad!"

The engine-driver looked down upon him very sternly, and said, "Now tell the truth; what were you put in prison for?"

"It was nothing very much," said poor Toad, colouring deeply. "I only borrowed a motor-car while the owners were at lunch; they had no need of it at the time. I didn't mean to steal it, really; but people—especially magistrates—take such harsh views of thoughtless and high-spirited actions."

The engine-driver looked very grave and said, "I fear that you have been indeed a wicked toad, and by rights I ought to give you up to offended justice. But you are evidently in sore trouble and distress, so I will not desert you. I don't hold with motor-cars, for one thing; and I don't hold with being ordered about by policemen when I'm on my own engine, for another. And the sight of an animal in tears always makes me feel queer and soft-hearted. So cheer up, Toad! I'll do my best, and we may beat them yet!"

They piled on more coals, shovelling furiously; the furnace roared, the sparks flew, the engine leapt and swung but still their pursuers slowly gained. The engine-driver, with a sigh, wiped his brow with a handful of cotton-waste, and said, "I'm afraid it's no good, Toad. You see, they are running light, and they have the better engine. There's just one thing left for us to do, and it's your only chance, so attend very carefully to what I tell you. A short way ahead of us is a long tunnel, and on the other side of that the line passes through a thick wood. Now, I will put on all the speed I can while we are running through the tunnel, but the other fellows will slow down a bit, naturally, for fear of an accident. When we are through, I will shut off steam and put on brakes as hard as I can, and the moment it's safe to do so you must jump and hide in the wood, before they get through the tunnel and see you. Then I will go full speed ahead again, and they can chase me if they like, for as long as they like, and as far as they like. Now mind and be ready to jump when I tell you!"

They piled on more coals, and the train shot into the tunnel, and the engine rushed and roared and rattled, till at last they shot out at the other end into fresh air and the peaceful moonlight, and saw the wood lying dark and helpful upon either side of the line. The driver shut off steam and put on brakes, the Toad got down on the step, and as the train slowed down to almost a walking pace he heard the driver call out, "Now, jump!"

Toad jumped, rolled down a short embankment, picked himself up unhurt, scrambled into the wood, and hid.

Peeping out, he saw his train get up speed again and disappear at a great pace. Then out of the tunnel burst the pursuing engine, roaring and whistling, her motley crew waving their various weapons and shouting, "Stop! stop! stop!" When they were past, the Toad had a hearty laugh—for the first time since he was thrown into prison.

But he soon stopped laughing when he came to consider that it was now very late and dark and cold, and he was in an unknown wood, with no money and no chance of supper, and still far from friends and home; and the dead silence of everything, after the roar and rattle of the train, was something of a shock. He dared not leave the shelter of the trees, so he struck into the wood, with the idea of leaving the railway as far as possible behind him.

After so many weeks within walls, he found the wood strange and unfriendly and inclined, he thought, to make fun of him. Nightjars, sounding their mechanical rattle, made him think that the wood was full of searching warders, closing in on him. An owl, swooping noiselessly towards him, brushed his shoulder with its wing, making him jump with the horrid certainty that it was a hand; then flitted off, moth-like, laughing its low ho! ho! ho; which Toad thought in very poor taste. Once he met a fox, who stopped, looked him up and down in a sarcastic sort of way, and said, "Hullo, washerwoman! Half a pair of socks and a pillow-case short this week! Mind it doesn't occur again!" and swaggered off, sniggering. Toad looked about for a stone to throw at him, but could not succeed in finding one, which vexed him more than anything. At last, cold, hungry, and tired out, he sought the shelter of a hollow tree, where with branches and dead leaves he made himself as comfortable a bed as he could, and slept soundly till the morning.

Chapter 9. Wayfarers All

The Water Rat was restless, and he did not exactly know why. To all appearance the summer's pomp was still at fullest height, and although in the tilled acres green had given way to gold, though rowans were reddening, and the woods were dashed here and there with a tawny fierceness, yet light and warmth and colour were still present in undiminished measure, clean of any chilly premonitions of the passing year. But the constant chorus of the orchards and hedges had shrunk to a casual evensong from a few yet unwearied performers; the robin was beginning to assert himself once more; and there was a feeling in the air of change and departure. The cuckoo, of course, had long been silent; but many another feathered friend, for months a part of the familiar landscape and its small society, was missing too, and it seemed that the ranks thinned steadily day by day. Rat, ever observant of all winged movement, saw that it was taking daily a southing tendency; and even as he lay in bed at night he thought he could make out, passing in the darkness overhead, the beat and quiver of impatient pinions, obedient to the peremptory call.

Nature's Grand Hotel has its Season, like the others. As the guests one by one pack, pay, and depart, and the seats at the table-d'hote shrink pitifully at each succeeding meal; as suites of rooms are closed, carpets taken up, and waiters sent away; those boarders who are staying on, en pension, until the next year's full re-opening, cannot help being somewhat affected by all these flittings and farewells, this eager discussion of plans, routes, and fresh quarters, this daily shrinkage in the stream of comradeship. One gets unsettled, depressed, and inclined to be querulous. Why this craving for change? Why not stay on quietly here, like us, and be jolly? You don't know this hotel out of the season, and what fun we have among ourselves, we fellows who remain and see the whole interesting year out. All very true, no doubt, the others always reply; we quite envy you—and some other year perhaps—but just now we have engagements—and there's the bus at the door—our time is up! So they depart, with a smile and a nod, and we miss them, and feel resentful. The Rat was a self-sufficing sort of animal, rooted to the land, and, whoever went, he stayed; still, he could not help noticing what was in the air, and feeling some of its influence in his bones.

It was difficult to settle down to anything seriously, with all this flitting going on. Leaving the water-side, where rushes stood thick and tall in a stream that was becoming sluggish and low, he wandered country-wards, crossed a field or two of pasturage already looking dusty and parched, and thrust into the great sea of wheat, yellow, wavy, and murmurous, full of quiet motion and small whisperings. Here he often loved to wander, through the forest of stiff strong stalks that carried their own golden sky away over his head—a sky that was always dancing, shimmering, softly talking; or swaying strongly to the passing wind and recovering itself with a toss and a merry laugh. Here, too, he had many small friends, a society complete in itself, leading full and busy lives, but always with a spare moment to gossip, and exchange news with a visitor. Today, however, though they were civil enough, the field-mice and harvest-mice seemed preoccupied. Many were digging and tunnelling busily; others, gathered together in small groups, examined plans and drawings of small flats, stated to be desirable and compact, and situated conveniently near the Stores. Some were hauling out dusty trunks and dress-baskets, others were already elbow-deep packing their belongings; while everywhere piles and bundles of wheat, oats, barley, beech-mast and nuts, lay about ready for transport.

"Here's old Ratty!" they cried as soon as they saw him. "Come and bear a hand, Rat, and don't stand about idle!"

"What sort of games are you up to?" said the Water Rat severely. "You know it isn't time to be thinking of winter quarters yet, by a long way!"

"O yes, we know that," explained a field-mouse rather shamefacedly; "but it's always as well to be in good time, isn't it? We really *must* get all the furniture and baggage and stores moved out of this before those horrid machines begin clicking round the fields; and then, you know, the best flats get picked up so quickly nowadays, and if you're late you have to put up with *anything*; and they want such a lot of doing up, too, before they're fit to move into. Of course, we're early, we know that; but we're only just making a start."

Today, however, though they were civil enough, the field-mice and harvest-mice seemed preoccupied.

"O, bother *starts*," said the Rat. "It's a splendid day. Come for a row, or a stroll along the hedges, or a picnic in the woods, or something."

"Well, I *think* not today, thank you," replied the field-mouse hurriedly. "Perhaps some *other* day—when we've more *time*—"

The Rat, with a snort of contempt, swung round to go, tripped over a hat-box, and fell, with undignified remarks.

"If people would be more careful," said a field-mouse rather stiffly, "and look where they're going, people wouldn't hurt themselves—and forget themselves. Mind that hold-all, Rat! You'd better sit down somewhere. In an hour or two we may be more free to attend to you."

"You won't be 'free,' as you call it, much this side of Christmas, I can see that," retorted the Rat grumpily, as he picked his way out of the field.

He returned somewhat despondently to his river again—his faithful, steady-going old river, which never packed up, flitted, or went into winter quarters.

In the osiers which fringed the bank he spied a swallow sitting. Presently it was joined by another, and then by a third; and the birds, fidgeting restlessly on their bough, talked together earnestly and low.

"What, *already*," said the Rat, strolling up to them. "What's the hurry? I call it simply ridiculous."

"O, we're not off yet, if that's what you mean," replied the first swallow. "We're only making plans and arranging things. Talking it over, you know—what route we're taking this year, and where we'll stop, and so on. That's half the fun!"

"Fun?" said the Rat; "now that's just what I don't understand. If you've *got* to leave this pleasant place, and your friends who will miss you, and your snug homes that you've just settled into, why, when the hour strikes I've no doubt you'll go bravely, and face all the trouble and discomfort and change and newness, and make believe that you're not very unhappy. But to want to talk about it, or even think about it, till you really need—"

"No, you don't understand, naturally," said the second swallow. "First, we feel it stirring within us, a sweet unrest; then back come the recollections one by one, like homing pigeons. They flutter through our dreams at night, they fly with us in our wheelings and circlings by day. We hunger to inquire of each other, to compare notes and assure ourselves that it was all really true, as one by one the scents and sounds and names of long-forgotten places come gradually back and beckon to us."

"Couldn't you stop on for just this year?" suggested the Water Rat, wistfully. "We'll all do our best to make you feel at home. You've no idea what good times we have here, while you are far away."

"I tried 'stopping on' one year," said the third swallow. "I had grown so fond of the place that when the time came I hung back and let the others go on without me. For a few weeks it was all well enough, but afterwards, O the weary length of the nights! The shivering, sunless days! The air so clammy and chill, and not an insect in an acre of it! No, it was no good; my courage broke down, and one cold, stormy night I took wing, flying well inland on account of the strong easterly gales. It was snowing hard as I beat through the passes of the great mountains, and I had a stiff fight to win through; but never shall I forget the blissful feeling of the hot sun again on my back as I sped down to the lakes that lay so blue and placid below me, and the taste of my first fat insect! The past was like a bad dream; the future was all happy holiday as I moved southwards week by week, easily, lazily, lingering as long as I dared, but always heeding the call! No, I had had my warning; never again did I think of disobedience."

"Ah, yes, the call of the South, of the South!" twittered the other two dreamily. "Its songs, its hues, its radiant air! O, do you remember—" and, forgetting the Rat, they slid into passionate reminiscence, while he listened fascinated, and his heart burned within him. In himself, too, he knew that it was vibrating at last, that chord hitherto dormant and unsuspected. The mere chatter of these southern-bound birds, their pale and second-hand reports, had yet power to awaken this wild new sensation and thrill him through and through with it; what would one moment of the real thing work in him—one passionate touch of the real southern sun, one waft of the authentic odor? With closed eyes he dared to dream a moment in full abandonment, and when he looked again the river seemed steely and chill, the green fields grey and lightless. Then his loyal heart seemed to cry out on his weaker self for its treachery.

"Why do you ever come back, then, at all?" he demanded of the swallows jealously. "What do you find to attract you in this poor drab little country?"

"And do you think," said the first swallow, "that the other call is not for us too, in its due season? The call of lush meadow-grass, wet orchards, warm, insect-haunted ponds, of browsing cattle, of haymaking, and all the farm-buildings clustering round the House of the perfect Eaves?"

"Do you suppose," asked the second one, "that you are the only living thing that craves with a hungry longing to hear the cuckoo's note again?"

"In due time," said the third, "we shall be home-sick once more for quiet water-lilies swaying on the surface of an English stream. But today all that seems pale and thin and very far away. Just now our blood dances to other music."

They fell a-twittering among themselves once more, and this time their intoxicating babble was of violet seas, tawny sands, and lizard-haunted walls.

Restlessly the Rat wandered off once more, climbed the slope that rose gently from the north bank of the river, and lay looking out towards the great ring of Downs that barred his vision further southwards—his simple horizon hitherto, his Mountains of the Moon, his limit behind which lay nothing he had cared to see or to know. Today, to him gazing South with a new-born need stirring in his heart, the clear sky over their long low outline seemed to pulsate with promise; today, the unseen was everything, the unknown the only real fact of life. On this side of the hills was now the real blank, on the other lay the crowded and coloured panorama that his inner eye was seeing so clearly. What seas lay beyond, green, leaping, and crested! What sun-bathed coasts, along which the white villas glittered against the olive woods! What quiet harbours, thronged with gallant shipping bound for purple islands of wine and spice, islands set low in languorous waters!

He rose and descended river-wards once more; then changed his mind and sought the side of the dusty lane. There, lying half-buried in the thick, cool under-hedge tangle that bordered it, he could muse on the metalled road and all the wondrous world that it led to; on all the wayfarers, too, that might have trodden it, and the fortunes and adventures they had gone to seek or found unseeking—out there, beyond—beyond!

Footsteps fell on his ear, and the figure of one that walked somewhat wearily came into view; and he saw that it was a Rat, and a very dusty one. The wayfarer, as he reached him, saluted with a gesture of courtesy that had something foreign about it—hesitated a moment—then with a pleasant smile turned from the track and sat down by his side in the cool herbage. He seemed tired, and the Rat let him rest unquestioned, understanding something of what was in his thoughts; knowing, too, the value all animals attach at times to mere silent companionship, when the weary muscles slacken and the mind marks time.

The wayfarer was lean and keen-featured, and somewhat bowed at the shoulders; his paws were thin and long, his eyes much wrinkled at the corners, and he wore small gold earrings in his neatly-set well-shaped ears. His knitted jersey was of a faded blue, his breeches, patched and stained, were based on a blue foundation, and his small belongings that he carried were tied up in a blue cotton handkerchief.

When he had rested awhile the stranger sighed, snuffed the air, and looked about him.

"That was clover, that warm whiff on the breeze," he remarked; "and those are cows we hear cropping the grass behind us and blowing softly between mouthfuls. There is a sound of distant reapers, and yonder rises a blue line of cottage smoke against the woodland. The river runs somewhere close by, for I hear the call of a moorhen, and I see by your build that you're a freshwater mariner. Everything seems asleep, and yet going on all the time. It is a goodly life that you lead, friend; no doubt the best in the world, if only you are strong enough to lead it!"

"Yes, it's *the* life, the only life, to live," responded the Water Rat dreamily, and without his usual whole-hearted conviction.

"I did not say exactly that," replied the stranger cautiously; "but no doubt it's the best. I've tried it, and I know. And because I've just tried it—six months of it—and know it's the best, here am I, footsore and hungry, tramping away from it, tramping southward, following the old call, back to the old life, *the* life which is mine and which will not let me go."

"Is this, then, yet another of them?" mused the Rat. "And where

The wayfarer saluted with a gesture of courtesy that had something foreign about it.

have you just come from?" he asked. He hardly dared to ask where he was bound for; he seemed to know the answer only too well.

"Nice little farm," replied the wayfarer, briefly. "Upalong in that direction"—he nodded northwards. "Never mind about it. I had everything I could want—everything I had any right to expect of life, and more; and here I am! Glad to be here all the same, though, glad to be here! So many miles further on the road, so many hours nearer to my heart's desire!"

His shining eyes held fast to the horizon, and he seemed to be listening for some sound that was wanting from that inland acreage, vocal as it was with the cheerful music of pasturage and farmyard.

"You are not one of *us*," said the Water Rat, "nor yet a farmer; nor even, I should judge, of this country."

"Right," replied the stranger. "I'm a seafaring rat, I am, and the port I originally hail from is Constantinople, though I'm a sort of a foreigner there too, in a manner of speaking. You will have heard of Constantinople, friend? A fair city, and an ancient and glorious one. And you may have heard, too, of Sigurd, King of Norway, and how he sailed thither with sixty ships, and how he and his men rode up through streets all canopied in their honour with purple and gold; and how the Emperor and Empress came down and banqueted with him on board his ship. When Sigurd returned home, many of his Northmen remained behind and entered the Emperor's body-guard, and my ancestor, a Norwegian born, stayed behind too, with the ships that Sigurd gave the Emperor. Seafarers we have ever been, and no wonder; as for me, the city of my birth is no more my home than any pleasant port between there and the London River. I know them all, and they know me. Set me down on any of their quays or foreshores, and I am home again."

"I suppose you go great voyages," said the Water Rat with growing interest. "Months and months out of sight of land, and provisions running short, and allowanced as to water, and your mind communing with the mighty ocean, and all that sort of thing?"

"By no means," said the Sea Rat frankly. "Such a life as you describe would not suit me at all. I'm in the coasting trade, and rarely out of sight of land. It's the jolly times on shore that appeal to me, as much as any seafaring. O, those southern seaports! The smell of them, the riding-lights at night, the glamour!"

"Well, perhaps you have chosen the better way," said the Water Rat, but rather doubtfully. "Tell me something of your coasting, then, if you have a mind to, and what sort of harvest an animal of spirit might hope to bring home from it to warm his latter days with gallant memories by the fireside; for my life, I confess to you, feels to me today somewhat narrow and circumscribed."

"My last voyage," began the Sea Rat, "that landed me eventually in this country, bound with high hopes for my inland farm, will serve as a good example of any of them, and, indeed, as an epitome of my highly-coloured life. Family troubles, as usual, began it. The domestic storm-cone was hoisted, and I shipped myself on board a small trading vessel bound from Constantinople, by classic seas whose every wave throbs with a deathless memory, to the Grecian Islands and the Levant. Those were golden days and balmy nights! In and out of harbour all the time—old friends everywhere—sleeping in some cool temple or ruined cistern during the heat of the day—feasting and song after sundown, under great stars set in a velvet sky! Thence we turned and coasted up the Adriatic, its shores swimming in an atmosphere of amber, rose, and aquamarine; we lay in wide land-locked harbours, we roamed through ancient and noble cities, until at last one morning, as the sun rose royally behind us, we rode into Venice down a path of gold. O, Venice is a fine city, wherein a rat can wander at his ease and take his pleasure! Or, when weary of wandering, can sit at the edge of the Grand Canal at night, feasting with his friends, when the air is full of music and the sky full of stars, and the lights flash and shimmer on the polished steel prows of the swaying gondolas, packed so that you could walk across the canal on them from side to side! And then the food—do you like shell-fish? Well, well, we won't linger over that now."

He was silent for a time; and the Water Rat, silent too and enthralled, floated on dream-canals and heard a phantom song pealing high between vaporous grey wave-lapped walls.

"Southwards we sailed again at last," continued the Sea Rat, "coasting down the Italian shore, till finally we made Palermo, and there I quitted for a long, happy spell on shore. I never stick too long to one ship; one gets narrow-minded and prejudiced. Besides, Sicily is one of my happy hunting-grounds. I know everybody there, and their ways just suit me. I spent many jolly weeks in the island, staying with friends up country. When I grew restless again I took advantage of a ship that was trading to Sardinia and Corsica; and very glad I was to feel the fresh breeze and the sea-spray in my face once more."

"But isn't it very hot and stuffy, down in the—hold, I think you call it?" asked the Water Rat.

The seafarer looked at him with the suspicion of a wink. "I'm an old hand," he remarked with much simplicity. "The captain's cabin's good enough for me."

"It's a hard life, by all accounts," murmured the Rat, sunk in deep thought.

"For the crew it is," replied the seafarer gravely, again with the ghost of a wink.

"From Corsica," he went on, "I made use of a ship that was taking wine to the mainland. We made Alassio in the evening, lay to, hauled up our wine-casks, and hove them overboard, tied one to the other by a long line. Then the crew took to the boats and rowed shorewards, singing as they went, and drawing after them the long bobbing procession of casks, like a mile of porpoises. On the sands they had horses waiting, which dragged the casks up the steep street of the little town with a fine rush and clatter and scramble. When the last cask was in, we went and refreshed and rested, and sat late into the night, drinking with our friends, and next morning I took to the great olive-woods for a spell and a rest. For now I had done with islands for the time, and ports and shipping were plentiful; so I led a lazy life among the peasants, lying and watching them work, or stretched high on the hillside with the blue Mediterranean far below me. And so at length, by easy stages, and partly on foot, partly by sea, to Marseilles, and the meeting of old shipmates, and the visiting of great ocean-bound vessels, and feasting once more. Talk of shell-fish! Why, sometimes I dream of the shell-fish of Marseilles, and wake up crying!"

"That reminds me," said the polite Water Rat; "you happened to mention that you were hungry, and I ought to have spoken earlier. Of course, you will stop and take your midday meal with me? My hole is close by; it is some time past noon, and you are very welcome to whatever there is."

"Now I call that kind and brotherly of you," said the Sea Rat. "I was indeed hungry when I sat down, and ever since I inadvertently happened to mention shell-fish, my pangs have been extreme. But couldn't you fetch it along out here? I am none too fond of going under hatches, unless I'm obliged to; and then, while we eat, I could tell you more concerning my voyages and the pleasant life I lead— at least, it is very pleasant to me, and by your attention I judge it commends itself to you; whereas if we go indoors it is a hundred to one that I shall presently fall asleep."

"That is indeed an excellent suggestion," said the Water Rat, and hurried off home. There he got out the luncheon-basket and packed a simple meal, in which, remembering the stranger's origin and preferences, he took care to include a yard of long French bread, a sausage out of which the garlic sang, some cheese which lay down and cried, and a long-necked straw-covered flask wherein lay bottled sunshine shed and garnered on far Southern slopes. Thus laden, he returned with all speed, and blushed for pleasure at the old seaman's commendations of his taste and judgment, as together they unpacked the basket and laid out the contents on the grass by the roadside.

The Sea Rat, as soon as his hunger was somewhat assuaged, continued the history of his latest voyage, conducting his simple hearer from port to port of Spain, landing him at Lisbon, Oporto, and Bordeaux, introducing him to the pleasant harbours of Cornwall and Devon, and so up the Channel to that final quayside, where, landing after winds long contrary, storm-driven and weather-beaten, he had caught the first magical hints and heraldings of another Spring, and, fired by these, had sped on a long tramp inland, hungry for the experiment of life on some quiet farmstead, very far from the weary beating of any sea.

Spell-bound and quivering with excitement, the Water Rat followed the Adventurer league by league, over stormy bays, through crowded roadsteads, across harbour bars on a racing tide, up winding rivers that hid their busy little towns round a sudden turn; and left him with a regretful sigh planted at his dull inland farm, about which he desired to hear nothing.

By this time their meal was over, and the Seafarer, refreshed and strengthened, his voice more vibrant, his eye lit with a brightness that seemed caught from some far-away sea-beacon, filled his glass with the red and glowing vintage of the South, and, leaning towards the Water Rat, compelled his gaze and held him, body and soul, while he talked. Those eyes were of the changing foam-streaked grey-green of leaping Northern seas; in the glass shone a hot ruby that seemed the very heart of the South, beating for him who had courage to respond to its pulsation. The twin lights, the shifting grey and the steadfast red, mastered the Water Rat and held him bound, fascinated, powerless. The quiet world outside their rays receded far away and ceased to be. And the talk, the wonderful talk flowed on—or was it speech entirely, or did it pass at times into song— chanty of the sailors weighing the dripping anchor, sonorous hum of the shrouds in a tearing North-Easter, ballad of the fisherman hauling his nets at sundown against an apricot sky, chords of guitar and mandoline from gondola or caique? Did it change into the cry of the wind, plaintive at first, angrily shrill as it freshened, rising to a tearing whistle, sinking to a musical trickle of air from the leech of the bellying sail? All these sounds the spell-bound listener seemed to hear, and with them the hungry complaint of the gulls and the sea-mews, the soft thunder of the breaking wave, the cry of the protesting shingle. Back into speech again it passed, and with beating heart he was following the adventures of a dozen seaports, the fights, the escapes, the rallies, the comradeships, the gallant undertakings; or he searched islands for treasure, fished in still lagoons and dozed day-long on warm white sand. Of deep-sea fishings he heard tell, and mighty silver gatherings of the mile-long net; of sudden perils, noise of breakers on a moonless night, or the tall bows of the great liner taking shape overhead through the fog; of the merry home-coming, the headland rounded, the harbour lights opened out; the groups seen dimly on the quay, the cheery hail, the splash of the hawser; the trudge up the steep little street towards the comforting glow of red-curtained windows.

Lastly, in his waking dream it seemed to him that the Adventurer had risen to his feet, but was still speaking, still holding him fast with his sea-grey eyes.

"And now," he was softly saying, "I take to the road again, holding on southwestwards for many a long and dusty day; till at last I reach the little grey sea town I know so well, that clings along one steep side of the harbour. There through dark doorways you look down flights of stone steps, overhung by great pink tufts of valerian and ending in a patch of sparkling blue water. The little boats that lie tethered to the rings and stanchions of the old sea-wall are gaily painted as those I clambered in and out of in my own childhood; the salmon leap on the flood tide, schools of mackerel flash and play past quay-sides and foreshores, and by the windows the great vessels glide, night and day, up to their moorings or forth to the open sea. There, sooner or later, the ships of all seafaring nations arrive; and there, at its destined hour, the ship of my choice will let go its anchor. I shall take my time, I shall tarry and bide, till at last the right one lies waiting for me, warped out into midstream, loaded low, her bowsprit pointing down harbour. I shall slip on board, by boat or along hawser; and then one morning I shall wake to the song and tramp of the sailors, the clink of the capstan, and the rattle of the anchor-chain coming merrily in. We shall break out the jib and the foresail, the white houses on the harbour side will glide slowly past us as she gathers steering-way, and the voyage will have begun! As she forges towards the headland she will clothe herself with canvas; and then, once outside, the sounding slap of great green seas as she heels to the wind, pointing South!

"And you, you will come too, young brother; for the days pass, and never return, and the South still waits for you. Take the Adventure, heed the call, now ere the irrevocable moment passes! 'Tis but a banging of the door behind you, a blithesome step forward, and you are out of the old life and into the new! Then some day, some day long hence, jog home here if you will, when the cup has been drained and the play has been played, and sit down by your quiet river with a store of goodly memories for company. You can easily overtake me on the road, for you are young, and I am ageing and go softly. I will linger, and look back; and at last I will surely see you coming, eager and light-hearted, with all the South in your face!"

The voice died away and ceased as an insect's tiny trumpet dwindles swiftly into silence; and the Water Rat, paralysed and staring, saw at last but a distant speck on the white surface of the road.

Mechanically he rose and proceeded to repack the luncheon-basket, carefully and without haste. Mechanically he returned home, gathered together a few small necessaries and special treasures he was fond of, and put them in a satchel; acting with slow deliberation, moving about the room like a sleep-walker; listening ever with parted lips. He swung the satchel over his shoulder, carefully selected a stout stick for his wayfaring, and with no haste, but with no hesitation at all, he stepped across the threshold just as the Mole appeared at the door.

"Why, where are you off to, Ratty?" asked the Mole in great surprise, grasping him by the arm.

"Going South, with the rest of them," murmured the Rat in a dreamy monotone, never looking at him. "Seawards first and then on shipboard, and so to the shores that are calling me!"

He pressed resolutely forward, still without haste, but with dogged fixity of purpose; but the Mole, now thoroughly alarmed, placed himself in front of him, and looking into his eyes saw that they were glazed and set and turned a streaked and shifting grey— not his friend's eyes, but the eyes of some other animal! Grappling with him strongly he dragged him inside, threw him down, and held him.

The Rat struggled desperately for a few moments, and then his strength seemed suddenly to leave him, and he lay still and exhausted, with closed eyes, trembling. Presently the Mole assisted him to rise and placed him in a chair, where he sat collapsed and shrunken into himself, his body shaken by a violent shivering, passing in time into an hysterical fit of dry sobbing. Mole made the door fast, threw the satchel into a drawer and locked it, and sat down quietly on the table by his friend, waiting for the strange seizure to pass. Gradually the Rat sank into a troubled doze, broken by starts and confused murmurings of things strange and wild and foreign to the unenlightened Mole; and from that he passed into a deep slumber.

Very anxious in mind, the Mole left him for a time and busied himself with household matters; and it was getting dark when he returned to the parlour and found the Rat where he had left him, wide awake indeed, but listless, silent, and dejected. He took one hasty glance at his eyes; found them, to his great gratification, clear and dark and brown again as before; and then sat down and tried to cheer him up and help him to relate what had happened to him.

Poor Ratty did his best, by degrees, to explain things; but how could he put into cold words what had mostly been suggestion? How recall, for another's benefit, the haunting sea voices that had sung to him, how reproduce at second-hand the magic of the Seafarer's hundred reminiscences? Even to himself, now the spell was broken and the glamour gone, he found it difficult to account for what had seemed, some hours ago, the inevitable and only thing. It is not surprising, then, that he failed to convey to the Mole any clear idea of what he had been through that day.

To the Mole this much was plain: the fit, or attack, had passed away, and had left him sane again, though shaken and cast down by the reaction. But he seemed to have lost all interest for the time in the things that went to make up his daily life, as well as in all pleasant forecastings of the altered days and doings that the changing season was surely bringing.

Casually, then, and with seeming indifference, the Mole turned his talk to the harvest that was being gathered in, the towering wagons and their straining teams, the growing ricks, and the large moon rising over bare acres dotted with sheaves. He talked of the reddening apples around, of the browning nuts, of jams and preserves and the distilling of cordials; till by easy stages such as these he reached midwinter, its hearty joys and its snug home life, and then he became simply lyrical.

By degrees the Rat began to sit up and to join in. His dull eye brightened, and he lost some of his listening air.

Presently the tactful Mole slipped away and returned with a pencil and a few half-sheets of paper, which he placed on the table at his friend's elbow.

"It's quite a long time since you did any poetry," he remarked. "You might have a try at it this evening, instead of—well, brooding over things so much. I've an idea that you'll feel a lot better when you've got something jotted down—if it's only just the rhymes."

The Rat pushed the paper away from him wearily, but the discreet Mole took occasion to leave the room, and when he peeped in again some time later, the Rat was absorbed and deaf to the world; alternately scribbling and sucking the top of his pencil. It is true that he sucked a good deal more than he scribbled; but it was joy to the Mole to know that the cure had at least begun.

Chapter 10. The Further Adventures of Toad

The front door of the hollow tree faced eastwards, so Toad was called at an early hour; partly by the bright sunlight streaming in on him, partly by the exceeding coldness of his toes, which made him dream that he was at home in bed in his own handsome room with the Tudor window, on a cold winter's night, and his bedclothes had got up, grumbling and protesting they couldn't stand the cold any longer, and had run downstairs to the kitchen fire to warm themselves; and he had followed, on bare feet, along miles and miles of icy stone-paved passages, arguing and beseeching them to be reasonable. He would probably have been aroused much earlier, had he not slept for some weeks on straw over stone flags, and almost forgotten the friendly feeling of thick blankets pulled well up round the chin.

Sitting up, he rubbed his eyes first and his complaining toes next, wondered for a moment where he was, looking round for familiar stone wall and little barred window; then, with a leap of the heart, remembered everything—his escape, his flight, his pursuit; remembered, first and best thing of all, that he was free!

Free! The word and the thought alone were worth fifty blankets. He was warm from end to end as he thought of the jolly world outside, waiting eagerly for him to make his triumphal entrance, ready to serve him and play up to him, anxious to help him and to keep him company, as it always had been in days of old before misfortune fell upon him. He shook himself and combed the dry leaves out of his hair with his fingers; and, his toilet complete, marched forth into the comfortable morning sun, cold but confident, hungry but hopeful, all nervous terrors of yesterday dispelled by rest and sleep and frank and heartening sunshine.

He had the world all to himself, that early summer morning. The dewy woodland, as he threaded it, was solitary and still: the green fields that succeeded the trees were his own to do as he liked with; the road itself, when he reached it, in that loneliness that was everywhere, seemed, like a stray dog, to be looking anxiously for company. Toad, however, was looking for something that could talk, and tell him clearly which way he ought to go. It is all very well, when you have a light heart, and a clear conscience, and money in your pocket, and nobody scouring the country for you to drag you off to prison again, to follow where the road beckons and points, not caring whither. The practical Toad cared very much indeed, and he could have kicked the road for its helpless silence when every minute was of importance to him.

The reserved rustic road was presently joined by a shy little brother in the shape of a canal, which took its hand and ambled along by its side in perfect confidence, but with the same tongue-tied, uncommunicative attitude towards strangers. "Bother them!" said Toad to himself. "But, anyhow, one thing's clear. They must both be coming *from* somewhere, and going *to* somewhere. You can't get over that, Toad, my boy!" So he marched on patiently by the water's edge.

Round a bend in the canal came plodding a solitary horse, stooping forward as if in anxious thought. From rope traces attached to his collar stretched a long line, taut, but dipping with his stride, the further part of it dripping pearly drops. Toad let the horse pass, and stood waiting for what the fates were sending him.

With a pleasant swirl of quiet water at its blunt bow the barge slid up alongside of him, its gaily painted gunwale level with the towing-path, its sole occupant a big stout woman wearing a linen sun-bonnet, one brawny arm laid along the tiller.

"A nice morning, ma'am!" she remarked to Toad, as she drew up level with him.

"I dare say it is, ma'am!" responded Toad politely, as he walked along the tow-path abreast of her. "I dare it *is* a nice morning to them that's not in sore trouble, like what I am. Here's my married daughter, she sends off to me post-haste to come to her at once; so off I comes, not knowing what may be happening or going to happen, but fearing the worst, as you will understand, ma'am, if you're a mother, too. And I've left my business to look after itself— I'm in the washing and laundering line, you must know, ma'am— and I've left my young children to look after themselves, and a more mischievous and troublesome set of young imps doesn't exist, ma'am; and I've lost all my money, and lost my way, and as for what may be happening to my married daughter, why, I don't like to think of it, ma'am!"

"Where might your married daughter be living, ma'am?" asked the barge-woman.

"She lives near to the river, ma'am," replied Toad. "Close to a fine house called Toad Hall, that's somewheres hereabouts in these parts. Perhaps you may have heard of it."

"Toad Hall? Why, I'm going that way myself," replied the barge-woman. "This canal joins the river some miles further on, a little above Toad Hall; and then it's an easy walk. You come along in the barge with me, and I'll give you a lift."

She steered the barge close to the bank, and Toad, with many humble and grateful acknowledgments, stepped lightly on board and sat down with great satisfaction. "Toad's luck again!" thought he. "I always come out on top!"

"So you're in the washing business, ma'am?" said the barge-woman politely, as they glided along. "And a very good business you've got too, I dare say, if I'm not making too free in saying so."

"Finest business in the whole country," said Toad airily. "All the gentry come to me—wouldn't go to anyone else if they were paid, they know me so well. You see, I understand my work thoroughly, and attend to it all myself. Washing, ironing, clear-starching, making up gents' fine shirts for evening wear—everything's done under my own eye!"

"But surely you don't *do* all that work yourself, ma'am?" asked the barge-woman respectfully.

"O, I have girls," said Toad lightly: "twenty girls or thereabouts, always at work. But you know what *girls* are, ma'am! Nasty little hussies, that's what *I* call 'em!"

"So do I, too," said the barge-woman with great heartiness. "But I dare say you set yours to rights, the idle trollops! And are you very fond of washing?"

"I love it," said Toad. "I simply dote on it. Never so happy as when I've got both arms in the wash-tub. But, then, it comes so easy to me! No trouble at all! A real pleasure, I assure you, ma'am!"

"What a bit of luck, meeting you!" observed the barge-woman, thoughtfully. "A regular piece of good fortune for both of us!"

"Why, what do you mean?" asked Toad, nervously.

"Well, look at me, now," replied the barge-woman. "*I* like washing, too, just the same as you do; and for that matter, whether I like it or not I have got to do all my own, naturally, moving about as I do. Now my husband, he's such a fellow for shirking his work and leaving the barge to me, that never a moment do I get for seeing to my own affairs. By rights he ought to be here now, either steering or attending to the horse, though luckily the horse has sense enough to attend to himself. Instead of which, he's gone off with the dog, to see if they can't pick up a rabbit for dinner somewhere. Says he'll catch me up at the next lock. Well, that's as may be—I don't trust him, once he gets off with that dog, who's worse than he is. But meantime, how am I to get on with my washing?"

"O, never mind about the washing," said Toad, not liking the subject. "Try and fix your mind on that rabbit. A nice fat young rabbit, I'll be bound. Got any onions?"

"I can't fix my mind on anything but my washing," said the barge-woman, "and I wonder you can be talking of rabbits, with such a joyful prospect before you. There's a heap of things of mine that you'll find in a corner of the cabin. If you'll just take one or two of the most necessary sort—I won't venture to describe them to a lady like you, but you'll recognise them at a glance—and put them through the wash-tub as we go along, why, it'll be a pleasure to you, as you rightly say, and a real help to me. You'll find a tub handy, and soap, and a kettle on the stove, and a bucket to haul up water from the canal with. Then I shall know you're enjoying yourself, instead of sitting here idle, looking at the scenery and yawning your head off."

"Here, you let me steer!" said Toad, now thoroughly frightened, "and then you can get on with your washing your own way. I might spoil your things, or not do 'em as you like. I'm more used to gentlemen's things myself. It's my special line."

"Let you steer?" replied the barge-woman, laughing. "It takes some practice to steer a barge properly. Besides, it's dull work, and I want you to be happy. No, you shall do the washing you are so fond of, and I'll stick to the steering that I understand. Don't try and deprive me of the pleasure of giving you a treat!"

Toad was fairly cornered. He looked for escape this way and that, saw that he was too far from the bank for a flying leap, and sullenly resigned himself to his fate. "If it comes to that," he thought in desperation, "I suppose any fool can *wash*!"

He fetched tub, soap, and other necessaries from the cabin, selected a few garments at random, tried to recollect what he had seen in casual glances through laundry windows, and set to.

A long half-hour passed, and every minute of it saw Toad getting crosser and crosser. Nothing that he could do to the things seemed to please them or do them good. He tried coaxing, he tried slapping, he tried punching; they smiled back at him out of the tub unconverted, happy in their original sin. Once or twice he looked nervously over his shoulder at the barge-woman, but she appeared to be gazing out in front of her, absorbed in her steering. His back ached badly, and he noticed with dismay that his paws were beginning to get all crinkly. Now Toad was very proud of his paws. He muttered under his breath words that should never pass the lips of either washerwomen or Toads; and lost the soap, for the fiftieth time.

A burst of laughter made him straighten himself and look round. The barge-woman was leaning back and laughing unrestrainedly, till the tears ran down her cheeks.

"I've been watching you all the time," she gasped. "I thought you must be a humbug all along, from the conceited way you talked. Pretty washerwoman you are! Never washed so much as a dish-clout in your life, I'll lay!"

Toad's temper, which had been simmering viciously for some time, now fairly boiled over, and he lost all control of himself.

"You common, low, *fat* barge-woman!" he shouted; "don't you dare to talk to your betters like that! Washerwoman indeed! I would have you to know that I am a Toad, a very well-known, respected, distinguished Toad! I may be under a bit of a cloud at present, but I will *not* be laughed at by a barge-woman!"

The woman moved nearer to him and peered under his bonnet keenly and closely. "Why, so you are!" she cried. "Well, I never! A horrid, nasty, crawly Toad! And in my nice clean barge, too! Now that is a thing that I will *not* have."

She relinquished the tiller for a moment. One big mottled arm shot out and caught Toad by a fore-leg, while the other gripped him fast by a hind-leg. Then the world turned suddenly upside down, the barge seemed to flit lightly across the sky, the wind whistled in his ears, and Toad found himself flying through the air, revolving rapidly as he went.

The water, when he eventually reached it with a loud splash, proved quite cold enough for his taste, though its chill was not sufficient to quell his proud spirit, or slake the heat of his furious temper. He rose to the surface spluttering, and when he had wiped the duck-weed out of his eyes the first thing he saw was the fat barge-woman looking back at him over the stern of the retreating barge and laughing; and he vowed, as he coughed and choked, to be even with her.

He struck out for the shore, but the cotton gown greatly impeded his efforts, and when at length he touched land he found it hard to climb up the steep bank unassisted. He had to take a minute or two's rest to recover his breath; then, gathering his wet skirts well over his arms, he started to run after the barge as fast as his legs would carry him, wild with indignation, thirsting for revenge.

The barge-woman was still laughing when he drew up level with her. "Put yourself through your mangle, washerwoman," she called out, "and iron your face and crimp it, and you'll pass for quite a decent-looking Toad!"

Toad never paused to reply. Solid revenge was what he wanted, not cheap, windy, verbal triumphs, though he had a thing or two in his mind that he would have liked to say. He saw what he wanted ahead of him. Running swiftly on he overtook the horse, unfastened the tow-rope and cast off, jumped lightly on the horse's back, and urged it to a gallop by kicking it vigorously in the sides. He steered for the open country, abandoning the tow-path, and swinging his steed down a rutty lane. Once he looked back, and saw that the barge had run aground on the other side of the canal, and the barge-woman was gesticulating wildly and shouting, "Stop, stop, stop!"

"I've heard that song before," said Toad, laughing, as he continued to spur his steed onward in its wild career.

The barge-horse was not capable of any very sustained effort, and its gallop soon subsided into a trot, and its trot into an easy walk; but Toad was quite contented with this, knowing that he, at any rate, was moving, and the barge was not. He had quite recovered his temper, now that he had done something he thought really clever; and he was satisfied to jog along quietly in the sun, steering his horse along by-ways and bridle-paths, and trying to forget how very long it was since he had had a square meal, till the canal had been left very far behind him.

He had travelled some miles, his horse and he, and he was feeling drowsy in the hot sunshine, when the horse stopped, lowered his head, and began to nibble the grass; and Toad, waking up, just saved himself from falling off by an effort. He looked about him and found he was on a wide common, dotted with patches of gorse and bramble as far as he could see. Near him stood a dingy gypsy caravan, and beside it a man was sitting on a bucket turned upside down, very busy smoking and staring into the wide world. A fire of sticks was burning near by, and over the fire hung an iron pot, and out of that pot came forth bubblings and gurglings, and a vague suggestive steaminess. Also smells—warm, rich, and varied smells—that twined and twisted and wreathed themselves at last into one complete, voluptuous, perfect smell that seemed like the very soul of Nature taking form and appearing to her children, a true Goddess, a mother of solace and comfort. Toad now knew well that he had not been really hungry before. What he had felt earlier in the day had been a mere trifling qualm. This was the real thing at last, and no mistake; and it would have to be dealt with speedily, too, or there would be trouble for somebody or something. He looked the gypsy over carefully, wondering vaguely whether it would be easier to fight him or cajole him. So there he sat, and sniffed and sniffed, and looked at the gypsy; and the gypsy sat and smoked, and looked at him.

Presently the gypsy took his pipe out of his mouth and remarked in a careless way, "Want to sell that there horse of yours?"

Toad was completely taken aback. He did not know that gypsies were very fond of horse-dealing, and never missed an opportunity, and he had not reflected that caravans were always on the move and took a deal of drawing. It had not occurred to him to turn the horse into cash, but the gypsy's suggestion seemed to smooth the way towards the two things he wanted so badly—ready money, and a solid breakfast.

"What?" he said, "me sell this beautiful young horse of mine? O, no; it's out of the question. Who's going to take the washing home to my customers every week? Besides, I'm too fond of him, and he simply dotes on me."

The gypsy remarked in a careless way, "Want to sell that there horse of yours?"

"Try and love a donkey," suggested the gypsy. "Some people do."

"You don't seem to see," continued Toad, "that this fine horse of mine is a cut above you altogether. He's a blood horse, he is, partly; not the part you see, of course—another part. And he's been a Prize Hackney, too, in his time—that was the time before you knew him, but you can still tell it on him at a glance, if you understand anything about horses. No, it's not to be thought of for a moment. All the same, how much might you be disposed to offer me for this beautiful young horse of mine?"

The gypsy looked the horse over, and then he looked Toad over with equal care, and looked at the horse again. "Shillin' a leg," he said briefly, and turned away, continuing to smoke and try to stare the wide world out of countenance.

"A shilling a leg?" cried Toad. "If you please, I must take a little time to work that out, and see just what it comes to."

He climbed down off his horse, and left it to graze, and sat down by the gypsy, and did sums on his fingers, and at last he said, "A shilling a leg? Why, that comes to exactly four shillings, and no more. O, no; I could not think of accepting four shillings for this beautiful young horse of mine."

"Well," said the gypsy, "I'll tell you what I will do. I'll make it five shillings, and that's three-and-sixpence more than the animal's worth. And that's my last word."

Then Toad sat and pondered long and deeply. For he was hungry and quite penniless, and still some way—he knew not how far— from home, and enemies might still be looking for him. To one in such a situation, five shillings may very well appear a large sum of money. On the other hand, it did not seem very much to get for a horse. But then, again, the horse hadn't cost him anything; so whatever he got was all clear profit. At last he said firmly, "Look here, gypsy! I tell you what we will do; and this is *my* last word. You shall hand me over six shillings and sixpence, cash down; and further, in addition thereto, you shall give me as much breakfast as I can possibly eat, at one sitting of course, out of that iron pot of yours that keeps sending forth such delicious and exciting smells. In return, I will make over to you my spirited young horse, with all the beautiful harness and trappings that are on him, freely thrown in. If that's not good enough for you, say so, and I'll be getting on. I know a man near here who's wanted this horse of mine for years."

The gypsy grumbled frightfully, and declared if he did a few more deals of that sort he'd be ruined. But in the end he lugged a dirty canvas bag out of the depths of his trouser pocket, and counted out six shillings and sixpence into Toad's paw. Then he disappeared into the caravan for an instant, and returned with a large iron plate and a knife, fork, and spoon. He tilted up the pot, and a glorious stream of hot rich stew gurgled into the plate. It was, indeed, the most beautiful stew in the world, being made of partridges, and pheasants, and chickens, and hares, and rabbits, and pea-hens, and guinea-fowls, and one or two other things. Toad took the plate on his lap, almost crying, and stuffed, and stuffed, and stuffed, and kept asking for more, and the gypsy never grudged it him. He thought that he had never eaten so good a breakfast in all his life.

When Toad had taken as much stew on board as he thought he could possibly hold, he got up and said good-bye to the gypsy, and took an affectionate farewell of the horse; and the gypsy, who knew the riverside well, gave him directions which way to go, and he set forth on his travels again in the best possible spirits. He was, indeed, a very different Toad from the animal of an hour ago. The sun was shining brightly, his wet clothes were quite dry again, he had money in his pocket once more, he was nearing home and friends and safety, and, most and best of all, he had had a substantial meal, hot and nourishing, and felt big, and strong, and careless, and self-confident.

As he tramped along gaily, he thought of his adventures and escapes, and how when things seemed at their worst he had always managed to find a way out; and his pride and conceit began to swell within him. "Ho, ho!" he said to himself as he marched along with his chin in the air, "what a clever Toad I am! There is surely no animal equal to me for cleverness in the whole world! My enemies shut me up in prison, encircled by sentries, watched night and day by warders; I walk out through them all, by sheer ability coupled with courage. They pursue me with engines, and policemen, and revolvers; I snap my fingers at them, and vanish, laughing, into space. I am, unfortunately, thrown into a canal by a woman fat of body and very evil-minded. What of it? I swim ashore, I seize her horse, I ride off in triumph, and I sell the horse for a whole pocketful of money and an excellent breakfast! Ho, ho! I am the Toad, the handsome, the popular, the successful Toad!" He got so puffed up with conceit that he made up a song as he walked in praise of himself, and sang it at the top of his voice, though there was no one to hear it but him. It was perhaps the most conceited song that any animal ever composed.

> *The world has held great Heroes,*
> *   As history-books have showed;*
> *But never a name to go down to fame*
> *   Compared with that of Toad!*
>
> *The clever men at Oxford*
> *   Know all that there is to be knowed.*
> *But they none of them know one half as much*
> *   As intelligent Mr. Toad!*
>
> *The animals sat in the Ark and cried,*
> *   Their tears in torrents flowed.*
> *Who was it said, "There's land ahead?"*
> *   Encouraging Mr. Toad!*
>
> *The army all saluted*
> *   As they marched along the road.*
> *Was it the King? Or Kitchener?*
> *   No. It was Mr. Toad.*
>
> *The Queen and her Ladies-in-waiting*
> *   Sat at the window and sewed.*
> *She cried, "Look! who's that* handsome *man?"*
> *   They answered, "Mr. Toad."*

There was a great deal more of the same sort, but too dreadfully conceited to be written down. These are some of the milder verses.

He sang as he walked, and he walked as he sang, and got more inflated every minute. But his pride was shortly to have a severe fall.

After some miles of country lanes he reached the high-road, and as he turned into it and glanced along its white length, he saw approaching him a speck that turned into a dot and then into a blob, and then into something very familiar; and a double note of warning, only too well known, fell on his delighted ear.

"This is something like!" said the excited Toad. "This is real life again, this is once more the great world from which I have been missed so long! I will hail them, my brothers of the wheel, and pitch them a yarn, of the sort that has been so successful hitherto; and they will give me a lift, of course, and then I will talk to them some more; and, perhaps, with luck, it may even end in my driving up to Toad Hall in a motor-car! That will be one in the eye for Badger!"

He stepped confidently out into the road to hail the motor-car, which came along at an easy pace, slowing down as it neared the lane; when suddenly he became very pale, his heart turned to water, his knees shook and yielded under him, and he doubled up and collapsed with a sickening pain in his interior. And well he might, the unhappy animal; for the approaching car was the very one he had stolen out of the yard of the Red Lion Hotel on that fatal day when all his troubles began! And the people in it were the very same people he had sat and watched at luncheon in the coffee-room!

He sank down in a shabby, miserable heap in the road, murmuring to himself in his despair, "It's all up! It's all over now! Chains and policemen again! Prison again! Dry bread and water again! O, what a fool I have been! What did I want to go strutting about the country for, singing conceited songs, and hailing people in broad day on the high-road, instead of hiding till nightfall and slipping home quietly by back ways! O hapless Toad! O ill-fated animal!"

The terrible motor-car drew slowly nearer and nearer, till at last he heard it stop just short of him. Two gentlemen got out and walked round the trembling heap of crumpled misery lying in the road, and one of them said, "O dear! this is very sad! Here is a poor old thing—a washerwoman apparently—who has fainted in the road! Perhaps she is overcome by the heat, poor creature; or possibly she has not had any food today. Let us lift her into the car and take her to the nearest village, where doubtless she has friends."

They tenderly lifted Toad into the motor-car and propped him up with soft cushions, and proceeded on their way.

When Toad heard them talk in so kind and sympathetic a way, and knew that he was not recognised, his courage began to revive, and he cautiously opened first one eye and then the other.

"Look!" said one of the gentlemen, "she is better already. The fresh air is doing her good. How do you feel now, ma'am?"

"Thank you kindly, sir," said Toad in a feeble voice, "I'm feeling a great deal better!"

"That's right," said the gentleman. "Now keep quite still, and, above all, don't try to talk."

"I won't," said Toad. "I was only thinking, if I might sit on the front seat there, beside the driver, where I could get the fresh air full in my face, I should soon be all right again."

"What a very sensible woman!" said the gentleman. "Of course you shall." So they carefully helped Toad into the front seat beside the driver, and on they went again.

Toad was almost himself again by now. He sat up, looked about him, and tried to beat down the tremors, the yearnings, the old cravings that rose up and beset him and took possession of him entirely.

"It is fate!" he said to himself. "Why strive? why struggle?" and he turned to the driver at his side.

"Please, sir," he said, "I wish you would kindly let me try and drive the car for a little. I've been watching you carefully, and it looks so easy and so interesting, and I should like to be able to tell my friends that once I had driven a motor-car!"

The driver laughed at the proposal, so heartily that the gentleman inquired what the matter was. When he heard, he said, to Toad's delight, "Bravo, ma'am! I like your spirit. Let her have a try, and look after her. She won't do any harm."

Toad eagerly scrambled into the seat vacated by the driver, took the steering-wheel in his hands, listened with affected humility to the instructions given him, and set the car in motion, but very slowly and carefully at first, for he was determined to be prudent.

The gentlemen behind clapped their hands and applauded, and Toad heard them saying, "How well she does it! Fancy a washerwoman driving a car as well as that, the first time!"

Toad went a little faster; then faster still, and faster.

He heard the gentlemen call out warningly, "Be careful, washerwoman!" And this annoyed him, and he began to lose his head.

The driver tried to interfere, but he pinned him down in his seat with one elbow, and put on full speed. The rush of air in his face, the hum of the engines, and the light jump of the car beneath him intoxicated his weak brain. "Washerwoman, indeed!" he shouted recklessly. "Ho! ho! I am the Toad, the motor-car snatcher, the prison-breaker, the Toad who always escapes! Sit still, and you shall know what driving really is, for you are in the hands of the famous, the skilful, the entirely fearless Toad!"

With a cry of horror the whole party rose and flung themselves on him. "Seize him!" they cried, "seize the Toad, the wicked animal who stole our motor-car! Bind him, chain him, drag him to the nearest police-station! Down with the desperate and dangerous Toad!"

Alas! they should have thought, they ought to have been more prudent, they should have remembered to stop the motor-car somehow before playing any pranks of that sort. With a half-turn of the wheel the Toad sent the car crashing through the low hedge that ran along the roadside. One mighty bound, a violent shock, and the wheels of the car were churning up the thick mud of a horse-pond.

Toad found himself flying through the air with the strong upward rush and delicate curve of a swallow. He liked the motion, and was just beginning to wonder whether it would go on until he developed wings and turned into a Toad-bird, when he landed on his back with a thump, in the soft rich grass of a meadow. Sitting up, he could just see the motor-car in the pond, nearly submerged; the gentlemen and the driver, encumbered by their long coats, were floundering helplessly in the water.

He picked himself up rapidly, and set off running across country as hard as he could, scrambling through hedges, jumping ditches, pounding across fields, till he was breathless and weary, and had to settle down into an easy walk. When he had recovered his breath somewhat, and was able to think calmly, he began to giggle, and from giggling he took to laughing, and he laughed till he had to sit down under a hedge. "Ho, ho!" he cried, in ecstasies of self-admiration, "Toad again! Toad, as usual, comes out on the top! Who was it got them to give him a lift? Who managed to get on the front seat for the sake of fresh air? Who persuaded them into letting him see if he could drive? Who landed them all in a horse-pond? Who escaped, flying gaily and unscathed through the air, leaving the narrow-minded, grudging, timid excursionists in the mud where they should rightly be? Why, Toad, of course; clever Toad, great Toad, *good* Toad!"

Then he burst into song again, and chanted with uplifted voice—

> *The motor-car went Poop-poop-poop,*
> *As it raced along the road.*
> *Who was it steered it into a pond?*
> *Ingenious Mr. Toad!*

"O, how clever I am! How clever, how clever, how very clev—"

A slight noise at a distance behind him made him turn his head and look. O horror! O misery! O despair!

About two fields off, a chauffeur in his leather gaiters and two large rural policemen were visible, running towards him as hard as they could go!

Poor Toad sprang to his feet and pelted away again, his heart in his mouth. "O, my!" he gasped, as he panted along, "what an *ass* I am! What a *conceited* and heedless ass! Swaggering again! Shouting and singing songs again! Sitting still and gassing again! O my! O my! O my!"

He glanced back, and saw to his dismay that they were gaining on him. On he ran desperately, but kept looking back, and saw that they still gained steadily. He did his best, but he was a fat animal, and his legs were short, and still they gained. He could hear them close behind him now. Ceasing to heed where he was going, he struggled on blindly and wildly, looking back over his shoulder at the now triumphant enemy, when suddenly the earth failed under his feet, he grasped at the air, and, splash! he found himself head over ears in deep water, rapid water, water that bore him along with a force he could not contend with; and he knew that in his blind panic he had run straight into the river!

He rose to the surface and tried to grasp the reeds and the rushes that grew along the water's edge close under the bank, but the stream was so strong that it tore them out of his hands. "O my!" gasped poor Toad, "if ever I steal a motor-car again! If ever I sing another conceited song"—then down he went, and came up breathless and spluttering. Presently he saw that he was approaching a big dark hole in the bank, just above his head, and as the stream bore him past he reached up with a paw and caught hold of the edge and held on. Then slowly and with difficulty he drew himself up out of the water, till at last he was able to rest his elbows on the edge of the hole. There he remained for some minutes, puffing and panting, for he was quite exhausted.

As he sighed and blew and stared before him into the dark hole, some bright small thing shone and twinkled in its depths, moving towards him. As it approached, a face grew up gradually around it, and it was a familiar face!

Brown and small, with whiskers.

Grave and round, with neat ears and silky hair.

It was the Water Rat!

Chapter 11. "Like Summer Tempests Came His Tears"

The Rat put out a neat little brown paw, gripped Toad firmly by the scruff of the neck, and gave a great hoist and a pull; and the water-logged Toad came up slowly but surely over the edge of the hole, till at last he stood safe and sound in the hall, streaked with mud and weed to be sure, and with the water streaming off him, but happy and high-spirited as of old, now that he found himself once more in the house of a friend, and dodgings and evasions were over, and he could lay aside a disguise that was unworthy of his position and wanted such a lot of living up to.

"O, Ratty!" he cried. "I've been through such times since I saw you last, you can't think! Such trials, such sufferings, and all so nobly borne! Then such escapes, such disguises, such subterfuges, and all so cleverly planned and carried out! Been in prison—got out of it, of course! Been thrown into a canal—swam ashore! Stole a horse— sold him for a large sum of money! Humbugged everybody—made 'em all do exactly what I wanted! Oh, I *am* a smart Toad, and no mistake! What do you think my last exploit was? Just hold on till I tell you—"

"Toad," said the Water Rat, gravely and firmly, "you go off upstairs at once, and take off that old cotton rag that looks as if it might formerly have belonged to some washerwoman, and clean yourself thoroughly, and put on some of my clothes, and try and come down looking like a gentleman if you *can*; for a more shabby, bedraggled, disreputable-looking object than you are I never set eyes on in my whole life! Now, stop swaggering and arguing, and be off! I'll have something to say to you later!"

Toad was at first inclined to stop and do some talking back at him. He had had enough of being ordered about when he was in prison, and here was the thing being begun all over again, apparently; and by a Rat, too! However, he caught sight of himself in the looking-glass over the hat-stand, with the rusty black bonnet perched rakishly over one eye, and he changed his mind and went very quickly and humbly upstairs to the Rat's dressing-room. There he had a thorough wash and brush-up, changed his clothes, and stood for a long time before the glass, contemplating himself with pride and pleasure, and thinking what utter idiots all the people must have been to have ever mistaken him for one moment for a washerwoman.

By the time he came down again luncheon was on the table, and very glad Toad was to see it, for he had been through some trying experiences and had taken much hard exercise since the excellent breakfast provided for him by the gypsy. While they ate Toad told the Rat all his adventures, dwelling chiefly on his own cleverness, and presence of mind in emergencies, and cunning in tight places; and rather making out that he had been having a gay and highly-coloured experience. But the more he talked and boasted, the more grave and silent the Rat became.

When at last Toad had talked himself to a standstill, there was silence for a while; and then the Rat said, "Now, Toady, I don't want to give you pain, after all you've been through already; but, seriously, don't you see what an awful ass you've been making of yourself? On your own admission you have been handcuffed, imprisoned, starved, chased, terrified out of your life, insulted, jeered at, and ignominiously flung into the water—by a woman, too! Where's the amusement in that? Where does the fun come in? And all because you must needs go and steal a motor-car. You know that you've never had anything but trouble from motor-cars from the moment you first set eyes on one. But if you *will* be mixed up with them—as you generally are, five minutes after you've started—why *steal* them? Be a cripple, if you think it's exciting; be a bankrupt, for a change, if you've set your mind on it: but why choose to be a convict? When are you going to be sensible, and think of your friends, and try and be a credit to them? Do you suppose it's any pleasure to me, for instance, to hear animals saying, as I go about, that I'm the chap that keeps company with gaol-birds?"

Now, it was a very comforting point in Toad's character that he was a thoroughly good-hearted animal and never minded being jawed by those who were his real friends. And even when most set upon a thing, he was always able to see the other side of the question. So although, while the Rat was talking so seriously, he kept saying to himself mutinously, "But it *was* fun, though! Awful fun!" and making strange suppressed noises inside him, k-i-ck-ck-ck, and poop-p-p, and other sounds resembling stifled snorts, or the opening of soda-water bottles, yet when the Rat had quite finished, he heaved a deep sigh and said, very nicely and humbly, "Quite right, Ratty! How *sound* you always are! Yes, I've been a conceited old ass, I can quite see that; but now I'm going to be a good Toad, and not do it anymore. As for motor-cars, I've not been at all so keen about them since my last ducking in that river of yours. The fact is, while I was hanging on to the edge of your hole and getting my breath, I had a sudden idea—a really brilliant idea—connected with motor-boats—there, there! don't take on so, old chap, and stamp, and upset things; it was only an idea, and we won't talk anymore about it now. We'll have our coffee, *and* a smoke, and a quiet chat, and then I'm going to stroll quietly down to Toad Hall, and get into clothes of my own, and set things going again on the old lines. I've had enough of adventures. I shall lead a quiet, steady, respectable life, pottering about my property, and improving it, and doing a little landscape gardening at times. There will always be a bit of dinner for my friends when they come to see me; and I shall keep a pony-chaise to jog about the country in, just as I used to in the good old days, before I got restless, and wanted to *do* things."

"Stroll quietly down to Toad Hall?" cried the Rat, greatly excited. "What are you talking about? Do you mean to say you haven't *heard?*"

"Heard what?" said Toad, turning rather pale. "Go on, Ratty! Quick! Don't spare me! What haven't I heard?"

"Do you mean to tell me," shouted the Rat, thumping with his little fist upon the table, "that you've heard nothing about the Stoats and Weasels?"

"What, the Wild Wooders?" cried Toad, trembling in every limb. "No, not a word! What have they been doing?"

"—And how they've been and taken Toad Hall?" continued the Rat.

Toad leaned his elbows on the table, and his chin on his paws; and a large tear welled up in each of his eyes, overflowed and splashed on the table, plop! plop!

"Go on, Ratty," he murmured presently; "tell me all. The worst is over. I am an animal again. I can bear it."

"When you—got—into that—that—trouble of yours," said

the Rat, slowly and impressively; "I mean, when you—disappeared from society for a time, over that misunderstanding about a—a machine, you know—"

Toad merely nodded.

"Well, it was a good deal talked about down here, naturally," continued the Rat, "not only along the river-side, but even in the Wild Wood. Animals took sides, as always happens. The river-bankers stuck up for you, and said you had been infamously treated, and there was no justice to be had in the land nowadays. But the Wild Wood animals said hard things, and served you right, and it was time this sort of thing was stopped. And they got very cocky, and went about saying you were done for this time! You would never come back again, never, never!"

Toad nodded once more, keeping silence.

"That's the sort of little beasts they are," the Rat went on. "But Mole and Badger, they stuck out, through thick and thin, that you would come back again soon, somehow. They didn't know exactly how, but somehow!"

Toad began to sit up in his chair again, and to smirk a little.

"They argued from history," continued the Rat. "They said that no criminal laws had ever been known to prevail against cheek and plausibility such as yours, combined with the power of a long purse. So they arranged to move their things in to Toad Hall, and sleep there, and keep it aired, and have it all ready for you when you turned up. They didn't guess what was going to happen, of course; still, they had their suspicions of the Wild Wood animals. Now I come to the most painful and tragic part of my story. One dark night—it was a *very* dark night, and blowing hard, too, and raining simply cats and dogs—a band of weasels, armed to the teeth, crept silently up the carriage-drive to the front entrance. Simultaneously, a body of desperate ferrets, advancing through the kitchen-garden, possessed themselves of the backyard and offices; while a company of skirmishing stoats who stuck at nothing occupied the conservatory and the billiard-room, and held the French windows opening on to the lawn.

"The Mole and the Badger were sitting by the fire in the smoking-room, telling stories and suspecting nothing, for it wasn't a night for any animals to be out in, when those bloodthirsty villains broke down the doors and rushed in upon them from every side. They made the best fight they could, but what was the good? They were unarmed, and taken by surprise, and what can two animals do against hundreds? They took and beat them severely with sticks, those two poor faithful creatures, and turned them out into the cold and the wet, with many insulting and uncalled-for remarks!"

Here the unfeeling Toad broke into a snigger, and then pulled himself together and tried to look particularly solemn.

"And the Wild Wooders have been living in Toad Hall ever since," continued the Rat; "and going on simply anyhow! Lying in bed half the day, and breakfast at all hours, and the place in such a mess (I'm told) it's not fit to be seen! Eating your grub, and drinking your drink, and making bad jokes about you, and singing vulgar songs, about—well, about prisons and magistrates, and policemen; horrid personal songs, with no humour in them. And they're telling the tradespeople and everybody that they've come to stay for good."

"O, have they!" said Toad getting up and seizing a stick. "I'll jolly soon see about that!"

"It's no good, Toad!" called the Rat after him. "You'd better come back and sit down; you'll only get into trouble."

But the Toad was off, and there was no holding him. He marched rapidly down the road, his stick over his shoulder, fuming and muttering to himself in his anger, till he got near his front gate, when suddenly there popped up from behind the palings a long yellow ferret with a gun.

"Who comes there?" said the ferret sharply.

"Stuff and nonsense!" said Toad, very angrily. "What do you mean by talking like that to me? Come out of that at once, or I'll—"

The ferret said never a word, but he brought his gun up to his shoulder. Toad prudently dropped flat in the road, and *bang!* a bullet whistled over his head.

The startled Toad scrambled to his feet and scampered off down the road as hard as he could; and as he ran he heard the ferret laughing and other horrid thin little laughs taking it up and carrying on the sound.

He went back, very crestfallen, and told the Water Rat.

"What did I tell you?" said the Rat. "It's no good. They've got sentries posted, and they are all armed. You must just wait."

Still, Toad was not inclined to give in all at once. So he got out the boat, and set off rowing up the river to where the garden front of Toad Hall came down to the waterside.

Arriving within sight of his old home, he rested on his oars and surveyed the land cautiously. All seemed very peaceful and deserted and quiet. He could see the whole front of Toad Hall, glowing in the evening sunshine, the pigeons settling by twos and threes along the straight line of the roof; the garden, a blaze of flowers; the creek that led up to the boat-house, the little wooden bridge that crossed it; all tranquil, uninhabited, apparently waiting for his return. He would try the boat-house first, he thought. Very warily he paddled up to the mouth of the creek, and was just passing under the bridge, when . . . *crash*!

A great stone, dropped from above, smashed through the bottom of the boat. It filled and sank, and Toad found himself struggling in deep water. Looking up, he saw two stoats leaning over the parapet of the bridge and watching him with great glee. "It will be your head next time, Toady!" they called out to him. The indignant Toad swam to shore, while the stoats laughed and laughed, supporting each other, and laughed again, till they nearly had two fits—that is, one fit each, of course.

The Toad retraced his weary way on foot, and related his disappointing experiences to the Water Rat once more.

"Well, *what* did I tell you?" said the Rat very crossly. "And, now, look here! See what you've been and done! Lost me my boat that I was so fond of, that's what you've done! And simply ruined that nice suit of clothes that I lent you! Really, Toad, of all the trying animals—I wonder you manage to keep any friends at all!"

The Toad saw at once how wrongly and foolishly he had acted. He admitted his errors and wrong-headedness and made a full apology to Rat for losing his boat and spoiling his clothes. And he wound up by saying, with that frank self-surrender which always disarmed his friend's criticism and won them back to his side, "Ratty! I see that I have been a headstrong and a wilful Toad! Henceforth, believe me, I will be humble and submissive, and will take no action without your kind advice and full approval!"

"If that is really so," said the good-natured Rat, already appeased, "then my advice to you is, considering the lateness of the hour, to sit down and have your supper, which will be on the table in a minute, and be very patient. For I am convinced that we can do nothing until we have seen the Mole and the Badger, and heard their latest news, and held conference and taken their advice in this difficult matter."

"Oh, ah, yes, of course, the Mole and the Badger," said Toad, lightly. "What's become of them, the dear fellows? I had forgotten all about them."

"Well may you ask!" said the Rat reproachfully. "While you were riding about the country in expensive motor-cars, and galloping proudly on blood-horses, and breakfasting on the fat of the land, those two poor devoted animals have been camping out in the open, in every sort of weather, living very rough by day and lying very hard by night; watching over your house, patrolling your boundaries, keeping a constant eye on the stoats and the weasels, scheming and planning and contriving how to get your property back for you. You don't deserve to have such true and loyal friends, Toad, you don't, really. Someday, when it's too late, you'll be sorry you didn't value them more while you had them!"

"I'm an ungrateful beast, I know," sobbed Toad, shedding bitter tears. "Let me go out and find them, out into the cold, dark night, and share their hardships, and try and prove by—Hold on a bit! Surely I heard the chink of dishes on a tray! Supper's here at last, hooray! Come on, Ratty!"

The Rat remembered that poor Toad had been on prison fare for a considerable time, and that large allowances had therefore to be made. He followed him to the table accordingly, and hospitably encouraged him in his gallant efforts to make up for past privations.

They had just finished their meal and resumed their armchairs, when there came a heavy knock at the door.

Toad was nervous, but the Rat, nodding mysteriously at him, went straight up to the door and opened it, and in walked Mr. Badger.

He had all the appearance of one who for some nights had been kept away from home and all its little comforts and conveniences. His shoes were covered with mud, and he was looking very rough and touzled; but then he had never been a very smart man, the Badger, at the best of times. He came solemnly up to Toad, shook him by the paw, and said, "Welcome home, Toad! Alas! what am I saying? Home, indeed! This is a poor home-coming. Unhappy Toad!" Then he turned his back on him, sat down to the table, drew his chair up, and helped himself to a large slice of cold pie.

Toad was quite alarmed at this very serious and portentous style of greeting; but the Rat whispered to him, "Never mind; don't take any notice; and don't say anything to him just yet. He's always rather low and despondent when he's wanting his victuals. In half an hour's time he'll be quite a different animal."

So they waited in silence, and presently there came another and a lighter knock. The Rat, with a nod to Toad, went to the door and ushered in the Mole, very shabby and unwashed, with bits of hay and straw sticking in his fur.

"Hooray! Here's old Toad!" cried the Mole, his face beaming. "Fancy having you back again!" And he began to dance round him. "We never dreamt you would turn up so soon! Why, you must have managed to escape, you clever, ingenious, intelligent Toad!"

The Rat, alarmed, pulled him by the elbow; but it was too late. Toad was puffing and swelling already.

"Clever? O, no!" he said. "I'm not really clever, according to my friends. I've only broken out of the strongest prison in England, that's all! And captured a railway train and escaped on it, that's all! And disguised myself and gone about the country humbugging everybody, that's all! O, no! I'm a stupid ass, I am! I'll tell you one or two of my little adventures, Mole, and you shall judge for yourself!"

"Well, well," said the Mole, moving towards the supper-table; "supposing you talk while I eat. Not a bite since breakfast! O my! O my!" And he sat down and helped himself liberally to cold beef and pickles.

Toad straddled on the hearth-rug, thrust his paw into his trouser-pocket and pulled out a handful of silver. "Look at that!" he cried, displaying it. "That's not so bad, is it, for a few minutes' work? And how do you think I done it, Mole? Horse-dealing! That's how I done it!"

"Go on, Toad," said the Mole, immensely interested.

"Toad, do be quiet, please!" said the Rat. "And don't you egg him on, Mole, when you know what he is; but please tell us as soon as possible what the position is, and what's best to be done, now that Toad is back at last."

"The position's about as bad as it can be," replied the Mole grumpily; "and as for what's to be done, why, blest if I know! The Badger and I have been round and round the place, by night and by day; always the same thing. Sentries posted everywhere, guns poked out at us, stones thrown at us; always an animal on the look-out, and when they see us, my! how they do laugh! That's what annoys me most!"

"It's a very difficult situation," said the Rat, reflecting deeply. "But I think I see now, in the depths of my mind, what Toad really ought to do. I will tell you. He ought to—"

"No, he oughtn't!" shouted the Mole, with his mouth full. "Nothing of the sort! You don't understand. What he ought to do is, he ought to—"

"Well, I shan't do it, anyway!" cried Toad, getting excited. "I'm not going to be ordered about by you fellows! It's my house we're talking about, and I know exactly what to do, and I'll tell you. I'm going to—"

By this time they were all three talking at once, at the top of their voices, and the noise was simply deafening, when a thin, dry voice made itself heard, saying, "Be quiet at once, all of you!" and instantly everyone was silent.

It was the Badger, who, having finished his pie, had turned round in his chair and was looking at them severely. When he saw that he had secured their attention, and that they were evidently waiting for him to address them, he turned back to the table again and reached out for the cheese. And so great was the respect commanded by the solid qualities of that admirable animal, that not another word was uttered until he had quite finished his repast and brushed the crumbs from his knees. The Toad fidgeted a good deal, but the Rat held him firmly down.

When the Badger had quite done, he got up from his seat and stood before the fireplace, reflecting deeply. At last he spoke.

"Toad!" he said severely. "You bad, troublesome little animal! Aren't you ashamed of yourself? What do you think your father, my old friend, would have said if he had been here tonight, and had known of all your goings on?"

Toad, who was on the sofa by this time, with his legs up, rolled over on his face, shaken by sobs of contrition.

"There, there!" went on the Badger, more kindly. "Never mind.

Stop crying. We're going to let bygones be bygones, and try and turn over a new leaf. But what the Mole says is quite true. The stoats are on guard, at every point, and they make the best sentinels in the world. It's quite useless to think of attacking the place. They're too strong for us."

"Then it's all over," sobbed the Toad, crying into the sofa cushions. "I shall go and enlist for a soldier, and never see my dear Toad Hall anymore!"

"Come, cheer up, Toady!" said the Badger. "There are more ways of getting back a place than taking it by storm. I haven't said my last word yet. Now I'm going to tell you a great secret."

Toad sat up slowly and dried his eyes. Secrets had an immense attraction for him, because he never could keep one, and he enjoyed the sort of unhallowed thrill he experienced when he went and told another animal, after having faithfully promised not to.

"There—is—an—underground—passage," said the Badger, impressively, "that leads from the river bank, quite near here, right up into the middle of Toad Hall."

"O, nonsense! Badger," said Toad, rather airily. "You've been listening to some of the yarns they spin in the public-houses about here. I know every inch of Toad Hall, inside and out. Nothing of the sort, I do assure you!"

"My young friend," said the Badger, with great severity, "your father, who was a worthy animal—a lot worthier than some others I know—was a particular friend of mine, and told me a great deal he wouldn't have dreamt of telling you. He discovered that passage—he didn't make it, of course; that was done hundreds of years before he ever came to live there—and he repaired it and cleaned it out, because he thought it might come in useful someday, in case of trouble or danger; and he showed it to me. 'Don't let my son know about it,' he said. 'He's a good boy, but very light and volatile in character, and simply cannot hold his tongue. If he's ever in a real fix, and it would be of use to him, you may tell him about the secret passage; but not before.'"

The other animals looked hard at Toad to see how he would take it. Toad was inclined to be sulky at first; but he brightened up immediately, like the good fellow he was.

"Well, well," he said; "perhaps I am a bit of a talker. A popular fellow such as I am—my friends get round me—we chaff, we sparkle, we tell witty stories—and somehow my tongue gets wagging. I have the gift of conversation. I've been told I ought to have a salon, whatever that may be. Never mind. Go on, Badger. How's this passage of yours going to help us?"

"I've found out a thing or two lately," continued the Badger. "I got Otter to disguise himself as a sweep and call at the back-door with brushes over his shoulder, asking for a job. There's going to be a big banquet tomorrow night. It's somebody's birthday—the Chief Weasel's, I believe—and all the weasels will be gathered together in the dining-hall, eating and drinking and laughing and carrying on, suspecting nothing. No guns, no swords, no sticks, no arms of any sort whatever!"

"But the sentinels will be posted as usual," remarked the Rat.

"Exactly," said the Badger; "that is my point. The weasels will trust entirely to their excellent sentinels. And that is where the passage comes in. That very useful tunnel leads right up under the butler's pantry, next to the dining-hall!"

"Aha! that squeaky board in the butler's pantry!" said Toad. "Now I understand it!"

"We shall creep out quietly into the butler's pantry—" cried the Mole.

"—with our pistols and swords and sticks—" shouted the Rat.

"—and rush in upon them," said the Badger.

"—and whack 'em, and whack 'em, and whack 'em!" cried the Toad in ecstasy, running round and round the room, and jumping over the chairs.

"Very well, then," said the Badger, resuming his usual dry manner, "our plan is settled, and there's nothing more for you to argue and squabble about. So, as it's getting very late, all of you go right off to bed at once. We will make all the necessary arrangements in the course of the morning tomorrow."

Toad, of course, went off to bed dutifully with the rest—he knew better than to refuse—though he was feeling much too excited to sleep. But he had had a long day, with many events crowded into it; and sheets and blankets were very friendly and comforting things, after plain straw, and not too much of it, spread on the stone floor of a draughty cell; and his head had not been many seconds on his pillow before he was snoring happily. Naturally, he dreamt a good deal; about roads that ran away from him just when he wanted them, and canals that chased him and caught him, and a barge that sailed into the banqueting-hall with his week's washing, just as he was giving a dinner-party; and he was alone in the secret passage, pushing onwards, but it twisted and turned round and shook itself, and sat up on its end; yet somehow, at the last, he found himself back in Toad Hall, safe and triumphant, with all his friends gathered round about him, earnestly assuring him that he really was a clever Toad.

He slept till a late hour next morning, and by the time he got down he found that the other animals had finished their breakfast some time before. The Mole had slipped off somewhere by himself, without telling anyone where he was going to. The Badger sat in the armchair, reading the paper, and not concerning himself in the slightest about what was going to happen that very evening. The Rat, on the other hand, was running round the room busily, with his arms full of weapons of every kind, distributing them in four little heaps on the floor, and saying excitedly under his breath, as he ran, "Here's-a-sword-for-the-Rat, here's-a-sword-for-the-Mole, here's-a-sword-for-the-Toad, here's-a-sword-for-the-Badger! Here's-a-pistol-for-the-Rat, here's-a-pistol-for-the-Mole, here's-a-pistol-for-the-Toad, here's-a-pistol-for-the-Badger!" And so on, in a regular, rhythmical way, while the four little heaps gradually grew and grew.

"That's all very well, Rat," said the Badger presently, looking at the busy little animal over the edge of his newspaper; "I'm not blaming you. But just let us once get past the stoats, with those detestable guns of theirs, and I assure you we shan't want any swords or pistols. We four, with our sticks, once we're inside the dining-hall, why, we shall clear the floor of all the lot of them in five minutes. I'd have done the whole thing by myself, only I didn't want to deprive you fellows of the fun!"

"It's as well to be on the safe side," said the Rat reflectively, polishing a pistol-barrel on his sleeve and looking along it.

The Toad, having finished his breakfast, picked up a stout stick and swung it vigorously, belabouring imaginary animals. "I'll learn 'em to steal my house!" he cried. "I'll learn 'em, I'll learn 'em!"

"Don't say 'learn 'em,' Toad," said the Rat, greatly shocked. "It's not good English."

"What are you always nagging at Toad for?" inquired the Badger, rather peevishly. "What's the matter with his English? It's the same what I use myself, and if it's good enough for me, it ought to be good enough for you!"

"I'm very sorry," said the Rat humbly. "Only I *think* it ought to be 'teach 'em,' not 'learn 'em.'"

"But we don't *want* to teach 'em," replied the Badger. "We want to *learn* 'em—learn 'em, learn 'em! And what's more, we're going to *do* it, too!"

"Oh, very well, have it your own way," said the Rat. He was getting rather muddled about it himself, and presently he retired into a corner, where he could be heard muttering, "Learn 'em, teach 'em, teach 'em, learn 'em!" till the Badger told him rather sharply to leave off.

Presently the Mole came tumbling into the room, evidently very pleased with himself. "I've been having such fun!" he began at once; "I've been getting a rise out of the stoats!"

"I hope you've been very careful, Mole?" said the Rat anxiously.

"I should hope so, too," said the Mole confidently. "I got the idea when I went into the kitchen, to see about Toad's breakfast being kept hot for him. I found that old washerwoman-dress that he came home in yesterday, hanging on a towel-horse before the fire. So I put it on, and the bonnet as well, and the shawl, and off I went to Toad Hall, as bold as you please. The sentries were on the look-out, of course, with their guns and their 'Who comes there?' and all the rest of their nonsense. 'Good morning, gentlemen!' says I, very respectful. 'Want any washing done today?'

"They looked at me very proud and stiff and haughty, and said, 'Go away, washerwoman! We don't do any washing on duty.' 'Or any other time?' says I. Ho, ho, ho! Wasn't I *funny*, Toad?"

"Poor, frivolous animal!" said Toad, very loftily. The fact is, he felt exceedingly jealous of Mole for what he had just done. It was exactly what he would have liked to have done himself, if only he had thought of it first, and hadn't gone and overslept himself.

"Some of the stoats turned quite pink," continued the Mole, "and the Sergeant in charge, he said to me, very short, he said, 'Now run away, my good woman, run away! Don't keep my men idling and talking on their posts.' 'Run away?' says I; 'it won't be me that'll be running away, in a very short time from now!'"

"O *Moly*, how could you?" said the Rat, dismayed.

The Badger laid down his paper.

"I could see them pricking up their ears and looking at each other," went on the Mole; "and the Sergeant said to them, 'Never mind *her*; she doesn't know what she's talking about.'"

"'O! don't I?' said I. 'Well, let me tell you this. My daughter, she washes for Mr. Badger, and that'll show you whether I know what I'm talking about; and *you*'ll know pretty soon, too! A hundred bloodthirsty badgers, armed with rifles, are going to attack Toad Hall this very night, by way of the paddock. Six boatloads of Rats, with pistols and cutlasses, will come up the river and effect a landing in the garden; while a picked body of Toads, known at the Die-hards, or the Death-or-Glory Toads, will storm the orchard and carry everything before them, yelling for vengeance. There won't be much left of you to wash, by the time they've done with you, unless you clear out while you have the chance!' Then I ran away, and when I was out of sight I hid; and presently I came creeping back along the ditch and took a peep at them through the hedge. They were all as nervous and flustered as could be, running all ways at once, and falling over each other, and everyone giving orders to everybody else and not listening; and the Sergeant kept sending off parties of stoats to distant parts of the grounds, and then sending other fellows to fetch 'em back again; and I heard them saying to each other, 'That's just like the weasels; they're to stop comfortably in the banqueting-hall, and have feasting and toasts and songs and all sorts of fun, while we must stay on guard in the cold and the dark, and in the end be cut to pieces by bloodthirsty Badgers!'"

"Oh, you silly ass, Mole!" cried Toad, "You've been and spoilt everything!"

"Mole," said the Badger, in his dry, quiet way, "I perceive you have more sense in your little finger than some other animals have in the whole of their fat bodies. You have managed excellently, and I begin to have great hopes of you. Good Mole! Clever Mole!"

The Toad was simply wild with jealousy, more especially as he couldn't make out for the life of him what the Mole had done that was so particularly clever; but, fortunately for him, before he could show temper or expose himself to the Badger's sarcasm, the bell rang for luncheon.

It was a simple but sustaining meal—bacon and broad beans, and a macaroni pudding; and when they had quite done, the Badger settled himself into an armchair, and said, "Well, we've got our work cut out for us tonight, and it will probably be pretty late before we're quite through with it; so I'm just going to take forty winks, while I can." And he drew a handkerchief over his face and was soon snoring.

The anxious and laborious Rat at once resumed his preparations, and started running between his four little heaps, muttering, "Here's-a-belt-for-the-Rat, here's-a-belt-for-the-Mole, here's-a-belt-for-the-Toad, here's-a-belt-for-the-Badger!" and so on, with every fresh accoutrement he produced, to which there seemed really no end; so the Mole drew his arm through Toad's, led him out into the open air, shoved him into a wicker-chair, and made him tell him all his adventures from beginning to end, which Toad was only too willing to do. The Mole was a good listener, and Toad, with no one to check his statements or to criticise in an unfriendly spirit, rather let himself go. Indeed, much that he related belonged more properly to the category of what-might-have-happened-had-I-only-thought-of-it-in-time-instead-of-ten-minutes-afterwards. Those are always the best and the raciest adventures; and why should they not be truly ours, as much as the somewhat inadequate things that really come off?

Chapter 12. The Return of Ulysses

When it began to grow dark, the Rat, with an air of excitement and mystery, summoned them back into the parlour, stood each of them up alongside of his little heap, and proceeded to dress them up for the coming expedition. He was very earnest and thoroughgoing about it, and the affair took quite a long time. First, there was a belt to go round each animal, and then a sword to be stuck into each belt, and then a cutlass on the other side to balance it. Then a pair of pistols, a policeman's truncheon, several sets of handcuffs, some bandages and sticking-plaster, and a flask and a sandwich-case. The Badger laughed good-humouredly and said, "All right, Ratty! It amuses you and it doesn't hurt me. I'm going to do all I've got to do with this here stick." But the Rat only said, "*Please*, Badger. You know I shouldn't like you to blame me afterwards and say I had forgotten *anything*!"

When all was quite ready, the Badger took a dark lantern in one paw, grasped his great stick with the other, and said, "Now then, follow me! Mole first, 'cos I'm very pleased with him; Rat next; Toad last. And look here, Toady! Don't you chatter so much as usual, or you'll be sent back, as sure as fate!"

The Toad was so anxious not to be left out that he took up the inferior position assigned to him without a murmur, and the animals set off. The Badger led them along by the river for a little way, and then suddenly swung himself over the edge into a hole in the river bank, a little above the water. The Mole and the Rat followed silently, swinging themselves successfully into the hole as they had seen the Badger do; but when it came to Toad's turn, of course he managed to slip and fall into the water with a loud splash and a squeal of alarm. He was hauled out by his friends, rubbed down and wrung out hastily, comforted, and set on his legs; but the Badger was seriously angry, and told him that the very next time he made a fool of himself he would most certainly be left behind.

So at last they were in the secret passage, and the cutting-out expedition had really begun!

It was cold, and dark, and damp, and low, and narrow, and poor

Toad began to shiver, partly from dread of what might be before him, partly because he was wet through. The lantern was far ahead, and he could not help lagging behind a little in the darkness. Then he heard the Rat call out warningly, "*Come* on, Toad!" and a terror seized him of being left behind, alone in the darkness, and he "came on" with such a rush that he upset the Rat into the Mole and the Mole into the Badger, and for a moment all was confusion. The Badger thought they were being attacked from behind, and, as there was no room to use a stick or a cutlass, drew a pistol, and was on the point of putting a bullet into Toad. When he found out what had really happened he was very angry indeed, and said, "Now this time that tiresome Toad *shall* be left behind!"

But Toad whimpered, and the other two promised that they would be answerable for his good conduct, and at last the Badger was pacified, and the procession moved on; only this time the Rat brought up the rear, with a firm grip on the shoulder of Toad.

So they groped and shuffled along, with their ears pricked up and their paws on their pistols, till at last the Badger said, "We ought by now to be pretty nearly under the Hall."

Then suddenly they heard, far away as it might be, and yet apparently nearly over their heads, a confused murmur of sound, as if people were shouting and cheering and stamping on the floor and hammering on tables. The Toad's nervous terrors all returned, but the Badger only remarked placidly, "They *are* going it, the Weasels!"

The passage now began to slope upwards; they groped onward a little further, and then the noise broke out again, quite distinct this time, and very close above them. "Ooo-ray-ooray-oo-ray-ooray!" they heard, and the stamping of little feet on the floor, and the clinking of glasses as little fists pounded on the table. "*What* a time they're having!" said the Badger. "Come on!" They hurried along the passage till it came to a full stop, and they found themselves standing under the trap-door that led up into the butler's pantry.

Such a tremendous noise was going on in the banqueting-hall that there was little danger of their being overheard. The Badger said, "Now, boys, all together!" and the four of them put their shoulders to the trap-door and heaved it back. Hoisting each other up, they found themselves standing in the pantry, with only a door between them and the banqueting-hall, where their unconscious enemies were carousing.

The noise, as they emerged from the passage, was simply deafening. At last, as the cheering and hammering slowly subsided, a voice could be made out saying, "Well, I do not propose to detain you much longer"—(great applause)—"but before I resume my seat"—(renewed cheering)—"I should like to say one word about our kind host, Mr. Toad. We all know Toad!"—(great laughter)— "*Good* Toad, *modest* Toad, *honest* Toad!" (shrieks of merriment).

"Only just let me get at him!" muttered Toad, grinding his teeth.

"Hold hard a minute!" said the Badger, restraining him with difficulty. "Get ready, all of you!"

"—Let me sing you a little song," went on the voice, "which I have composed on the subject of Toad"—(prolonged applause).

Then the Chief Weasel—for it was he—began in a high, squeaky voice:

> *Toad he went a-pleasuring*
> *Gaily down the street—*

The Badger drew himself up, took a firm grip of his stick with both paws, glanced round at his comrades, and cried—

"The hour is come! Follow me!"

And flung the door open wide.

My!

What a squealing and a squeaking and a screeching filled the air!

Well might the terrified weasels dive under the tables and spring madly up at the windows! Well might the ferrets rush wildly for the fireplace and get hopelessly jammed in the chimney! Well might tables and chairs be upset, and glass and china be sent crashing on the floor, in the panic of that terrible moment when the four Heroes strode wrathfully into the room! The mighty Badger, his whiskers bristling, his great cudgel whistling through the air; Mole, black and grim, brandishing his stick and shouting his awful war-cry, "A Mole! A Mole!" Rat, desperate and determined, his belt bulging with weapons of every age and every variety; Toad, frenzied with excitement and injured pride, swollen to twice his ordinary size, leaping into the air and emitting Toad-whoops that chilled them to the marrow! "Toad he went a-pleasuring!" he yelled. "*I'll* pleasure 'em!" and he went straight for the Chief Weasel. They were but four in all, but to the panic-stricken weasels the hall seemed full of monstrous animals, grey, black, brown and yellow, whooping and flourishing enormous cudgels; and they broke and fled with squeals of terror and dismay, this way and that, through the windows, up the chimney, anywhere to get out of reach of those terrible sticks.

The affair was soon over. Up and down, the whole length of the hall, strode the four Friends, whacking with their sticks at every head that showed itself; and in five minutes the room was cleared. Through the broken windows the shrieks of terrified weasels escaping across the lawn were borne faintly to their ears; on the floor lay prostrate some dozen or so of the enemy, on whom the Mole was busily engaged in fitting handcuffs. The Badger, resting from his labours, leant on his stick and wiped his honest brow.

"Mole," he said, "you're the best of fellows! Just cut along outside and look after those stoat-sentries of yours, and see what they're doing. I've an idea that, thanks to you, we shan't have much trouble from *them* tonight!"

The Mole vanished promptly through a window; and the Badger bade the other two set a table on its legs again, pick up knives and forks and plates and glasses from the debris on the floor, and see if they could find materials for a supper. "I want some grub, I do," he said, in that rather common way he had of speaking. "Stir your stumps, Toad, and look lively! We've got your house back for you, and you don't offer us so much as a sandwich."

Toad felt rather hurt that the Badger didn't say pleasant things to him, as he had to the Mole, and tell him what a fine fellow he was, and how splendidly he had fought; for he was rather particularly pleased with himself and the way he had gone for the Chief Weasel and sent him flying across the table with one blow of his stick. But he bustled about, and so did the Rat, and soon they found some guava jelly in a glass dish, and a cold chicken, a tongue that had hardly been touched, some trifle, and quite a lot of lobster salad; and in the pantry they came upon a basketful of French rolls and any quantity of cheese, butter, and celery. They were just about to sit down when the Mole clambered in through the window, chuckling, with an armful of rifles.

"It's all over," he reported. "From what I can make out, as soon as the stoats, who were very nervous and jumpy already, heard the shrieks and the yells and the uproar inside the hall, some of them threw down their rifles and fled. The others stood fast for a bit, but when the weasels came rushing out upon them they thought they were betrayed; and the stoats grappled with the weasels, and the weasels fought to get away, and they wrestled and wriggled and punched each other, and rolled over and over, till most of 'em rolled into the river! They've all disappeared by now, one way or another; and I've got their rifles. So *that's* all right!"

"Excellent and deserving animal!" said the Badger, his mouth full of chicken and trifle. "Now, there's just one more thing I want you to do, Mole, before you sit down to your supper along of us; and I wouldn't trouble you only I know I can trust you to see a thing done, and I wish I could say the same of everyone I know. I'd send Rat, if he wasn't a poet. I want you to take those fellows on the floor there upstairs with you, and have some bedrooms cleaned out and tidied up and made really comfortable. See that they sweep *under* the beds, and put clean sheets and pillow-cases on, and turn down one corner of the bed-clothes, just as you know it ought to be done; and have a can of hot water, and clean towels, and fresh cakes of soap, put in each room. And then you can give them a licking a-piece, if it's any satisfaction to you, and put them out by the back-door, and we shan't see any more of *them*, I fancy. And then come along and have some of this cold tongue. It's first rate. I'm very pleased with you, Mole!"

The goodnatured Mole picked up a stick, formed his prisoners up in a line on the floor, gave them the order "Quick march!" and led his squad off to the upper floor. After a time, he appeared again, smiling, and said that every room was ready, and as clean as a new pin. "And I didn't have to lick them, either," he added. "I thought, on the whole, they had had licking enough for one night, and the weasels, when I put the point to them, quite agreed with me, and said they wouldn't think of troubling me. They were very penitent, and said they were extremely sorry for what they had done, but it was all the fault of the Chief Weasel and the stoats, and if ever they could do anything for us at any time to make up, we had only got to mention it. So I gave them a roll a-piece, and let them out at the back, and off they ran, as hard as they could!"

Then the Mole pulled his chair up to the table, and pitched into the cold tongue; and Toad, like the gentleman he was, put all his jealousy from him, and said heartily, "Thank you kindly, dear Mole, for all your pains and trouble tonight, and especially for your cleverness this morning!" The Badger was pleased at that, and said, "There spoke my brave Toad!" So they finished their supper in great joy and contentment, and presently retired to rest between clean sheets, safe in Toad's ancestral home, won back by matchless valour, consummate strategy, and a proper handling of sticks.

The following morning, Toad, who had overslept himself as usual, came down to breakfast disgracefully late, and found on the table a certain quantity of egg-shells, some fragments of cold and leathery toast, a coffee-pot three-fourths empty, and really very little else; which did not tend to improve his temper, considering that, after all, it was his own house. Through the French windows of the breakfast-room he could see the Mole and the Water Rat sitting in wicker-chairs out on the lawn, evidently telling each other stories; roaring with laughter and kicking their short legs up in the air. The Badger, who was in an armchair and deep in the morning paper, merely looked up and nodded when Toad entered the room. But Toad knew his man, so he sat down and made the best breakfast he could, merely observing to himself that he would get square with the others sooner or later. When he had nearly finished, the Badger looked up and remarked rather shortly: "I'm sorry, Toad, but I'm afraid there's a heavy morning's work in front of you. You see, we really ought to have a Banquet at once, to celebrate this affair. It's expected of you—in fact, it's the rule."

"O, all right!" said the Toad, readily. "Anything to oblige. Though why on earth you should want to have a Banquet in the morning I cannot understand. But you know I do not live to please myself, but merely to find out what my friends want, and then try and arrange it for 'em, you dear old Badger!"

"Don't pretend to be stupider than you really are," replied the Badger, crossly; "and don't chuckle and splutter in your coffee while you're talking; it's not manners. What I mean is, the Banquet will be at night, of course, but the invitations will have to be written and got off at once, and you've got to write 'em. Now, sit down at that table—there's stacks of letter-paper on it, with 'Toad Hall' at the top in blue and gold—and write invitations to all our friends, and if you stick to it we shall get them out before luncheon. And *I'll* bear a hand, too; and take my share of the burden. *I'll* order the Banquet."

"What!" cried Toad, dismayed. "Me stop indoors and write a lot of rotten letters on a jolly morning like this, when I want to go around my property, and set everything and everybody to rights, and swagger about and enjoy myself! Certainly not! I'll be—I'll see you—Stop a minute, though! Why, of course, dear Badger! What is my pleasure or convenience compared with that of others! You wish it done, and it shall be done. Go, Badger, order the Banquet, order what you like; then join our young friends outside in their innocent mirth, oblivious of me and my cares and toils. I sacrifice this fair morning on the altar of duty and friendship!"

The Badger looked at him very suspiciously, but Toad's frank, open countenance made it difficult to suggest any unworthy motive in this change of attitude. He quitted the room, accordingly, in the direction of the kitchen, and as soon as the door had closed behind him, Toad hurried to the writing-table. A fine idea had occurred to him while he was talking. He *would* write the invitations; and he would take care to mention the leading part he had taken in the fight, and how he had laid the Chief Weasel flat; and he would hint at his adventures, and what a career of triumph he had to tell about; and on the fly-leaf he would set out a sort of a programme of entertainment for the evening—something like this, as he sketched it out in his head:

SPEECH . . . BY TOAD
(There will be other speeches by *Toad* during the evening.)

ADDRESS . . . BY TOAD
Synopsis
Our Prison System—The Waterways of Old England—
Horse-dealing, and how to deal—Property, its rights and its
duties—Back to the Land—A Typical English Squire.

SONG . . . BY TOAD
(*Composed by himself.*)

OTHER COMPOSITIONS . . . BY TOAD
will be sung in the course of the evening
by the *Composer*.

The idea pleased him mightily, and he worked very hard and got all the letters finished by noon, at which hour it was reported to him that there was a small and rather bedraggled weasel at the door, inquiring timidly whether he could be of any service to the gentlemen. Toad swaggered out and found it was one of the prisoners of the previous evening, very respectful and anxious to please. He patted him on the head, shoved the bundle of invitations into his paw, and told him to cut along quick and deliver them as fast as he could, and if he liked to come back again in the evening, perhaps there might be a shilling for him, or, again, perhaps there mightn't; and the poor weasel seemed really quite grateful, and hurried off eagerly to do his mission.

When the other animals came back to luncheon, very boisterous and breezy after a morning on the river, the Mole, whose conscience had been pricking him, looked doubtfully at Toad, expecting to find him sulky or depressed. Instead, he was so uppish and inflated that the Mole began to suspect something; while the Rat and the Badger exchanged significant glances.

As soon as the meal was over, Toad thrust his paws deep into his trouser-pockets, remarked casually, "Well, look after yourselves, you fellows! Ask for anything you want!" and was swaggering off in the direction of the garden, where he wanted to think out an idea or two for his coming speeches, when the Rat caught him by the arm.

Toad rather suspected what he was after, and did his best to get away; but when the Badger took him firmly by the other arm he began to see that the game was up. The two animals conducted him between them into the small smoking-room that opened out of the entrance-hall, shut the door, and put him into a chair. Then they both stood in front of him, while Toad sat silent and regarded them with much suspicion and ill-humour.

"Now, look here, Toad," said the Rat. "It's about this Banquet, and very sorry I am to have to speak to you like this. But we want you to understand clearly, once and for all, that there are going to be no speeches and no songs. Try and grasp the fact that on this occasion we're not arguing with you; we're just telling you."

Toad saw that he was trapped. They understood him, they saw through him, they had got ahead of him. His pleasant dream was shattered.

"Mayn't I sing them just one *little* song?" he pleaded piteously.

"No, not *one* little song," replied the Rat firmly, though his heart bled as he noticed the trembling lip of the poor disappointed Toad. "It's no good, Toady; you know well that your songs are all conceit and boasting and vanity; and your speeches are all self-praise and—and—well, and gross exaggeration and—and—"

"And gas," put in the Badger, in his common way.

"It's for your own good, Toady," went on the Rat. "You know you *must* turn over a new leaf sooner or later, and now seems a splendid time to begin; a sort of turning-point in your career. Please don't think that saying all this doesn't hurt me more than it hurts you."

Toad remained a long while plunged in thought. At last he raised his head, and the traces of strong emotion were visible on his features. "You have conquered, my friends," he said in broken accents. "It was, to be sure, but a small thing that I asked—merely leave to blossom and expand for yet one more evening, to let myself go and hear the tumultuous applause that always seems to me—somehow—to bring out my best qualities. However, you are right, I know, and I am wrong. Henceforth I will be a very different Toad. My friends, you shall never have occasion to blush for me again. But, O dear, O dear, this is a hard world!"

And, pressing his handkerchief to his face, he left the room, with faltering footsteps.

"Badger," said the Rat, "*I* feel like a brute; I wonder what *you* feel like?"

"O, I know, I know," said the Badger gloomily. "But the thing had to be done. This good fellow has got to live here, and hold his own, and be respected. Would you have him a common laughing-stock, mocked and jeered at by stoats and weasels?"

"Of course not," said the Rat. "And, talking of weasels, it's lucky we came upon that little weasel, just as he was setting out with Toad's invitations. I suspected something from what you told me, and had a look at one or two; they were simply disgraceful.

I confiscated the lot, and the good Mole is now sitting in the blue boudoir, filling up plain, simple invitation cards."

* * * * *

At last the hour for the banquet began to draw near, and Toad, who on leaving the others had retired to his bedroom, was still sitting there, melancholy and thoughtful. His brow resting on his paw, he pondered long and deeply. Gradually his countenance cleared, and he began to smile long, slow smiles. Then he took to giggling in a shy, self-conscious manner. At last he got up, locked the door, drew the curtains across the windows, collected all the chairs in the room and arranged them in a semicircle, and took up his position in front of them, swelling visibly. Then he bowed, coughed twice, and, letting himself go, with uplifted voice he sang, to the enraptured audience that his imagination so clearly saw.

Toad's Last Little Song!

The Toad—came—home!
There was panic in the parlours and howling in the halls,
There was crying in the cow-sheds and shrieking in the stalls,
When the Toad—came—home!

When the Toad—came—home!
There was smashing in of window and crashing in of door,
There was chivvying of weasels that fainted on the floor,
When the Toad—came—home!

Bang! go the drums!
The trumpeters are tooting and the soldiers are saluting,
And the cannon they are shooting and the motor-cars are hooting,
As the—Hero—comes!

Shout—Hoo-ray!
And let each one of the crowd try and shout it very loud,
In honour of an animal of whom you're justly proud,
For it's Toad's—great—day!

He sang this very loud, with great unction and expression; and when he had done, he sang it all over again.

Then he heaved a deep sigh; a long, long, long sigh.

Then he dipped his hairbrush in the water-jug, parted his hair in the middle, and plastered it down very straight and sleek on each side of his face; and, unlocking the door, went quietly down the stairs to greet his guests, who he knew must be assembling in the drawing-room.

All the animals cheered when he entered, and crowded round to congratulate him and say nice things about his courage, and his cleverness, and his fighting qualities; but Toad only smiled faintly, and murmured, "Not at all!" Or, sometimes, for a change, "On the contrary!" Otter, who was standing on the hearthrug, describing to an admiring circle of friends exactly how he would have managed things had he been there, came forward with a shout, threw his arm round Toad's neck, and tried to take him round the room in triumphal progress; but Toad, in a mild way, was rather snubby to him, remarking gently, as he disengaged himself, "Badger's was the mastermind; the Mole and the Water Rat bore the brunt of the fighting; I merely served in the ranks and did little or nothing." The animals were evidently puzzled and taken aback by this unexpected attitude of his; and Toad felt, as he moved from one guest to the other, making his modest responses, that he was an object of absorbing interest to everyone.

The Badger had ordered everything of the best, and the banquet was a great success. There was much talking and laughter and chaff among the animals, but through it all Toad, who of course was in the chair, looked down his nose and murmured pleasant nothings to the animals on either side of him. At intervals he stole a glance at the Badger and the Rat, and always when he looked they were staring at each other with their mouths open; and this gave him the greatest satisfaction. Some of the younger and livelier animals, as the evening wore on, got whispering to each other that things were not so amusing as they used to be in the good old days; and there were some knockings on the table and cries of "Toad! Speech! Speech from Toad! Song! Mr. Toad's song!" But Toad only shook his head gently, raised one paw in mild protest, and, by pressing delicacies on his guests, by topical small-talk, and by earnest inquiries after members of their families not yet old enough to appear at social functions, managed to convey to them that this dinner was being run on strictly conventional lines.

He was indeed an altered Toad!

* * * * *

After this climax, the four animals continued to lead their lives, so rudely broken in upon by civil war, in great joy and contentment, undisturbed by further risings or invasions. Toad, after due consultation with his friends, selected a handsome gold chain and locket set with pearls, which he dispatched to the gaoler's daughter with a letter that even the Badger admitted to be modest, grateful, and appreciative; and the engine-driver, in his turn, was properly thanked and compensated for all his pains and trouble. Under severe compulsion from the Badger, even the barge-woman was, with some trouble, sought out and the value of her horse discreetly made good to her; though Toad kicked terribly at this, holding himself to be an instrument of Fate, sent to punish fat women with mottled arms who couldn't tell a real gentleman when they saw one. The amount involved, it was true, was not very burdensome, the gypsy's valuation being admitted by local assessors to be approximately correct.

Sometimes, in the course of long summer evenings, the friends would take a stroll together in the Wild Wood, now successfully tamed so far as they were concerned; and it was pleasing to see how respectfully they were greeted by the inhabitants, and how the mother-weasels would bring their young ones to the mouths of their holes, and say, pointing, "Look, baby! There goes the great Mr. Toad! And that's the gallant Water Rat, a terrible fighter, walking along o' him! And yonder comes the famous Mr. Mole, of whom you so often have heard your father tell!" But when their infants were fractious and quite beyond control, they would quiet them by telling how, if they didn't hush them and not fret them, the terrible grey Badger would up and get them. This was a base libel on Badger, who, though he cared little about Society, was rather fond of children; but it never failed to have its full effect.

The Golden Age

Prologue: The Olympians

Looking back to those days of old, ere the gate shut behind me, I can see now that to children with a proper equipment of parents these things would have worn a different aspect. But to those whose nearest were aunts and uncles, a special attitude of mind may be allowed. They treated us, indeed, with kindness enough as to the needs of the flesh, but after that with indifference (an indifference, as I recognise, the result of a certain stupidity), and therewith the commonplace conviction that your child is merely animal. At a very early age I remember realising in a quite impersonal and kindly way the existence of that stupidity, and its tremendous influence in the world; while there grew up in me, as in the parallel case of Caliban upon Setebos, a vague sense of a ruling power, wilful and freakish, and prone to the practice of vagaries—"just choosing so": as, for instance, the giving of authority over us to these hopeless and incapable creatures, when it might far more reasonably have been given to ourselves over them. These elders, our betters by a trick of chance, commanded no respect, but only a certain blend of envy—of their good luck—and pity—for their inability to make use of it. Indeed, it was one of the most hopeless features in their character (when we troubled ourselves to waste a thought on them: which wasn't often) that, having absolute licence to indulge in the pleasures of life, they could get no good of it. They might dabble in the pond all day, hunt the chickens, climb trees in the most uncompromising Sunday clothes; they were free to issue forth and buy gunpowder in the full eye of the sun—free to fire cannons and explode mines on the lawn: yet they never did any one of these things. No irresistible Energy haled them to church o' Sundays; yet they went there regularly of their own accord, though they betrayed no greater delight in the experience than ourselves.

On the whole, the existence of these Olympians seemed to be entirely void of interests, even as their movements were confined and slow, and their habits stereotyped and senseless. To anything but appearances they were blind. For them the orchard (a place elf-haunted, wonderful!) simply produced so many apples and cherries:

or it didn't, when the failures of Nature were not infrequently ascribed to us. They never set foot within fir-wood or hazel-copse, nor dreamt of the marvels hid therein. The mysterious sources—sources as of old Nile—that fed the duck-pond had no magic for them. They were unaware of Indians, nor recked they anything of bisons or of pirates (with pistols!), though the whole place swarmed with such portents. They cared not about exploring for robbers' caves, nor digging for hidden treasure. Perhaps, indeed, it was one of their best qualities that they spent the greater part of their time stuffily indoors.

To be sure, there was an exception in the curate, who would receive unblenching the information that the meadow beyond the orchard was a prairie studded with herds of buffalo, which it was our delight, moccasined and tomahawked, to ride down with those whoops that announce the scenting of blood. He neither laughed nor sneered, as the Olympians would have done; but possessed of a serious idiosyncrasy, he would contribute such lots of valuable suggestion as to the pursuit of this particular sort of big game that, as it seemed to us, his mature age and eminent position could scarce have been attained without a practical knowledge of the creature in its native lair. Then, too, he was always ready to constitute himself a hostile army or a band of marauding Indians on the shortest possible notice: in brief, a distinctly able man, with talents, so far as we could judge, immensely above the majority. I trust he is a bishop by this time—he had all the necessary qualifications, as we knew.

These strange folk had visitors sometimes—stiff and colourless Olympians like themselves, equally without vital interests and intelligent pursuits: emerging out of the clouds, and passing away again to drag on an aimless existence somewhere out of our ken. Then brute force was pitilessly applied. We were captured, washed, and forced into clean collars: silently submitting, as was our wont, with more contempt than anger. Anon, with unctuous hair and faces stiffened in a conventional grin, we sat and listened to the usual platitudes. How could reasonable people spend their precious time so? That was ever our wonder as we bounded forth at last—to the old clay-pit to make pots, or to hunt bears among the hazels.

It was incessant matter for amazement how these Olympians would talk over our heads—during meals, for instance—of this or the other social or political inanity, under the delusion that these pale phantasms of reality were among the importances of life. We illuminati, eating silently, our heads full of plans and conspiracies, could have told them what real life was. We had just left it outside, and were all on fire to get back to it. Of course we didn't waste the revelation on them; the futility of imparting our ideas had long been demonstrated. One in thought and purpose, linked by the necessity of combating one hostile fate, a power antagonistic ever—a power we lived to evade—we had no confidants save ourselves. This strange anaemic order of beings was further removed from us, in fact, than the kindly beasts who shared our natural existence in the sun. The estrangement was fortified by an abiding sense of injustice, arising from the refusal of the Olympians ever to defend, retract, or admit themselves in the wrong, or to accept similar concessions on our part. For instance, when I flung the cat out of an upper window (though I did it from no ill-feeling, and it didn't hurt the cat), I was ready, after a moment's reflection, to own I was wrong, as a gentleman should. But was the matter allowed to end there? I trow not. Again, when Harold was locked up in his room all day, for assault and battery upon a neighbour's pig—an action he would have scorned, being indeed on the friendliest terms with the porker in question—there was no handsome expression of regret on the discovery of the real culprit. What Harold had felt was not so much the imprisonment—indeed he had very soon escaped by the window, with assistance from his allies, and had only gone back in time for his release—as the Olympian habit. A word would have set all right; but of course that word was never spoken.

Well! The Olympians are all past and gone. Somehow the sun does not seem to shine so brightly as it used; the trackless meadows of old time have shrunk and dwindled away to a few poor acres. A saddening doubt, a dull suspicion, creeps over me. *Et in Arcadia ego*—I certainly did once inhabit Arcady. Can it be I too have become an Olympian?

A Holiday

The masterful wind was up and out, shouting and chasing, the lord of the morning. Poplars swayed and tossed with a roaring swish; dead leaves sprang aloft, and whirled into space; and all the clear-swept heaven seemed to thrill with sound like a great harp.

It was one of the first awakenings of the year. The earth stretched herself, smiling in her sleep; and everything leapt and pulsed to the stir of the giant's movement. With us it was a whole holiday; the occasion a birthday—it matters not whose. Someone of us had had presents, and pretty conventional speeches, and had glowed with that sense of heroism which is no less sweet that nothing has been done to deserve it. But the holiday was for all, the rapture of awakening Nature for all, the various outdoor joys of puddles and sun and hedge-breaking for all. Colt-like I ran through the meadows, frisking happy heels in the face of Nature laughing responsive. Above, the sky was bluest of the blue; wide pools left by the winter's floods flashed the colour back, true and brilliant; and the soft air thrilled with the germinating touch that seemed to kindle something in my own small person as well as in the rash primrose already lurking in sheltered haunts. Out into the brimming sun-bathed world I sped, free of lessons, free of discipline and correction, for one day at least. My legs ran of themselves, and though I heard my name called faint and shrill behind, there was no stopping for me. It was only Harold, I concluded, and his legs, though shorter than mine, were good for a longer spurt than this. Then I heard it called again, but this time more faintly, with a pathetic break in the middle; and I pulled up short, recognising Charlotte's plaintive note.

She panted up anon, and dropped on the turf beside me. Neither had any desire for talk; the glow and the glory of existing on this perfect morning were satisfaction full and sufficient.

"Where's Harold?" I asked presently.

"Oh, he's just playin' muffin-man, as usual," said Charlotte with petulance. "Fancy wanting to be a muffin-man on a whole holiday!"

It was a strange craze, certainly; but Harold, who invented his own games and played them without assistance, always stuck staunchly to a new fad, till he had worn it quite out. Just at present he was a muffin-man, and day and night he went through passages and up and down staircases, ringing a noiseless bell and offering phantom muffins to invisible wayfarers. It sounds a poor sort of sport; and yet—to pass along busy streets of your own building, forever ringing an imaginary bell and offering airy muffins of your own make to a bustling thronging crowd of your own creation—there were points about the game, it cannot be denied, though it seemed scarce in harmony with this radiant wind-swept morning!

"And Edward, where is he?" I questioned again.

"He's coming along by the road," said Charlotte. "He'll be crouching in the ditch when we get there, and he's going to be a grizzly bear and spring out on us, only you mustn't say I told you, 'cos it's to be a surprise."

"All right," I said magnanimously. "Come on and let's be surprised." But I could not help feeling that on this day of days even a grizzly felt misplaced and common.

Sure enough an undeniable bear sprang out on us as we dropped into the road; then ensued shrieks, growlings, revolver-shots, and unrecorded heroisms, till Edward condescended at last to roll over and die, bulking large and grim, an unmitigated grizzly. It was an understood thing, that whoever took upon himself to be a bear must eventually die, sooner or later, even if he were the eldest born; else, life would have been all strife and carnage, and the Age of Acorns have displaced our hard-won civilisation. This little affair concluded with satisfaction to all parties concerned, we rambled along the road, picking up the defaulting Harold by the way, muffinless now and in his right and social mind.

"What would you do?" asked Charlotte presently—the book of the moment always dominating her thoughts until it was sucked dry and cast aside—"what would you do if you saw two lions in the road, one on each side, and you didn't know if they was loose or if they was chained up?"

"Do?" shouted Edward, valiantly, "I should—I should—I should—"

His boastful accents died away into a mumble: "Dunno what I should do."

"Shouldn't do anything," I observed after consideration; and really it would be difficult to arrive at a wiser conclusion.

"If it came to *doing*," remarked Harold, reflectively, "the lions would do all the doing there was to do, wouldn't they?"

"But if they was *good* lions," rejoined Charlotte, "they would do as they would be done by."

"Ah, but how are you to know a good lion from a bad one?" said Edward. "The books don't tell you at all, and the lions ain't marked any different."

"Why, there aren't any good lions," said Harold, hastily.

"Oh yes, there are, heaps and heaps," contradicted Edward. "Nearly all the lions in the story-books are good lions. There was Androcles' lion, and St. Jerome's lion, and—and—the Lion and the Unicorn—"

"He beat the Unicorn," observed Harold, dubiously, "all round the town."

"That *proves* he was a good lion," cried Edward triumphantly. "But the question is, how are you to tell 'em when you see 'em?"

"*I* should ask Martha," said Harold of the simple creed.

Edward snorted contemptuously, then turned to Charlotte. "Look here," he said; "let's play at lions, anyhow, and I'll run on to that corner and be a lion—I'll be two lions, one on each side of the road—and you'll come along, and you won't know whether I'm chained up or not, and that'll be the fun!"

"No, thank you," said Charlotte, firmly; "you'll be chained up till I'm quite close to you, and then you'll be loose, and you'll tear me in pieces, and make my frock all dirty, and p'raps you'll hurt me as well. *I* know your lions!"

"No, I won't; I swear I won't," protested Edward. "I'll be quite a new lion this time—something you can't even imagine." And he raced off to his post. Charlotte hesitated; then she went timidly on, at each step growing less Charlotte, the mummer of a minute, and more the anxious Pilgrim of all time. The lion's wrath waxed terrible at her approach; his roaring filled the startled air. I waited until they were both thoroughly absorbed, and then I slipped through the hedge out of the trodden highway, into the vacant meadow spaces.

It was not that I was unsociable, nor that I knew Edward's lions to the point of satiety; but the passion and the call of the divine morning were high in my blood.

Earth to earth! That was the frank note, the joyous summons of the day; and they could not but jar and seem artificial, these human discussions and pretences, when boon Nature, reticent no more, was singing that full-throated song of hers that thrills and claims control of every fibre. The air was wine; the moist earth-smell, wine; the lark's song, the wafts from the cow-shed at top of the field, the pant and smoke of a distant train—all were wine—or song, was it? or odour, this unity they all blended into? I had no words then to describe it, that earth-effluence of which I was so conscious; nor, indeed, have I found words since. I ran sideways, shouting; I dug glad heels into the squelching soil; I splashed diamond showers from puddles with a stick; I hurled clods skywards at random, and presently I somehow found myself singing. The words were mere nonsense—irresponsible babble; the tune was an improvisation, a weary, unrhythmic thing of rise and fall: and yet it seemed to me a genuine utterance, and just at that moment the one thing fitting and right and perfect. Humanity would have rejected it with scorn. Nature, everywhere singing in the same key, recognised and accepted it without a flicker of dissent.

All the time the hearty wind was calling to me companionably from where he swung and bellowed in the tree-tops. "Take me for guide today," he seemed to plead. "Other holidays you have tramped it in the track of the stolid, unswerving sun; a belated truant, you have dragged a weary foot homeward with only a pale, expressionless moon for company. Today why not I, the trickster, the hypocrite? I, who whip round corners and bluster, relapse and evade, then rally and pursue! I can lead you the best and rarest dance of any; for I am the strong capricious one, the lord of misrule, and I alone am irresponsible and unprincipled, and obey no law." And for me, I was ready enough to fall in with the fellow's humour; was not this a whole holiday? So we sheered off together, arm-in-arm, so to speak; and with fullest confidence I took the jigging, thwartwise course my chainless pilot laid for me.

A whimsical comrade I found him, ere he had done with me. Was it in jest, or with some serious purpose of his own, that he brought me plump upon a pair of lovers, silent, face to face o'er a discreet unwinking stile? As a rule this sort of thing struck me as the most pitiful tomfoolery. Two calves rubbing noses through a gate were natural and right and within the order of things; but that human beings, with salient interests and active pursuits beckoning them on from every side, could thus—! Well, it was a thing to hurry past, shamed of face, and think on no more. But this morning everything I met seemed to be accounted for and set in tune by that same magical touch in the air; and it was with a certain surprise that I found myself regarding these fatuous ones with kindliness instead of contempt, as I rambled by, unheeded of them. There was indeed some reconciling influence abroad, which could bring the like antics into harmony with bud and growth and the frolic air.

A puff on the right cheek from my wilful companion sent me off at a fresh angle, and presently I came in sight of the village church, sitting solitary within its circle of elms. From forth the vestry window projected two small legs, gyrating, hungry for foothold, with larceny—not to say sacrilege—in their every wriggle: a godless sight for a supporter of the Establishment. Though the rest was hidden, I knew the legs well enough; they were usually attached to the body of Bill Saunders, the peerless bad boy of the village. Bill's coveted booty, too, I could easily guess at that; it came from the Vicar's store of biscuits, kept (as I knew) in a cupboard along with his official trappings.

For a moment I hesitated; then I passed on my way. I protest I was not on Bill's side; but then, neither was I on the Vicar's, and there was something in this immoral morning which seemed to say that perhaps, after all, Bill had as much right to the biscuits as the Vicar, and would certainly enjoy them better; and anyhow it was a disputable point, and no business of mine. Nature, who had accepted me for ally, cared little who had the world's biscuits, and assuredly was not going to let any friend of hers waste his time in playing policeman for Society.

He was tugging at me anew, my insistent guide; and I felt sure, as I rambled off in his wake, that he had more holiday matter to show me. And so, indeed, he had; and all of it was to the same lawless tune. Like a black pirate flag on the blue ocean of air, a hawk hung ominous; then, plummet-wise, dropped to the hedgerow, whence there rose, thin and shrill, a piteous voice of squealing.

By the time I got there a whisk of feathers on the turf—like scattered playbills—was all that remained to tell of the tragedy just enacted. Yet Nature smiled and sang on, pitiless, gay, impartial. To her, who took no sides, there was every bit as much to be said for the hawk as for the chaffinch. Both were her children, and she would show no preferences.

Further on, a hedgehog lay dead athwart the path—nay, more than dead; decadent, distinctly; a sorry sight for one that had known the fellow in more bustling circumstances. Nature might at least have paused to shed one tear over this rough-jacketed little son of hers, for his wasted aims, his cancelled ambitions, his whole career of usefulness cut suddenly short. But not a bit of it! Jubilant as ever, her song went bubbling on, and "Death-in-Life," and again, "Life-in-Death," were its alternate burdens. And looking round, and seeing the sheep-nibbled heels of turnips that dotted the ground, their hearts eaten out of them in frost-bound days now over and done, I seemed to discern, faintly, a something of the stern meaning in her valorous chant.

My invisible companion was singing also, and seemed at times to be chuckling softly to himself, doubtless at thought of the strange new lessons he was teaching me; perhaps, too, at a special bit of waggishness he had still in store. For when at last he grew weary of such insignificant earthbound company, he deserted me at a certain spot I knew; then dropped, subsided, and slunk away into nothingness. I raised my eyes, and before me, grim and lichened, stood the ancient whipping-post of the village; its sides fretted with the initials of a generation that scorned its mute lesson, but still clipped by the stout rusty shackles that had tethered the wrists of such of that generation's ancestors as had dared to mock at order and law. Had I been an infant Sterne, here was a grand chance for sentimental output! As things were, I could only hurry homewards, my moral tail well between my legs, with an uneasy feeling, as I glanced back over my shoulder, that there was more in this chance than met the eye.

And outside our gate I found Charlotte, alone and crying. Edward, it seemed, had persuaded her to hide, in the full expectation of being duly found and ecstatically pounced upon; then he had caught sight of the butcher's cart, and, forgetting his obligations, had rushed off for a ride. Harold, it further appeared, greatly coveting tadpoles, and top-heavy with the eagerness of possession, had fallen into the pond. This, in itself, was nothing; but on attempting to sneak in by the back-door, he had rendered up his duckweed-bedabbled person into the hands of an aunt, and had been promptly sent off to bed; and this, on a holiday, was very much. The moral of the whipping-post was working itself out; and I was not in the least surprised when, on reaching home, I was seized upon and accused of doing something I had never even thought of. And my frame of mind was such, that I could only wish most heartily that I had done it.

A White-washed Uncle

In our small lives that day was eventful when another uncle was to come down from town, and submit his character and qualifications (albeit unconsciously) to our careful criticism. Previous uncles had been weighed in the balance, and—alas!—found grievously wanting. There was Uncle Thomas—a failure from the first. Not that his disposition was malevolent, nor were his habits such as to unfit him for decent society; but his rooted conviction seemed to be that the reason of a child's existence was to serve as a butt for senseless adult jokes—or what, from the accompanying guffaws of laughter, appeared to be intended for jokes. Now, we were anxious that he should have a perfectly fair trial; so in the tool-house, between breakfast and lessons, we discussed and examined all his witticisms, one by one, calmly, critically, dispassionately. It was no good; we could not discover any salt in them. And as only a genuine gift of humour could have saved Uncle Thomas—for he pretended to naught besides—he was reluctantly writ down a hopeless impostor.

Uncle George—the youngest—was distinctly more promising. He accompanied us cheerily round the establishment—suffered himself to be introduced to each of the cows, held out the right hand of fellowship to the pig, and even hinted that a pair of pink-eyed Himalayan rabbits might arrive—unexpectedly—from town someday. We were just considering whether in this fertile soil an apparently accidental remark on the solid qualities of guinea-pigs or ferrets might haply blossom and bring forth fruit, when our governess appeared on the scene. Uncle George's manner at once underwent a complete and contemptible change. His interest in rational topics seemed, "like a fountain's sickening pulse," to flag and ebb away; and though Miss Smedley's ostensible purpose was to take Selina for her usual walk, I can vouch for it that Selina spent her morning ratting, along with the keeper's boy and me; while, if Miss Smedley walked with anyone, it would appear to have been with Uncle George.

But despicable as his conduct had been, he underwent no hasty condemnation. The defection was discussed in all its bearings, but it seemed sadly clear at last that this uncle must possess some innate badness of character and fondness for low company. We who from daily experience knew Miss Smedley like a book—were we not only too well aware that she had neither accomplishments nor charms, no characteristic, in fact, but an inbred viciousness of temper and disposition? True, she knew the dates of the English kings by heart; but how could that profit Uncle George, who, having passed into the army, had ascended beyond the need of useful information? Our bows and arrows, on the other hand, had been freely placed at his disposal; and a soldier should not have hesitated in his choice a moment. No: Uncle George had fallen from grace, and was unanimously damned. And the non-arrival of the Himalayan rabbits was only another nail in his coffin. Uncles, therefore, were just then a heavy and lifeless market, and there was little inclination to deal. Still it was agreed that Uncle William, who had just returned from India, should have as fair a trial as the others; more especially as romantic possibilities might well be embodied in one who had held the gorgeous East in fee.

Selina had kicked my shins—like the girl she is!—during a scuffle in the passage, and I was still rubbing them with one hand when I found that the uncle-on-approbation was half-heartedly shaking the other. A florid, elderly man, and unmistakably nervous, he dropped our grimy paws in succession, and, turning very red, with an awkward simulation of heartiness, "Well, h' are y' all?" he said, "Glad to see me, eh?" As we could hardly, in justice, be expected to have formed an opinion on him at that early stage, we could but look at each other in silence; which scarce served to relieve the tension of the situation. Indeed, the cloud never really lifted during his stay. In talking it over later, someone put forward the suggestion that he must at some time or other have committed a stupendous crime; but I could not bring myself to believe that the man, though evidently unhappy, was really guilty of anything; and I caught him once or twice looking at us with evident kindliness, though seeing himself observed, he blushed and turned away his head.

When at last the atmosphere was clear of this depressing influence, we met despondently in the potato-cellar—all of us, that is, but Harold, who had been told off to accompany his relative to the station; and the feeling was unanimous, that, as an uncle, William could not be allowed to pass. Selina roundly declared him a beast, pointing out that he had not even got us a half-holiday; and, indeed, there seemed little to do but to pass sentence. We were about to put it, when Harold appeared on the scene; his red face, round eyes, and mysterious demeanour, hinting at awful portents. Speechless he stood a space: then, slowly drawing his hand from the pocket of his knickerbockers, he displayed on a dirty palm one—two—three—four half-crowns! We could but gaze—tranced, breathless, mute; never had any of us seen, in the aggregate, so much bullion before. Then Harold told his tale.

"I took the old fellow to the station," he said, "and as we went along I told him all about the station-master's family, and how I had seen the porter kissing our housemaid, and what a nice fellow he was, with no airs, or affectation about him, and anything I thought would be of interest; but he didn't seem to pay much attention, but walked along puffing his cigar, and once I thought—I'm not certain, but I *thought*—I heard him say, 'Well, thank God, that's over!' When we got to the station he stopped suddenly, and said, 'Hold on a minute!' Then he shoved these into my hand in a frightened sort of way; and said, 'Look here, youngster! These are for you and the other kids. Buy what you like—make little beasts of yourselves—only don't tell the old people, mind! Now cut away home!' So I cut."

A solemn hush fell on the assembly, broken first by the small Charlotte. "I didn't know," she observed dreamily, "that there were such good men anywhere in the world. I hope he'll die tonight, for then he'll go straight to heaven!" But the repentant Selina bewailed herself with tears and sobs, refusing to be comforted; for that in her haste she had called this white-souled relative a beast.

"I'll tell you what we'll do," said Edward, the master-mind, rising—as he always did—to the situation: "We'll christen the piebald pig after him—the one that hasn't got a name yet. And that'll show we're sorry for our mistake!"

"I—I christened that pig this morning," Harold guiltily confessed; "I christened it after the curate. I'm very sorry—but he came and bowled to me last night, after you others had all been sent to bed early—and somehow I felt I *had* to do it!"

"Oh, but that doesn't count," said Edward hastily; "because we weren't all there. We'll take that christening off, and call it Uncle William. And you can save up the curate for the next litter!"

And the motion being agreed to without a division, the House went into Committee of Supply.

Alarums and Excursions

"Let's pretend," suggested Harold, "that we're Cavaliers and Roundheads; and *you* be a Roundhead!"

"O bother," I replied drowsily, "we pretended that yesterday; and it's not my turn to be a Roundhead, anyhow." The fact is, I was lazy, and the call to arms fell on indifferent ears. We three younger ones were stretched at length in the orchard. The sun was hot, the season merry June, and never (I thought) had there been such wealth and riot of buttercups throughout the lush grass. Green-and-gold was the dominant key that day. Instead of active "pretence" with its shouts and perspiration, how much better—I held—to lie at ease and pretend to one's self, in green and golden fancies, slipping the husk and passing, a careless lounger, through a sleepy imaginary world all gold and green! But the persistent Harold was not to be fobbed off.

"Well, then," he began afresh, "let's pretend we're Knights of the Round Table; and (with a rush) *I'll* be Lancelot!"

"I won't play unless I'm Lancelot," I said. I didn't mean it really, but the game of Knights always began with this particular contest.

"O *please*," implored Harold. "You know when Edward's here I never get a chance of being Lancelot. I haven't been Lancelot for weeks!"

Then I yielded gracefully. "All right," I said. "I'll be Tristram."

"O, but you can't," cried Harold again. "Charlotte has always been Tristram. She won't play unless she's allowed to be Tristram! Be somebody else this time."

Charlotte said nothing, but breathed hard, looking straight before her. The peerless hunter and harper was her special hero of romance, and rather than see the part in less appreciative hands, she would even have returned sadly to the stuffy schoolroom.

"I don't care," I said: "I'll be anything. I'll be Sir Kay. Come on!"

Then once more in this country's story the mail-clad knights paced through the greenwood shaw, questing adventure, redressing wrong; and bandits, five to one, broke and fled discomfited to their caves. Once again were damsels rescued, dragons disembowelled, and giants, in every corner of the orchard, deprived of their already superfluous number of heads; while Palamides the Saracen waited for us by the well, and Sir Breuse Saunce Pite vanished in craven flight before the skilled spear that was his terror and his bane. Once more the lists were dight in Camelot, and all was gay with shimmer of silk and gold; the earth shook with thunder of horses, ash-staves flew in splinters; and the firmament rang to the clash of sword on helm. The varying fortune of the day swung doubtful— now on this side, now on that; till at last Lancelot, grim and great, thrusting through the press, unhorsed Sir Tristram (an easy task), and bestrode her, threatening doom; while the Cornish knight, forgetting hard-won fame of old, cried piteously, "You're hurting me, I tell you! and you're tearing my frock!" Then it happed that Sir Kay, hurtling to the rescue, stopped short in his stride, catching sight suddenly, through apple-boughs, of a gleam of scarlet afar off; while the confused tramp of many horses, mingled with talk and laughter, was borne to our ears.

"What is it?" inquired Tristram, sitting up and shaking out her curls; while Lancelot forsook the clanging lists and trotted nimbly to the hedge.

I stood spell-bound for a moment longer, and then, with a cry of "Soldiers!" I was off to the hedge, Charlotte picking herself up and scurrying after.

Down the road they came, two and two, at an easy walk; scarlet flamed in the eye, bits jingled and saddles squeaked delightfully; while the men, in a halo of dust, smoked their short clays like the heroes they were. In a swirl of intoxicating glory the troop clinked and clattered by, while we shouted and waved, jumping up and down, and the big jolly horsemen acknowledged the salute with easy condescension. The moment they were past we were through the hedge and after them. Soldiers were not the common stuff of everyday life. There had been nothing like this since the winter before last, when on a certain afternoon—bare of leaf and monochrome in its hue of sodden fallow and frost-nipt copse— suddenly the hounds had burst through the fence with their mellow cry, and all the paddock was for the minute reverberant of thudding hoof and dotted with glancing red. But this was better, since it could only mean that blows and bloodshed were in the air.

"Is there going to be a battle?" panted Harold, hardly able to keep up for excitement.

"Of course there is," I replied. "We're just in time. Come on!"

Perhaps I ought to have known better; and yet—? The pigs and poultry, with whom we chiefly consorted, could instruct us little concerning the peace that in these latter days lapped this sea-girt realm. In the schoolroom we were just now dallying with the Wars of the Roses; and did not legends of the country-side inform us how Cavaliers had once galloped up and down these very lanes from their quarters in the village? Here, now, were soldiers unmistakable; and if their business was not fighting, what was it? Sniffing the joy of battle, we followed hard on their tracks.

"Won't Edward be sorry," puffed Harold, "that he's begun that beastly Latin?"

It did, indeed, seem hard. Edward, the most martial spirit of us all, was drearily conjugating *amo* (of all verbs) between four walls; while Selina, who ever thrilled ecstatic to a red coat, was struggling with the uncouth German tongue. "Age," I reflected, "carries its penalties."

It was a grievous disappointment to us that the troop passed through the village unmolested. Every cottage, I pointed out to my companions, ought to have been loopholed, and strongly held. But no opposition was offered to the soldiers, who, indeed, conducted themselves with a recklessness and a want of precaution that seemed simply criminal.

At the last cottage a transitory gleam of common sense flickered across me, and, turning on Charlotte, I sternly ordered her back.

The small maiden, docile but exceedingly dolorous, dragged reluctant feet homewards, heavy at heart that she was to behold no stout fellows slain that day; but Harold and I held steadily on, expecting every instant to see the environing hedges crackle and spit forth the leaden death.

"Will they be Indians?" inquired my brother (meaning the enemy); "or Roundheads, or what?"

I reflected. Harold always required direct, straightforward answers—not faltering suppositions.

"They won't be Indians," I replied at last; "nor yet Roundheads. There haven't been any Roundheads seen about here for a long time. They'll be Frenchmen."

Harold's face fell. "All right," he said; "Frenchmen'll do; but I did hope they'd be Indians."

"If they were going to be Indians," I explained, "I—I don't think I'd go on. Because when Indians take you prisoner they scalp you first, and then burn you at a stake. But Frenchmen don't do that sort of thing."

"Are you quite sure?" asked Harold doubtfully.

"Quite," I replied. "Frenchmen only shut you up in a thing called the Bastille; and then you get a file sent in to you in a loaf of bread, and saw the bars through, and slide down a rope, and they all fire at you—but they don't hit you—and you run down to the seashore as hard as you can, and swim off to a British frigate, and there you are!"

Harold brightened up again. The programme was rather attractive.

"If they try to take us prisoner," he said, "we—we won't run, will we?"

Meanwhile, the craven foe was a long time showing himself; and we were reaching strange outland country, uncivilised, wherein lions might be expected to prowl at nightfall. I had a stitch in my side, and both Harold's stockings had come down. Just as I was beginning to have gloomy doubts of the proverbial courage of Frenchmen, the officer called out something, the men closed up, and, breaking into a trot, the troops—already far ahead—vanished out of our sight. With a sinking at the heart, I began to suspect we had been fooled.

"Are they charging?" cried Harold, weary, but rallying gamely.

"I think not," I replied doubtfully. "When there's going to be a charge, the officer always makes a speech, and then they draw their swords and the trumpets blow, and—but let's try a short cut. We may catch them up yet."

So we struck across the fields and into another road, and pounded down that, and then over more fields, panting, down-hearted, yet hoping for the best. The sun went in, and a thin drizzle began to fall; we were muddy, breathless, almost dead beat; but we blundered on, till at last we struck a road more brutally, more callously unfamiliar than any road I ever looked upon. Not a hint nor a sign of friendly direction or assistance on the dogged white face of it. There was no longer any disguising it—we were hopelessly lost. The small rain continued steadily, the evening began to come on. Really there are moments when a fellow is justified in crying; and I would have cried too, if Harold had not been there. That right-minded child regarded an elder brother as a veritable god; and I could see that he felt himself as secure as if a whole Brigade of Guards hedged him round with protecting bayonets. But I dreaded sore lest he should begin again with his questions.

As I gazed in dumb appeal on the face of unresponsive nature, the sound of nearing wheels sent a pulse of hope through my being; increasing to rapture as I recognised in the approaching vehicle the familiar carriage of the old doctor. If ever a god emerged from a machine, it was when this heaven-sent friend, recognising us, stopped and jumped out with a cheery hail. Harold rushed up to him at once. "Have you been there?" he cried. "Was it a jolly fight? who beat? were there many people killed?"

The doctor appeared puzzled. I briefly explained the situation.

"I see," said the doctor, looking grave and twisting his face this way and that. "Well, the fact is, there isn't going to be any battle today. It's been put off, on account of the change in the weather. You will have due notice of the renewal of hostilities. And now you'd better jump in and I'll drive you home. You've been running a fine rig! Why, you might have both been taken and shot as spies!"

This special danger had never even occurred to us. The thrill of it accentuated the cosey homelike feeling of the cushions we nestled into as we rolled homewards. The doctor beguiled the journey with blood-curdling narratives of personal adventure in the tented field, he having followed the profession of arms (so it seemed) in every quarter of the globe. Time, the destroyer of all things beautiful, subsequently revealed the baselessness of these legends; but what of that? There are higher things than truth; and we were almost reconciled, by the time we were dropped at our gate, to the fact that the battle had been postponed.

The Finding of the Princess

It was the day I was promoted to a tooth-brush. The girls, irrespective of age, had been thus distinguished some time before; why, we boys could never rightly understand, except that it was part and parcel of a system of studied favouritism on behalf of creatures both physically inferior and (as was shown by a fondness for tale-bearing) of weaker mental fibre. It was not that we yearned after these strange instruments in themselves; Edward, indeed, applied his to the scrubbing-out of his squirrel's cage, and for personal use, when a superior eye was grim on him, borrowed Harold's or mine, indifferently; but the nimbus of distinction that clung to them—that we coveted exceedingly. What more, indeed, was there to ascend to, before the remote, but still possible, razor and strop?

Perhaps the exaltation had mounted to my head; or nature and the perfect morning joined to him at disaffection; anyhow, having breakfasted, and triumphantly repeated the collect I had broken down in the last Sunday—'twas one without rhythm or alliteration: a most objectionable collect—having achieved thus much, the small natural man in me rebelled, and I vowed, as I straddled and spat about the stable-yard in feeble imitation of the coachman, that lessons might go to the Inventor of them. It was only geography that morning, anyway: and the practical thing was worth any quantity of bookish theoretic; as for me, I was going on my travels, and imports and exports, populations and capitals, might very well wait while I explored the breathing, coloured world outside.

True, a fellow-rebel was wanted; and Harold might, as a rule, have been counted on with certainty. But just then Harold was very proud. The week before he had "gone into tables," and had been endowed with a new slate, having a miniature sponge attached, wherewith we washed the faces of Charlotte's dolls, thereby producing an unhealthy pallor which struck terror into the child's heart, always timorous regarding epidemic visitations. As to "tables," nobody knew exactly what they were, least of all Harold; but it was a step over the heads of the rest, and therefore a subject for self-adulation and—generally speaking—airs; so that Harold, hugging his slate and his chains, was out of the question now. In such a matter, girls were worse than useless, as wanting the necessary tenacity of will and contempt for self-constituted authority. So eventually I slipped through the hedge a solitary protestant, and issued forth on the lane what time the rest of the civilised world was sitting down to lessons.

The scene was familiar enough; and yet, this morning, how different it all seemed! The act, with its daring, tinted everything with new, strange hues; affecting the individual with a sort of bruised feeling just below the pit of the stomach, that was intensified whenever his thoughts flew back to the ink-stained, smelly schoolroom. And could this be really me? or was I only contemplating, from the schoolroom aforesaid, some other jolly young mutineer, faring forth under the genial sun? Anyhow, here was the friendly well, in its old place, halfway up the lane. Hither the yoke-shouldering village-folk were wont to come to fill their clinking buckets; when the drippings made worms of wet in the thick dust of the road. They had flat wooden crosses inside each pail, which floated on the top and (we were instructed) served to prevent the water from slopping over. We used to wonder by what magic this strange principle worked, and who first invented the crosses, and whether he got a peerage for it. But indeed the well was a centre of mystery, for a hornet's nest was somewhere hard by, and the very thought was fearsome. Wasps we knew well and disdained, storming them in their fastnesses. But these great Beasts, vestured in angry orange, three stings from which—so 'twas averred—would kill a horse, these were of a different kidney, and their warning drone suggested prudence and retreat. At this time neither villagers nor hornets encroached on the stillness: lessons, apparently, pervaded all Nature. So, after dabbling awhile in the well—what boy has ever passed a bit of water without messing in it?—I scrambled through the hedge, avoiding the hornet-haunted side, and struck into the silence of the copse.

If the lane had been deserted, this was loneliness become personal. Here mystery lurked and peeped; here brambles caught and held with a purpose of their own, and saplings whipped the face with human spite. The copse, too, proved vaster in extent, more direfully drawn out, than one would ever have guessed from its frontage on the lane: and I was really glad when at last the wood opened and sloped down to a streamlet brawling forth into the sunlight. By this cheery companion I wandered along, conscious of little but that Nature, in providing store of water-rats, had thoughtfully furnished provender of right-sized stones. Rapids, also, there were, telling of canoes and portages—crinkling bays and inlets—caves for pirates and hidden treasures—the wise Dame had forgotten nothing—till at last, after what lapse of time I know not, my further course, though not the stream's, was barred by some six feet of stout wire netting, stretched from side to side, just where a thick hedge, arching till it touched, forbade all further view.

The excitement of the thing was becoming thrilling. A Black Flag must surely be fluttering close by. Here was evidently a malignant contrivance of the Pirates, designed to baffle our gun-boats when we dashed up-stream to shell them from their lair. A gun-boat, indeed, might well have hesitated, so stout was the netting, so close the hedge: but I spied where a rabbit was wont to pass, close down by the water's edge; where a rabbit could go a boy could follow, albeit stomach-wise and with one leg in the stream; so the passage was achieved, and I stood inside, safe but breathless at the sight.

Gone was the brambled waste, gone the flickering tangle of woodland. Instead, terrace after terrace of shaven sward, stone-edged, urn-cornered, stepped delicately down to where the stream, now tamed and educated, passed from one to another marble basin, in which on occasion gleams of red hinted at gold-fish in among the spreading water-lilies. The scene lay silent and slumbrous in the brooding noonday sun: the drowsing peacock squatted humped on the lawn, no fish leapt in the pools, nor bird declared himself from the environing hedges. Self-confessed it was here, then, at last the Garden of Sleep!

Two things, in those old days, I held in especial distrust: gamekeepers and gardeners. Seeing, however, no baleful apparitions of either nature, I pursued my way between rich flower-beds, in search of the necessary Princess. Conditions declared her presence patently as trumpets; without this centre such surroundings could not exist. A pavilion, gold-topped, wreathed with lush jessamine, beckoned with a special significance over close-set shrubs. There, if anywhere, She should be enshrined. Instinct, and some knowledge of the habits of princesses, triumphed; for (indeed) there She was! In no tranced repose, however, but laughingly, struggling to disengage her hand from the grasp of a grown-up man who occupied the marble bench with her. (As to age, I suppose now that the two swung in respective scales that pivoted on twenty. But children heed no minor distinctions; to them, the inhabited world is composed of the two main divisions: children and upgrown people; the latter being in no way superior to the former—only hopelessly different. These two, then, belonged to the grown-up section.) I paused, thinking it strange they should prefer seclusion when there were fish to be caught, and butterflies to hunt in the sun outside; and as I cogitated thus, the grown-up man caught sight of me.

"Hallo, sprat!" he said, with some abruptness, "where do you spring from?"

"I came up the stream," I explained politely and comprehensively, "and I was only looking for the Princess."

"Then you are a water-baby," he replied. "And what do you think of the Princess, now you've found her?"

"I think she is lovely," I said (and doubtless I was right, having never learned to flatter). "But she's wide-awake, so I suppose somebody has kissed her!"

This very natural deduction moved the grown-up man to laughter; but the Princess, turning red and jumping up, declared that it was time for lunch.

"Come along, then," said the grown-up man; "and you too, Water-baby; come and have something solid. You must want it."

I accompanied them, without any feeling of false delicacy. The world, as known to me, was spread with food each several mid-day, and the particular table one sat at seemed a matter of no importance. The palace was very sumptuous and beautiful, just what a palace ought to be; and we were met by a stately lady, rather more grown-up than the Princess—apparently her mother.

My friend the Man was very kind, and introduced me as the Captain, saying I had just run down from Aldershot. I didn't know where Aldershot was, but had no manner of doubt that he was perfectly right. As a rule, indeed, grown-up people are fairly correct on matters of fact; it is in the higher gift of imagination that they are so sadly to seek.

The lunch was excellent and varied. Another gentleman in

beautiful clothes—a lord, presumably—lifted me into a high carved chair, and stood behind it, brooding over me like a Providence. I endeavoured to explain who I was and where I had come from, and to impress the company with my own tooth-brush and Harold's tables; but either they were stupid—or is it a characteristic of Fairyland that everyone laughs at the most ordinary remarks? My friend the Man said good-naturedly, "All right, Water-baby; you came up the stream, and that's good enough for us." The lord—a reserved sort of man, I thought—took no share in the conversation.

After lunch I walked on the terrace with the Princess and my friend the Man, and was very proud. And I told him what I was going to be, and he told me what he was going to be; and then I remarked, "I suppose you two are going to get married?" He only laughed, after the Fairy fashion. "Because if you aren't," I added, "you really ought to": meaning only that a man who discovered a Princess, living in the right sort of Palace like this, and didn't marry her there and then, was false to all recognised tradition.

They laughed again, and my friend suggested I should go down to the pond and look at the gold-fish, while they went for a stroll.

I was sleepy, and assented; but before they left me, the grown-up man put two half-crowns in my hand, for the purpose, he explained, of treating the other water-babies. I was so touched by this crowning mark of friendship that I nearly cried; and thought much more of his generosity than of the fact that the Princess, ere she moved away, stooped down and kissed me.

I watched them disappear down the path—how naturally arms seem to go round waists in Fairyland!—and then, my cheek on the cool marble, lulled by the trickle of water, I slipped into dreamland out of real and magic world alike.

When I woke, the sun had gone in, a chill wind set all the leaves a-whispering, and the peacock on the lawn was harshly calling up the rain. A wild unreasoning panic possessed me, and I sped out of the garden like a guilty thing, wriggled through the rabbit-run, and threaded my doubtful way homewards, hounded by nameless terrors. The half-crowns happily remained solid and real to the touch; but could I hope to bear such treasure safely through the brigand-haunted wood? It was a dirty, weary little object that entered its home, at nightfall, by the unassuming aid of the scullery-window:

and only to be sent tealess to bed seemed infinite mercy to him. Officially tealess, that is; for, as was usual after such escapades, a sympathetic housemaid, coming delicately by backstairs, stayed him with chunks of cold pudding and condolence, till his small skin was tight as any drum. Then, nature asserting herself, I passed into the comforting kingdom of sleep, where, a golden carp of fattest build, I oared it in translucent waters with a new half-crown snug under right fin and left; and thrust up a nose through water-lily leaves to be kissed by a rose-flushed Princess.

Sawdust and Sin

A belt of rhododendrons grew close down to one side of our pond; and along the edge of it many things flourished rankly. If you crept through the undergrowth and crouched by the water's rim, it was easy—if your imagination were in healthy working order—to transport yourself in a trice to the heart of a tropical forest. Overhead the monkeys chattered, parrots flashed from bough to bough, strange large blossoms shone around you, and the push and rustle of great beasts moving unseen thrilled you deliciously. And if you lay down with your nose an inch or two from the water, it was not long ere the old sense of proportion vanished clean away. The glittering insects that darted to and fro on its surface became sea-monsters dire, the gnats that hung above them swelled to albatrosses, and the pond itself stretched out into a vast inland sea, whereon a navy might ride secure, and whence at any moment the hairy scalp of a sea-serpent might be seen to emerge.

It is impossible, however, to play at tropical forests properly, when homely accents of the human voice intrude; and all my hopes of seeing a tiger seized by a crocodile while drinking (vide picture-books, passim) vanished abruptly, and earth resumed her old dimensions, when the sound of Charlotte's prattle somewhere hard by broke in on my primeval seclusion. Looking out from the bushes, I saw her trotting towards an open space of lawn the other side the pond, chattering to herself in her accustomed fashion, a doll tucked under either arm, and her brow knit with care. Propping up her double burden against a friendly stump, she sat down in front of them, as full of worry and anxiety as a Chancellor on a Budget night.

Her victims, who stared resignedly in front of them, were recognisable as Jerry and Rosa. Jerry hailed from far Japan: his hair was straight and black; his one garment cotton, of a simple blue; and his reputation was distinctly bad. Jerome was his proper name, from his supposed likeness to the holy man who hung in a print on the staircase; though a shaven crown was the only thing in common 'twixt Western saint and Eastern sinner. Rosa was typical British, from her flaxen poll to the stout calves she displayed so liberally, and in character she was of the blameless order of those who have not yet been found out.

I suspected Jerry from the first; there was a latent devilry in his slant eyes as he sat there moodily, and knowing what he was capable of, I scented trouble in store for Charlotte. Rosa I was not so sure about; she sat demurely and upright, and looked far away into the tree-tops in a visionary, world-forgetting sort of way; yet the prim purse of her mouth was somewhat overdone, and her eyes glittered unnaturally.

"Now, I'm going to begin where I left off," said Charlotte, regardless of stops, and thumping the turf with her fist excitedly: "and you must pay attention, 'cos this is a treat, to have a story told you before you're put to bed. Well, so the White Rabbit scuttled off down the passage and Alice hoped he'd come back 'cos he had a waistcoat on and her flamingo flew up a tree—but we haven't got to that part yet—you must wait a minute, and—where had I got to?"

Jerry only remained passive until Charlotte had got well under way, and then began to heel over quietly in Rosa's direction. His head fell on her plump shoulder, causing her to start nervously.

Charlotte seized and shook him with vigour, "O Jerry," she cried piteously, "if you're not going to be good, how ever shall I tell you my story?"

Jerry's face was injured innocence itself. "Blame if you like, Madam," he seemed to say, "the eternal laws of gravitation, but not a helpless puppet, who is also an orphan and a stranger in the land."

"Now we'll go on," began Charlotte once more. "So she got into the garden at last—I've left out a lot, but you won't care, I'll tell you some other time—and they were all playing croquet, and that's where the flamingo comes in, and the Queen shouted out, 'Off with her head!'"

At this point Jerry collapsed forward, suddenly and completely, his bald pate between his knees. Charlotte was not very angry this time. The sudden development of tragedy in the story had evidently been too much for the poor fellow. She straightened him out, wiped his nose, and, after trying him in various positions, to which he refused to adapt himself, she propped him against the shoulder of the (apparently) unconscious Rosa. Then my eyes were opened, and the full measure of Jerry's infamy became apparent. This, then, was what he had been playing up for. The fellow had designs. I resolved to keep him under close observation.

"If you'd been in the garden," went on Charlotte, reproachfully, "and flopped down like that when the Queen said, 'Off with his head!' she'd have offed with your head; but Alice wasn't that sort of girl at all. She just said, 'I'm not afraid of you, you're nothing but a pack of cards'—oh, dear! I've got to the end already, and I hadn't begun hardly! I never can make my stories last out! Never mind, I'll tell you another one."

Jerry didn't seem to care, now he had gained his end, whether the stories lasted out or not. He was nestling against Rosa's plump form with a look of satisfaction that was simply idiotic; and one arm had disappeared from view—was it round her waist? Rosa's natural blush seemed deeper than usual, her head inclined shyly—it must have been round her waist.

"If it wasn't so near your bedtime," continued Charlotte, reflectively, "I'd tell you a nice story with a bogy in it. But you'd be frightened, and you'd dream of bogies all night. So I'll tell you one about a White Bear, only you mustn't scream when the bear says 'Wow,' like I used to, 'cos he's a good bear really—"

Here Rosa fell flat on her back in the deadest of faints. Her limbs were rigid, her eyes glassy; what had Jerry been doing? It must have been something very bad, for her to take on like that. I scrutinised him carefully, while Charlotte ran to comfort the damsel. He appeared to be whistling a tune and regarding the scenery. If I only possessed Jerry's command of feature, I thought to myself, half regretfully, I would never be found out in anything.

"It's all your fault, Jerry," said Charlotte, reproachfully, when the lady had been restored to consciousness: "Rosa's as good as gold, except when you make her wicked. I'd put you in the corner, only a stump hasn't got a corner—wonder why that is? Thought everything had corners. Never mind, you'll have to sit with your face to the wall—*so*. Now you can sulk if you like!"

Jerry seemed to hesitate a moment between the bliss of indulgence in sulks with a sense of injury, and the imperious summons of beauty waiting to be wooed at his elbow; then, carried away by his passion, he fell sideways across Rosa's lap. One arm stuck stiffly upwards, as in passionate protestation; his amorous countenance was full of entreaty. Rosa hesitated—wavered—and yielded, crushing his slight frame under the weight of her full-bodied surrender.

Charlotte had stood a good deal, but it was possible to abuse even her patience. Snatching Jerry from his lawless embraces, she reversed him across her knee, and then—the outrage offered to the whole superior sex in Jerry's hapless person was too painful to witness; but though I turned my head away, the sound of brisk slaps continued to reach my tingling ears. When I looked again, Jerry was sitting up as before; his garment, somewhat crumpled, was restored to its original position; but his pallid countenance was set hard. Knowing as I did, only too well, what a volcano of passion and shame must be seething under that impassive exterior, for the moment I felt sorry for him.

Rosa's face was still buried in her frock; it might have been shame, it might have been grief for Jerry's sufferings. But the callous Japanese never even looked her way. His heart was exceeding bitter within him. In merely following up his natural impulses he had run his head against convention, and learnt how hard a thing it was; and the sunshiny world was all black to him.

Even Charlotte softened somewhat at the sight of his rigid misery. "If you'll say you're sorry, Jerome," she said, "I'll say I'm sorry, too."

Jerry only dropped his shoulders against the stump and stared out in the direction of his dear native Japan, where love was no sin, and smacking had not been introduced. Why had he ever left it? He would go back tomorrow—and yet there were obstacles: another grievance. Nature, in endowing Jerry with every grace of form and feature, along with a sensitive soul, had somehow forgotten the gift of locomotion.

There was a crackling in the bushes behind me, with sharp short pants as of a small steam-engine, and Rollo, the black retriever, just released from his chain by some friendly hand, burst through the underwood, seeking congenial company. I joyfully hailed him to stop and be a panther; but he sped away round the pond, upset Charlotte with a boisterous caress, and seizing Jerry by the middle, disappeared with him down the drive. Charlotte raved, panting behind the swift-footed avenger of crime; Rosa lay dishevelled, bereft of consciousness; Jerry himself spread helpless arms to heaven, and I almost thought I heard a cry for mercy, a tardy promise of amendment; but it was too late. The Black Man had got Jerry at last; and though the tear of sensibility might moisten the eye, no one who really knew him could deny the justice of his fate.

"Young Adam Cupid"

No one would have suspected Edward of being in love, but that after breakfast, with an over-acted carelessness, "Anybody who likes," he said, "can feed my rabbits," and he disappeared, with a jauntiness that deceived nobody, in the direction of the orchard. Now, kingdoms might totter and reel, and convulsions change the map of Europe; but the iron unwritten law prevailed, that each boy severely fed his own rabbits. There was good ground, then, for suspicion and alarm; and while the lettuce-leaves were being drawn through the wires, Harold and I conferred seriously on the situation.

It may be thought that the affair was none of our business; and indeed we cared little as individuals. We were only concerned as members of a corporation, for each of whom the mental or physical ailment of one of his fellows might have far-reaching effects. It was thought best that Harold, as least open to suspicion of motive, should be despatched to probe and peer. His instructions were, to proceed by a report on the health of our rabbits in particular; to glide gently into a discussion on rabbits in general, their customs, practices, and vices; to pass thence, by a natural transition, to the female sex, the inherent flaws in its composition, and the reasons for regarding it (speaking broadly) as dirt. He was especially to be very diplomatic, and then to return and report progress. He departed on his mission gaily; but his absence was short, and his return, discomfited and in tears, seemed to betoken some want of parts for diplomacy. He had found Edward, it appeared, pacing the orchard, with the sort of set smile that mountebanks wear in their precarious antics, fixed painfully on his face, as with pins. Harold had opened well, on the rabbit subject, but, with a fatal confusion between the abstract and the concrete, had then gone on to remark that Edward's lop-eared doe, with her long hindlegs and contemptuous twitch of the nose, always reminded him of Sabina Larkin (a nine-year-old damsel, child of a neighbouring farmer): at which point Edward, it would seem, had turned upon and savagely maltreated him, twisting his arm and punching him in the short ribs. So that Harold returned to the rabbit-hutches preceded by long-drawn wails: anon wishing, with sobs, that he were a man, to kick his love-lorn brother: anon lamenting that ever he had been born.

I was not big enough to stand up to Edward personally, so I had to console the sufferer by allowing him to grease the wheels of the donkey-cart—a luscious treat that had been specially reserved for me, a week past, by the gardener's boy, for putting in a good word on his behalf with the new kitchen-maid. Harold was soon all smiles and grease; and I was not, on the whole, dissatisfied with the significant hint that had been gained as to the *fons et origo mali.*

Fortunately, means were at hand for resolving any doubts on the subject, since the morning was Sunday, and already the bells were ringing for church. Lest the connexion may not be evident at first sight, I should explain that the gloomy period of church-time, with its enforced inaction and its lack of real interest—passed, too, within sight of all that the village held of fairest—was just the one when a young man's fancies lightly turned to thoughts of love. For such trifling the rest of the week afforded no leisure; but in church— well, there was really nothing else to do! True, naughts-and-crosses might be indulged in on fly-leaves of prayer-books while the Litany dragged its slow length along; but what balm or what solace could be found for the sermon? Naturally the eye, wandering here and there among the serried ranks, made bold, untrammelled choice among our fair fellow-supplicants. It was in this way that, some months earlier, under the exceptional strain of the Athanasian Creed, my roving fancy had settled upon the baker's wife as a fit object for a life-long devotion. Her riper charms had conquered a heart which none of her be-muslined, tittering juniors had been able to subdue; and that she was already wedded had never occurred to me as any bar to my affection. Edward's general demeanour, then, during morning service, was safe to convict him; but there was also a special test for the particular case. It happened that we sat in a transept, and, the Larkins being behind us, Edward's only chance of feasting on Sabina's charms was in the all-too fleeting interval when we swung round eastwards. I was not mistaken. During the singing of the Benedictus the impatient one made several false starts, and at last he slewed fairly round before "As it was in the beginning, is now, and ever shall be" was half finished. The evidence was conclusive: a court of law could have desired no better.

The fact being patent, the next thing was to grapple with it; and my mind was fully occupied during the sermon. There was really nothing unfair or unbrotherly in my attitude. A philosophic affection such as mine own, which clashed with nothing, was (I held) permissible; but the volcanic passions in which Edward indulged about once a quarter were a serious interference with business. To make matters worse, next week there was a circus coming to the neighbourhood, to which we had all been strictly forbidden to go; and without Edward no visit in contempt of law and orders could be successfully brought off. I had sounded him as to the circus on our way to church, and he had replied briefly that the very thought of a clown made him sick. Morbidity could no further go. But the sermon came to an end without any line of conduct having suggested itself; and I walked home in some depression, feeling sadly that Venus was in the ascendant and in direful opposition, while Auriga—the circus star—drooped declinant, perilously near the horizon.

By the irony of fate, Aunt Eliza, of all people, turned out to be the *Dea ex machina*. The thing fell out in this wise. It was that lady's obnoxious practice to issue forth, of a Sunday afternoon, on a visit of state to such farmers and cottagers as dwelt at hand; on which occasion she was wont to hale a reluctant boy along with her, from the mixed motives of propriety and his soul's health. Much cudgelling of brains, I suppose, had on that particular day made me torpid and unwary. Anyhow, when a victim came to be sought for, I fell an easy prey, while the others fled scatheless and whooping. Our first visit was to the Larkins. Here ceremonial might be viewed in its finest flower, and we conducted ourselves, like Queen Elizabeth when she trod the measure, "high and disposedly." In the low, oak-panelled parlour, cake and currant wine were set forth, and after courtesies and compliments exchanged, Aunt Eliza, greatly condescending, talked the fashions with Mrs Larkin; while the farmer and I, perspiring with the unusual effort, exchanged remarks on the mutability of the weather and the steady fall in the price of corn. (Who would have thought, to hear us, that only two short days ago we had confronted each other on either side of a hedge—I triumphant, provocative, derisive; he flushed, wroth, cracking his whip, and volleying forth profanity? So powerful is all-subduing ceremony!) Sabina the while, demurely seated with a *Pilgrim's*

Progress on her knee, and apparently absorbed in a brightly coloured presentment of "Apollyon Straddling Right across the Way," eyed me at times with shy interest; but repelled all Aunt Eliza's advances with a frigid politeness for which I could not sufficiently admire her.

"It's surprising to me," I heard my aunt remark presently, "how my eldest nephew, Edward, despises little girls. I heard him tell Charlotte the other day that he wished he could exchange her for a pair of Japanese guinea-pigs. It made the poor child cry. Boys are so heartless!" (I saw Sabina stiffen as she sat, and her tip-tilted nose twitched scornfully.) "Now this boy here——" (my soul descended into my very boots. Could the woman have intercepted any of my amorous glances at the baker's wife?) "Now this boy," my aunt went on, "is more human altogether. Only yesterday he took his sister to the baker's shop, and spent his only penny buying her sweets. I thought it showed such a nice disposition. I wish Edward were more like him!"

I breathed again. It was unnecessary to explain my real motives for that visit to the baker's. Sabina's face softened, and her contemptuous nose descended from its altitude of scorn; she gave me one shy glance of kindness, and then concentrated her attention upon Mercy knocking at the Wicket Gate. I felt awfully mean as regarded Edward; but what could I do? I was in Gaza, gagged and bound; the Philistines hemmed me in.

The same evening the storm burst, the bolt fell, and—to continue the metaphor—the atmosphere grew serene and clear once more. The evening service was shorter than usual, the vicar, as he ascended the pulpit steps, having dropped two pages out of his sermon-case—unperceived by any but ourselves, either at the moment or subsequently when the hiatus was reached; so as we joyfully shuffled out I whispered Edward that by racing home at top speed we should make time to assume our bows and arrows (laid aside for the day) and play at Indians and buffaloes with Aunt Eliza's fowls—already strolling roostwards, regardless of their doom—before that sedately stepping lady could return. Edward hung at the door, wavering; the suggestion had unhallowed charms.

At that moment Sabina issued primly forth, and, seeing Edward, put out her tongue at him in the most exasperating manner conceivable; then passed on her way, her shoulders rigid, her dainty head held high. A man can stand very much in the cause of love: poverty, aunts, rivals, barriers of every sort—all these only serve to fan the flame. But personal ridicule is a shaft that reaches the very vitals. Edward led the race home at a speed which one of Ballantyne's heroes might have equalled but never surpassed; and that evening the Indians dispersed Aunt Eliza's fowls over several square miles of country, so that the tale of them remaineth incomplete unto this day. Edward himself, cheering wildly, pursued the big Cochin-China cock till the bird sank gasping under the drawing-room window, whereat its mistress stood petrified; and after supper, in the shrubbery, smoked a half-consumed cigar he had picked up in the road, and declared to an awe-stricken audience his final, his immitigable, resolve to go into the army.

The crisis was past, and Edward was saved! . . . And yet . . . *sunt lachrymae rerem* . . . to me watching the cigar-stump alternately pale and glow against the dark background of laurel, a vision of a tip-tilted nose, of a small head poised scornfully, seemed to hover on the gathering gloom—seemed to grow and fade and grow again, like the grin of the Cheshire cat—pathetically, reproachfully even; and the charms of the baker's wife slipped from my memory like snow-wreaths in thaw. After all, Sabina was nowise to blame: why should the child be punished? Tomorrow I would give them the slip, and stroll round by her garden promiscuous-like, at a time when the farmer was safe in the rick-yard. If nothing came of it, there was no harm done; and if on the contrary . . . !

The Burglars

It was much too fine a night to think of going to bed at once, and so, although the witching hour of nine P.M. had struck, Edward and I were still leaning out of the open window in our nightshirts, watching the play of the cedar-branch shadows on the moonlit lawn, and planning schemes of fresh devilry for the sunshiny morrow. From below, strains of the jocund piano declared that the Olympians were enjoying themselves in their listless, impotent way; for the new curate had been bidden to dinner that night, and was at the moment unclerically proclaiming to all the world that he feared no foe. His discordant vociferations doubtless started a train of thought in Edward's mind, for the youth presently remarked, a propos of nothing that had been said before, "I believe the new curate's rather gone on Aunt Maria."

I scouted the notion. "Why, she's quite old," I said. (She must have seen some five-and-twenty summers.)

"Of course she is," replied Edward, scornfully. "It's not her, it's her money he's after, you bet!"

"Didn't know she had any money," I observed timidly.

"Sure to have," said my brother, with confidence. "Heaps and heaps."

Silence ensued, both our minds being busy with the new situation thus presented—mine, in wonderment at this flaw that so often declared itself in enviable natures of fullest endowment—in a grown-up man and a good cricketer, for instance, even as this curate; Edward's (apparently), in the consideration of how such a state of things, supposing it existed, could be best turned to his own advantage.

"Bobby Ferris told me," began Edward in due course, "that there was a fellow spooning his sister once—"

"What's spooning?" I asked meekly.

"Oh, *I* dunno," said Edward, indifferently. "It's—it's—it's just a thing they do, you know. And he used to carry notes and messages and things between 'em, and he got a shilling almost every time."

"What, from each of 'em?" I innocently inquired.

Edward looked at me with scornful pity. "Girls never have any money," he briefly explained. "But she did his exercises and got him out of rows, and told stories for him when he needed it—and much better ones than he could have made up for himself. Girls are useful in some ways. So he was living in clover, when unfortunately they went and quarrelled about something."

"Don't see what that's got to do with it," I said.

"Nor don't I," rejoined Edward. "But anyhow the notes and things stopped, and so did the shillings. Bobby was fairly cornered, for he had bought two ferrets on tick, and promised to pay a shilling a week, thinking the shillings were going on forever, the silly young ass. So when the week was up, and he was being dunned for the shilling, he went off to the fellow and said, 'Your broken-hearted Bella implores you to meet her at sundown—by the hollow oak, as of old, be it only for a moment. Do not fail!' He got all that out of some rotten book, of course. The fellow looked puzzled and said—

"'What hollow oak? I don't know any hollow oak.'

"'Perhaps it was the Royal Oak?' said Bobby promptly, 'cos he saw he had made a slip, through trusting too much to the rotten book; but this didn't seem to make the fellow any happier."

"Should think not," I said, "the Royal Oak's an awful low sort of pub."

"I know," said Edward. "Well, at last the fellow said, 'I think I know what she means: the hollow tree in your father's paddock. It happens to be an elm, but she wouldn't know the difference. All right: say I'll be there.' Bobby hung about a bit, for he hadn't got his money. 'She was crying awfully,' he said. Then he got his shilling."

"And wasn't the fellow riled," I inquired, "when he got to the place and found nothing?"

"He found Bobby," said Edward, indignantly. "Young Ferris was a gentleman, every inch of him. He brought the fellow another message from Bella: 'I dare not leave the house. My cruel parents immure me closely. If you only knew what I suffer. Your broken-hearted Bella.' Out of the same rotten book. This made the fellow a little suspicious, 'cos it was the old Ferrises who had been keen about the thing all through: the fellow, you see, had tin."

"But what's that got to—" I began again.

"Oh, *I* dunno," said Edward, impatiently. "I'm telling you just what Bobby told me. He got suspicious, anyhow, but he couldn't exactly call Bella's brother a liar, so Bobby escaped for the time. But when he was in a hole next week, over a stiff French exercise, and tried the same sort of game on his sister, she was too sharp for him, and he got caught out. Somehow women seem more mistrustful than men. They're so beastly suspicious by nature, you know."

"*I* know," said I. "But did the two—the fellow and the sister— make it up afterwards?"

"I don't remember about that," replied Edward, indifferently; "but Bobby got packed off to school a whole year earlier than his people meant to send him—which was just what he wanted. So you see it all came right in the end!"

I was trying to puzzle out the moral of this story—it was evidently meant to contain one somewhere—when a flood of golden lamplight mingled with the moon rays on the lawn, and Aunt Maria and the new curate strolled out on the grass below us, and took the direction of a garden-seat that was backed by a dense laurel shrubbery reaching round in a half-circle to the house. Edward mediated moodily. "If we only knew what they were talking about," said he, "you'd soon see whether I was right or not. Look here! Let's send the kid down by the porch to reconnoitre!"

"Harold's asleep," I said; "it seems rather a shame—"

"Oh, rot!" said my brother; "he's the youngest, and he's got to do as he's told!"

So the luckless Harold was hauled out of bed and given his sailing-orders. He was naturally rather vexed at being stood up suddenly on the cold floor, and the job had no particular interest for him; but he was both staunch and well disciplined. The means of exit were simple enough. A porch of iron trellis came up to within easy reach of the window, and was habitually used by all three of us, when modestly anxious to avoid public notice. Harold climbed deftly down the porch like a white rat, and his night-gown glimmered a moment on the gravel walk ere he was lost to sight in the darkness of the shrubbery. A brief interval of silence ensued, broken suddenly by a sound of scuffle, and then a shrill, long-drawn squeal, as of metallic surfaces in friction. Our scout had fallen into the hands of the enemy!

Indolence alone had made us devolve the task of investigation on our younger brother. Now that danger had declared itself, there was no hesitation. In a second we were down the side of the porch, and crawling Cherokee-wise through the laurels to the back of the garden-seat. Piteous was the sight that greeted us. Aunt Maria was on the seat, in a white evening frock, looking—for an aunt—really quite nice. On the lawn stood an incensed curate, grasping our small brother by a large ear, which—judging from the row he was making—seemed on the point of parting company with the head it adorned. The gruesome noise he was emitting did not really affect us otherwise than aesthetically. To one who has tried both, the wail of genuine physical anguish is easy distinguishable from the pumped-up ad misericordiam blubber. Harold's could clearly be recognised as belonging to the latter class. "Now, you young—" (whelp, *I* think it was, but Edward stoutly maintains it was devil), said the curate, sternly; "tell us what you mean by it!"

"Well, leggo of my ear then!" shrilled Harold, "and I'll tell you the solemn truth!"

"Very well," agreed the curate, releasing him; "now go ahead, and don't lie more than you can help."

We abode the promised disclosure without the least misgiving; but even we had hardly given Harold due credit for his fertility of resource and powers of imagination.

"I had just finished saying my prayers," began that young gentleman, slowly, "when I happened to look out of the window, and on the lawn I saw a sight which froze the marrow in my veins! A burglar was approaching the house with snake-like tread! He had a scowl and a dark lantern, and he was armed to the teeth!"

We listened with interest. The style, though unlike Harold's native notes, seemed strangely familiar.

"Go on," said the curate, grimly.

"Pausing in his stealthy career," continued Harold, "he gave a low whistle. Instantly the signal was responded to, and from the adjacent shadows two more figures glided forth. The miscreants were both armed to the teeth."

"Excellent," said the curate; "proceed."

"The robber chief," pursued Harold, warming to his work, "joined his nefarious comrades, and conversed with them in silent tones. His expression was truly ferocious, and I ought to have said that he was armed to the t—"

"There, never mind his teeth," interrupted the curate, rudely; "there's too much jaw about you altogether. Hurry up and have done."

"I was in a frightful funk," continued the narrator, warily guarding his ear with his hand, "but just then the drawing-room window opened, and you and Aunt Maria came out—I mean emerged. The burglars vanished silently into the laurels, with horrid implications!"

The curate looked slightly puzzled. The tale was well sustained, and certainly circumstantial. After all, the boy might have really seen something. How was the poor man to know—though the chaste and lofty diction might have supplied a hint—that the whole yarn was a free adaptation from the last Penny Dreadful lent us by the knife-and-boot boy?

"Why did you not alarm the house?" he asked.

"'Cos I was afraid," said Harold, sweetly, "that p'raps they mightn't believe me!"

"But how did you get down here, you naughty little boy?" put in Aunt Maria.

Harold was hard pressed—by his own flesh and blood, too!

At that moment Edward touched me on the shoulder and glided off through the laurels. When some ten yards away he gave a low whistle. I replied by another. The effect was magical. Aunt Maria started up with a shriek. Harold gave one startled glance around, and then fled like a hare, made straight for the back-door, burst in upon the servants at supper, and buried himself in the broad bosom of the cook, his special ally. The curate faced the laurels—hesitatingly. But Aunt Maria flung herself on him. "O Mr. Hodgitts!" I heard her cry, "you are brave! for my sake do not be rash!" He was not rash. When I peeped out a second later, the coast was entirely clear.

By this time there were sounds of a household timidly emerging; and Edward remarked to me that perhaps we had better be off. Retreat was an easy matter. A stunted laurel gave a leg up on to the garden wall, which led in its turn to the roof of an out-house, up which, at a dubious angle, we could crawl to the window of the box-room. This overland route had been revealed to us one day by the domestic cat, when hard pressed in the course of an otter-hunt, in which the cat—somewhat unwillingly—was filling the title role; and it had proved distinctly useful on occasions like the present. We were snug in bed—minus some cuticle from knees and elbows— and Harold, sleepily chewing something sticky, had been carried up in the arms of the friendly cook, ere the clamour of the burglar-hunters had died away.

The curate's undaunted demeanour, as reported by Aunt Maria, was generally supposed to have terrified the burglars into flight, and much kudos accrued to him thereby. Some days later, however, when he had dropped in to afternoon tea, and was making a mild curatorial joke about the moral courage required for taking the last piece of bread-and-butter, I felt constrained to remark dreamily, and as it were to the universe at large, "Mr. Hodgitts! you are brave! for my sake, do not be rash!"

Fortunately for me, the vicar was also a caller on that day; and it was always a comparatively easy matter to dodge my long-coated friend in the open.

A Harvesting

The year was in its yellowing time, and the face of Nature a study in old gold. "A field or, *semée*, with garbs of the same": it may be false Heraldry—Nature's generally is—but it correctly blazons the display that Edward and I considered from the rickyard gate, Harold was not on in this scene, being stretched upon the couch of pain; the special disorder stomachic, as usual.

The evening before, Edward, in a fit of unwonted amiability, had deigned to carve me out a turnip lantern, an art-and-craft he was peculiarly deft in; and Harold, as the interior of the turnip flew out in scented fragments under the hollowing knife, had eaten largely thereof: regarding all such jetsam as his special perquisite. Now he was dreeing his weird, with such assistance as the chemist could afford. But Edward and I, knowing that this particular field was to be carried today, were revelling in the privilege of riding in the empty waggons from the rickyard back to the sheaves, whence we returned toilfully on foot, to career it again over the billowy acres in these great galleys of a stubble sea. It was the nearest approach to sailing that we inland urchins might compass: and hence it ensued, that such stirring scenes as Sir Richard Grenville on the *Revenge*, the smoke-wreathed Battle of the Nile, and the Death of Nelson, had all been enacted in turn on these dusty quarter decks, as they swayed and bumped afield.

Another waggon had shot its load, and was jolting out through the rickyard gate, as we swung ourselves in, shouting, over its tail. Edward was the first up, and, as I gained my feet, he clutched me in a death-grapple. I was a privateersman, he proclaimed, and he the captain of the British frigate *Terpsichore*, of—I forget the precise number of guns. Edward always collared the best parts to himself; but I was holding my own gallantly, when I suddenly discovered that the floor we battled on was swarming with earwigs. Shrieking, I hurled free of him, and rolled over the tail-board on to the stubble. Edward executed a war-dance of triumph on the deck of the retreating galleon; but I cared little for that. I knew *he* knew that I wasn't afraid of him, but that I was—and terribly—of earwigs, "those mortal bugs o' the field." So I let him disappear, shouting lustily for all hands to repel boarders, while I strolled inland, down the village.

There was a touch of adventure in the expedition. This was not our own village, but a foreign one, distant at least a mile. One felt that sense of mingled distinction and insecurity which is familiar to the traveller: distinction, in that folk turned the head to note you curiously; insecurity, by reason of the ever-present possibility of missiles on the part of the more juvenile inhabitants, a class eternally conservative. Elated with isolation, I went even more nose-in-air than usual: and "even so," I mused, "might Mungo Park have threaded the trackless African forest and . . ." Here I plumped against a soft, but resisting body.

Recalled to my senses by the shock, I fell back in the attitude every boy under these circumstances instinctively adopts—both elbows well up over the ears. I found myself facing a tall elderly man, clean-shaven, clad in well-worn black—a clergyman evidently; and I noted at once a far-away look in his eyes, as if they were used to another plane of vision, and could not instantly focus things terrestrial, being suddenly recalled thereto. His figure was bent in apologetic protest: "I ask a thousand pardons, sir," he said; "I am really so very absent-minded. I trust you will forgive me."

Now most boys would have suspected chaff under this courtly style of address. I take infinite credit to myself for recognising at once the natural attitude of a man to whom his fellows were gentlemen all, neither Jew nor Gentile, clean nor unclean. Of course, I took the blame on myself; adding, that I was very absent-minded too—which was indeed the case.

"I perceive," he said pleasantly, "that we have something in common. I, an old man, dream dreams; you, a young one, see visions. Your lot is the happier. And now—" his hand had been resting all this time on a wicket-gate—"you are hot, it is easily seen; the day is advanced, Virgo is the Zodiacal sign. Perhaps I may offer you some poor refreshment, if your engagements will permit."

My only engagement that afternoon was an arithmetic lesson, and I had not intended to keep it in any case; so I passed in, while he held the gate open politely, murmuring, "*Venit Hesperus ite, capellae*: come, little kid!" and then apologising abjectly for a familiarity which (he said) was less his than the Roman poet's. A straight flagged walk led up to the cool-looking old house, and my host, lingering in his progress at this rose-tree and that, forgot all about me at least twice, waking up and apologising humbly after each lapse. During these intervals I put two and two together, and identified him as the Rector: a bachelor, eccentric, learned exceedingly, round whom the crust of legend was already beginning to form; to myself an object of special awe, in that he was alleged to have written a real book. "Heaps o' books," Martha, my informant, said; but I knew the exact rate of discount applicable to Martha's statements.

We passed eventually through a dark hall into a room which struck me at once as the ideal I had dreamed but failed to find. None of your feminine fripperies here! None of your chair-backs and tidies! This man, it was seen, groaned under no aunts. Stout volumes in calf and vellum lined three sides; books sprawled or hunched themselves on chairs and tables; books diffused the pleasant odour of printers' ink and bindings; topping all, a faint aroma of tobacco cheered and heartened exceedingly, as under foreign skies the flap and rustle over the wayfarer's head of the Union Jack—the old flag of emancipation! And in one corner, book-piled like the rest of the furniture, stood a piano.

This I hailed with a squeal of delight. "Want to strum?" inquired my friend, as if it was the most natural wish in the world—his eyes were already straying towards another corner, where bits of writing-table peeped out from under a sort of Alpine system of book and foolscap.

"O, but may I?" I asked in doubt. "At home I'm not allowed to— only beastly exercises!"

"Well, you can strum here, at all events," he replied; and murmuring absently, *Age, dic Latinum, barbite, carmen*, he made his way, mechanically guided as it seemed, to the irresistible writing-table. In ten seconds he was out of sight and call. A great book open on his knee, another propped up in front, a score or so disposed within easy reach, he read and jotted with an absorption almost passionate. I might have been in Boeotia, for any consciousness he had of me. So with a light heart I turned to and strummed.

Those who painfully and with bleeding feet have scaled the crags

of mastery over musical instruments have yet their loss in this—
that the wild joy of strumming has become a vanished sense. Their
happiness comes from the concord and the relative value of the notes
they handle: the pure, absolute quality and nature of each note in
itself are only appreciated by the strummer. For some notes have all
the sea in them, and some cathedral bells; others a woodland joyance
and a smell of greenery; in some fauns dance to the merry reed,
and even the grave centaurs peep out from their caves. Some bring
moonlight, and some the deep crimson of a rose's heart; some are
blue, some red, and others will tell of an army with silken standards
and march-music. And throughout all the sequence of suggestion,
up above the little white men leap and peep, and strive against the
imprisoning wires; and all the big rosewood box hums as it were full
of hiving bees.

Spent with the rapture, I paused a moment and caught my
friend's eye over the edge of a folio. "But as for these Germans," he
began abruptly, as if we had been in the middle of a discussion, "the
scholarship is there, I grant you; but the spark, the fine perception,
the happy intuition, where is it? They get it all from us!"

"They get nothing whatever from *us*," I said decidedly: the word
German only suggesting Bands, to which Aunt Eliza was bitterly
hostile.

"You think not?" he rejoined, doubtfully, getting up and walking
about the room. "Well, I applaud such fairness and temperance in
so young a critic. They are qualities—in youth—as rare as they
are pleasing. But just look at Schrumpffius, for instance—how he
struggles and wrestles with a simple γάρ in this very passage here!"

I peeped fearfully through the open door, half-dreading to see
some sinuous and snark-like conflict in progress on the mat; but all
was still. I saw no trouble at all in the passage, and I said so.

"Precisely," he cried, delighted. "To you, who possess the natural
scholar's faculty in so happy a degree, there is no difficulty at all.
But to this Schrumpffius—" But here, luckily for me, in came the
housekeeper, a clean-looking woman of staid aspect.

"Your tea is in the garden," she said, as if she were correcting
a faulty emendation. "I've put some cakes and things for the little
gentleman; and you'd better drink it before it gets cold."

He waved her off and continued his stride, brandishing an aorist over my devoted head. The housekeeper waited unmoved till there fell a moment's break in his descant; and then, "You'd better drink it before it gets cold," she observed again, impassively. The wretched man cast a deprecating look at me. "Perhaps a little tea would be rather nice," he observed, feebly; and to my great relief he led the way into the garden. I looked about for the little gentleman, but, failing to discover him, I concluded he was absent-minded too, and attacked the "cakes and things" with no misgivings.

After a most successful and most learned tea a something happened which, small as I was, never quite shook itself out of my memory. To us at parley in an arbour over the high road, there entered, slouching into view, a dingy tramp, satellited by a frowsy woman and a pariah dog; and, catching sight of us, he set up his professional whine; and I looked at my friend with the heartiest compassion, for I knew well from Martha—it was common talk—that at this time of day he was certainly and surely penniless. Morn by morn he started forth with pockets lined; and each returning evening found him with never a sou. All this he proceeded to explain at length to the tramp, courteously and even shamefacedly, as one who was in the wrong; and at last the gentleman of the road, realising the hopelessness of his case, set to and cursed him with gusto, vocabulary, and abandonment. He reviled his eyes, his features, his limbs, his profession, his relatives and surroundings; and then slouched off, still oozing malice and filth. We watched the party to a turn in the road, where the woman, plainly weary, came to a stop. Her lord, after some conventional expletives demanded of him by his position, relieved her of her bundle, and caused her to hang on his arm with a certain rough kindness of tone, and in action even a dim approach to tenderness; and the dingy dog crept up for one lick at her hand.

"See," said my friend, bearing somewhat on my shoulder, "how this strange thing, this love of ours, lives and shines out in the unlikeliest of places! You have been in the fields in early morning? Barren acres, all! But only stoop—catch the light thwartwise—and all is a silver network of gossamer! So the fairy filaments of this strange thing underrun and link together the whole world. Yet it is not the old imperious god of the fatal bow—ἔρως ἀνίκατε μάχαν not that—nor even the placid respectable στοργή—but something still unnamed, perhaps more mysterious, more divine! Only one must stoop to see it, old fellow, one must stoop!"

The dew was falling, the dusk closing, as I trotted briskly homewards down the road. Lonely spaces everywhere, above and around. Only Hesperus hung in the sky, solitary, pure, ineffably far-drawn and remote; yet infinitely heartening, somehow, in his valorous isolation.

Snowbound

Twelfth-night had come and gone, and life next morning seemed a trifle flat and purposeless. But yester-eve and the mummers were here! They had come striding into the old kitchen, powdering the red brick floor with snow from their barbaric bedizenments; and stamping, and crossing, and declaiming, till all was whirl and riot and shout. Harold was frankly afraid: unabashed, he buried himself in the cook's ample bosom. Edward feigned a manly superiority to illusion, and greeted these awful apparitions familiarly, as Dick and Harry and Joe. As for me, I was too big to run, too rapt to resist the magic and surprise. Whence came these outlanders, breaking in on us with song and ordered masque and a terrible clashing of wooden swords? And after these, what strange visitants might we not look for any quiet night, when the chestnuts popped in the ashes, and the old ghost stories drew the awe-stricken circle close? Old Merlin, perhaps, "all furred in black sheep-skins, and a russet gown, with a bow and arrows, and bearing wild geese in his hand!" Or stately Ogier the Dane, recalled from Faery, asking his way to the land that once had need of him! Or even, on some white night, the Snow-Queen herself, with a chime of sleigh-bells and the patter of reindeers' feet, with sudden halt at the door flung wide, while aloft the Northern Lights went shaking attendant spears among the quiet stars!

This morning, house-bound by the relentless, indefatigable snow, I was feeling the reaction Edward, on the contrary, being violently stage-struck on this his first introduction to the real Drama, was striding up and down the floor, proclaiming "Here be I, King Gearge the Third," in a strong Berkshire accent. Harold, accustomed, as the youngest, to lonely antics and to sports that asked no sympathy, was absorbed in "clubmen": a performance consisting in a measured progress round the room arm-in-arm with an imaginary companion of reverend years, with occasional halts at imaginary clubs, where—imaginary steps being leisurely ascended—imaginary papers were glanced at, imaginary scandal was discussed with elderly shakings of the head, and—regrettable to say—imaginary glasses were lifted lipwards. Heaven only knows how the germ of this dreary pastime first found way into his small-boyish being. It was his own invention, and he was proportionately proud of it. Meanwhile, Charlotte and I, crouched in the window-seat, watched, spell-stricken, the whirl and eddy and drive of the innumerable snow-flakes, wrapping our cheery little world in an uncanny uniform, ghastly in line and hue.

Charlotte was sadly out of spirits. Having "countered" Miss Smedley at breakfast, during some argument or other, by an apt quotation from her favourite classic (the *Fairy Book*) she had been gently but firmly informed that no such things as fairies ever really existed. "Do you mean to say it's all lies?" asked Charlotte, bluntly. Miss Smedley deprecated the use of any such unladylike words in any connection at all. "These stories had their origin, my dear," she explained, "in a mistaken anthropomorphism in the interpretation of nature. But though we are now too well informed to fall into similar errors, there are still many beautiful lessons to be learned from these myths—"

"But how can you learn anything," persisted Charlotte, "from what doesn't exist?" And she left the table defiant, howbeit depressed.

"Don't you mind *her*," I said, consolingly; "how can she know anything about it? Why, she can't even throw a stone properly!"

"Edward says they're all rot, too," replied Charlotte, doubtfully.

"Edward says everything's rot," I explained, "now he thinks he's going into the Army. If a thing's in a book it *must* be true, so that settles it!"

Charlotte looked almost reassured. The room was quieter now, for Edward had got the dragon down and was boring holes in him with a purring sound. Harold was ascending the steps of the Athenaeum with a jaunty air—suggestive rather of the Junior Carlton. Outside, the tall elm-tops were hardly to be seen through the feathery storm. "The sky's a-falling," quoted Charlotte, softly; "I must go and tell the king." The quotation suggested a fairy story, and I offered to read to her, reaching out for the book. But the Wee Folk were under a cloud; sceptical hints had embittered the chalice. So I was fain to fetch *Arthur*—second favourite with Charlotte for his dames riding errant, and an easy first with us boys for his spear-splintering crash of tourney and hurtle against hopeless odds. Here again, however, I proved unfortunate—what ill-luck made the book open at the sorrowful history of Balin and Balan? "And he vanished anon," I read: "and so he heard an horne blow, as it had been the death of a beast. 'That blast,' said Balin, 'is blowen for me, for I am the prize, and yet am I not dead.'" Charlotte began to cry: she knew the rest too well. I shut the book in despair. Harold emerged from behind the armchair. He was sucking his thumb (a thing which members of the Reform are seldom seen to do), and he stared wide-eyed at his tear stained sister. Edward put off his histrionics, and rushed up to her as the consoler—a new part for him.

"I know a jolly story," he began. "Aunt Eliza told it me. It was when she was somewhere over in that beastly abroad"—(he had once spent a black month of misery at Dinan)—"and there was a fellow there who had got two storks. And one stork died—it was the she-stork." ("What did it die of?" put in Harold.) "And the other stork was quite sorry, and moped, and went on, and got very miserable. So they looked about and found a duck, and introduced it to the stork. The duck was a drake, but the stork didn't mind, and they loved each other and were as jolly as could be. By and by another duck came along—a real she-duck this time—and when the drake saw her he fell in love, and left the stork, and went and proposed to the duck: for she was very beautiful. But the poor stork who was left, he said nothing at all to anybody, but just pined and pined and pined away, till one morning he was found quite dead! But the ducks lived happily ever afterwards!"

This was Edward's idea of a jolly story! Down again went the corners of poor Charlotte's mouth. Really Edward's stupid inability to see the real point in anything was *too* annoying! It was always so. Years before, it being necessary to prepare his youthful mind for a domestic event that might lead to awkward questionings at a time when there was little leisure to invent appropriate answers, it was delicately inquired of him whether he would like to have a little brother, or perhaps a little sister? He considered the matter carefully in all its bearings, and finally declared for a Newfoundland pup. Any boy more "gleg at the uptak" would have met his parents halfway, and eased their burden. As it was, the matter had to be approached all over again from a fresh standpoint. And now, while Charlotte turned away sniffingly, with a hiccough that told of an overwrought soul, Edward, unconscious (like Sir Isaac's Diamond) of the mischief he had done, wheeled round on Harold with a shout.

"I want a live dragon," he announced: "you've got to be my dragon!"

"Leave me go, will you?" squealed Harold, struggling stoutly. "I'm playin' at something else. How can I be a dragon and belong to all the clubs?"

"But wouldn't you like to be a nice scaly dragon, all green," said Edward, trying persuasion, "with a curly tail and red eyes, and breathing real smoke and fire?"

Harold wavered an instant: Pall-Mall was still strong in him. The next he was grovelling on the floor. No saurian ever swung a tail so scaly and so curly as his. Clubland was a thousand years away. With horrific pants he emitted smokiest smoke and fiercest fire.

"Now I want a Princess," cried Edward, clutching Charlotte ecstatically; "and *you* can be the doctor, and heal me from the dragon's deadly wound."

Of all professions I held the sacred art of healing in worst horror and contempt. Cataclysmal memories of purge and draught crowded thick on me, and with Charlotte—who courted no barren honours—I made a break for the door. Edward did likewise, and the hostile forces clashed together on the mat, and for a brief space things were mixed and chaotic and Arthurian. The silvery sound of the luncheon-bell restored an instant peace, even in the teeth of clenched antagonisms like ours. The Holy Grail itself, "sliding athwart a sunbeam," never so effectually stilled a riot of warring passions into sweet and quiet accord.

What They Talked About

Edward was standing ginger-beer like a gentleman, happening, as the one that had last passed under the dentist's hands, to be the capitalist of the flying hour. As in all well-regulated families, the usual tariff obtained in ours—half-a-crown a tooth; one shilling only if the molar were a loose one. This one, unfortunately—in spite of Edward's interested affectation of agony—had been shaky undisguised; but the event was good enough to run to ginger-beer. As financier, however, Edward had claimed exemption from any servile duties of procurement, and had swaggered about the garden while I fetched from the village post-office, and Harold stole a tumbler from the pantry. Our preparations complete, we were sprawling on the lawn; the staidest and most self respecting of the rabbits had been let loose to grace the feast, and was lopping demurely about the grass, selecting the juiciest plantains; while Selina, as the eldest lady present, was toying, in her affected feminine way, with the first full tumbler, daintily fishing for bits of broken cork.

"Hurry up, can't you?" growled our host; "what are you girls always so beastly particular for?"

"Martha says," explained Harold (thirsty too, but still just), "that if you swallow a bit of cork, it swells, and it swells, and it swells inside you, till you—"

"O bosh!" said Edward, draining the glass with a fine pretence of indifference to consequences, but all the same (as I noticed) dodging the floating cork-fragments with skill and judgment.

"O, it's all very well to say bosh," replied Harold, nettled; "but everyone knows it's true but you. Why, when Uncle Thomas was here last, and they got up a bottle of wine for him, he took just one tiny sip out of his glass, and then he said, 'Poo, my goodness, that's corked!' And he wouldn't touch it. And they had to get a fresh bottle up. The funny part was, though, I looked in his glass afterwards, when it was brought out into the passage, and there wasn't any cork in it at all! So I drank it all off, and it was very good!"

"You'd better be careful, young man!" said his elder brother, regarding him severely. "D' you remember that night when the

Mummers were here, and they had mulled port, and you went round and emptied all the glasses after they had gone away?"

"Ow! I did feel funny that night," chuckled Harold. "Thought the house was comin' down, it jumped about so; and Martha had to carry me up to bed, 'cos the stairs was goin' all waggity!"

We gazed searchingly at our graceless junior; but it was clear that he viewed the matter in the light of a phenomenon rather than of a delinquency.

A third bottle was by this time circling; and Selina, who had evidently waited for it to reach her, took a most unfairly long pull, and then jumping up and shaking out her frock, announced that she was going for a walk. Then she fled like a hare; for it was the custom of our Family to meet with physical coercion any independence of action in individuals.

"She's off with those Vicarage girls again," said Edward, regarding Selina's long black legs twinkling down the path. "She goes out with them every day now; and as soon as ever they start, all their heads go together and they chatter, chatter, chatter the whole blessed time! I can't make out what they find to talk about. They never stop; it's gabble, gabble, gabble right along, like a nest of young rooks!"

"P'raps they talk about birds'-eggs," I suggested sleepily (the sun was hot, the turf soft, the ginger-beer potent); "and about ships, and buffaloes, and desert islands; and why rabbits have white tails; and whether they'd sooner have a schooner or a cutter; and what they'll be when they're men—at least, I mean there's lots of things to talk about, if you *want* to talk."

"Yes; but they don't talk about those sort of things at all," persisted Edward. "How *can* they? They don't *know* anything; they can't *do* anything—except play the piano, and nobody would want to talk about *that*; and they don't care about anything—anything sensible, I mean. So what *do* they talk about?"

"I asked Martha once," put in Harold; "and she said, 'Never *you* mind; young ladies has lots of things to talk about that young gentlemen can't understand.'"

"I don't believe it," Edward growled.

"Well, that's what she *said*, anyway," rejoined Harold, indifferently. The subject did not seem to him of first-class importance, and it was hindering the circulation of the ginger-beer.

We heard the click of the front-gate. Through a gap in the hedge we could see the party setting off down the road. Selina was in the middle: a Vicarage girl had her by either arm; their heads were together, as Edward had described; and the clack of their tongues came down the breeze like the busy pipe of starlings on a bright March morning.

"What *do* they talk about, Charlotte?" I inquired, wishing to pacify Edward. "You go out with them sometimes."

"I don't know," said poor Charlotte, dolefully. "They make me walk behind, 'cos they say I'm too little, and mustn't hear. And I *do* want to so," she added.

"When any lady comes to see Aunt Eliza," said Harold, "they both talk at once all the time. And yet each of 'em seems to hear what the other one's saying. I can't make out how they do it. Grown-up people are so clever!"

"The Curate's the funniest man," I remarked. "He's always saying things that have no sense in them at all, and then laughing at them as if they were jokes. Yesterday, when they asked him if he'd have some more tea he said, 'Once more unto the breach, dear friends, once more,' and then sniggered all over. I didn't see anything funny in that. And then somebody asked him about his button-hole and he said, ''Tis but a little faded flower,' and exploded again. I thought it very stupid."

"O *him*," said Edward contemptuously: "he can't help it, you know; it's a sort of way he's got. But it's these girls I can't make out. If they've anything really sensible to talk about, how is it nobody knows what it is? And if they haven't—and we know they *can't* have, naturally—why don't they shut up their jaw? This old rabbit here— *he* doesn't want to talk. He's got something better to do." And Edward aimed a ginger-beer cork at the unruffled beast, who never budged.

"O but rabbits *do* talk," interposed Harold. "I've watched them often in their hutch. They put their heads together and their noses go up and down, just like Selina's and the Vicarage girls'. Only of course I can't hear what they're saying."

"Well, if they do," said Edward, unwillingly, "I'll bet they don't talk such rot as those girls do!"—which was ungenerous, as well as unfair; for it had not yet transpired—nor has it to this day—*what* Selina and her friends talked about.

The Argonauts

The advent of strangers, of whatever sort, into our circle, had always been a matter of grave dubiety and suspicion; indeed, it was generally a signal for retreat into caves and fastnesses of the earth, into unthreaded copses or remote outlying cowsheds, whence we were only to be extricated by wily nursemaids, rendered familiar by experience with our secret runs and refuges. It was not surprising therefore that the heroes of classic legend, when first we made their acquaintance, failed to win our entire sympathy at once. "Confidence," says somebody, "is a plant of slow growth"; and these stately dark-haired demi-gods, with names hard to master and strange accoutrements, had to win a citadel already strongly garrisoned with a more familiar soldiery. Their chill foreign goddesses had no such direct appeal for us as the mocking malicious fairies and witches of the North; we missed the pleasant alliance of the animal—the fox who spread the bushiest of tails to convey us to the enchanted castle, the frog in the well, the raven who croaked advice from the tree; and—to Harold especially—it seemed entirely wrong that the hero should ever be other than the youngest brother of three. This belief, indeed, in the special fortune that ever awaited the youngest brother, as such—the "Borough-English" of Faery—had been of baleful effect on Harold, producing a certain self-conceit and perkiness that called for physical correction. But even in our admonishment we were on his side; and as we distrustfully eyed these new arrivals, old Saturn himself seemed something of a parvenu.

Even strangers, however, we may develop into sworn comrades; and these gay swordsmen, after all, were of the right stuff. Perseus, with his cap of darkness and his wonderful sandals, was not long in winging his way to our hearts; Apollo knocked at Admetus' gate in something of the right fairy fashion; Psyche brought with her an orthodox palace of magic, as well as helpful birds and friendly ants. Ulysses, with his captivating shifts and strategies, broke down the final barrier, and henceforth the band was adopted and admitted into our freemasonry.

I had been engaged in chasing Farmer Larkin's calves—his special pride—round the field, just to show the man we hadn't forgotten him, and was returning through the kitchen-garden with a conscience at peace with all men, when I happened upon Edward, grubbing for worms in the dung-heap. Edward put his worms into his hat, and we strolled along together, discussing high matters of state. As we reached the tool-shed, strange noises arrested our steps; looking in, we perceived Harold, alone, rapt, absorbed, immersed in the special game of the moment. He was squatting in an old pig-trough that had been brought in to be tinkered; and as he rhapsodised, anon he waved a shovel over his head, anon dug it into the ground with the action of those who would urge Canadian canoes. Edward strode in upon him.

"What rot are you playing at now?" he demanded sternly.

Harold flushed up, but stuck to his pig-trough like a man. "I'm Jason," he replied, defiantly; "and this is the *Argo*. The other fellows are here too, only you can't see them; and we're just going through the Hellespont, so don't you come bothering." And once more he plied the wine-dark sea.

Edward kicked the pig-trough contemptuously.

"Pretty sort of *Argo* you've got!" said he.

Harold began to get annoyed. "I can't help it," he replied. "It's the best sort of *Argo* I can manage, and it's all right if you only pretend enough; but *you* never could pretend one bit."

Edward reflected. "Look here," he said presently; "why shouldn't we get hold of Farmer Larkin's boat, and go right away up the river in a real *Argo*, and look for Medea, and the Golden Fleece, and everything? And I'll tell you what, I don't mind your being Jason, as you thought of it first."

Harold tumbled out of the trough in the excess of his emotion. "But we aren't allowed to go on the water by ourselves," he cried.

"No," said Edward, with fine scorn: "we aren't allowed; and Jason wasn't allowed either, I daresay—but he *went!*"

Harold's protest had been merely conventional: he only wanted to be convinced by sound argument. The next question was, How about the girls? Selina was distinctly handy in a boat: the difficulty about her was, that if she disapproved of the expedition—and, morally considered, it was not exactly a Pilgrim's Progress—she might go and tell; she having just reached that disagreeable age when one begins to develop a conscience. Charlotte, for her part, had a habit of day-dreams, and was as likely as not to fall overboard in one of her rapt musings. To be sure, she would dissolve in tears when she found herself left out; but even that was better than a watery tomb. In fine, the public voice—and rightly, perhaps—was against the admission of the skirted animal: spite the precedent of Atalanta, who was one of the original crew.

"And now," said Edward, "who's to ask Farmer Larkin? I can't; last time I saw him he said when he caught me again he'd smack my head. *You'll* have to."

I hesitated, for good reasons. "You know those precious calves of his?" I began.

Edward understood at once. "All right," he said; "then we won't ask him at all. It doesn't much matter. He'd only be annoyed, and that would be a pity. Now let's set off."

We made our way down to the stream, and captured the farmer's boat without let or hindrance, the enemy being engaged in the hayfields. This "river," so called, could never be discovered by us in any atlas; indeed our *Argo* could hardly turn in it without risk of shipwreck. But to us 'twas Orinoco, and the cities of the world dotted its shores. We put the *Argo*'s head upstream, since that led away from the Larkin province; Harold was faithfully permitted to be Jason, and we shared the rest of the heroes among us. Then launching forth from Thessaly, we threaded the Hellespont with shouts, breathlessly dodged the Clashing Rocks, and coasted under the lee of the Siren-haunted isles. Lemnos was fringed with meadow-sweet, dog-roses dotted the Mysian shore, and the cheery call of the haymaking folk sounded along the coast of Thrace.

After some hour or two's seafaring, the prow of the *Argo* embedded itself in the mud of a landing-place, plashy with the tread of cows and giving on to a lane that led towards the smoke of human habitations. Edward jumped ashore, alert for exploration, and strode off without waiting to see if we followed; but I lingered behind, having caught sight of a moss-grown water-gate hard by, leading into a garden that from the brooding quiet lapping it round, appeared to portend magical possibilities.

Indeed the very air within seemed stiller, as we circumspectly passed through the gate; and Harold hung back shamefaced, as if we were crossing the threshold of some private chamber, and ghosts of old days were hustling past us. Flowers there were, everywhere; but they drooped and sprawled in an overgrowth hinting at indifference; the scent of heliotrope possessed the place, as if actually hung in solid festoons from tall untrimmed hedge to hedge. No basket-chairs, shawls, or novels dotted the lawn with colour; and on the garden-front of the house behind, the blinds were mostly drawn. A grey old sun-dial dominated the central sward, and we moved towards it instinctively, as the most human thing visible. An antique motto ran round it, and with eyes and fingers we struggled at the decipherment.

"*Time: Tryeth: Trothe:*" spelt out Harold at last. "I wonder what that means?"

I could not enlighten him, nor meet his further questions as to the inner mechanism of the thing, and where you wound it up.

I had seen these instruments before, of course, but had never fully understood their manner of working.

We were still puzzling our heads over the contrivance, when I became aware that Medea herself was moving down the path from the house. Dark-haired, supple, of a figure lightly poised and swayed, but pale and listless—I knew her at once, and having come out to find her, naturally felt no surprise at all. But Harold, who was trying to climb on the top of the sun-dial, having a cat-like fondness for the summit of things, started and fell prone, barking his chin and filling the pleasance with lamentation.

Medea skimmed the ground swallow-like, and in a moment was on her knees comforting him—wiping the dirt out of his chin with her own dainty handkerchief—and vocal with soft murmur of consolation.

"You needn't take on so about him," I observed, politely. "He'll cry for just one minute, and then he'll be all right."

My estimate was justified. At the end of his regulation time Harold stopped crying suddenly, like a clock that had struck its hour; and with a serene and cheerful countenance wriggled out of Medea's embrace, and ran for a stone to throw at an intrusive blackbird.

"O you boys!" cried Medea, throwing wide her arms with abandonment. "Where have you dropped from? How dirty you are! I've been shut up here for a thousand years, and all that time I've never seen anyone under a hundred and fifty! Let's play at something, at once!"

"Rounders is a good game," I suggested. "Girls can play at rounders. And we could serve up to the sun-dial here. But you want a bat and a ball, and some more people."

She struck her hands together tragically. "I haven't a bat," she cried, "or a ball, or more people, or anything sensible whatever. Never mind; let's play at hide-and-seek in the kitchen-garden. And we'll race there, up to that walnut-tree; I haven't run for a century!"

She was so easy a victor, nevertheless, that I began to doubt, as I panted behind, whether she had not exaggerated her age by a year or two. She flung herself into hide-and-seek with all the gusto and abandonment of the true artist, and as she flitted away and reappeared, flushed and laughing divinely, the pale witch-maiden seemed to fall away from her, and she moved rather as that other girl I had read about, snatched from fields of daffodil to reign in shadow below, yet permitted once again to visit earth, and light, and the frank, caressing air.

Tired at last, we strolled back to the old sun-dial, and Harold, who never relinquished a problem unsolved, began afresh, rubbing his finger along the faint incisions, "*Time tryeth trothe.* Please, I want to know what that means."

Medea's face drooped low over the sun-dial, till it was almost hidden in her fingers. "That's what I'm here for," she said presently, in quite a changed, low voice. "They shut me up here—they think I'll forget—but I never will—never, never! And he, too—but I don't know—it is so long—I don't know!"

Her face was quite hidden now. There was silence again in the old garden. I felt clumsily helpless and awkward; beyond a vague idea of kicking Harold, nothing remedial seemed to suggest itself.

None of us had noticed the approach of another she-creature— one of the angular and rigid class—how different from our dear comrade! The years Medea had claimed might well have belonged to her; she wore mittens, too—a trick I detested in woman. "Lucy!" she said, sharply, in a tone with *aunt* writ large over it; and Medea started up guiltily.

"You've been crying," said the newcomer, grimly regarding her through spectacles. "And pray who are these exceedingly dirty little boys?"

"Friends of mine, aunt," said Medea, promptly, with forced

cheerfulness. "I—I've known them a long time. I asked them to come."

The aunt sniffed suspiciously. "You must come indoors, dear," she said, "and lie down. The sun will give you a headache. And you little boys had better run away home to your tea. Remember, you should not come to pay visits without your nursemaid."

Harold had been tugging nervously at my jacket for some time, and I only waited till Medea turned and kissed a white hand to us as she was led away. Then I ran. We gained the boat in safety; and "What an old dragon!" said Harold.

"Wasn't she a beast!" I replied. "Fancy the sun giving anyone a headache! But Medea was a real brick. Couldn't we carry her off?"

"We could if Edward was here," said Harold, confidently.

The question was, What had become of that defaulting hero? We were not left long in doubt. First, there came down the lane the shrill and wrathful clamour of a female tongue, then Edward, running his best, and then an excited woman hard on his heel. Edward tumbled into the bottom of the boat, gasping, "Shove her off!" And shove her off we did, mightily, while the dame abused us from the bank in the self-same accents in which Alfred hurled defiance at the marauding Dane.

"That was just like a bit out of *Westward Ho!*" I remarked approvingly, as we sculled down the stream. "But what had you been doing to her?"

"Hadn't been doing anything," panted Edward, still breathless. "I went up into the village and explored, and it was a very nice one, and the people were very polite. And there was a blacksmith's forge there, and they were shoeing horses, and the hoofs fizzled and smoked, and smelt so jolly! I stayed there quite a long time. Then I got thirsty, so I asked that old woman for some water, and while she was getting it her cat came out of the cottage, and looked at me in a nasty sort of way, and said something I didn't like. So I went up to it just to—to teach it manners, and somehow or other, next minute it was up an apple-tree, spitting, and I was running down the lane with that old thing after me."

Edward was so full of his personal injuries that there was no interesting him in Medea at all. Moreover, the evening was closing in, and it was evident that this cutting-out expedition must be kept for another day. As we neared home, it gradually occurred to us that perhaps the greatest danger was yet to come; for the farmer must have missed his boat ere now, and would probably be lying in wait for us near the landing-place. There was no other spot admitting of debarcation on the home side; if we got out on the other, and made for the bridge, we should certainly be seen and cut off. Then it was that I blessed my stars that our elder brother was with us that day—he might be little good at pretending, but in grappling with the stern facts of life he had no equal. Enjoining silence, he waited till we were but a little way from the fated landing-place, and then brought us in to the opposite bank. We scrambled out noiselessly, and—the gathering darkness favouring us—crouched behind a willow, while Edward pushed off the empty boat with his foot. The old *Argo*, borne down by the gentle current, slid and grazed along the rushy bank; and when she came opposite the suspected ambush, a stream of imprecation told us that our precaution had not been wasted. We wondered, as we listened, where Farmer Larkin, who was bucolically bred and reared, had acquired such range and wealth of vocabulary. Fully realising at last that his boat was derelict, abandoned, at the mercy of wind and wave—as well as out of his reach—he strode away to the bridge, about a quarter of a mile further down; and as soon as we heard his boots clumping on the planks, we nipped out, recovered the craft, pulled across, and made the faithful vessel fast to her proper moorings. Edward was anxious to wait and exchange courtesies and compliments with the disappointed farmer, when he should confront us on the opposite bank; but wiser counsels prevailed. It was possible that the piracy was not yet laid at our particular door: Ulysses, I reminded him, had reason to regret a similar act of bravado, and—were he here— would certainly advise a timely retreat. Edward held but a low opinion of me as a counsellor; but he had a very solid respect for Ulysses.

The Roman Road

All the roads of our neighbourhood were cheerful and friendly, having each of them pleasant qualities of their own; but this one seemed different from the others in its masterful suggestion of a serious purpose, speeding you along with a strange uplifting of the heart. The others tempted chiefly with their treasures of hedge and ditch; the rapt surprise of the first lords-and-ladies, the rustle of a field-mouse, splash of a frog; while cool noses of brother-beasts were pushed at you through gate or gap. A loiterer you had need to be, did you choose one of them—so many were the tiny hands thrust out to detain you, from this side and that. But this other was of a sterner sort, and even in its shedding off of bank and hedgerow as it marched straight and full for the open downs, it seemed to declare its contempt for adventitious trappings to catch the shallow-pated. When the sense of injustice or disappointment was heavy on me, and things were very black within, as on this particular day, the road of character was my choice for that solitary ramble, when I turned my back for an afternoon on a world that had unaccountably declared itself against me.

"The Knights' Road," we children had named it, from a sort of feeling that, if from any quarter at all, it would be down this track we might someday see Lancelot and his peers come pacing on their great war-horses—supposing that any of the stout band still survived, in nooks and unexplored places. Grown-up people sometimes spoke of it as the "Pilgrims' Way"; but I didn't know much about pilgrims—except Walter in the Horselberg story. Him I sometimes saw, breaking with haggard eyes out of yonder copse, and calling to the pilgrims as they hurried along on their desperate march to the Holy City, where peace and pardon were awaiting them. "All roads lead to Rome," I had once heard somebody say; and I had taken the remark very seriously, of course, and puzzled over it many days. There must have been some mistake, I concluded at last; but of one road at least I intuitively felt it to be true. And my belief was clinched by something that fell from Miss Smedley during a history lesson, about a strange road that ran right down the middle of England till it reached the coast, and then began again in France, just opposite, and so on undeviating, through city and vineyard, right from the misty Highlands to the Eternal City. Uncorroborated, any statement of Miss Smedley's usually fell on incredulous ears; but here, with the road itself in evidence, she seemed, once, in a way, to have strayed into truth.

Rome! It was fascinating to think that it lay at the other end of this white ribbon that rolled itself off from my feet over the distant downs. I was not quite so uninstructed as to imagine I could reach it that afternoon; but someday, I thought, if things went on being as unpleasant as they were now—someday, when Aunt Eliza had gone on a visit—we would see.

I tried to imagine what it would be like when I got there. The Coliseum I knew, of course, from a woodcut in the history-book: so to begin with I plumped that down in the middle. The rest had to be patched up from the little grey market-town where twice a year we went to have our hair cut; hence, in the result, Vespasian's amphitheatre was approached by muddy little streets, wherein the Red Lion and the Blue Boar, with Somebody's Entire along their front, and "Commercial Room" on their windows; the doctor's house, of substantial red-brick; and the façade of the New Wesleyan Chapel, which we thought very fine, were the chief architectural ornaments: while the Roman populace pottered about in smocks and corduroys, twisting the tails of Roman calves and inviting each other to beer in musical Wessex. From Rome I drifted on to other cities, dimly heard of—Damascus, Brighton (Aunt Eliza's ideal), Athens, and Glasgow, whose glories the gardener sang; but there was a certain sameness in my conception of all of them: that Wesleyan chapel would keep cropping up everywhere. It was easier to go a-building among those dream-cities where no limitations were imposed, and one was sole architect, with a free hand. Down a delectable street of cloud-built palaces I was mentally pacing, when I happened upon the Artist.

He was seated at work by the roadside, at a point whence the cool large spaces of the downs, juniper-studded, swept grandly westwards. His attributes proclaimed him of the artist tribe: besides, he wore knickerbockers like myself—a garb confined, I was aware, to boys and artists. I knew I was not to bother him with questions, nor look over his shoulder and breathe in his ear—they didn't like it, this genus irritabile; but there was nothing about staring in my code of instructions, the point having somehow been overlooked: so, squatting down on the grass, I devoted myself to a passionate absorbing of every detail. At the end of five minutes there was not a button on him that I could not have passed an examination in; and the wearer himself of that homespun suit was probably less familiar with its pattern and texture than I was. Once he looked up, nodded, half held out his tobacco pouch—mechanically, as it were—then, returning it to his pocket, resumed his work, and I my mental photography.

After another five minutes or so had passed he remarked, without looking my way: "Fine afternoon we're having: going far today?"

"No, I'm not going any farther than this," I replied; "I *was* thinking of going on to Rome: but I've put it off."

"Pleasant place, Rome," he murmured; "you'll like it." It was some minutes later that he added: "But I wouldn't go just now, if I were you—too jolly hot."

"*You* haven't been to Rome, have you?" I inquired.

"Rather," he replied, briefly; "I live there."

This was too much, and my jaw dropped as I struggled to grasp the fact that I was sitting there talking to a fellow who lived in Rome. Speech was out of the question: besides, I had other things to do. Ten solid minutes had I already spent in an examination of him as a mere stranger and artist; and now the whole thing had to be done over again, from the changed point of view. So I began afresh, at the crown of his soft hat, and worked down to his solid British shoes, this time investing everything with the new Roman halo; and at last I managed to get out: "But you don't really live there, do you?" never doubting the fact, but wanting to hear it repeated.

"Well," he said, good-naturedly overlooking the slight rudeness of my query, "I live there as much as I live anywhere—about half the year sometimes. I've got a sort of a shanty there. You must come and see it someday."

"But do you live anywhere else as well?" I went on, feeling the forbidden tide of questions surging up within me.

"O yes, all over the place," was his vague reply. "And I've got a diggings somewhere off Piccadilly."

"Where's that?" I inquired.

"Where's what?" said he. "Oh, Piccadilly! It's in London."

"Have you a large garden?" I asked; "and how many pigs have you got?"

"I've no garden at all," he replied, sadly, "and they don't allow me to keep pigs, though I'd like to, awfully. It's very hard."

"But what do you do all day, then," I cried, "and where do you go and play, without any garden, or pigs, or things?"

"When I want to play," he said, gravely, "I have to go and play in the street; but it's poor fun, I grant you. There's a goat, though, not far off, and sometimes I talk to him when I'm feeling lonely; but he's very proud."

"Goats *are* proud," I admitted. "There's one lives near here, and if you say anything to him at all, he hits you in the wind with his head. You know what it feels like when a fellow hits you in the wind?"

"I do, well," he replied, in a tone of proper melancholy, and painted on.

"And have you been to any other places," I began again, presently, "besides Rome and Piccy-what's-his-name?"

"Heaps," he said. "I'm a sort of Ulysses—seen men and cities, you know. In fact, about the only place I never got to was the Fortunate Island."

I began to like this man. He answered your questions briefly and to the point, and never tried to be funny. I felt I could be confidential with him.

"Wouldn't you like," I inquired, "to find a city without any people in it at all?"

He looked puzzled. "I'm afraid I don't quite understand," said he.

"I mean," I went on eagerly, "a city where you walk in at the gates, and the shops are all full of beautiful things, and the houses furnished as grand as can be, and there isn't anybody there whatever! And you go into the shops, and take anything you want—chocolates and magic lanterns and injirubber balls—and there's nothing to pay; and you choose your own house and live there and do just as you like, and never go to bed unless you want to!"

The artist laid down his brush. "That *would* be a nice city," he said. "Better than Rome. You can't do that sort of thing in

Rome—or in Piccadilly either. But I fear it's one of the places I've never been to."

"And you'd ask your friends," I went on, warming to my subject—"only those you really like, of course—and they'd each have a house to themselves—there'd be lots of houses—and no relations at all, unless they promised they'd be pleasant, and if they weren't they'd have to go."

"So you wouldn't have any relations?" said the artist. "Well, perhaps you're right. We have tastes in common, I see."

"I'd have Harold," I said, reflectively, "and Charlotte. They'd like it awfully. The others are getting too old. Oh, and Martha—I'd have Martha, to cook and wash up and do things. You'd like Martha. She's ever so much nicer than Aunt Eliza. She's my idea of a real lady."

"Then I'm sure I should like her," he replied, heartily, "and when I come to—what do you call this city of yours? Nephelo—something, did you say?"

"I—I don't know," I replied, timidly. "I'm afraid it hasn't got a name—yet."

The artist gazed out over the downs. "'The poet says, dear city of Cecrops,'" he said, softly, to himself, "'and wilt not thou say, dear city of Zeus?' That's from Marcus Aurelius," he went on, turning again to his work. "You don't know him, I suppose; you will someday."

"Who's he?" I inquired.

"Oh, just another fellow who lived in Rome," he replied, dabbing away.

"O dear!" I cried, disconsolately. "What a lot of people seem to live at Rome, and I've never even been there! But I think I'd like *my* city best."

"And so would I," he replied with unction. "But Marcus Aurelius wouldn't, you know."

"Then we won't invite him," I said, "will we?"

"*I* won't if you won't," said he. And that point being settled, we were silent for a while.

"Do you know," he said, presently, "I've met one or two fellows from time to time who have been to a city like yours—perhaps it was the same one. They won't talk much about it—only broken hints, now and then; but they've been there sure enough. They don't seem to care about anything in particular—and everything's the same to them, rough or smooth; and sooner or later they slip off and disappear; and you never see them again. Gone back, I suppose."

"Of course," said I. "Don't see what they ever came away for; *I* wouldn't—to be told you've broken things when you haven't, and stopped having tea with the servants in the kitchen, and not allowed to have a dog to sleep with you. But *I've* known people, too, who've gone there."

The artist stared, but without incivility.

"Well, there's Lancelot," I went on. "The book says he died, but it never seemed to read right, somehow. He just went away, like Arthur. And Crusoe, when he got tired of wearing clothes and being respectable. And all the nice men in the stones who don't marry the Princess, 'cos only one man ever gets married in a book, you know. They'll be there!"

"And the men who never come off," he said, "who try like the rest, but get knocked out, or somehow miss—or break down or get bowled over in the melee—and get no Princess, nor even a second-class kingdom—some of them'll be there, I hope?"

"Yes, if you like," I replied, not quite understanding him; "if they're friends of yours, we'll ask 'em, of course."

"What a time we shall have!" said the artist, reflectively; "and how shocked old Marcus Aurelius will be!"

The shadows had lengthened uncannily, a tide of golden haze was flooding the grey-green surface of the downs, and the artist began to put his traps together, preparatory to a move. I felt very low; we would have to part, it seemed, just as we were getting on so well together. Then he stood up, and he was very straight and tall, and the sunset was in his hair and beard as he stood there, high over me. He took my hand like an equal. "I've enjoyed our conversation very much," he said. "That was an interesting subject you started, and we haven't half exhausted it. We shall meet again, I hope."

"Of course we shall," I replied, surprised that there should be any doubt about it.

"In Rome, perhaps?" said he.

"Yes, in Rome," I answered, "or Piccy-the-other-place, or somewhere."

"Or else," said he, "in that other city—when we've found the way there. And I'll look out for you, and you'll sing out as soon as you see me. And we'll go down the street arm-in-arm, and into all the shops, and then I'll choose my house, and you'll choose your house, and we'll live there like princes and good fellows."

"Oh, but you'll stay in my house, won't you?" I cried; "wouldn't ask everybody; but I'll ask *you*."

He affected to consider a moment; then "Right!" he said: "I believe you mean it, and I *will* come and stay with you. I won't go to anybody else, if they ask me ever so much. And I'll stay quite a long time, too, and I won't be any trouble."

Upon this compact we parted, and I went down-heartedly from the man who understood me, back to the house where I never could do anything right. How was it that everything seemed natural and sensible to him, which these uncles, vicars, and other grown-up men took for the merest tomfoolery? Well, he would explain this, and many another things, when we met again. The Knights' Road! How it always brought consolation! Was he possibly one of those vanished knights I had been looking for so long? Perhaps he would be in armour next time—why not? He would look well in armour, I thought. And I would take care to get there first, and see the sunlight flash and play on his helmet and shield, as he rode up the High Street of the Golden City.

Meantime, there only remained the finding it—an easy matter.

The Secret Drawer

It must surely have served as a boudoir for the ladies of old time, this little used, rarely entered chamber where the neglected old bureau stood. There was something very feminine in the faint hues of its faded brocades, in the rose and blue of such bits of china as yet remained, and in the delicate old-world fragrance of pot-pourri from the great bowl—blue and white, with funny holes in its cover—that stood on the bureau's flat top. Modern aunts disdained this out-of-the-way, back-water, upstairs room, preferring to do their accounts and grapple with their correspondence in some central position more in the whirl of things, whence one eye could be kept on the carriage-drive, while the other was alert for malingering servants and marauding children. Those aunts of a former generation—I sometimes felt—would have suited our habits better. But even by us children, to whom few places were private or reserved, the room was visited but rarely. To be sure, there was nothing particular in it that we coveted or required— only a few spindle-legged gilt-backed chairs; an old harp, on which, so the legend ran, Aunt Eliza herself used once to play, in years remote, unchronicled; a corner-cupboard with a few pieces of china; and the old bureau. But one other thing the room possessed, peculiar to itself; a certain sense of privacy—a power of making the intruder feel that he *was* intruding—perhaps even a faculty of hinting that someone might have been sitting on those chairs, writing at the bureau, or fingering the china, just a second before one entered. No such violent word as "haunted" could possibly apply to this pleasant old-fashioned chamber, which indeed we all rather liked; but there was no doubt it was reserved and stand-offish, keeping itself to itself.

Uncle Thomas was the first to draw my attention to the possibilities of the old bureau. He was pottering about the house one afternoon, having ordered me to keep at his heels for company— he was a man who hated to be left one minute alone—when his eye fell on it. "H'm! Sheraton!" he remarked. (He had a smattering of most things, this uncle, especially the vocabularies.) Then he let down the flap, and examined the empty pigeon-holes and dusty panelling. "Fine bit of inlay," he went on: "good work, all of it. I know the sort. There's a secret drawer in there somewhere." Then, as I breathlessly drew near, he suddenly exclaimed: "By Jove, I do want to smoke!" and wheeling round he abruptly fled for the garden, leaving me with the cup dashed from my lips. What a strange thing, I mused, was this smoking, that takes a man suddenly, be he in the court, the camp, or the grove, grips him like an Afreet, and whirls him off to do its imperious behests! Would it be even so with myself, I wondered, in those unknown grown-up years to come?

But I had no time to waste in vain speculations. My whole being was still vibrating to those magic syllables, "secret drawer"; and that particular chord had been touched that never fails to thrill responsive to such words as *cave*, *trap-door*, *sliding-panel*, *bullion*, *ingots*, or *Spanish dollars*. For, besides its own special bliss, who ever heard of a secret drawer with nothing in it? And oh, I did want money so badly! I mentally ran over the list of demands which were pressing me the most imperiously.

First, there was the pipe I wanted to give George Jannaway. George, who was Martha's young man, was a shepherd, and a great ally of mine; and the last fair he was at, when he bought his sweetheart fairings, as a right-minded shepherd should, he had purchased a lovely snake expressly for me; one of the wooden sort, with joints, waggling deliciously in the hand; with yellow spots on a green ground, sticky and strong-smelling, as a fresh-painted snake ought to be; and with a red-flannel tongue, pasted cunningly into its jaws. I loved it much, and took it to bed with me every night, till what time its spinal cord was loosed and it fell apart, and went the way of all mortal joys. I thought it so nice of George to think of me at the fair, and that's why I wanted to give him a pipe. When the young year was chill and lambing-time was on, George inhabited a little wooden house on wheels, far out on the wintry downs, and saw no faces but such as were sheepish and woolly and mute; and when he and Martha were married, she was going to carry his dinner out to him every day, two miles; and after it, perhaps he would smoke my pipe. It seemed an idyllic sort of existence, for both the parties concerned; but a pipe of quality, a pipe fitted to be part of a life such as this, could not be procured (so Martha informed me) for a less sum than eighteen pence. And meantime——!

Then there was the fourpence I owed Edward; not that he was bothering me for it, but I knew he was in need of it himself, to pay back Selina, who wanted it to make up a sum of two shillings, to buy Harold an ironclad for his approaching birthday—H.M.S. *Majestic*, now lying uselessly careened in the toyshop window, just when her country had such sore need of her.

And then there was that boy in the village who had caught a young squirrel, and I had never yet possessed one, and he wanted a shilling for it, but I knew that for ninepence in cash—but what was the good of these sorry, threadbare reflections? I had wants enough to exhaust any possible find of bullion, even if it amounted to half a sovereign. My only hope now lay in the magic drawer, and here I was standing and letting the precious minutes slip by. Whether "findings" of this sort could, morally speaking, be considered "keepings," was a point that did not occur to me.

The room was very still as I approached the bureau—possessed, it seemed to be, by a sort of hush of expectation. The faint odour of orris-root that floated forth as I let down the flap, seemed to identify itself with the yellows and browns of the old wood, till hue and scent were of one quality and interchangeable.

Even so, ere this, the pot-pourri had mixed itself with the tints of the old brocade, and brocade and pot-pourri had long been one.

With expectant fingers I explored the empty pigeon-holes and sounded the depths of the softly-sliding drawers. No books that I knew of gave any general recipe for a quest like this; but the glory, should I succeed unaided, would be all the greater.

To him who is destined to arrive, the fates never fail to afford, on the way, their small encouragements; in less than two minutes, I had come across a rusty button-hook. This was truly magnificent. In the nursery there existed, indeed, a general button-hook, common to either sex; but none of us possessed a private and special button-hook, to lend or refuse as suited the high humour of the moment. I pocketed the treasure carefully and proceeded. At the back of another drawer, three old foreign stamps told me I was surely on the high road to fortune.

Following on these bracing incentives, came a dull blank period of unrewarded search. In vain I removed all the drawers and felt over every inch of the smooth surfaces, from front to back. Never a knob, spring or projection met the thrilling finger-tips; unyielding the old bureau stood, stoutly guarding its secret, if secret it really had. I began to grow weary and disheartened. This was not the first time that Uncle Thomas had proved shallow, uninformed, a guide into blind alleys where the echoes mocked you. Was it any good persisting longer? Was anything any good whatever? In my mind I began to review past disappointments, and life seemed one long record of failure and of non-arrival. Disillusioned and depressed, I left my work and went to the window. The light was ebbing from the room, and outside seemed to be collecting itself on the horizon for its concentrated effort of sunset. Far down the garden, Uncle Thomas was holding Edward in the air reversed, and smacking him. Edward, gurgling hysterically, was striking blind fists in the direction where he judged his uncle's stomach should rightly be; the contents of his pockets—a motley show—were strewing the lawn. Somehow, though I had been put through a similar performance an hour or two ago, myself, it all seemed very far away and cut off from me.

Westwards the clouds were massing themselves in a low violet bank; below them, to north and south, as far round as eye could reach, a narrow streak of gold ran out and stretched away, straight along the horizon. Somewhere very far off, a horn was being blown, clear and thin; it sounded like the golden streak grown audible, while the gold seemed the visible sound. It pricked my ebbing courage, this blended strain of music and colour, and I turned for a last effort; and Fortune thereupon, as if half-ashamed of the unworthy game she had been playing with me, relented, opening her clenched fist. Hardly had I put my hand once more to the obdurate wood, when with a sort of small sigh, almost a sob—as it were—of relief, the secret drawer sprang open.

I drew it out and carried it to the window, to examine it in the failing light. Too hopeless had I gradually grown, in my dispiriting search, to expect very much; and yet at a glance I saw that my basket of glass lay in fragments at my feet. No ingots or dollars were here, to crown me the little Monte Cristo of a week. Outside, the distant horn had ceased its gnat-song, the gold was paling to primrose, and everything was lonely and still. Within, my confident little castles were tumbling down like card-houses, leaving me stripped of estate, both real and personal, and dominated by the depressing reaction.

And yet—as I looked again at the small collection that lay within that drawer of disillusions, some warmth crept back to my heart as I recognised that a kindred spirit to my own had been at the making of it. Two tarnished gilt buttons—naval, apparently—a portrait of a monarch unknown to me, cut from some antique print and deftly coloured by hand in just my own bold style of brush-work—some foreign copper coins, thicker and clumsier of make than those I hoarded myself—and a list of birds' eggs, with names of the places where they had been found. Also, a ferret's muzzle, and a twist of tarry string, still faintly aromatic. It was a real boy's hoard, then, that I had happened upon. He too had found out the secret drawer, this happy starred young person; and here he had stowed away his treasures, one by one, and had cherished them secretly awhile; and then—what? Well, one would never know now the reason why these priceless possessions still lay here unreclaimed; but across the void stretch of years I seemed to touch hands a moment with my little comrade of seasons long since dead.

I restored the drawer, with its contents, to the trusty bureau, and heard the spring click with a certain satisfaction. Some other boy, perhaps, would someday release that spring again. I trusted he would be equally appreciative. As I opened the door to go, I could hear from the nursery at the end of the passage shouts and yells, telling that the hunt was up. Bears, apparently, or bandits, were on the evening bill of fare, judging by the character of the noises. In another minute I would be in the thick of it, in all the warmth and light and laughter. And yet—what a long way off it all seemed, both in space and time, to me yet lingering on the threshold of that old-world chamber!

"Exit Tyrannus"

The eventful day had arrived at last, the day which, when first named, had seemed—like all golden dates that promise anything definite—so immeasurably remote. When it was first announced, a fortnight before, that Miss Smedley was really going, the resultant ecstasies had occupied a full week, during which we blindly revelled in the contemplation and discussion of her past tyrannies, crimes, malignities; in recalling to each other this or that insult, dishonour, or physical assault, sullenly endured at a time when deliverance was not even a small star on the horizon; and in mapping out the golden days to come, with special new troubles of their own, no doubt, since this is but a work-a-day world, but at least free from one familiar scourge. The time that remained had been taken up by the planning of practical expressions of the popular sentiment. Under Edward's masterly direction, arrangements had been made for a flag to be run up over the hen-house at the very moment when the fly, with Miss Smedley's boxes on top and the grim oppressor herself inside, began to move off down the drive. Three brass cannons, set on the brow of the sunk-fence, were to proclaim our deathless sentiments in the ears of the retreating foe: the dogs were to wear ribbons, and later—but this depended on our powers of evasiveness and dissimulation—there might be a small bonfire, with a cracker or two, if the public funds could bear the unwonted strain.

I was awakened by Harold digging me in the ribs, and "She's going today!" was the morning hymn that scattered the clouds of sleep. Strange to say, it was with no corresponding jubilation of spirits that I slowly realised the momentous fact. Indeed, as I dressed, a dull disagreeable feeling that I could not define grew within me—something like a physical bruise. Harold was evidently feeling it too, for after repeating "She's going today!" in a tone more befitting the Litany, he looked hard in my face for direction as to how the situation was to be taken. But I crossly bade him look sharp and say his prayers and not bother me. What could this gloom portend, that on a day of days like the present seemed to hang my heavens with black?

Down at last and out in the sun, we found Edward before us, swinging on a gate, and chanting a farm-yard ditty in which all the beasts appear in due order, jargoning in their several tongues, and every verse begins with the couplet—

Now, my lads, come with me,
Out in the morning early!

The fateful exodus of the day had evidently slipped his memory entirely. I touched him on the shoulder. "She's going today!" I said. Edward's carol subsided like a water-tap turned off. "So she is!" he replied, and got down at once off the gate: and we returned to the house without another word.

At breakfast Miss Smedley behaved in a most mean and uncalled-for manner. The right divine of governesses to govern wrong includes no right to cry. In thus usurping the prerogative of their victims, they ignore the rules of the ring, and hit below the belt. Charlotte was crying, of course; but that counted for nothing. Charlotte even cried when the pigs' noses were ringed in due season; thereby evoking the cheery contempt of the operators, who asserted they liked it, and doubtless knew. But when the cloud-compeller, her bolts laid aside, resorted to tears, mutinous humanity had a right to feel aggrieved, and placed in a false and difficult position. What would the Romans have done, supposing Hannibal had cried? History has not even considered the possibility. Rules and precedents should be strictly observed on both sides; when they are violated, the other party is justified in feeling injured.

There were no lessons that morning, naturally—another grievance! The fitness of things required that we should have struggled to the last in a confused medley of moods and tenses, and parted forever, flushed with hatred, over the dismembered corpse of the multiplication table. But this thing was not to be; and I was free to stroll by myself through the garden, and combat, as best I might, this growing feeling of depression. It was a wrong system altogether, I thought, this going of people one had got used to. Things ought always to continue as they had been. Change there must be, of course; pigs, for instance, came and went with disturbing frequency—

Fired their ringing shot and passed,
Hotly charged and sank at last—

but Nature had ordered it so, and in requital had provided for rapid successors. Did you come to love a pig, and he was taken from you, grief was quickly assuaged in the delight of selection from the new litter. But now, when it was no question of a peerless pig, but only of a governess, Nature seemed helpless, and the future held no litter of oblivion. Things might be better, or they might be worse, but they would never be the same; and the innate conservatism of youth asks neither poverty nor riches, but only immunity from change.

Edward slouched up alongside of me presently, with a hang-dog look on him, as if he had been caught stealing jam. "What a lark it'll be when she's really gone!" he observed, with a swagger obviously assumed.

"Grand fun!" I replied, dolorously; and conversation flagged.

We reached the hen-house, and contemplated the banner of freedom lying ready to flaunt the breezes at the supreme moment.

"Shall you run it up," I asked, "when the fly starts, or—or wait a little till it's out of sight?"

Edward gazed around him dubiously. "We're going to have some rain, I think," he said; "and—and it's a new flag. It would be a pity to spoil it. P'raps I won't run it up at all."

Harold came round the corner like a bison pursued by Indians. "I've polished up the cannons," he cried, "and they look grand! Mayn't I load 'em now?"

"You leave 'em alone," said Edward, severely, "or you'll be blowing yourself up" (consideration for others was not usually Edward's strong point). "Don't touch the gunpowder till you're told, or you'll get your head smacked."

Harold fell behind, limp, squashed, obedient. "She wants me to write to her," he began, presently. "Says she doesn't mind the spelling, if I'll only write. Fancy her saying that!"

"Oh, shut up, will you?" said Edward, savagely; and once more we were silent, with only our thoughts for sorry company.

"Let's go off to the copse," I suggested timidly, feeling that something had to be done to relieve the tension, "and cut more new bows and arrows."

"She gave me a knife my last birthday," said Edward, moodily, never budging. "It wasn't much of a knife—but I wish I hadn't lost it."

"When my legs used to ache," I said, "she sat up half the night, rubbing stuff on them. I forgot all about that till this morning."

"There's the fly!" cried Harold suddenly. "I can hear it scrunching on the gravel."

Then for the first time we turned and stared one another in the face.

* * * * *

The fly and its contents had finally disappeared through the gate: the rumble of its wheels had died away; and no flag floated defiantly in the sun, no cannons proclaimed the passing of a dynasty. From out the frosted cake of our existence Fate had cut an irreplaceable segment; turn which way we would, the void was present. We sneaked off in different directions, mutually undesirous of company; and it seemed borne in upon me that I ought to go and dig my garden right over, from end to end. It didn't actually want digging; on the other hand, no amount of digging could affect it, for good or for evil; so I worked steadily, strenuously, under the hot sun, stifling thought in action. At the end of an hour or so, I was joined by Edward.

"I've been chopping up wood," he explained, in a guilty sort of way, though nobody had called on him to account for his doings.

"What for?" I inquired, stupidly. "There's piles and piles of it chopped up already."

"I know," said Edward; "but there's no harm in having a bit over. You never can tell what may happen. But what have you been doing all this digging for?"

"You said it was going to rain," I explained, hastily; "so I thought I'd get the digging done before it came. Good gardeners always tell you that's the right thing to do."

"It did look like rain at one time," Edward admitted; "but it's passed off now. Very queer weather we're having. I suppose that's why I've felt so funny all day."

"Yes, I suppose it's the weather," I replied. "*I've* been feeling funny too."

The weather had nothing to do with it, as we well knew. But we would both have died rather than have admitted the real reason.

The Blue Room

That nature has her moments of sympathy with man has been noted often enough—and generally as a new discovery; to us, who had never known any other condition of things, it seemed entirely right and fitting that the wind sang and sobbed in the poplar tops, and in the lulls of it, sudden spirts of rain spattered the already dusty roads, on that blusterous March day when Edward and I awaited, on the station platform, the arrival of the new tutor. Needless to say, this arrangement had been planned by an aunt, from some fond idea that our shy, innocent young natures would unfold themselves during the walk from the station, and that on the revelation of each other's more solid qualities that must then inevitably ensue, an enduring friendship springing from mutual respect might be firmly based. A pretty dream—nothing more. For Edward, who foresaw that the brunt of tutorial oppression would have to be borne by him, was sulky, monosyllabic, and determined to be as negatively disagreeable as good manners would permit. It was therefore evident that I would have to be spokesman and purveyor of hollow civilities, and I was none the more amiable on that account; all courtesies, welcomes, explanations, and other court-chamberlain kind of business, being my special aversion. There was much of the tempestuous March weather in the hearts of both of us, as we sullenly glowered along the carriage-windows of the slackening train.

One is apt, however, to misjudge the special difficulties of a situation; and the reception proved, after all, an easy and informal matter. In a trainful so uniformly bucolic, a tutor was readily recognisable; and his portmanteau had been consigned to the luggage-cart, and his person conveyed into the lane, before I had discharged one of my carefully considered sentences. I breathed more easily, and, looking up at our new friend as we stepped out together, remembered that we had been counting on something altogether more arid, scholastic, and severe. A boyish eager face and a petulant pince-nez—untidy hair—a head of constant quick turns like a robin's, and a voice that kept breaking into alto—these were all very strange and new, but not in the least terrible.

He proceeded jerkily through the village, with glances on this side and that; and "Charming," he broke out presently; "quite too charming and delightful!"

I had not counted on this sort of thing, and glanced for help to Edward, who, hands in pockets, looked grimly down his nose. He had taken his line, and meant to stick to it.

Meantime our friend had made an imaginary spy-glass out of his fist, and was squinting through it at something I could not perceive. "What an exquisite bit!" he burst out; "fifteenth century—no—yes, it is!"

I began to feel puzzled, not to say alarmed. It reminded me of the butcher in the *Arabian Nights*, whose common joints, displayed on the shop-front, took to a startled public the appearance of dismembered humanity. This man seemed to see the strangest things in our dull, familiar surroundings.

"Ah!" he broke out again, as we jogged on between hedgerows: "and that field now—backed by the downs—with the rain-cloud brooding over it—that's all David Cox—every bit of it!"

"That field belongs to Farmer Larkin," I explained politely, for of course he could not be expected to know. "I'll take you over to Farmer Cox's tomorrow, if he's a friend of yours; but there's nothing to see there."

Edward, who was hanging sullenly behind, made a face at me, as if to say, "What sort of lunatic have we got here?"

"It has the true pastoral character, this country of yours," went on our enthusiast: "with just that added touch in cottage and farmstead, relics of a bygone art, which makes our English landscape so divine, so unique!"

Really this grasshopper was becoming a burden. These familiar fields and farms, of which we knew every blade and stick, had done nothing that I knew of to be bespattered with adjectives in this way. I had never thought of them as divine, unique, or anything else. They were—well, they were just themselves, and there was an end of it. Despairingly I jogged Edward in the ribs, as a sign to start rational conversation, but he only grinned and continued obdurate.

"You can see the house now," I remarked, presently; "and that's Selina, chasing the donkey in the paddock—or is it the donkey chasing Selina? I can't quite make out; but it's *them*, anyhow."

Needless to say, he exploded with a full charge of adjectives. "Exquisite!" he rapped out; "so mellow and harmonious! and so entirely in keeping!" (I could see from Edward's face that he was thinking who ought to be in keeping.) "Such possibilities of romance, now, in those old gables!"

"If you mean the garrets," I said, "there's a lot of old furniture in them; and one is generally full of apples; and the bats get in sometimes, under the eaves, and flop about till we go up with hairbrushes and things and drive 'em out; but there's nothing else in them that I know of."

"Oh, but there must be more than bats," he cried. "Don't tell me there are no ghosts. I shall be deeply disappointed if there aren't any ghosts."

I did not think it worth while to reply, feeling really unequal to this sort of conversation; besides, we were nearing the house, when my task would be ended. Aunt Eliza met us at the door, and in the cross-fire of adjectives that ensued—both of them talking at once, as grown-up folk have a habit of doing—we two slipped round to the back of the house, and speedily put several solid acres between us and civilisation, for fear of being ordered in to tea in the drawing-room. By the time we returned, our new importation had gone up to dress for dinner, so till the morrow at least we were free of him.

Meanwhile the March wind, after dropping a while at sundown, had been steadily increasing in volume; and although I fell asleep at my usual hour, about midnight I was wakened by the stress and cry of it. In the bright moonlight, wind-swung branches tossed and swayed eerily across the blinds; there was rumbling in chimneys, whistling in keyholes, and everywhere a clamour and a call. Sleep was out of the question, and, sitting up in bed, I looked round. Edward sat up too. "I was wondering when you were going to wake," he said. "It's no good trying to sleep through this. I vote we get up and do something."

"I'm game," I replied. "Let's play at being in a ship at sea" (the plaint of the old house under the buffeting wind suggested this, naturally); "and we can be wrecked on an island, or left on a raft, whichever you choose; but I like an island best myself, because there's more things on it."

Edward on reflection negatived the idea. "It would make too

much noise," he pointed out. "There's no fun playing at ships, unless you can make a jolly good row."

The door creaked, and a small figure in white slipped cautiously in. "Thought I heard you talking," said Charlotte. "We don't like it; we're afraid—Selina too. She'll be here in a minute. She's putting on her new dressing-gown she's so proud of."

His arms round his knees, Edward cogitated deeply until Selina appeared, barefooted, and looking slim and tall in the new dressing-gown. Then, "Look here," he exclaimed; "now we're all together, I vote we go and explore!"

"You're always wanting to explore," I said. "What on earth is there to explore for in this house?"

"Biscuits!" said the inspired Edward.

"Hooray! Come on!" chimed in Harold, sitting up suddenly. He had been awake all the time, but had been shamming asleep, lest he should be fagged to do anything.

It was indeed a fact, as Edward had remembered, that our thoughtless elders occasionally left the biscuits out, a prize for the night-walking adventurer with nerves of steel.

Edward tumbled out of bed, and pulled a baggy old pair of knickerbockers over his bare shanks. Then he girt himself with a belt, into which he thrust, on the one side a large wooden pistol, on the other an old single-stick; and finally he donned a big slouch-hat—once an uncle's—that we used for playing Guy Fawkes and Charles-the-Second up-a-tree in. Whatever the audience, Edward, if possible, always dressed for his parts with care and conscientiousness; while Harold and I, true Elizabethans, cared little about the mounting of the piece, so long as the real dramatic heart of it beat sound.

Our commander now enjoined on us a silence deep as the grave, reminding us that Aunt Eliza usually slept with an open door, past which we had to file.

"But we'll take the short cut through the Blue Room," said the wary Selina.

"Of course," said Edward, approvingly. "I forgot about that. Now then! You lead the way!"

The Blue Room had in prehistoric times been added to by taking in a superfluous passage, and so not only had the advantage of two doors, but enabled us to get to the head of the stairs without passing the chamber wherein our dragon-aunt lay couched. It was rarely occupied, except when a casual uncle came down for the night. We entered in noiseless file, the room being plunged in darkness, except for a bright strip of moonlight on the floor, across which we must pass for our exit. On this our leading lady chose to pause, seizing the opportunity to study the hang of her new dressing-gown. Greatly satisfied thereat, she proceeded, after the feminine fashion, to peacock and to pose, pacing a minuet down the moonlit patch with an imaginary partner. This was too much for Edward's histrionic instincts, and after a moment's pause he drew his single-stick, and with flourishes meet for the occasion, strode onto the stage. A struggle ensued on approved lines, at the end of which Selina was stabbed slowly and with unction, and her corpse borne from the chamber by the ruthless cavalier. The rest of us rushed after in a clump, with capers and gesticulations of delight; the special charm of the performance lying in the necessity for its being carried out with the dumbest of dumb shows.

Once out on the dark landing, the noise of the storm without told us that we had exaggerated the necessity for silence; so, grasping the tails of each other's nightgowns even as Alpine climbers rope themselves together in perilous places, we fared stoutly down the staircase-moraine, and across the grim glacier of the hall, to where a faint glimmer from the half-open door of the drawing-room beckoned to us like friendly hostel-lights. Entering, we found that our thriftless seniors had left the sound red heart of a fire, easily coaxed into a cheerful blaze; and biscuits—a plateful—smiled at us in an encouraging sort of way, together with the halves of a lemon, already once squeezed but still suckable. The biscuits were righteously shared, the lemon segments passed from mouth to mouth; and as we squatted round the fire, its genial warmth consoling our unclad limbs, we realised that so many nocturnal perils had not been braved in vain.

"It's a funny thing," said Edward, as we chatted, "how I hate this room in the daytime. It always means having your face washed, and your hair brushed, and talking silly company talk. But tonight it's really quite jolly. Looks different, somehow."

"I never can make out," I said, "what people come here to tea for.

They can have their own tea at home if they like—they're not poor people—with jam and things, and drink out of their saucer, and suck their fingers and enjoy themselves; but they come here from a long way off, and sit up straight with their feet off the bars of their chairs, and have one cup, and talk the same sort of stuff every time."

Selina sniffed disdainfully. "You don't know anything about it," she said. "In society you have to call on each other. It's the proper thing to do."

"Pooh! *You're* not in society," said Edward, politely; "and, what's more, you never will be."

"Yes, I shall, someday," retorted Selina; "but I shan't ask you to come and see me, so there!"

"Wouldn't come if you did," growled Edward.

"Well, you won't get the chance," rejoined our sister, claiming her right of the last word. There was no heat about these little amenities, which made up—as we understood it—the art of polite conversation.

"I don't like society people," put in Harold from the sofa, where he was sprawling at full length—a sight the daylight hours would have blushed to witness. "There were some of 'em here this afternoon, when you two had gone off to the station. Oh, and I found a dead mouse on the lawn, and I wanted to skin it, but I wasn't sure I knew how, by myself; and they came out into the garden and patted my head—I wish people wouldn't do that—and one of 'em asked me to pick her a flower. Don't know why she couldn't pick it herself; but I said, 'All right, I will if you'll hold my mouse.' But she screamed, and threw it away; and Augustus (the cat) got it, and ran away with it. I believe it was really his mouse all the time, 'cos he'd been looking about as if he had lost something, so I wasn't angry with *him*; but what did *she* want to throw away my mouse for?"

"You have to be careful with mice," reflected Edward; "they're such slippery things. Do you remember we were playing with a dead mouse once on the piano, and the mouse was Robinson Crusoe, and the piano was the island, and somehow Crusoe slipped down inside the island, into its works, and we couldn't get him out, though we tried rakes and all sorts of things, till the tuner came. And that wasn't till a week after, and then—"

Here Charlotte, who had been nodding solemnly, fell over into the fender; and we realised that the wind had dropped at last, and the house was lapped in a great stillness. Our vacant beds seemed to be calling to us imperiously; and we were all glad when Edward gave the signal for retreat. At the top of the staircase Harold unexpectedly turned mutinous, insisting on his right to slide down the banisters in a free country. Circumstances did not allow of argument; I suggested frog's-marching instead, and frog's-marched he accordingly was, the procession passing solemnly across the moonlit Blue Room, with Harold horizontal and limply submissive. Snug in bed at last, I was just slipping off into slumber when I heard Edward explode, with chuckle and snort.

"By Jove!" he said; "I forgot all about it. The new tutor's sleeping in the Blue Room!"

"Lucky he didn't wake up and catch us," I grunted, drowsily; and both of us, without another thought on the matter, sank into well-earned repose.

Next morning we came down to breakfast braced to grapple with fresh adversity, but were surprised to find our garrulous friend of the previous day—he was late in making his appearance—strangely silent and (apparently) preoccupied. Having polished off our porridge, we ran out to feed the rabbits, explaining to them that a beast of a tutor would prevent their enjoying so much of our society as formerly.

On returning to the house at the fated hour appointed for study, we were thunderstruck to see the station-cart disappearing down the drive, freighted with our new acquaintance. Aunt Eliza was brutally uncommunicative; but she was overheard to remark casually that she thought the man must be a lunatic. In this theory we were only too ready to concur, dismissing thereafter the whole matter from our minds.

Some weeks later it happened that Uncle Thomas, while paying us a flying visit, produced from his pocket a copy of the latest weekly, *Psyche: a Journal of the Unseen*; and proceeded laboriously to rid himself of much incomprehensible humour, apparently at our expense. We bore it patiently, with the forced grin demanded by convention, anxious to get at the source of inspiration, which it presently appeared lay in a paragraph circumstantially describing our modest and humdrum habitation. "Case III," it began. "The following particulars were communicated by a young member of the Society, of undoubted probity and earnestness, and are a chronicle of actual and recent experience." A fairly accurate description of the house followed, with details that were unmistakable; but to this there succeeded a flood of meaningless drivel about apparitions, nightly visitants, and the like, writ in a manner betokening a disordered mind, coupled with a feeble imagination. The fellow was not even original. All the old material was there—the storm at night, the haunted chamber, the white lady, the murder re-enacted, and so on—already worn threadbare in many a Christmas Number. No one was able to make head or tail of the stuff, or of its connexion with our quiet mansion; and yet Edward, who had always suspected the man, persisted in maintaining that our tutor of a brief span was, somehow or other, at the bottom of it.

A Falling Out

Harold told me the main facts of this episode some time later—in bits, and with reluctance. It was not a recollection he cared to talk about. The crude blank misery of a moment is apt to leave a dull bruise which is slow to depart, if it ever does so entirely; and Harold confesses to a twinge or two, still, at times, like the veteran who brings home a bullet inside him from martial plains over sea.

He knew he was a brute the moment he had done it; Selina had not meant to worry, only to comfort and assist. But his soul was one raw sore within him, when he found himself shut up in the schoolroom after hours, merely for insisting that 7 times 7 amounted to 47. The injustice of it seemed so flagrant. Why not 47 as much as 49? One number was no prettier than the other to look at, and it was evidently only a matter of arbitrary taste and preference, and, anyhow, it had always been 47 to him, and would be to the end of time. So when Selina came in out of the sun, leaving the Trappers or the Far West behind her, and putting off the glory of being an Apache squaw in order to hear him his tables and win his release, Harold turned on her venomously, rejected her kindly overtures, and ever drove his elbow into her sympathetic ribs, in his determination to be left alone in the glory of sulks. The fit passed directly, his eyes were opened, and his soul sat in the dust as he sorrowfully began to cast about for some atonement heroic enough to salve the wrong.

Of course poor Selina looked for no sacrifice nor heroics whatever: she didn't even want him to say he was sorry. If he would only make it up, she would have done the apologising part herself. But that was not a boy's way. Something solid, Harold felt, was due from him; and until that was achieved, making-up must not be thought of, in order that the final effect might not be spoilt. Accordingly, when his release came, and poor Selina hung about, trying to catch his eye, Harold, possessed by the demon of a distorted motive, avoided her steadily—though he was bleeding inwardly at every minute of delay—and came to me instead. Needless to say, I approved his plan highly; it was so much more high-toned than just going and making-up tamely, which anyone could do; and a girl who had been jobbed in the ribs by a hostile elbow could not be expected for a moment to overlook it, without the liniment of an offering to soothe her injured feelings.

"I know what she wants most," said Harold. "She wants that set of tea-things in the toy-shop window, with the red and blue flowers on 'em; she's wanted it for months, 'cos her dolls are getting big enough to have real afternoon tea; and she wants it so badly that she won't walk that side of the street when we go into the town. But it costs five shillings!"

Then we set to work seriously, and devoted the afternoon to a realisation of assets and the composition of a Budget that might have been dated without shame from Whitehall. The result worked out as follows:

	s.	d.
By one uncle, unspent through having been lost for nearly a week—turned up at last in the straw of the dog-kennel	2	6
By advance from me on security of next uncle, and failing that, to be called in at Christmas	1	0
By shaken out of missionary-box with the help of a knife-blade. (They were our own pennies and a forced levy)	0	4
By bet due from Edward, for walking across the field where Farmer Larkin's bull was, and Edward bet him twopence he wouldn't —called in with difficulty	0	2
By advance from Martha, on no security at all, only you mustn't tell your aunt	1	0
Total	5	0

and at last we breathed again.

The rest promised to be easy. Selina had a tea-party at five on the morrow, with the chipped old wooden tea-things that had served her successive dolls from babyhood. Harold would slip off directly after dinner, going alone, so as not to arouse suspicion, as we were not allowed to go into the town by ourselves. It was nearly two miles to our small metropolis, but there would be plenty of time for him to go and return, even laden with the olive-branch neatly packed in shavings; besides, he might meet the butcher, who was his friend and would give him a lift. Then, finally, at five, the rapture of the new tea-service, descended from the skies; and, retribution made, making-up at last, without loss of dignity. With the event before us, we thought it a small thing that twenty-four hours more of alienation and pretended sulks must be kept up on Harold's part; but Selina, who naturally knew nothing of the treat in store for her, moped for the rest of the evening, and took a very heavy heart to bed.

When next day the hour for action arrived, Harold evaded Olympian attention with an easy modesty born of long practice, and made off for the front gate. Selina, who had been keeping her eye upon him, thought he was going down to the pond to catch frogs, a joy they had planned to share together, and made after him; but Harold, though he heard her footsteps, continued sternly on his high mission, without even looking back; and Selina was left to wander disconsolately among flower-beds that had lost—for her—all scent and colour. I saw it all, and although cold reason approved our line of action, instinct told me we were brutes.

Harold reached the town—so he recounted afterwards—in record time, having run most of the way for fear the tea-things, which had reposed six months in the window, should be snapped up by some other conscience-stricken lacerator of a sister's feelings; and it seemed hardly credible to find them still there, and their owner willing to part with them for the price marked on the ticket. He paid his money down at once, that there should be no drawing back from the bargain; and then, as the things had to be taken out of the window and packed, and the afternoon was yet young, he thought he might treat himself to a taste of urban joys and la vie de Boheme. Shops came first, of course, and he flattened his nose successively against the window with the india-rubber balls in it, and the clock-work locomotive; and against the barber's window, with wigs on blocks, reminding him of uncles, and shaving-cream that looked so good to eat; and the grocer's window, displaying more currants than the whole British population could possibly consume without a special effort; and the window of the bank, wherein gold was thought so little of that it was dealt about in shovels. Next there was the market-place, with all its clamorous joys; and when a runaway calf came down the street like a cannon-ball, Harold felt that he had not lived in vain. The whole place was so brimful of excitement that he had quite forgotten the why and the wherefore of his being there, when a sight of the church clock recalled him to his better self, and sent him flying out of the town, as he realised he had only just time enough left to get back in. If he were after his appointed hour, he would not only miss his high triumph, but probably would be detected as a transgressor of bounds—a crime before which a private opinion on multiplication sank to nothingness. So he jogged along on his homeward way, thinking of many things, and probably talking to himself a good deal, as his habit was, and had covered nearly half the distance, when suddenly—a deadly sinking in the pit of his stomach—a paralysis of every limb—around him a world extinct of light and music—a black sun and a reeling sky—he had forgotten the tea-things!

It was useless, it was hopeless, all was over, and nothing could now be done; nevertheless he turned and ran back wildly, blindly, choking with the big sobs that evoked neither pity nor comfort from a merciless mocking world around; a stitch in his side, dust in his eyes, and black despair clutching at his heart. So he stumbled on, with leaden legs and bursting sides, till—as if Fate had not yet dealt him her last worst buffet—on turning a corner in the road he almost ran under the wheels of a dog-cart, in which, as it pulled up, was apparent the portly form of Farmer Larkin, the arch-enemy, whose ducks he had been shying stones at that very morning!

Had Harold been in his right and unclouded senses, he would have vanished through the hedge some seconds earlier, rather than pain the farmer by any unpleasant reminiscences which his appearance might call up; but as things were, he could only stand and blubber hopelessly, caring, indeed, little now what further ill might befall him. The farmer, for his part, surveyed the desolate figure with some astonishment, calling out in no unfriendly accents, "Why, Master Harold! whatever be the matter? Baint runnin' away, be ee?"

Then Harold, with the unnatural courage born of desperation, flung himself on the step, and climbing into the cart, fell in the straw at the bottom of it, sobbing out that he wanted to go back, go back! The situation had a vagueness; but the farmer, a man of action rather than words, swung his horse round smartly, and they were in the town again by the time Harold had recovered himself sufficiently to furnish some details. As they drove up to the shop, the woman was waiting at the door with the parcel; and hardly a minute seemed to have elapsed since the black crisis, ere they were bowling along swiftly home, the precious parcel hugged in a close embrace.

And now the farmer came out in quite a new and unexpected light. Never a word did he say of broken fences and hurdles, of trampled crops and harried flocks and herds. One would have thought the man had never possessed a head of livestock in his life. Instead, he was deeply interested in the whole dolorous quest of the tea-things, and sympathised with Harold on the disputed point in mathematics as if he had been himself at the same stage of education. As they neared home, Harold found himself, to his surprise, sitting up and chatting to his new friend like man to man; and before he was dropped at a convenient gap in the garden hedge, he had promised that when Selina gave her first public tea-party, little Miss Larkin should be invited to come and bring her whole sawdust family along with her; and the farmer appeared as pleased and proud as if he had been asked to a garden-party at Marlborough House. Really, those Olympians have certain good points, far down in them. I shall have to leave off abusing them someday.

At the hour of five, Selina, having spent the afternoon searching for Harold in all his accustomed haunts, sat down disconsolately to tea with her dolls, who ungenerously refused to wait beyond the appointed hour. The wooden tea-things seemed more chipped than usual; and the dolls themselves had more of wax and sawdust, and less of human colour and intelligence about them, than she ever remembered before. It was then that Harold burst in, very dusty, his stockings at his heels, and the channels ploughed by tears still showing on his grimy cheeks; and Selina was at last permitted to know that he had been thinking of her ever since his ill-judged exhibition of temper, and that his sulks had not been the genuine article, nor had he gone frogging by himself. It was a very happy hostess who dispensed hospitality that evening to a glassy-eyed stiff-kneed circle; and many a dollish gaucherie, that would have been severely checked on ordinary occasions, was as much overlooked as if it had been a birthday.

But Harold and I, in our stupid masculine way, thought all her happiness sprang from possession of the long-coveted tea-service.

"Lusisti Satis"

Among the many fatuous ideas that possessed the Olympian noddle, this one was pre-eminent; that, being Olympians, they could talk quite freely in our presence on subjects of the closest import to us, so long as names, dates, and other landmarks were ignored. We were supposed to be denied the faculty for putting two and two together; and, like the monkeys, who very sensibly refrain from speech lest they should be set to earn their livings, we were careful to conceal our capabilities for a simple syllogism. Thus we were rarely taken by surprise, and so were considered by our disappointed elders to be apathetic and to lack the divine capacity for wonder.

Now the daily output of the letter-bag, with the mysterious discussions that ensued thereon, had speedily informed us that Uncle Thomas was intrusted with a mission—a mission, too, affecting ourselves. Uncle Thomas's missions were many and various; a self-important man, one liking the business while protesting that he sank under the burden, he was the missionary, so to speak, of our remote habitation. The matching a ribbon, the running down to the stores, the interviewing a cook—these and similar duties lent constant colour and variety to his vacant life in London and helped to keep down his figure. When the matter, however, had in our presence to be referred to with nods and pronouns, with significant hiatuses and interpolations in the French tongue, then the red flag was flown, the storm-cone hoisted, and by a studious pretence of inattention we were not long in plucking out the heart of the mystery.

To clinch our conclusion, we descended suddenly and together on Martha; proceeding, however, not by simple inquiry as to facts—that would never have done—but by informing her that the air was full of school and that we knew all about it, and then challenging denial. Martha was a trusty soul, but a bad witness for the defence, and we soon had it all out of her. The word had gone forth, the school had been selected; the necessary sheets were hemming even now; and Edward was the designated and appointed victim.

It had always been before us as an inevitable bourne, this strange unknown thing called school; and yet—perhaps I should say consequently—we had never seriously set ourselves to consider what it really meant. But now that the grim spectre loomed imminent, stretching lean hands for one of our flock, it behoved us to face the situation, to take soundings in this uncharted sea and find out whither we were drifting. Unfortunately, the data in our possession were absolutely insufficient, and we knew not whither to turn for exact information. Uncle Thomas could have told us all about it, of course; he had been there himself, once, in the dim and misty past. But an unfortunate conviction, that Nature had intended him for a humourist, tainted all his evidence, besides making it wearisome to hear. Again, of such among our contemporaries as we had approached, the trumpets gave forth an uncertain sound. According to some, it meant larks, revels, emancipation, and a foretaste of the bliss of manhood. According to others—the majority, alas!—it was a private and peculiar Hades, that could give the original institution points and a beating. When Edward was observed to be swaggering round with a jaunty air and his chest stuck out, I knew that he was contemplating his future from the one point of view. When, on the contrary, he was subdued and unaggressive, and sought the society of his sisters, I recognised that the other aspect was in the ascendant. "You can always run away, you know," I used to remark consolingly on these latter occasions; and Edward would brighten up wonderfully at the suggestion, while Charlotte melted into tears before her vision of a brother with blistered feet and an empty belly, passing nights of frost 'neath the lee of windy haystacks.

It was to Edward, of course, that the situation was chiefly productive of anxiety; and yet the ensuing change in my own circumstances and position furnished me also with food for grave reflexion. Hitherto I had acted mostly to orders. Even when I had devised and counselled any particular devilry, it had been carried out on Edward's approbation, and—as eldest—at his special risk. Henceforward I began to be anxious of the bugbear Responsibility, and to realise what a soul-throttling thing it is. True, my new position would have its compensations.

Edward had been masterful exceedingly, imperious, perhaps a little narrow; impassioned for hard facts, and with scant sympathy for make-believe. I should now be free and untrammelled; in the conception and carrying out of a scheme, I could accept and reject to better artistic purpose.

It would, moreover, be needless to be a Radical anymore. Radical I never was, really, by nature or by sympathy. The part had been thrust on me one day, when Edward proposed to foist the House of Lords on our small Republic. The principles of the thing he set forth learnedly and well, and it all sounded promising enough, till he went on to explain that, for the present at least, he proposed to be the House of Lords himself. We others were to be the Commons. There would be promotions, of course, he added, dependent on service and on fitness, and open to both sexes; and to me in especial he held out hopes of speedy advancement. But in its initial stages the thing wouldn't work properly unless he were first and only Lord. Then I put my foot down promptly, and said it was all rot, and I didn't see the good of any House of Lords at all. "Then you must be a low Radical!" said Edward, with fine contempt. The inference seemed hardly necessary, but what could I do? I accepted the situation, and said firmly, Yes, I was a low Radical. In this monstrous character I had been obliged to masquerade ever since; but now I could throw it off, and look the world in the face again.

And yet, did this and other gains really out-balance my losses? Henceforth I should, it was true, be leader and chief; but I should also be the buffer between the Olympians and my little clan. To Edward this had been nothing; he had withstood the impact of Olympus without flinching, like Teneriffe or Atlas unremoved. But was I equal to the task? And was there not rather a danger that for the sake of peace and quietness I might be tempted to compromise, compound, and make terms? sinking thus, by successive lapses, into the Blameless Prig? I don't mean, of course, that I thought out my thoughts to the exact point here set down. In those fortunate days of old one was free from the hard necessity of transmuting the vague idea into the mechanical inadequate medium of words. But the feeling was there, that I might not possess the qualities of character for so delicate a position.

The unnatural halo round Edward got more pronounced, his own demeanour more responsible and dignified, with the arrival of his new clothes. When his trunk and play-box were sent in, the approaching cleavage between our brother, who now belonged to the future, and ourselves, still claimed by the past, was accentuated indeed. His name was painted on each of them, in large letters, and after their arrival their owner used to disappear mysteriously, and be found eventually wandering round his luggage, murmuring to himself, "Edward——" in a rapt, remote sort of way. It was a weakness, of course, and pointed to a soft spot in his character; but those who can remember the sensation of first seeing their names in print will not think hardly of him.

As the short days sped by and the grim event cast its shadow longer and longer across our threshold, an unnatural politeness, a civility scarce canny, began to pervade the air. In those latter hours Edward himself was frequently heard to say "Please," and also "Would you mind fetchin' that ball?" while Harold and I would sometimes actually find ourselves trying to anticipate his wishes. As for the girls, they simply grovelled. The Olympians, too, in their uncouth way, by gift of carnal delicacies and such-like indulgence, seemed anxious to demonstrate that they had hitherto misjudged this one of us. Altogether the situation grew strained and false, and I think a general relief was felt when the end came.

We all trooped down to the station, of course; it is only in later years that the farce of "seeing people off" is seen in its true colours. Edward was the life and soul of the party; and if his gaiety struck one at times as being a trifle overdone, it was not a moment to be critical. As we tramped along, I promised him I would ask Farmer Larkin not to kill any more pigs till he came back for the holidays, and he said he would send me a proper catapult—the real lethal article, not a kid's plaything. Then suddenly, when we were about halfway down, one of the girls fell a-snivelling.

The happy few who dare to laugh at the woes of sea-sickness will perhaps remember how, on occasion, the sudden collapse of a fellow-voyager before their very eyes has caused them hastily to revise their self-confidence and resolve to walk more humbly for the future. Even so it was with Edward, who turned his head aside, feigning an interest in the landscape. It was but for a moment; then he recollected the hat he was wearing—a hard bowler, the first of that sort he had ever owned. He took it off, examined it, and felt it over. Something about it seemed to give him strength, and he was a man once more.

At the station, Edward's first care was to dispose his boxes on the platform so that everyone might see the labels and the lettering thereon. One did not go to school for the first time every day! Then he read both sides of his ticket carefully; shifted it to every one of his pockets in turn; and finally fell to chinking of his money, to keep his courage up. We were all dry of conversation by this time, and could only stand round and stare in silence at the victim decked for the altar. And, as I looked at Edward, in new clothes of a manly cut, with a hard hat upon his head, a railway ticket in one pocket and money of his own in the other—money to spend as he liked and no questions asked!—I began to feel dimly how great was the gulf already yawning betwixt us. Fortunately I was not old enough to realise, further, that here on this little platform the old order lay at its last gasp, and that Edward might come back to us, but it would not be the Edward of yore, nor could things ever be the same again.

When the train steamed up at last, we all boarded it impetuously with the view of selecting the one peerless carriage to which Edward might be intrusted with the greatest comfort and honour; and as each one found the ideal compartment at the same moment, and vociferously maintained its merits, he stood some chance for a time of being left behind. A porter settled the matter by heaving him through the nearest door; and as the train moved off, Edward's head was thrust out of the window, wearing on it an unmistakable first-quality grin that he had been saving up somewhere for the supreme moment. Very small and white his face looked, on the long side of the retreating train. But the grin was visible, undeniable, stoutly maintained; till a curve swept him from our sight, and he was borne away in the dying rumble, out of our placid backwater, out into the busy world of rubs and knocks and competition, out into the New Life.

When a crab has lost a leg, his gait is still more awkward than his wont, till Time and healing Nature make him *totus teres atque rotundus* once more. We straggled back from the station disjointedly; Harold, who was very silent, sticking close to me, his last slender prop while the girls in front, their heads together, were already reckoning up the weeks to the holidays. Home at last, Harold suggested one or two occupations of a spicy and contraband flavour, but though we did our manful best there was no knocking any interest out of them.

Then I suggested others, with the same want of success. Finally we found ourselves sitting silent on an upturned wheelbarrow, our chins on our fists, staring haggardly into the raw new conditions of our changed life, the ruins of a past behind our backs.

And all the while Selina and Charlotte were busy stuffing Edward's rabbits with unwonted forage, bilious and green; polishing up the cage of his mice till the occupants raved and swore like householders in spring-time; and collecting materials for new bows and arrows, whips, boats, guns, and four-in-hand harness, against the return of Ulysses. Little did they dream that the hero, once back from Troy and all its onsets, would scornfully condemn their clumsy but laborious armoury as rot and humbug and only fit for kids! This, with many another like awakening, was mercifully hidden from them. Could the veil have been lifted, and the girls permitted to see Edward as he would appear a short three months hence, ragged of attire and lawless of tongue, a scorner of tradition and an adept in strange new physical tortures, one who would in the same half-hour dismember a doll and shatter a hallowed belief—in fine, a sort of swaggering Captain, fresh from the Spanish Main—could they have had the least hint of this, well, then perhaps——. But which of us is of mental fibre to stand the test of a glimpse into futurity? Let us only hope that, even with certain disillusionment ahead, the girls would have acted precisely as they did.

And perhaps we have reason to be very grateful that, both as children and long afterwards, we are never allowed to guess how the absorbing pursuit of the moment will appear, not only to others, but to ourselves, a very short time hence. So we pass, with a gusto and a heartiness that to an onlooker would seem almost pathetic, from one droll devotion to another misshapen passion; and who shall care to play Rhadamanthus, to appraise the record, and to decide how much of it is solid achievement, and how much the merest child's play?

Dream Days

The Twenty-first of October

In the matter of general culture and attainments, we youngsters stood on pretty level ground. True, it was always happening that one of us would be singled out at any moment, freakishly, and without regard to his own preferences, to wrestle with the inflections of some idiotic language long rightly dead; while another, from some fancied artistic tendency which always failed to justify itself, might be told off without warning to hammer out scales and exercises, and to bedew the senseless keys with tears of weariness or of revolt. But in subjects common to either sex, and held to be necessary even for him whose ambition soared no higher than to crack a whip in a circus-ring—in geography, for instance, arithmetic, or the weary doings of kings and queens—each would have scorned to excel. And, indeed, whatever our individual gifts, a general dogged determination to shirk and to evade kept us all at much the same dead level—a level of Ignorance tempered by insubordination.

Fortunately there existed a wide range of subjects, of healthier tone than those already enumerated, in which we were free to choose for ourselves, and which we would have scorned to consider education; and in these we freely followed each his own particular line, often attaining an amount of special knowledge which struck our ignorant elders as simply uncanny. For Edward, the uniforms, accoutrements, colours, and mottoes of the regiments composing the British Army had a special glamour. In the matter of facings he was simply faultless; among chevrons, badges, medals, and stars, he moved familiarly; he even knew the names of most of the colonels in command; and he would squander sunny hours prone on the lawn, heedless of challenge from bird or beast, poring over a tattered Army List. My own accomplishment was of another character—took, as it seemed to me, a wider and a more untrammelled range. Dragoons might have swaggered in Lincoln green, riflemen might have donned sporrans over tartan trews, without exciting notice or comment from me. But did you seek precise information as to the fauna of the American continent, then you had come to the right shop. Where and why the bison "wallowed"; how beaver were to be trapped and wild turkeys stalked; the grizzly and how to handle him, and the pretty pressing ways of the constrictor—in fine, the haunts and the habits of all that burrowed, strutted, roared, or wriggled between the Atlantic and the Pacific—all this knowledge I took for my province. By the others my equipment was fully recognized. Supposing a book with a bear-hunt in it made its way into the house, and the atmosphere was electric with excitement; still, it was necessary that I should first decide whether the slot had been properly described and properly followed up, ere the work could be stamped with full approval. A writer might have won fame throughout the civilized globe for his trappers and his realistic backwoods, and all went for nothing. If his pemmican were not properly compounded I damned his achievement, and it was heard no more of.

Harold was hardly old enough to possess a special subject of his own. He had his instincts, indeed, and at bird's-nesting they almost amounted to prophecy. Where we others only suspected eggs, surmised possible eggs, hinted doubtfully at eggs in the neighbourhood, Harold went straight for the right bush, bough, or hole as if he carried a divining-rod. But this faculty belonged to the class of mere gifts, and was not to be ranked with Edward's lore regarding facings, and mine as to the habits of prairie-dogs, both gained by painful study and extensive travel in those "realms of gold," the Army List and Ballantyne.

Selina's subject, quite unaccountably, happened to be naval history. There is no laying down rules as to subjects; you just possess them—or rather, they possess you—and their genesis or protoplasm is rarely to be tracked down. Selina had never so much as seen the sea; but for that matter neither had I ever set foot on the American continent, the by-ways of which I knew so intimately. And just as I, if set down without warning in the middle of the Rocky Mountains, would have been perfectly at home, so Selina, if a genie had dropped her suddenly on Portsmouth Hard, could have given points to most of its frequenters. From the days of Blake down to the death of Nelson (she never condescended further), Selina had taken spiritual part in every notable engagement of the British Navy; and even in the dark days when she had to pick up skirts and flee, chased by an ungallant De Ruyter or Van Tromp, she was yet cheerful in the consciousness that ere long she would be gleefully hammering the fleets of the world, in the glorious times to follow. When that golden period arrived, Selina was busy indeed; and, while loving best to stand where the splinters were flying the thickest, she was also a careful and critical student of seamanship and of maneuver. She knew the order in which the great line-of-battle ships moved into action, the vessels they respectively engaged, the moment when each let go its anchor, and which of them had a spring on its cable (while not understanding the phrase, she carefully noted the fact); and she habitually went into an engagement on the quarter-deck of the gallant ship that reserved its fire the longest.

At the time of Selina's weird seizure I was unfortunately away from home, on a loathsome visit to an aunt; and my account is therefore feebly compounded from hearsay. It was an absence I never ceased to regret—scoring it up, with a sense of injury, against the aunt. There was a splendid uselessness about the whole performance that specially appealed to my artistic sense. That it should have been Selina, too, who should break out this way—Selina, who had just become a regular subscriber to the "Young Ladies' Journal," and who allowed herself to be taken out to strange teas with an air of resignation palpably assumed—this was a special joy, and served to remind me that much of this dreaded convention that was creeping over us might be, after all, only veneer. Edward also was absent, getting licked into shape at school; but to him the loss was nothing. With his stern practical bent he wouldn't have seen any sense in it— to recall one of his favourite expressions. To Harold, however, for whom the gods had always cherished a special tenderness, it was granted, not only to witness, but also, priestlike, to feed the sacred fire itself. And if at the time he paid the penalty exacted by the sordid unimaginative ones who temporarily rule the roast, he must ever after, one feels sure, have carried inside him some of the white gladness of the acolyte who, greatly privileged, has been permitted to swing a censer at the sacring of the very Mass.

October was mellowing fast, and with it the year itself; full of tender hints, in woodland and hedgerow, of a course well-nigh completed. From all sides that still afternoon you caught the quick breathing and sob of the runner nearing the goal. Preoccupied and possessed, Selina had strayed down the garden and out into the pasture beyond, where, on a bit of rising ground that dominated the garden on one side and the downs with the old coach-road on the other, she had cast herself down to chew the cud of fancy. There she was presently joined by Harold, breathless and very full of his latest grievance.

"I asked him not to," he burst out. "I said if he'd only please wait a bit and Edward would be back soon, and it couldn't matter to *him*, and the pig wouldn't mind, and Edward'd be pleased and everybody'd be happy. But he just said he was very sorry, but bacon didn't wait for nobody. So I told him he was a regular beast, and then I came away. And—and I b'lieve they're doing it now!"

"Yes, he's a beast," agreed Selina, absently. She had forgotten all about the pig-killing. Harold kicked away a freshly thrown-up mole-hill, and prodded down the hole with a stick. From the direction of Farmer Larkin's demesne came a long-drawn note of sorrow, a thin cry and appeals telling that the stout soul of a black Berkshire pig was already faring down the stony track to Hades.

"D' you know what day it is?" said Selina presently, in a low voice, looking far away before her.

Harold did not appear to know, nor yet to care. He had laid open his mole-run for a yard or so, and was still grubbing at it absorbedly.

"It's Trafalgar Day," went on Selina, trancedly; "Trafalgar Day—and nobody cares!"

Something in her tone told Harold that he was not behaving quite becomingly. He didn't exactly know in what manner; still, he abandoned his mole-hunt for a more courteous attitude of attention.

"Over there," resumed Selina—she was gazing out in the direction of the old high road—"over there the coaches used to go by. Uncle Thomas was telling me about it the other day. And the people used to watch for 'em coming, to tell the time by, and p'r'aps to get their parcels. And one morning—they wouldn't be expecting anything different—one morning, first there would be a cloud of dust, as usual, and then the coach would come racing by, and then they would know! For the coach would be dressed in laurel, all laurel from stem to stern! And the coachman would be wearing laurel, and the guard would be wearing laurel; and then they would know, then they would know!"

Harold listened in respectful silence. He would much rather have been hunting the mole, who must have been a mile away by this time if he had his wits about him. But he had all the natural instincts of a gentleman; of whom it is one of the principal marks, if not the complete definition, never to show signs of being bored.

Selina rose to her feet, and paced the turf restlessly with a short quarter-deck walk.

"Why can't we *do* something?" she burst out presently. "*He*—he did everything—why can't we do anything for him?"

"*Who* did everything?" inquired Harold, meekly. It was useless wasting further longings on that mole. Like the dead, he travelled fast.

"Why, Nelson, of course," said Selina, shortly, still looking restlessly around for help or suggestion.

"But he's—he's *dead*, isn't he?" asked Harold, slightly puzzled.

"What's that got to do with it?" retorted his sister, resuming her caged-lion promenade.

Harold was somewhat taken aback. In the case of the pig, for instance, whose last outcry had now passed into stillness, he had considered the chapter as finally closed. Whatever innocent mirth the holidays might hold in store for Edward, that particular pig, at least, would not be a contributor. And now he was given to understand that the situation had not materially changed! He would have to revise his ideas, it seemed. Sitting up on end, he looked towards the garden for assistance in the task. Thence, even as he gazed, a tiny column of smoke rose straight up into the still air. The gardener had been sweeping that afternoon, and now, an unconscious priest, was offering his sacrifice of autumn leaves to the calm-eyed goddess of changing hues and chill forebodings who was moving slowly about the land that golden afternoon. Harold was up and off in a moment, forgetting Nelson, forgetting the pig, the mole, the Larkin betrayal, and Selina's strange fever of conscience. Here was fire, real fire, to play with, and that was even better than messing with water, or remodelling the plastic surface of the earth. Of all the toys the world provides for right-minded persons, the original elements rank easily the first.

But Selina sat on where she was, her chin on her fists; and her fancies whirled and drifted, here and there, in curls and eddies, along with the smoke she was watching. As the quick-footed dusk of the short October day stepped lightly over the garden, little red tongues of fire might be seen to leap and vanish in the smoke. Harold, anon staggering under armfuls of leaves, anon stoking vigorously, was discernible only at fitful intervals. It was another sort of smoke that the inner eye of Selina was looking upon—a smoke that hung in sullen banks round the masts and the hulls of the fighting ships; a smoke from beneath which came thunder and the crash and the splinter-rip, the shout of the boarding-party, the choking sob of the gunner stretched by his gun; a smoke from out of which at last she saw, as through a riven pall, the radiant spirit of the Victor, crowned with the coronal of a perfect death, leap in full assurance up into the ether that Immortals breathe. The dusk was glooming towards darkness when she rose and moved slowly down towards the beckoning fire; something of the priestess in her stride, something of the devotee in the set purpose of her eye.

The leaves were well alight by this time, and Harold had just added an old furze bush, which flamed and crackled stirringly.

"Go 'n' get some more sticks," ordered Selina, "and shavings, 'n' chunks of wood, 'n' anything you can find. Look here—in the kitchen-garden there's a pile of old pea-sticks. Fetch as many as you can carry, and then go back and bring some more!"

"But I say—" began Harold, amazedly, scarce knowing his sister, and with a vision of a frenzied gardener, pea-stickless and threatening retribution.

"Go and fetch 'em quick!" shouted Selina, stamping with impatience.

Harold ran off at once, true to the stern system of discipline in which he had been nurtured. But his eyes were like round O's, and as he ran he talked fast to himself, in evident disorder of mind.

The pea-sticks made a rare blaze, and the fire, no longer smouldering sullenly, leapt up and began to assume the appearance of a genuine bonfire. Harold, awed into silence at first, began to jump round it with shouts of triumph. Selina looked on grimly, with knitted brow; she was not yet fully satisfied. "Can't you get any more sticks?" she said presently. "Go and hunt about. Get some old hampers and matting and things out of the tool-house. Smash up that old cucumber frame Edward shoved you into, the day we were playing scouts and Mohicans. Stop a bit! Hooray! I know. You come along with me."

Hard by there was a hot-house, Aunt Eliza's special pride and joy, and even grimly approved of by the gardener. At one end, in an out-house adjoining, the necessary firing was stored; and to this sacred fuel, of which we were strictly forbidden to touch a stick, Selina went straight. Harold followed obediently, prepared for any crime after that of the pea-sticks, but pinching himself to see if he were really awake.

"You bring some coals," said Selina briefly, without any palaver or pro-and-con discussion. "Here's a basket. *I'll* manage the faggots!"

In a very few minutes there was little doubt about its being a genuine bonfire and no paltry makeshift. Selina, a Maenad now, hatless and tossing disordered locks, all the dross of the young lady purged out of her, stalked around the pyre of her own purloining, or prodded it with a pea-stick. And as she prodded she murmured at intervals, "I knew there was something we could do! It isn't much—but still it's *something*!"

The gardener had gone home to his tea. Aunt Eliza had driven out for hers a long way off, and was not expected back till quite late; and this far end of the garden was not overlooked by any windows. So the Tribute blazed on merrily unchecked. Villagers far away, catching sight of the flare, muttered something about "them young devils at their tricks again," and trudged on beer-wards. Never a thought of what day it was, never a thought for Nelson, who preserved their honest pint-pots, to be paid for in honest pence, and saved them from litres and decimal coinage. Nearer at hand, frightened rabbits popped up and vanished with a flick of white tails; scared birds fluttered among the branches, or sped across the glade to quieter sleeping-quarters; but never a bird nor a beast gave a thought to the hero to whom they owed it that each year their little homes of horsehair, wool, or moss, were safe stablished 'neath the flap of the British flag; and that Game Laws, quietly permanent, made *la chasse* a terror only to their betters. No one seemed to know, nor to care, nor to sympathise. In all the ecstasy of her burnt-offering and sacrifice, Selina stood alone.

And yet— not quite alone! For, as the fire was roaring at its best, certain stars stepped delicately forth on the surface of the immensity above, and peered down doubtfully—with wonder at first, then with interest, then with recognition, with a start of glad surprise. *They* at least knew all about it, *they* understood. Among *them* the Name was a daily familiar word; his story was a part of the music to which they swung, himself was their fellow and their mate and comrade. So they peeped, and winked, and peeped again, and called to their laggard brothers to come quick and see.

* * * * *

The best of life is but intoxication, and Selina, who during her brief inebriation had lived in an ecstasy as golden as our drab existence affords, had to experience the inevitable bitterness of awakening sobriety, when the dying down of the flames into sullen embers coincided with the frenzied entrance of Aunt Eliza on the scene. It was not so much that she was at once and forever disrated, broke, sent before the mast, and branded as one on whom no reliance could be placed, even with Edward safe at school, and myself under the distant vigilance of an aunt; that her pocket money was stopped indefinitely, and her new Church Service, the pride of her last birthday, removed from her own custody and placed under the control of a Trust. She sorrowed rather because she had dragged poor Harold, against his better judgment, into a most horrible scrape, and moreover because, when the reaction had fairly set in, when the exaltation had fizzled away and the young-lady portion of her had crept timorously back to its wonted lodging, she could only see herself as a plain fool, unjustified, undeniable, without a shadow of an excuse or explanation.

As for Harold, youth and a short memory made his case less pitiful than it seemed to his more sensitive sister. True, he started upstairs to his lonely cot bellowing dismally, before him a dreary future of pains and penalties, sufficient to last to the crack of doom. Outside his door, however, he tumbled over Augustus the cat, and made capture of him; and at once his mourning was changed into a song of triumph, as he conveyed his prize into port. For Augustus, who detested above all things going to bed with little boys, was ever more knave than fool, and the trapper who was wily enough to ensnare him had achieved something notable. Augustus, when he realized that his fate was sealed, and his night's lodging settled, wisely made the best of things, and listened, with a languorous air of complete comprehension, to the incoherent babble concerning pigs and heroes, moles and bonfires, which served Harold for a self-sung lullaby. Yet it may be doubted whether Augustus was one of those rare fellows who thoroughly understood.

But Selina knew no more of this source of consolation than of the sympathy with which the stars were winking above her; and it was only after some sad interval of time, and on a very moist pillow, that she drifted into that quaint inconsequent country where you may meet your own pet hero strolling down the road, and commit what hair-brained oddities you like, and everybody understands and appreciates.

Dies Irae

Those memorable days that move in procession, their heads just out of the mist of years long dead—the most of them are full-eyed as the dandelion that from dawn to shade has steeped itself in sunlight. Here and there in their ranks, however, moves a forlorn one who is blind—blind in the sense of the dulled window-pane on which the pelting raindrops have mingled and run down, obscuring sunshine and the circling birds, happy fields, and storied garden; blind with the spatter of a misery uncomprehended, unanalysed, only felt as something corporeal in its buffeting effects.

Martha began it; and yet Martha was not really to blame. Indeed, that was half the trouble of it—no solid person stood full in view, to be blamed and to make atonement. There was only a wretched, impalpable condition to deal with. Breakfast was just over; the sun was summoning us, imperious as a herald with clamour of trumpet; I ran upstairs to her with a broken bootlace in my hand, and there she was, crying in a corner, her head in her apron. Nothing could be got from her but the same dismal succession of sobs that would not have done, that struck and hurt like a physical beating; and meanwhile the sun was getting impatient, and I wanted my bootlace.

Inquiry below stairs revealed the cause. Martha's brother was dead, it seemed—her sailor brother Billy; drowned in one of those strange far-off seas it was our dream to navigate one day. We had known Billy well, and appreciated him. When an approaching visit of Billy to his sister had been announced, we had counted the days to it. When his cheery voice was at last heard in the kitchen and we had descended with shouts, first of all he had to exhibit his tattooed arms, always a subject for fresh delight and envy and awe; then he was called upon for tricks, jugglings, and strange, fearful gymnastics; and lastly came yarns, and more yarns, and yarns till bedtime. There had never been anyone like Billy in his own particular sphere; and now he was drowned, they said, and Martha was miserable, and—and I couldn't get a new bootlace. They told me that Billy would never come back any more, and I stared out of the window at the sun which came back, right enough, every day, and their news conveyed nothing whatever to me. Martha's sorrow hit home a little, but only because the actual sight and sound of it gave me a dull, bad sort of pain low down inside—a pain not to be actually located. Moreover, I was still wanting my bootlace.

This was a poor sort of a beginning to a day that, so far as outside conditions went, had promised so well. I rigged up a sort of jurymast of a bootlace with a bit of old string, and wandered off to look up the girls, conscious of a jar and a discordance in the scheme of things. The moment I entered the schoolroom something in the air seemed to tell me that here, too, matters were strained and awry. Selina was staring listlessly out of the window, one foot curled round her leg. When I spoke to her she jerked a shoulder testily, but did not condescend to the civility of a reply. Charlotte, absolutely unoccupied, sprawled in a chair, and there were signs of sniffles about her, even at that early hour. It was but a trifling matter that had caused all this electricity in the atmosphere, and the girls' manner of taking it seemed to me most unreasonable. Within the last few days the time had come round for the despatch of a hamper to Edward at school. Only one hamper a term was permitted him, so its preparation was a sort of blend of revelry and religious ceremony. After the main corpus of the thing had been carefully selected and safely bestowed —the pots of jam, the cake, the sausages, and the apples that filled up corners so nicely—after the last package had been wedged in, the girls had deposited their own private and personal offerings on the top. I forget their precise nature; anyhow, they were nothing of any particular practical use to a boy. But they had involved some contrivance and labour, some skimping of pocket money, and much delightful cloud-building as to the effect on their enraptured recipient. Well, yesterday there had come a terse acknowledgment from Edward, heartily commending the cakes and the jam, stamping the sausages with the seal of Smith major's approval, and finally hinting that, fortified as he now was, nothing more was necessary but a remittance of five shillings in postage stamps to enable him to face the world armed against every buffet of fate. That was all. Never a word or a hint of the personal tributes or of his appreciation of them. To us—to Harold and me, that is—the letter seemed natural and sensible enough. After all, provender was the main thing, and five shillings stood for a complete equipment against the most unexpected turns of luck. The presents were very well in their way—very nice, and so on—but life was a serious matter, and the contest called for cakes and half-crowns to carry it on, not gew-gaws and knitted mittens and the like. The girls, however, in their obstinate way, persisted in taking their own view of the slight. Hence it was that I received my second rebuff of the morning.

Somewhat disheartened, I made my way downstairs and out into the sunlight, where I found Harold playing conspirators by himself on the gravel. He had dug a small hole in the walk and had laid an imaginary train of powder thereto; and, as he sought refuge in the laurels from the inevitable explosion, I heard him murmur: " 'My God!' said the Czar, 'my plans are frustrated!' " It seemed an excellent occasion for being a black puma. Harold liked black pumas, on the whole, as well as any animal we were familiar with. So I launched myself on him, with the appropriate howl, rolling him over on the gravel.

Life may be said to be composed of things that come off and things that don't come off. This thing, unfortunately, was one of the things that didn't come off. From beneath me I heard a shrill cry of, "Oh, it's my sore knee!" And Harold wriggled himself free from the puma's clutches, bellowing dismally. Now, I honestly didn't know he had a sore knee, and, what's more, he knew I didn't know he had a sore knee. According to boy-ethics, therefore, his attitude was wrong, sore knee or not, and no apology was due from me. I made half-way advances, however, suggesting we should lie in ambush by the edge of the pond and cut off the ducks as they waddled down in simple, unsuspecting single file; then hunt them as bisons flying scattered over the vast prairie. A fascinating pursuit this, and strictly illicit. But Harold would none of my overtures, and retreated to the house wailing with full lungs.

Things were getting simply infernal. I struck out blindly for the open country; and even as I made for the gate a shrill voice from a window bade me keep off the flower-beds. When the gate had swung to behind me with a vicious click I felt better, and after ten minutes along the road it began to grow on me that some radical change was needed, that I was in a blind alley, and that this intolerable state of things must somehow cease. All that I could do

I had already done. As well-meaning a fellow as ever stepped was
pounding along the road that day, with an exceeding sore heart; one
who only wished to live and let live, in touch with his fellows, and
appreciating what joys life had to offer. What was wanted now was
a complete change of environment. Somewhere in the world, I felt
sure, justice and sympathy still resided. There were places called
pampas, for instance, that sounded well. League upon league of
grass, with just an occasional wild horse, and not a relation within
the horizon! To a bruised spirit this seemed a sane and a healing
sort of existence. There were other pleasant corners, again, where
you dived for pearls and stabbed sharks in the stomach with your
big knife. No relations would be likely to come interfering with you
when thus blissfully occupied. And yet I did not wish—just yet—to
have done with relations entirely. They should be made to feel their
position first, to see themselves as they really were, and to wish—
when it was too late—that they had behaved more properly.

Of all professions, the army seemed to lend itself the most
thoroughly to the scheme. You enlisted, you followed the drum,
you marched, fought, and ported arms, under strange skies, through
unrecorded years. At last, at long last, your opportunity would come,
when the horrors of war were flickering through the quiet country-
side where you were cradled and bred, but where the memory of
you had long been dim. Folk would run together, clamorous, palsied
with fear; and among the terror-stricken groups would figure certain
aunts. "What hope is left us?" they would ask themselves, "save in
the clemency of the General, the mysterious, invincible General, of
whom men tell such romantic tales?" And the army would march
in, and the guns would rattle and leap along the village street, and,
last of all, you—you, the General, the fabled hero—you would
enter, on your coal-black charger, your pale set face seamed by an
interesting sabre-cut. And then—but every boy has rehearsed this
familiar piece a score of times. You are magnanimous, in fine—that
goes without saying; you have a coal-black horse, and a sabre-cut,
and you can afford to be very magnanimous. But all the same you
give them a good talking-to.

This pleasant conceit simply ravished my soul for some twenty
minutes, and then the old sense of injury began to well up afresh,
and to call for new plasters and soothing syrups. This time I took

refuge in happy thoughts of the sea. The sea was my real sphere, after all. On the sea, in especial, you could combine distinction with lawlessness, whereas the army seemed to be always weighted by a certain plodding submission to discipline. To be sure, by all accounts, the life was at first a rough one. But just then I wanted to suffer keenly; I wanted to be a poor devil of a cabin boy, kicked, beaten, and sworn at—for a time. Perhaps some hint, some inkling of my sufferings might reach their ears. In due course the sloop or felucca would turn up—it always did—the rakish-looking craft, black of hull, low in the water, and bristling with guns; the jolly Roger flapping overhead, and myself for sole commander. By and by, as usually happened, an East Indiaman would come sailing along full of relations—not a necessary relation would be missing. And the crew should walk the plank, and the captain should dance from his own yard-arm, and then I would take the passengers in hand—that miserable group of well-known figures cowering on the quarter-deck!—and then—and then the same old performance: the air thick with magnanimity. In all the repertory of heroes, none is more truly magnanimous than your pirate chief.

When at last I brought myself back from the future to the actual present, I found that these delectable visions had helped me over a longer stretch of road than I had imagined; and I looked around and took my bearings. To the right of me was a long low building of grey stone, new, and yet not smugly so; new, and yet possessing distinction, marked with a character that did not depend on lichen or on crumbling semi-effacement of moulding and mullion. Strangers might have been puzzled to classify it; to me, an explorer from earliest years, the place was familiar enough. Most folk called it "The Settlement"; others, with quite sufficient conciseness for our neighbourhood, spoke of "them there fellows up by Halliday's"; others again, with a hint of derision, named them the "monks." This last title I supposed to be intended for satire, and knew to be fatuously wrong. I was thoroughly acquainted with monks—in books—and well knew the cut of their long frocks, their shaven polls, and their fascinating big dogs, with brandy-bottles round their necks, incessantly hauling happy travellers out of the snow. The only dog at the settlement was an Irish terrier, and the good fellows who owned him, and were owned by him, in common, wore clothes of the most nondescript order, and mostly cultivated side-whiskers. I had wandered up there one day, searching (as usual) for something I never found, and had been taken in by them and treated as friend and comrade. They had made me free of their ideal little rooms, full of books and pictures, and clean of the antimacassar taint; they had shown me their chapel, high, hushed, and faintly scented, beautiful with a strange new beauty born both of what it had and what it had not—that too familiar dowdiness of common places of worship. They had also fed me in their dining-hall, where a long table stood on trestles plain to view, and all the woodwork was natural, unpainted, healthily scrubbed, and redolent of the forest it came from. I brought away from that visit, and kept by me for many days, a sense of cleanness, of the freshness that pricks the senses—the freshness of cool spring water; and the large swept spaces of the rooms, the red tiles, and the oaken settles, suggested a comfort that had no connection with padded upholstery.

On this particular morning I was in much too unsociable a mind for paying friendly calls. Still, something in the aspect of the place harmonized with my humour, and I worked my way round to the back, where the ground, after affording level enough for a kitchen-garden, broke steeply away. Both the word Gothic and the thing itself were still unknown to me, yet doubtless the architecture of the place, consistent throughout, accounted for its sense of comradeship in my hour of disheartenment. As I mused there, with the low, grey, purposeful-looking building before me, and thought of my pleasant friends within, and what good times they always seemed to be having, and how they larked with the Irish terrier, whose footing was one of a perfect equality, I thought of a certain look in their faces, as if they had a common purpose and a business, and were acting under orders thoroughly recognized and understood. I remembered, too, something that Martha had told me, about these same fellows doing "a power o' good," and other hints I had collected vaguely, of renouncements, rules, self-denials, and the like. Thereupon, out of the depths of my morbid soul swam up a new and fascinating idea; and at once the career of arms seemed over-acted and stale, and piracy, as a profession, flat and unprofitable. This, then, or something like it, should be my vocation and my revenge. A severer line of business, perhaps, such as I had read of; something that included black bread and a hair-shirt. There should be vows, too—irrevocable, blood-curdling vows; and an iron grating. This iron grating was the most necessary feature of all, for I intended that on the other side of it my relations should range themselves—I mentally ran over the catalogue, and saw that the whole gang was present, all in their proper places—a sad-eyed row, combined in tristful appeal. "We see our error now," they would say; "we were always dull dogs, slow to catch—especially in those akin to us—the finer qualities of soul! We misunderstood you, misappreciated you, and we own up to it. And now—"

"Alas, my dear friends," I would strike in here, waving towards them an ascetic hand—one of the emaciated sort, that lets the light shine through at the fingertips—"Alas, you come too late! This conduct is fitting and meritorious on your part, and indeed I always expected it of you, sooner or later; but the die is cast, and you may go home again and bewail at your leisure this too tardy repentance of yours. For me, I am vowed and dedicated, and my relations henceforth are austerity and holy works. Once a month, should you wish it, it shall be your privilege to come and gaze at me through this very solid grating; but—" Whack!

A well-aimed clod of garden soil, whizzing just past my ear, starred on a tree-trunk behind, spattering me with dirt. The present came back to me in a flash, and I nimbly took cover behind the trees, realizing that the enemy was up and abroad, with ambuscades, alarms, and thrilling sallies. It was the gardener's boy, I knew well enough; a red proletariat, who hated me just because I was a gentleman. Hastily picking up a nice sticky clod in one hand, with the other I delicately projected my hat beyond the shelter of the tree-trunk. I had not fought with Red-skins all these years for nothing.

As I had expected, another clod, of the first class for size and stickiness, took my poor hat full in the centre. Then, Ajax-like, shouting terribly, I issued from shelter and discharged my ammunition. Woe then for the gardener's boy, who, unprepared, skipping in premature triumph, took the clod full in his stomach! He, the foolish one, witless on whose side the gods were fighting that day, discharged yet other missiles, wavering and wide of the mark; for his wind had been taken with the first clod, and he shot wildly, as one already desperate and in flight. I got another clod in at short range; we clinched on the brow of the hill, and rolled down to the bottom together. When he had shaken himself free and regained his legs, he trotted smartly off in the direction of his mother's cottage; but over his shoulder he discharged at me both imprecation and deprecation, menace mixed up with an under-current of tears.

But as for me, I made off smartly for the road, my frame tingling, my head high, with never a backward look at the Settlement of suggestive aspect, or at my well-planned future which lay in fragments around it. Life had its jollities, then; life was action, contest, victory! The present was rosy once more, surprises lurked on every side, and I was beginning to feel villainously hungry.

Just as I gained the road a cart came rattling by, and I rushed for it, caught the chain that hung below, and swung thrillingly between the dizzy wheels, choked and blinded with delicious-smelling dust, the world slipping by me like a streaky ribbon below, till the driver licked at me with his whip, and I had to descend to earth again. Abandoning the beaten track, I then struck homewards through the fields; not that the way was very much shorter, but rather because on that route one avoided the bridge, and had to splash through the stream and get refreshingly wet. Bridges were made for narrow folk, for people with aims and vocations which compelled abandonment of many of life's highest pleasures. Truly wise men called on each element alike to minister to their joy, and while the touch of sun-bathed air, the fragrance of garden soil, the ductible qualities of mud, and the spark-whirling rapture of playing with fire, had each their special charm, they did not overlook the bliss of getting their feet wet. As I came forth on the common Harold broke out of an adjoining copse and ran to meet me, the morning rain-clouds all blown away from his face. He had made a new squirrel-stick, it seemed. Made it all himself; melted the lead and everything! I examined the instrument critically, and pronounced it absolutely magnificent. As we passed in at our gate the girls were distantly visible, gardening with a zeal in cheerful contrast to their heartsick lassitude of the morning.

"There's bin another letter come today," Harold explained, "and the hamper got joggled about on the journey, and the presents worked down into the straw and all over the place. One of 'em turned up inside the cold duck. And that's why they weren't found at first. And Edward said, Thanks *awfully*!"

I did not see Martha again until we were all re-assembled at tea-time, when she seemed red-eyed and strangely silent, neither scolding nor finding fault with anything. Instead, she was very kind and thoughtful with jams and things, feverishly pressing unwonted delicacies on us, who wanted little pressing enough. Then suddenly, when I was busiest, she disappeared; and Charlotte whispered me presently that she had heard her go to her room and lock herself in. This struck me as a funny sort of proceeding.

Mutabile Semper

She stood on the other side of the garden fence, and regarded me gravely as I came down the road. Then she said, "Hi—o!" and I responded, "Hullo!" and pulled up somewhat nervously.

To tell the truth, the encounter was not entirely unexpected on my part. The previous Sunday I had seen her in church, and after service it had transpired who she was, this new-comer, and what aunt she was staying with. That morning a volunteer had been called for, to take a note to the Parsonage, and rather to my own surprise I had found myself stepping forward with alacrity, while the others had become suddenly absorbed in various pursuits, or had sneaked unobtrusively out of view. Certainly I had not yet formed any deliberate plan of action; yet I suppose I recollected that the road to the Parsonage led past her aunt's garden.

She began the conversation, while I hopped backwards and forwards over the ditch, feigning a careless ease.

"Saw you in church on Sunday," she said; "only you looked different then. All dressed up, and your hair quite smooth, and brushed up at the sides, and oh, so shiny! What do they put on it to make it shine like that? Don't you hate having your hair brushed?" she ran on, without waiting for an answer. "How your boots squeaked when you came down the aisle! When mine squeak, I walk in all the puddles till they stop. Think I'll get over the fence."

This she proceeded to do in a businesslike way, while, with my hands deep in my pockets, I regarded her movements with silent interest, as those of some strange new animal.

"I've been gardening," she explained, when she had joined me, "but I didn't like it. There's so many worms about today. I hate worms. Wish they'd keep out of the way when I'm digging."

"Oh, I like worms when I'm digging," I replied heartily, "seem to make things more lively, don't they?"

She reflected. "Shouldn't mind 'em so much if they were warm and *dry*," she said, "but—" here she shivered, and somehow I liked her for it, though if it had been my own flesh and blood hoots of derision would have instantly assailed her.

From worms we passed, naturally enough, to frogs, and thence to pigs, aunts, gardeners, rocking-horses, and other fellow-citizens of our common kingdom. In five minutes we had each other's confidences, and I seemed to have known her for a lifetime. Somehow, on the subject of one's self it was easier to be frank and communicative with her than with one's female kin. It must be, I supposed, because she was less familiar with one's faulty, tattered past.

"I was watching you as you came along the road," she said presently, "and you had your head down and your hands in your pockets, and you weren't throwing stones at anything, or whistling, or jumping over things; and I thought perhaps you'd bin scolded, or got a stomachache."

"No," I answered shyly, "it wasn't that. Fact is, I was—I often—but it's a secret."

There I made an error in tactics. That enkindling word set her dancing round me, half beseeching, half imperious. "Oh, do tell it me!" she cried. "You must! I'll never tell anyone else at all, I vow and declare I won't!"

Her small frame wriggled with emotion, and with imploring eyes she jigged impatiently just in front of me. Her hair was tumbled bewitchingly on her shoulders, and even the loss of a front tooth—a loss incidental to her age—seemed but to add a piquancy to her face.

"You won't care to hear about it," I said, wavering. "Besides, I can't explain exactly. I think I won't tell you." But all the time I knew I should have to.

"But I *do* care," she wailed plaintively. "I didn't think you'd be so unkind!"

This would never do. That little downward tug at either corner of the mouth—I knew the symptom only too well!

"It's like this," I began stammeringly. "This bit of road here—up as far as that corner—you know it's a horrid dull bit of road. I'm always having to go up and down it, and I know it so well, and I'm so sick of it. So whenever I get to that corner, I just—well, I go right off to another place!"

"What sort of a place?" she asked, looking round her gravely.

"Of course it's just a place I imagine," I went on hurriedly and rather shamefacedly: "but it's an awfully nice place—the nicest place you ever saw. And I always go off there in church, or during joggraphy lessons."

"I'm sure it's not nicer than my home," she cried patriotically. "Oh, you ought to see my home—it's lovely! We've got—"

"Yes it is, ever so much nicer," I interrupted. "I mean"—I went on apologetically—"of course I know your home's beautiful and all that. But this *must* be nicer, 'cos if you want anything at all, you've only *got* to want it, and you can have it!"

"That sounds jolly," she murmured. "Tell me more about it, please. Tell me how you get there, first."

"I—don't—quite—know—exactly," I replied. "I just go. But generally it begins by—well, you're going up a broad, clear river in a sort of a boat. You're not rowing or anything—you're just moving along. And there's beautiful grass meadows on both sides, and the river's very full, quite up to the level of the grass. And you glide along by the edge. And the people are haymaking there, and playing games, and walking about; and they shout to you, and you shout back to them, and they bring you things to eat out of their baskets, and let you drink out of their bottles; and some of 'em are the nice people you read about in books. And so at last you come to the Palace steps—great broad marble steps, reaching right down to the water. And there at the steps you find every sort of boat you can imagine—schooners, and punts, and row-boats, and little men-of-war. And you have any sort of boating you want to—rowing, or sailing, or shoving about in a punt!"

"I'd go sailing," she said decidedly: "and I'd steer. No, *you'd* have to steer, and I'd sit about on the deck. No, I wouldn't though; I'd row—at least I'd make you row, and I'd steer. And then we'd—Oh, no! I'll tell you what we do! We'd just sit in a punt and dabble!"

"Of course we'll do just what you like," I said hospitably; but already I was beginning to feel my liberty of action somewhat curtailed by this exigent visitor I had so rashly admitted into my sanctum.

"I don't think we'd boat at all," she finally decided. "It's always so *wobbly*. Where do you come to next?"

"You go up the steps," I continued, "and in at the door, and the very first place you come to is the Chocolate-room!"

She brightened up at this, and I heard her murmur with gusto, "Chocolate-room!"

"It's got every sort of chocolate you can think of," I went on: "soft chocolate, with sticky stuff inside, white and pink, what girls like; and hard shiny chocolate, that cracks when you bite it, and takes such a nice long time to suck!"

"I like the soft stuff best," she said: "'cos you can eat such a lot more of it!" This was to me a new aspect of the chocolate question, and I regarded her with interest and some respect. With us, chocolate was none too common a thing, and, whenever we happened to come by any, we resorted to the quaintest devices in order to make it last out. Still, legends had reached us of children who actually had, from time to time, as much chocolate as they could possibly eat; and here, apparently, was one of them.

"You can have all the creams," I said magnanimously, "and I'll eat the hard sticks, 'cos I like 'em best."

"Oh, but you mustn't!" she cried impetuously. "You must eat the same as I do! It isn't nice to want to eat different. I'll tell you what— you must give me all the chocolate, and then I'll give you—I'll give you what you ought to have!"

"Oh, all right," I said, in a subdued sort of way. It seemed a little hard to be put under a sentimental restriction like this in one's own Chocolate-room.

"In the next room you come to," I proceeded, "there's fizzy drinks! There's a marble-slab business all round the room, and little silver taps; and you just turn the right tap, and have any kind of fizzy drink you want."

"What fizzy drinks are there?" she inquired.

"Oh, all sorts," I answered hastily, hurrying on. (She might restrict my eatables, but I'd be hanged if I was going to have her meddle with my drinks.) "Then you go down the corridor, and at the back of the palace there's a great big park—the finest park you ever saw. And there's ponies to ride on, and carriages and carts; and a little railway, all complete, engine and guard's van and all; and you work it yourself, and you can go first-class, or in the van, or on the engine, just whichever you choose."

"I'd go on the engine," she murmured dreamily. "No, I wouldn't, I'd—"

"Then there's all the soldiers," I struck in. Really the line had to be drawn somewhere, and I could not have my railway system disorganized and turned upside down by a mere girl. "There's any quantity of 'em, fine big soldiers, and they all belong to me. And a row of brass cannons all along the terrace! And every now and then I give the order, and they fire off all the guns!"

"No, they don't," she interrupted hastily. "I won't have 'em fire off any guns. You must tell 'em not to. I hate guns, and as soon as they begin firing I shall run right away!"

"But—but that's what they're *there* for," I protested, aghast.

"I don't care," she insisted. "They mustn't do it. They can walk about behind me if they like, and talk to me, and carry things. But they mustn't fire off any guns."

I was sadly conscious by this time that in this brave palace of mine, wherein I was wont to swagger daily, irresponsible and unquestioned, I was rapidly becoming—so to speak—a mere lodger. The idea of my fine big soldiers being told off to "carry things"! I was not inclined to tell her any more, though there still remained plenty more to tell.

"Any other boys there?" she asked presently, in a casual sort of way.

"Oh yes," I unguardedly replied. "Nice chaps, too. We'll have great—"

Then I recollected myself. "We'll play with them, of course," I went on. "But you are going to be *my* friend, aren't you? And you'll come in *my* boat, and we'll travel in the guard's van together, and I'll stop the soldiers firing off their guns!"

But she looked mischievously away, and—do what I would—I could not get her to promise.

Just then the striking of the village clock awoke within me another clamorous timepiece, reminding me of mid-day mutton a good half-mile away, and of penalties and curtailments attaching to a late appearance. We took a hurried farewell of each other, and before we parted I got from her an admission that she might be gardening again that afternoon, if only the worms would be less aggressive and give her a chance.

"Remember," I said as I turned to go, "you mustn't tell anybody about what I've been telling you!"

She appeared to hesitate, swinging one leg to and fro while she regarded me sideways with half-shut eyes.

"It's a dead secret," I said artfully. "A secret between us two, and nobody knows it except ourselves!"

Then she promised, nodding violently, big-eyed, her mouth pursed up small. The delight of revelation, and the bliss of possessing a secret, run each other very close. But the latter generally wins—for a time.

I had passed the mutton stage and was weltering in warm rice pudding, before I found leisure to pause and take in things generally; and then a glance in the direction of the window told me, to my dismay, that it was raining hard. This was annoying in every way, for, even if it cleared up later, the worms—I knew well from experience—would be offensively numerous and frisky. Sulkily I said grace and accompanied the others upstairs to the schoolroom; where I got out my paint-box and resolved to devote myself seriously to Art, which of late I had much neglected. Harold got hold of a sheet of paper and a pencil, retired to a table in the corner, squared his elbows, and protruded his tongue. Literature had always been his form of artistic expression.

Selina had a fit of the fidgets, bred of the unpromising weather, and, instead of settling down to something on her own account, must needs walk round and annoy us artists, intent on embodying our conceptions of the ideal. She had been looking over my shoulder some minutes before I knew of it; or I would have had a word or two to say upon the subject.

"I suppose you call that thing a ship," she remarked contemptuously. "Who ever heard of a pink ship? Hoo-hoo!"

I stifled my wrath, knowing that in order to score properly it was necessary to keep a cool head.

"There is a pink ship," I observed with forced calmness, "lying in the toy-shop window now. You can go and look at it if you like. D' you suppose you know more about ships than the fellows who make 'em?"

Selina, baffled for the moment, returned to the charge presently.

"Those are funny things, too," she observed. "S'pose they're meant to be trees. But they're *blue*."

"They *are* trees," I replied with severity; "and they *are* blue. They've *got* to be blue, 'cos you stole my gamboge last week, so I can't mix up any green."

"*Didn't* steal your gamboge," declared Selina, haughtily, edging away, however, in the direction of Harold. "And I wouldn't tell lies, either, if I was you, about a dirty little bit of gamboge."

I preserved a discreet silence. After all, I knew *she* knew she stole my gamboge.

The moment Harold became conscious of Selina's stealthy approach, he dropped his pencil and flung himself flat upon the table, protecting thus his literary efforts from chilling criticism by the interposed thickness of his person. From somewhere in his interior proceeded a heart-rending compound of squeal and whistle, as of escaping steam—long-drawn, ear-piercing, unvarying in note.

"I only just wanted to see," protested Selina, struggling to uproot his small body from the scrawl it guarded. But Harold clung limpet-like to the table edge, and his shrill protest continued to deafen humanity and to threaten even the serenities of Olympus. The time seemed come for a demonstration in force. Personally I cared little what soul-outpourings of Harold were priated by Selina—she was pretty sure to get hold of them sooner or later—and indeed I rather welcomed the diversion as favourable to the undisturbed pursuit of Art. But the clannishness of sex has its unwritten laws. Boys, as such, are sufficiently put upon, maltreated, trodden under, as it is. Should they fail to hang together in perilous times, what disasters, what ignominies may not be looked for? Possibly even an extinction of the tribe. I dropped my paint brush and sailed shouting into the fray.

The result for a short space hung dubious. There is a period of life when the difference of a year or two in age far outweighs the minor advantage of sex. Then the gathers of Selina's frock came away with a sound like the rattle of distant musketry; and this calamity it was, rather than mere brute compulsion, that quelled her indomitable spirit.

The female tongue is mightier than the sword, as I soon had good reason to know, when Selina, her riven garment held out at length, avenged her discomfiture with the Greek-fire of personalities and abuse. Every black incident in my short, but not stainless, career—every error, every folly, every penalty ignobly suffered—were paraded before me as in a magic-lantern show. The information, however, was not particularly new to me, and the effect was staled by previous rehearsals. Besides, a victory remains a victory, whatever the moral character of the triumphant general.

Harold chuckled and crowed as he dropped from the table, revealing the document over which so many gathers had sighed their short lives out. "*You* can read it if you like," he said to me gratefully. "It's only a death-letter."

It had never been possible to say what Harold's particular amusement of the hour might turn out to be. One thing only was certain, that it would be something improbable, unguessable, not to be foretold. Who, for instance, in search of relaxation, would ever dream of choosing the drawing-up of a testamentary disposition of property? Yet this was the form taken by Harold's latest craze; and in justice this much had to be said for him, that in the christening of his amusement he had gone right to the heart of the matter. The words "will" and "testament" have various meanings and uses; but about the signification of "death-letter" there can be no manner of doubt. I smoothed out the crumpled paper and read. In actual form it deviated considerably from that usually adopted by family solicitors of standing, the only resemblance, indeed, lying in the absence of punctuation.

"my dear edward (it ran) when I die I leave all my muny to you my walkin sticks wips my crop my sord and gun bricks forts and all things i have goodbye my dear charlotte when die I leave you my wach and cumpus and pencel case my salors and camperdown my picteres and evthing goodbye your loving brother armen my dear Martha I love you very much i leave you my garden my mice and rabets my plants in pots when I die please take care of them my dear——" *Catera desunt.*

"Why, you're not leaving *me* anything!" exclaimed Selina, indignantly. "You're a regular mean little boy, and I'll take back the last birthday present I gave you!"

"I don't care," said Harold, repossessing himself of the document. "I *was* going to leave you something, but I shan't now, 'cos you tried to read my death-letter before I was dead!"

"Then I'll write a death-letter myself," retorted Selina, scenting an artistic vengeance: "and I shan't leave you a single thing!" And she went off in search of a pencil.

The tempest within-doors had kept my attention off the

condition of things without. But now a glance through the window told me that the rain had entirely ceased, and that everything was bathed instead in a radiant glow of sunlight, more golden than any gamboge of mine could possibly depict. Leaving Selina and Harold to settle their feud by a mutual disinheritance, I slipped from the room and escaped into the open air, eager to pick up the loose end of my new friendship just where I had dropped it that morning. In the glorious reaction of the sunshine after the downpour, with its moist warm smells, bespanglement of greenery, and inspiriting touch of rain-washed air, the parks and palaces of the imagination glowed with a livelier iris, and their blurred beauties shone out again with fresh blush and palpitation. As I sped along to the tryst, again I accompanied my new comrade along the corridors of my pet palace into which I had so hastily introduced her; and on reflection I began to see that it wouldn't work properly. I had made a mistake, and those were not the surroundings in which she was most fitted to shine. However, it really did not matter much; I had other palaces to place at her disposal—plenty of 'em; and on a further acquaintance with and knowledge of her tastes, no doubt I could find something to suit her.

There was a real Arabian one, for instance, which I visited but rarely—only just when I was in the fine Oriental mood for it; a wonder of silk hangings, fountains of rosewater, pavilions, and minarets. Hundreds of silent, well-trained slaves thronged the stairs and alleys of this establishment, ready to fetch and carry for her all day, if she wished it; and my brave soldiers would be spared the indignity. Also there were processions through the bazaar at odd moments—processions with camels, elephants, and palanquins. Yes, she was more suited for the East, this imperious young person; and I determined that thither she should be personally conducted as soon as ever might be.

I reached the fence and climbed up two bars of it, and leaning over I looked this way and that for my twin-souled partner of the morning. It was not long before I caught sight of her, only a short distance away. Her back was towards me and—well, one can never foresee exactly how one will find things—she was talking to a Boy.

Of course there are boys and boys, and Lord knows I was never narrow. But this was the parson's son from an adjoining village, a red-headed boy and as common a little beast as ever stepped. He cultivated ferrets—his only good point; and it was evidently through the medium of this art that he was basely supplanting me, for her head was bent absorbedly over something he carried in his hands. With some trepidation I called out, "Hi!" But answer there was none. Then again I called, "Hi!" but this time with a sickening sense of failure and of doom. She replied only by a complex gesture, decisive in import if not easily described. A petulant toss of the head, a jerk of the left shoulder, and a backward kick of the left foot, all delivered at once—that was all, and that was enough. The red-headed boy never even condescended to glance my way. Why, indeed, should he? I dropped from the fence without another effort, and took my way homewards along the weary road.

Little inclination was left to me, at first, for any solitary visit to my accustomed palace, the pleasures of which I had so recently tasted in company; and yet after a minute or two I found myself, from habit, sneaking off there much as usual. Presently I became aware of a certain solace and consolation in my newly-recovered independence of action. Quit of all female whims and fanciful restrictions, I rowed, sailed, or punted, just as I pleased; in the Chocolate-room I cracked and nibbled the hard sticks, with a certain contempt for those who preferred the soft, veneered article; and I mixed and quaffed countless fizzy drinks without dread of any prohibitionist. Finally, I swaggered into the park, paraded all my soldiers on the terrace, and, bidding them take the time from me, gave the order to fire off all the guns.

The Magic Ring

Grown-up people really ought to be more careful. Among themselves it may seem but a small thing to give their word and take back their word. For them there are so many compensations. Life lies at their feet, a party-coloured india-rubber ball; they may kick it this way or kick it that, it turns up blue, yellow, or green, but always coloured and glistening. Thus one sees it happen almost every day, and, with a jest and a laugh, the thing is over, and the disappointed one turns to fresh pleasure, lying ready to his hand. But with those who are below them, whose little globe is swayed by them, who rush to build star-pointing alhambras on their most casual word, they really ought to be more careful.

In this case of the circus, for instance, it was not as if we had led up to the subject. It was they who began it entirely—prompted thereto by the local newspaper. "What, a circus!" said they, in their irritating, casual way: "that would be nice to take the children to. Wednesday would be a good day. Suppose we go on Wednesday. Oh, and pleats are being worn again, with rows of deep braid," etc.

What the others thought I know not: what they said, if they said anything, I did not comprehend. For me the house was bursting, walls seemed to cramp and to stifle, the roof was jumping and lifting. Escape was the imperative thing—to escape into the open air, to shake off bricks and mortar, and to wander in the unfrequented places of the earth, the more properly to take in the passion and the promise of the giddy situation.

Nature seemed prim and staid that day, and the globe gave no hint that it was flying round a circus ring of its own. Could they really be true, I wondered, all those bewildering things I had heard tell of circuses? Did long-tailed ponies really walk on their hind-legs and fire off pistols? Was it humanly possible for clowns to perform one-half of the bewitching drolleries recorded in history? And how, oh, how dare I venture to believe that, from off the backs of creamy Arab steeds, ladies of more than earthly beauty discharged themselves through paper hoops? No, it was not altogether possible, there must have been some exaggeration. Still, I would be content with very little, I would take a low percentage—a very small proportion of the circus myth would more than satisfy me. But again, even supposing that history were, once in a way, no liar, could it be that I myself was really fated to look upon this thing in the flesh and to live through it, to survive the rapture? No, it was altogether too much. Something was bound to happen, one of us would develop measles, the world would blow up with a loud explosion. I must not dare, I must not presume, to entertain the smallest hope. I must endeavour sternly to think of something else.

Needless to say, I thought, I dreamed of nothing else, day or night. Waking, I walked arm-in-arm with a clown, and cracked a portentous whip to the brave music of a band. Sleeping, I pursued—perched astride of a coal-black horse—a princess all gauze and spangles, who always managed to keep just one unattainable length ahead. In the early morning Harold and I, once fully awake, cross-exammed each other as to the possibilities of this or that circus tradition, and exhausted the lore long ere the first housemaid was stirring. In this state of exaltation we slipped onward to what promised to be a day of all white days—which brings me right back to my text, that grown-up people really ought to be more careful.

I had known it could never really be; I had said so to myself a dozen times. The vision was too sweetly ethereal for embodiment. Yet the pang of the disillusionment was none the less keen and sickening, and the pain was as that of a corporeal wound. It seemed strange and foreboding, when we entered the breakfast-room, not to find everybody cracking whips, jumping over chairs, and whooping in ecstatic rehearsal of the wild reality to come. The situation became grim and pallid indeed, when I caught the expressions "garden-party" and "my mauve tulle," and realized that they both referred to that very afternoon. And every minute, as I sat silent and listened, my heart sank lower and lower, descending relentlessly like a clock-weight into my boot soles.

Throughout my agony I never dreamed of resorting to a direct question, much less a reproach. Even during the period of joyful anticipation some fear of breaking the spell had kept me from any bald circus talk in the presence of them. But Harold, who was built in quite another way, so soon as he discerned the drift of their conversation and heard the knell of all his hopes, filled the room with wail and clamour of bereavement. The grinning welkin rang with "Circus!" "Circus!" shook the window-panes; the mocking walls re-echoed "Circus!" Circus he would have, and the whole circus, and nothing but the circus. No compromise for him, no evasions, no fallacious, unsecured promises to pay. He had drawn his cheque on the Bank of Expectation, and it had got to be cashed then and there; else he would yell, and yell himself into a fit, and come out of it and yell again. Yelling should be his profession, his art, his mission, his career. He was qualified, he was resolute, and he was in no hurry to retire from the business.

The noisy ones of the world, if they do not always shout themselves into the imperial purple, are sure at least of receiving attention. If they cannot sell everything at their own price, one thing—silence—must, at any cost, be purchased of them. Harold accordingly had to be consoled by the employment of every specious fallacy and base-born trick known to those whose doom it is to handle children. For me their hollow cajolery had no interest, I could pluck no consolation out of their bankrupt though prodigal pledges. I only waited till that hateful, well-known "Some other time, dear!" told me that hope was finally dead. Then I left the room without any remark. It made it worse—if anything could—to hear that stale, worn-out old phrase, still supposed by those dullards to have some efficacy.

To nature, as usual, I drifted by instinct, and there, out of the track of humanity, under a friendly hedgerow had my black hour unseen. The world was a globe no longer, space was no more filled with whirling circuses of spheres. That day the old beliefs rose up and asserted themselves, and the earth was flat again—ditch-riddled, stagnant, and deadly flat. The undeviating roads crawled straight and white, elms dressed themselves stiffly along inflexible hedges, all nature, centrifugal no longer, sprawled flatly in lines out to its farthest edge, and I felt just like walking out to that terminus, and dropping quietly off. Then, as I sat there, morosely chewing bits of stick, the recollection came back to me of certain fascinating advertisements I had spelled out in the papers—advertisements of great and happy men, owning big ships of tonnage running into four figures, who yet craved, to the extent of public supplication, for the sympathetic cooperation of youths as apprentices. I did not rightly know what apprentices might be, nor whether I was yet big enough to be styled a youth; but one thing seemed clear, that, by some such means as this, whatever the intervening hardships, I could eventually visit all the circuses of the world—the circuses of merry France and gaudy Spain, of Holland and Bohemia, of China and Peru. Here was a plan worth thinking out in all its bearings; for something had presently to be done to end this intolerable state of things.

Mid-day, and even feeding-time, passed by gloomily enough, till a small disturbance occurred which had the effect of releasing some of the electricity with which the air was charged. Harold, it should be explained, was of a very different mental mould, and never brooded, moped, nor ate his heart out over any disappointment. One wild outburst—one dissolution of a minute into his original elements of air and water, of tears and outcry—so much insulted nature claimed. Then he would pull himself together, iron out his countenance with a smile, and adjust himself to the new condition of things.

If the gods are ever grateful to man for anything, it is when he is so good as to display a short memory. The Olympians were never slow to recognize this quality of Harold's, in which, indeed, their salvation lay, and on this occasion their gratitude had taken the practical form of a fine fat orange, tough-rinded as oranges of those days were wont to be. This he had eviscerated in the good old-fashioned manner, by biting out a hole in the shoulder, inserting a lump of sugar therein, and then working it cannily till the whole soul and body of the orange passed glorified through the sugar into his being. Thereupon, filled full of orange-juice and iniquity, he conceived a deadly snare. Having deftly patted and squeezed the orange-skin till it resumed its original shape, he filled it up with water, inserted a fresh lump of sugar in the orifice, and, issuing forth, blandly proffered it to me as I sat moodily in the doorway dreaming of strange wild circuses under tropic skies.

Such a stale old dodge as this would hardly have taken me in at ordinary moments. But Harold had reckoned rightly upon the disturbing effect of ill-humour, and had guessed, perhaps, that I thirsted for comfort and consolation, and would not criticize too closely the source from which they came. Unthinkingly I grasped the golden fraud, which collapsed at my touch, and squirted its contents, into my eyes and over my collar, till the nethermost parts of me were damp with the water that had run down my neck. In an instant I had Harold down, and, with all the energy of which I was capable, devoted myself to grinding his head into the gravel; while he, realizing that the closure was applied, and that the time for discussion or argument was past, sternly concentrated his powers on kicking me in the stomach.

Some people can never allow events to work themselves out quietly. At this juncture one of Them swooped down on the scene, pouring shrill, misplaced abuse on both of us: on me for ill-treating my younger brother, whereas it was distinctly I who was the injured and the deceived; on him for the high offense of assault and battery on a clean collar—a collar which I had myself deflowered and defaced, shortly before, in sheer desperate ill-temper. Disgusted and defiant we fled in different directions, rejoining each other later in the kitchen-garden; and as we strolled along together, our short feud forgotten, Harold observed, gloomily: "I should like to be a cave-man, like Uncle George was tellin' us about: with a flint hatchet and no clothes, and live in a cave and not know anybody!"

"And if anyone came to see us we didn't like," I joined in, catching on to the points of the idea, "we'd hit him on the head with the hatchet till he dropped down dead."

"And then," said Harold, warming up, "we'd drag him into the cave and *skin him!*"

For a space we gloated silently over the fair scene our imaginations had conjured up. It was *blood* we felt the need of just then. We wanted no luxuries, nothing dear-bought nor far-fetched. Just plain blood, and nothing else, and plenty of it.

Blood, however, was not to be had. The time was out of joint, and we had been born too late. So we went off to the greenhouse, crawled into the heating arrangement underneath, and played at the dark and dirty and unrestricted life of cave-men till we were heartily sick of it. Then we emerged once more into historic times, and went off to the road to look for something living and sentient to throw stones at.

Nature, so often a cheerful ally, sometimes sulks and refuses to play. When in this mood she passes the word to her underlings, and all the little people of fur and feather take the hint and slip home quietly by back streets. In vain we scouted, lurked, crept, and ambuscaded. Everything that usually scurried, hopped, or fluttered—the small society of the undergrowth—seemed to have engagements elsewhere. The horrid thought that perhaps they had all gone off to the circus occurred to us simultaneously, and we humped ourselves up on the fence and felt bad. Even the sound of approaching wheels failed to stir any interest in us. When you are bent on throwing stones at something, humanity seems obtrusive and better away. Then suddenly we both jumped off the fence together, our faces clearing. For our educated ear had told us that the approaching rattle could only proceed from a dog-cart, and we felt sure it must be the funny man.

We called him the funny man because he was sad and serious, and said little, but gazed right into our souls, and made us tell him just what was on our minds at the time, and then came out with some magnificently luminous suggestion that cleared every cloud away. What was more, he would then go off with us at once and play the thing right out to its finish, earnestly and devotedly, putting all other things aside. So we called him the funny man, meaning only that he was different from those others who thought it incumbent on them to play the painful mummer. The ideal as opposed to the real man was what we meant, only we were not acquainted with the phrase. Those others, with their laboured jests and clumsy contortions, doubtless flattered themselves that *they* were funny men; we, who had to sit through and applaud the painful performance, knew better.

He pulled up to a walk as soon as he caught sight of us, and the dog-cart crawled slowly along till it stopped just opposite. Then he leant his chin on his hand and regarded us long and soulfully, yet said he never a word; while we jigged up and down in the dust, grinning bashfully but with expectation. For you never knew exactly what this man might say or do.

"You look bored," he remarked presently; "thoroughly bored. Or else—let me see; you're not married, are you?"

He asked this in such sad earnestness that we hastened to assure him we were not married, though we felt he ought to have known that much; we had been intimate for some time.

"Then it's only boredom," he said. "Just satiety and world-weariness. Well, if you assure me you aren't married you can climb into this cart and I'll take you for a drive. I'm bored, too. I want to do something dark and dreadful and exciting."

We clambered in, of course, yapping with delight and treading all over his toes; and as we set off, Harold demanded of him imperiously whither he was going.

"My wife," he replied, "has ordered me to go and look up the curate and bring him home to tea. Does that sound sufficiently exciting for you?"

Our faces fell. The curate of the hour was not a success, from our point of view. He was not a funny man, in any sense of the word.

"—but I'm not going to," he added, cheerfully. "Then I was to stop at some cottage and ask—what was it? There was nettle-rash mixed up in it, I'm sure. But never mind, I've forgotten, and it doesn't matter. Look here, we're three desperate young fellows who stick at nothing. Suppose we go off to the circus?"

Of certain supreme moments it is not easy to write. The varying shades and currents of emotion may indeed be put into words by those specially skilled that way; they often are, at considerable length. But the sheer, crude article itself—the strong, live thing that leaps up inside you and swells and strangles you, the dizziness of revulsion that takes the breath like cold water —who shall depict this and live? All I knew was that I would have died then and there, cheerfully, for the funny man; that I longed for red Indians to spring out from the hedge on the dog-cart, just to show what I would do; and that, with all this, I could not find the least little word to say to him.

Harold was less taciturn. With shrill voice, uplifted in solemn chant, he sang the great spheral circus-song, and the undying glory of the Ring. Of its timeless beginning he sang, of its fashioning by cosmic forces, and of its harmony with the stellar plan. Of horses he sang, of their strength, their swiftness, and their docility as to tricks. Of clowns again, of the glory of knavery, and of the eternal type that shall endure. Lastly he sang of Her—the Woman of the Ring—flawless, complete, untrammelled in each subtly curving limb; earth's highest output, time's noblest expression. At least, he doubtless sang all these things and more—he certainly seemed to; though all that was distinguishable, was,

"We're-goin'-to-the-circus!" and then, once more, "We're-goin'-to-the-circus!"—the sweet rhythmic phrase repeated again and again. But indeed I cannot be quite sure, for I heard confusedly, as in a dream. Wings of fire sprang from the old mare's shoulders. We whirled on our way through purple clouds, and earth and the rattle of wheels were far away below.

The dream and the dizziness were still in my head when I found myself, scarce conscious of intermediate steps, seated actually in the circus at last, and took in the first sniff of that intoxicating circus smell that will stay by me while this clay endures. The place was beset by a hum and a glitter and a mist; suspense brooded large o'er the blank, mysterious arena. Strung up to the highest pitch of expectation, we knew not from what quarter, in what divine shape, the first surprise would come.

A thud of unseen hoofs first set us aquiver; then a crash of cymbals, a jangle of bells, a hoarse applauding roar, and Coralie was in the midst of us, whirling past 'twixt earth and sky, now erect, flushed, radiant, now crouched to the flowing mane; swung and tossed and moulded by the maddening dance-music of the band. The mighty whip of the count in the frock-coat marked time with pistol-shots; his war-cry, whooping clear above the music, fired the blood with a passion for splendid deeds, as Coralie, laughing, exultant, crashed through the paper hoops. We gripped the red cloth in front of us, and our souls sped round and round with Coralie, leaping with her, prone with her, swung by mane or tail with her. It was not only the ravishment of her delirious feats, nor her cream-coloured horse of fairy breed, long-tailed, roe-footed, an enchanted prince surely, if ever there was one! It was her more than mortal beauty—displayed, too, under conditions never vouchsafed to us before—that held us spell-bound. What princess had arms so dazzlingly white, or went delicately clothed in such pink and spangles? Hitherto we had known the outward woman as but a drab thing, hour-glass shaped, nearly legless, bunched here, constricted there; slow of movement, and given to deprecating lusty action of limb. Here was a revelation! From henceforth our imaginations would have to be revised and corrected up to date. In one of those swift rushes the mind makes in high-strung moments, I saw myself and Coralie, close enfolded, pacing the world together, o'er hill and plain, through storied cities, past rows of applauding relations—I in my Sunday knickerbockers, she in her pink and spangles.

Summers sicken, flowers fail and die, all beauty but rides round the ring and out at the portal; even so Coralie passed in her turn, poised sideways, panting, on her steed; lightly swayed as a tulip-bloom, bowing on this side and on that as she disappeared; and with her went my heart and my soul, and all the light and the glory and the entrancement of the scene.

Harold woke up with a gasp. "Wasn't she beautiful?" he said, in quite a subdued way for him. I felt a momentary pang. We had been friendly rivals before, in many an exploit; but here was altogether a more serious affair. Was this, then, to be the beginning of strife and coldness, of civil war on the hearthstone and the sundering of old ties? Then I recollected the true position of things, and felt very sorry for Harold; for it was inexorably written that he would have to give way to me, since I was the elder. Rules were not made for nothing, in a sensibly constructed universe.

There was little more to wait for, now Coralie had gone; yet I lingered still, on the chance of her appearing again. Next moment the clown tripped up and fell flat, with magnificent artifice, and at once fresh emotions began to stir. Love had endured its little hour, and stern ambition now asserted itself. Oh, to be a splendid fellow like this, self-contained, ready of speech, agile beyond conception, braving the forces of society, his hand against everyone, yet always getting the best of it! What freshness of humour, what courtesy to dames, what triumphant ability to discomfit rivals, frock-coated and moustached though they might be! And what a grand, self-confident straddle of the legs! Who could desire a finer career than to go through life thus gorgeously equipped! Success was his key-note, adroitness his panoply, and the mellow music of laughter his instant reward. Even Coralie's image wavered and receded. I would come back to her in the evening, of course; but I would be a clown all the working hours of the day.

The short interval was ended: the band, with long-drawn chords, sounded a prelude touched with significance; and the programme, in letters overtopping their fellows, proclaimed Zephyrine, the Bride of the Desert, in her unequalled bareback equestrian interlude. So sated was I already with beauty and with wit, that I hardly dared hope for a fresh emotion. Yet her title was tinged with romance, and Coralie's display had aroused in me an interest in her sex which even herself had failed to satisfy entirely.

Brayed in by trumpets, Zephyrine swung passionately into the arena. With a bound she stood erect, one foot upon each of her supple, plunging Arabs; and at once I knew that my fate was sealed, my chapter closed, and the Bride of the Desert was the one bride for me. Black was her raiment, great silver stars shone through it, caught in the dusky twilight of her gauze; black as her own hair were the two mighty steeds she bestrode. In a tempest they thundered by, in a whirlwind, a scirocco of tan; her cheeks bore the kiss of an Eastern sun, and the sand-storms of her native desert were her satellites. What was Coralie, with her pink silk, her golden hair and slender limbs, beside this magnificent, full-figured Cleopatra? In a twinkling we were scouring the desert—she and I and the two coal-black horses. Side by side, keeping pace in our swinging gallop, we distanced the ostrich, we outstrode the zebra; and, as we went, it seemed the wilderness blossomed like the rose.

* * * * *

I know not rightly how we got home that evening. On the road there were everywhere strange presences, and the thud of phantom hoofs encircled us. In my nose was the pungent circus-smell; the crack of the whip and the frank laugh of the clown were in my ears. The funny man thoughtfully abstained from conversation, and left our illusion quite alone, sparing us all jarring criticism and analysis; and he gave me no chance, when he deposited us at our gate, to get rid of the clumsy expressions of gratitude I had been laboriously framing. For the rest of the evening, distraught and silent, I only heard the march-music of the band, playing on in some corner of my brain. When at last my head touched the pillow, in a trice I was with Zephyrine, riding the boundless Sahara, cheek to cheek, the world well lost; while at times, through the sand-clouds that encircled us, glimmered the eyes of Coralie, touched, one fancied, with something of a tender reproach.

Its Walls Were as of Jasper

In the long winter evenings, when we had the picture-books out on the floor, and sprawled together over them with elbows deep in the hearth-rug, the first business to be gone through was the process of allotment. All the characters in the pictures had to be assigned and dealt out among us, according to seniority, as far as they would go. When once that had been satisfactorily completed, the story was allowed to proceed; and thereafter, in addition to the excitement of the plot, one always possessed a personal interest in some particular member of the cast, whose successes or rebuffs one took as so much private gain or loss.

For Edward this was satisfactory enough. Claiming his right of the eldest, he would annex the hero in the very frontispiece; and for the rest of the story his career, if chequered at intervals, was sure of heroic episodes and a glorious close. But his juniors, who had to put up with characters of a clay more mixed—nay, sometimes with undiluted villany—were hard put to it on occasion to defend their other selves (as it was strict etiquette to do) from ignominy perhaps only too justly merited.

Edward was indeed a hopeless grabber. In the "Buffalo-book," for instance (so named from the subject of its principal picture, though indeed it dealt with varied slaughter in every zone), Edward was the stalwart, bearded figure, with yellow leggings and a powder-horn, who undauntedly discharged the fatal bullet into the shoulder of the great bull bison, charging home to within a yard of his muzzle. To me was allotted the subsidiary character of the friend who had succeeded in bringing down a cow; while Harold had to be content to hold Edward's spare rifle in the background, with evident signs of uneasiness. Farther on, again, where the magnificent chamois sprang rigid into mid-air, Edward, crouched dizzily against the precipice-face, was the sportsman from whose weapon a puff of white smoke was floating away. A bare-kneed guide was all that fell to my share, while poor Harold had to take the boy with the haversack, or abandon, for this occasion at least, all Alpine ambitions.

Of course the girls fared badly in this book, and it was not surprising that they preferred the *Pilgrim's Progress* (for instance), where women had a fair show, and there was generally enough of 'em to go round; or a good fairy story, wherein princesses met with a healthy appreciation. But indeed we were all best pleased with a picture wherein the characters just fitted us, in number, sex, and qualifications; and this, to us, stood for artistic merit.

All the Christmas numbers, in their gilt frames on the nursery-wall, had been gone through and allotted long ago; and in these, sooner or later, each one of us got a chance to figure in some satisfactory and brightly coloured situation. Few of the other pictures about the house afforded equal facilities. They were generally wanting in figures, and even when these were present they lacked dramatic interest. In this picture that I have to speak about, although the characters had a stupid way of not doing anything, and apparently not wanting to do anything, there was at least a sufficiency of them; so in due course they were allotted, too.

In itself the picture, which—in its ebony and tortoise-shell frame—hung in a corner of the dining-room, had hitherto possessed no special interest for us, and would probably never have been dealt with at all but for a revolt of the girls against a succession of books on sport, in which the illustrator seemed to have forgotten that there were such things as women in the world. Selina accordingly made for it one rainy morning, and announced that she was the lady seated in the centre, whose gown of rich, flowered brocade fell in such straight, severe lines to her feet, whose cloak of dark blue was held by a jewelled clasp, and whose long, fair hair was crowned with a diadem of gold and pearl. Well, we had no objection to that; it seemed fair enough, especially to Edward, who promptly proceeded to "grab" the armour-man who stood leaning on his shield at the lady's right hand. A dainty and delicate armour-man this! And I confess, though I knew it was all right and fair and orderly, I felt a slight pang when he passed out of my reach into Edward's possession. His armour was just the sort I wanted myself—scalloped and fluted and shimmering and spotless; and, though he was but a boy by his beardless face and golden hair, the shattered spear-shaft in his grasp proclaimed him a genuine fighter and fresh from some such agreeable work. Yes, I grudged Edward the armour-man, and when he said I could have the fellow on the other side, I hung back and said I'd think about it.

This fellow had no armour nor weapons, but wore a plain jerkin with a leather pouch—a mere civilian—and with one hand he pointed to a wound in his thigh. I didn't care about him, and when Harold eagerly put in his claim I gave way and let him have the man. The cause of Harold's anxiety only came out later. It was the wound he coveted, it seemed. He wanted to have a big, sore wound of his very own, and go about and show it to people, and excite their envy or win their respect. Charlotte was only too pleased to take the child-angel seated at the lady's feet, grappling with a musical instrument much too big for her. Charlotte wanted wings badly, and, next to those, a guitar or a banjo. The angel, besides, wore an amber necklace, which took her fancy immensely.

This left the picture allotted, with the exception of two or three more angels, who peeped or perched behind the main figures with a certain subdued drollery in their faces, as if the thing had gone on long enough, and it was now time to upset something or kick up a row of some sort. We knew these good folk to be saints and angels, because we had been told they were; otherwise we should never have guessed it. Angels, as we knew them in our Sunday books, were vapid, colourless, uninteresting characters, with straight up-and-down sort of figures, white night-gowns, white wings, and the same straight yellow hair parted in the middle. They were serious, even melancholy; and we had no desire to have any traffic with them. These bright bejewelled little persons, however, piquant of face and radiant of feather, were evidently hatched from quite a different egg, and we felt we might have interests in common with them. Short-nosed, shock-headed, with mouths that went up at the corners and with an evident disregard for all their fine clothes, they would be the best of good company, we felt sure, if only we could manage to get at them. One doubt alone disturbed my mind. In games requiring agility, those wings of theirs would give them a tremendous pull. Could they be trusted to play fair? I asked Selina, who replied scornfully that angels *always* played fair. But I went back and had another look at the brown-faced one peeping over the back of the lady's chair, and still I had my doubts.

When Edward went off to school a great deal of adjustment and re-allotment took place, and all the heroes of illustrated literature were at my call, did I choose to possess them. In this particular case, however, I made no haste to seize upon the armour-man. Perhaps it was because I wanted a *fresh* saint of my own, not a stale saint that Edward had been for so long a time. Perhaps it was rather that, ever since I had elected to be saintless, I had got into the habit of strolling off into the background, and amusing myself with what I found there.

A very fascinating background it was, and held a great deal, though so tiny. Blue and red, like gems. Then a white road ran, with wilful, uncalled-for loops, up a steep, conical hill, crowned with towers, bastioned walls, and belfries; and down the road the little knights came riding, two and two. The hill on one side descended to water, tranquil, far-reaching, and blue; and a very curly ship lay at anchor, with one mast having an odd sort of crow's-nest at the top of it.

There was plenty to do in this pleasant land. The annoying thing about it was, one could never penetrate beyond a certain point. I might wander up that road as often as I liked, I was bound to be brought up at the gateway, the funny galleried, top-heavy gateway, of the little walled town. Inside, doubtless, there were high jinks going on; but the password was denied to me. I could get on board a boat and row up as far as the curly ship, but around the headland I might not go. On the other side, of a surety, the shipping lay thick. The merchants walked on the quay, and the sailors sang as they swung out the corded bales. But as for me, I must stay down in the meadow, and imagine it all as best I could.

Once I broached the subject to Charlotte, and found, to my surprise, that she had had the same joys and encountered the same disappointments in this delectable country. She, too, had walked up that road and flattened her nose against that portcullis; and she pointed out something that I had overlooked—to wit, that if you rowed off in a boat to the curly ship, and got hold of a rope, and clambered aboard of her, and swarmed up the mast, and got into the crow's-nest, you could just see over the headland, and take in at your ease the life and bustle of the port. She proceeded to describe all the fun that was going on there, at such length and with so much particularity that I looked at her suspiciously. "Why, you talk as if you'd been in that crow's-nest yourself!" I said. Charlotte answered nothing, but pursed her mouth up and nodded violently for some minutes; and I could get nothing more out of her. I felt rather hurt. Evidently she had managed, somehow or other, to get up into that crow's-nest. Charlotte had got ahead of me on this occasion.

It was necessary, no doubt, that grown-up people should dress themselves up and go forth to pay calls. I don't mean that we saw any sense in the practice. It would have been so much more reasonable to stay at home in your old clothes and play. But we recognized that these folk had to do many unaccountable things, and after all it was *their* life, and not ours, and we were not in a position to criticize. Besides, they had many habits more objectionable than this one, which to us generally meant a free and untrammelled afternoon, wherein to play the devil in our own way. The case was different, however, when the press-gang was abroad, when prayers and excuses were alike disregarded, and we were forced into the service, like native levies impelled toward the foe less by the inherent righteousness of the cause than by the indisputable rifles of their white allies. This was unpardonable and altogether detestable. Still, the thing happened, now and again; and when it did, there was no arguing about it. The order was for the front, and we just had to shut up and march.

Selina, to be sure, had a sneaking fondness for dressing up and paying calls, though she pretended to dislike it, just to keep on the soft side of public opinion. So I thought it extremely mean in her to have the earache on that particular afternoon when Aunt Eliza ordered the pony-carriage and went on the war-path. I was ordered also, in the same breath as the pony-carriage; and, as we eventually trundled off, it seemed to me that the utter waste of that afternoon, for which I had planned so much, could never be made up nor atoned for in all the tremendous stretch of years that still lay before me.

The house that we were bound for on this occasion was a "big house"; a generic title applied by us to the class of residence that had a long carriage-drive through rhododendrons; and a portico propped by fluted pillars; and a grave butler who bolted back swing-doors, and came down steps, and pretended to have entirely forgotten his familiar intercourse with you at less serious moments; and a big hall, where no boots or shoes or upper garments were allowed to lie about frankly and easily, as with us; and where, finally, people were apt to sit about dressed up as if they were going on to a party.

The lady who received us was effusive to Aunt Eliza and hollowly gracious to me. In ten seconds they had their heads together and were hard at it talking *clothes*. I was left high and dry on a straight-backed chair, longing to kick the legs of it, yet not daring. For a time I was content to stare; there was lots to stare at, high and low and around. Then the inevitable fidgets came on, and scratching one's legs mitigated slightly, but did not entirely disperse them. My two warders were still deep in clothes; I slipped off my chair and edged cautiously around the room, exploring, examining, recording.

Many strange, fine things lay along my route—pictures and gimcracks on the walls, trinkets and globular old watches and snuff-boxes on the tables; and I took good care to finger everything within reach thoroughly and conscientiously. Some articles, in addition, I smelt. At last in my orbit I happened on an open door, half concealed by the folds of a curtain. I glanced carefully around. They were still deep in clothes, both talking together, and I slipped through.

This was altogether a more sensible sort of room that I had got into; for the walls were honestly upholstered with books, though these for the most part glimmered provokingly through the glass doors of their tall cases. I read their titles longingly, breathing on every accessible pane of glass, for I dared not attempt to open the doors, with the enemy encamped so near. In the window, though, on a high sort of desk, there lay, all by itself, a most promising-looking book, gorgeously bound. I raised the leaves by one corner, and like scent from a pot-pourri jar there floated out a brief vision of blues and reds, telling of pictures, and pictures all highly coloured! Here was the right sort of thing at last, and my afternoon would not be entirely wasted. I inclined an ear to the door by which I had entered. Like the brimming tide of a full-fed river the grand, eternal, inexhaustible clothes-problem bubbled and eddied and surged along. It seemed safe enough. I slid the book off its desk with some difficulty, for it was very fine and large, and staggered with it to the hearthrug—the only fit and proper place for books of quality, such as this.

They were excellent hearthrugs in that house; soft and wide, with the thickest of pile, and one's knees sank into them most comfortably. When I got the book open there was a difficulty at first in making the great stiff pages lie down. Most fortunately the coal-scuttle was actually at my elbow, and it was easy to find a flat bit of coal to lay on the refractory page. Really, it was just as if everything had been arranged for me. This was not such a bad sort of house after all.

The beginnings of the thing were gay borders—scrolls and strap-work and diapered backgrounds, a maze of colour, with small misshapen figures clambering cheerily up and down everywhere. But first I eagerly scanned what text there was in the middle, in order to get a hint of what it was all about. Of course I was not going to waste any time in reading. A clue, a sign-board, a finger-post was all I required. To my dismay and disgust it was all in a stupid foreign language! Really, the perversity of some people made one at times almost despair of the whole race. However, the pictures remained; pictures never lied, never shuffled nor evaded; and as for the story, I could invent it myself.

Over the page I went, shifting the bit of coal to a new position; and, as the scheme of the picture disengaged itself from out the medley of colour that met my delighted eyes, first there was a warm sense of familiarity, then a dawning recognition, and then—O then! along with blissful certainty came the imperious need to clasp my stomach with both hands, in order to repress the shout of rapture that struggled to escape—it was my own little city!

I knew it well enough, I recognized it at once, though I had never been quite so near it before. Here was the familiar gateway, to the left that strange, slender tower with its grim, square head shot far above the walls; to the right, outside the town, the hill—as of old—broke steeply down to the sea. But today everything was bigger and fresher and clearer, the walls seemed newly hewn, gay carpets were hung out over them, fair ladies and long-haired children peeped and crowded on the battlements. Better still, the portcullis was up—I could even catch a glimpse of the sunlit square within—and a dainty company was trooping through the gate on horseback, two and two. Their horses, in trappings that swept the ground, were gay as themselves; and *they* were the gayest crew, for dress and bearing, I had ever yet beheld. It could mean nothing else but a wedding,

I thought, this holiday attire, this festal and solemn entry; and, wedding or whatever it was, I meant to be there. This time I would not be balked by any grim portcullis; this time I would slip in with the rest of the crowd, find out just what my little town was like, within those exasperating walls that had so long confronted me, and, moreover, have my share of the fun that was evidently going on inside. Confident, yet breathless with expectation, I turned the page.

Joy! At last I was in it, at last I was on the right side of those provoking walls; and, needless to say, I looked about me with much curiosity. A public place, clearly, though not such as I was used to. The houses at the back stood on a sort of colonnade, beneath which the people jostled and crowded. The upper stories were all painted with wonderful pictures. Above the straight line of the roofs the deep blue of a cloudless sky stretched from side to side. Lords and ladies thronged the foreground, while on a dais in the centre a gallant gentleman, just alighted off his horse, stooped to the fingers of a girl as bravely dressed out as Selina's lady between the saints; and round about stood venerable personages, robed in the most variegated clothing. There were boys, too, in plenty, with tiny red caps on their thick hair; and their shirts had bunched up and worked out at the waist, just as my own did so often, after chasing anybody; and each boy of them wore an odd pair of stockings, one blue and the other red. This system of attire went straight to my heart. I had tried the same thing so often, and had met with so much discouragement; and here, at last, was my justification, painted deliberately in a grown-up book! I looked about for my saint-friends—the armour-man and the other fellow—but they were not to be seen. Evidently they were unable to get off duty, even for a wedding, and still stood on guard in that green meadow down below. I was disappointed, too, that not an angel was visible. One or two of them, surely, could easily have been spared for an hour, to run up and see the show; and they would have been thoroughly at home here, in the midst of all the colour and the movement and the fun.

But it was time to get on, for clearly the interest was only just beginning. Over went the next page, and there we were, the whole crowd of us, assembled in a noble church. It was not easy to make out exactly what was going on; but in the throng I was delighted to recognize my angels at last, happy and very much at home. They had managed to get leave off, evidently, and must have run up the hill and scampered breathlessly through the gate; and perhaps they cried a little when they found the square empty, and thought the fun must be all over. Two of them had got hold of a great wax candle apiece, as much as they could stagger under, and were tittering sideways at each other as the grease ran bountifully over their clothes. A third had strolled in among the company, and was chatting to a young gentleman, with whom she appeared to be on the best of terms. Decidedly, this was the right breed of angel for us. None of your sick-bed or night nursery business for them!

Well, no doubt they were now being married, He and She, just as always happened. And then, of course, they were going to live happily ever after; and *that* was the part I wanted to get to. Storybooks were so stupid, always stopping at the point where they became really nice; but this picture-story was only in its first chapters, and at last I was to have a chance of knowing *how* people lived happily ever after. We would all go home together, He and She, and the angels, and I; and the armour-man would be invited to come and stay. And then the story would really begin, at the point where those other ones always left off. I turned the page, and found myself free of the dim and splendid church and once more in the open country.

This was all right; this was just as it should be. The sky was a fleckless blue, the flags danced in the breeze, and our merry bridal party, with jest and laughter, jogged down to the water-side. I was through the town by this time, and out on the other side of the hill, where I had always wanted to be; and, sure enough, there was the harbour, all thick with curly ships. Most of them were piled high with wedding-presents—bales of silk, and gold and silver plate, and comfortable-looking bags suggesting bullion; and the gayest ship of all lay close up to the carpeted landing-stage. Already the bride was stepping daintily down the gangway, her ladies following primly, one by one; a few minutes more and we should all be aboard, the hawsers would splash in the water, the sails would fill and strain. From the deck I should see the little walled town recede and sink and grow dim, while every plunge of our bows brought us nearer to the happy island—it was an island we were bound for, I knew well! Already I could see the island-people waving hands on the crowded quay, whence the little houses ran up the hill to the castle, crowning all with its towers and battlements. Once more we should ride together, a merry procession, clattering up the steep street and through the grim gateway; and then we should have arrived, then we should all dine together, then we should have reached home! And then—

Ow! Ow! Ow!

Bitter it is to stumble out of an opalescent dream into the cold daylight; cruel to lose in a second a sea-voyage, an island, and a castle that was to be practically your own; but cruellest and bitterest of all to know, in addition to your loss, that the fingers of an angry aunt have you tight by the scruff of your neck. My beautiful book was gone too—ravished from my grasp by the dressy lady, who joined in the outburst of denunciation as heartily as if she had been a relative—and naught was left me but to blubber dismally, awakened of a sudden to the harshness of real things and the unnumbered hostilities of the actual world. I cared little for their reproaches, their abuse; but I sorrowed heartily for my lost ship, my vanished island, my uneaten dinner, and for the knowledge that, if I wanted any angels to play with, I must henceforth put up with the anaemic, night-gowned nonentities that hovered over the bed of the Sunday-school child in the pages of the *Sabbath Improver*.

I was led ignominiously out of the house, in a pulpy, watery state, while the butler handled his swing doors with a stony, impassive countenance, intended for the deception of the very elect, though it did not deceive me. I knew well enough that next time he was off duty, and strolled around our way, we should meet in our kitchen as man to man, and I would punch him and ask him riddles, and he would teach me tricks with corks and bits of string. So his unsympathetic manner did not add to my depression.

I maintained a diplomatic blubber long after we had been packed into our pony-carriage and the lodge-gate had clicked behind us, because it served as a sort of armour-plating against heckling and argument and abuse, and I was thinking hard and wanted to be let alone. And the thoughts that I was thinking were two.

First I thought, "I've got ahead of Charlotte *this* time!"

And next I thought, "When I've grown up big, and have money of my own, and a full-sized walking-stick, I will set out early one morning, and never stop till I get to that little walled town." There ought to be no real difficulty in the task. It only meant asking here and asking there, and people were very obliging, and I could describe every stick and stone of it.

As for the island which I had never even seen, that was not so easy. Yet I felt confident that somehow, at some time, sooner or later, I was destined to arrive.

A Saga of the Seas

It happened one day that some ladies came to call, who were not at all the sort I was used to. They suffered from a grievance, so far as I could gather, and the burden of their plaint was Man—Men in general and Man in particular. (Though the words were but spoken, I could clearly discern the capital M in their acid utterance.)

Of course I was not present officially, so to speak. Down below, in my sub-world of chair-legs and hearthrugs and the undersides of sofas, I was working out my own floor-problems, while they babbled on far above my head, considering me as but a chair-leg, or even something lower in the scale. Yet I was listening hard all the time, with that respectful consideration one gives to all grown-up people's remarks, so long as one knows no better.

It seemed a serious indictment enough, as they rolled it out. In tact, considerateness, and right appreciation, as well as in taste and aesthetic sensibilities—we failed at every point, we breeched and bearded prentice-jobs of Nature; and I began to feel like collapsing on the carpet from sheer spiritual anaemia. But when one of them, with a swing of her skirt, prostrated a whole regiment of my brave tin soldiers, and never apologized nor even offered her aid toward revivifying the battle-line, I could not help feeling that in tactfulness and consideration for others she was still a little to seek. And I said as much, with some directness of language.

That was the end of me, from a society point of view. Rudeness to visitors was the unpardonable sin, and in two seconds I had my marching orders, and was sullenly wending my way to the St. Helena of the nursery. As I climbed the stair, my thoughts reverted somehow to a game we had been playing that very morning. It was the good old game of Rafts—a game that will be played till all the oceans are dry and all the trees in the world are felled—and after. And we were all crowded together on the precarious little platform, and Selina occupied every bit as much room as I did, and Charlotte's legs didn't dangle over any more than Harold's. The pitiless sun overhead beat on us all with tropic impartiality, and the hungry sharks, whose fins scored the limitless Pacific stretching out on every side, were impelled by an appetite that made no exceptions as to sex. When we shared the ultimate biscuit and circulated the last water-keg, the girls got an absolute fourth apiece, and neither more nor less; and the only partiality shown was entirely in favour of Charlotte, who was allowed to perceive and to hail the saviour-sail on the horizon. And this was only because it was her turn to do so, not because she happened to be this or that. Surely, the rules of the raft were the rules of life, and in what, then, did these visitor-ladies' grievance consist?

Puzzled and a little sulky, I pushed open the door of the deserted nursery, where the raft that had rocked beneath so many hopes and fears still occupied the ocean-floor. To the dull eye, that merely tarries upon the outsides of things, it might have appeared unromantic and even unraftlike, consisting only as it did of a round sponge-bath on a bald deal towel-horse placed flat on the floor. Even to myself much of the recent raft-glamour seemed to have departed as I half-mechanically stepped inside and curled myself up in it for a solitary voyage. Once I was in, however, the old magic and mystery returned in full flood, when I discovered that the inequalities of the towel-horse caused the bath to rock, slightly, indeed, but easily and incessantly. A few minutes of this delightful motion, and one was fairly launched. So those women below didn't want us? Well, there were other women, and other places, that did. And this was going to be no scrambling raft-affair, but a full-blooded voyage of the Man, equipped and purposeful, in search of what was his rightful own.

Whither should I shape my course, and what sort of vessel should I charter for the voyage? The shipping of all England was mine to pick from, and the far corners of the globe were my rightful inheritance. A frigate, of course, seemed the natural vehicle for a boy of spirit to set out in. And yet there was something rather "uppish" in commanding a frigate at the very first set-off, and little spread was left for the ambition. Frigates, too, could always be acquired later by sheer adventure; and your real hero generally saved up a square-rigged ship for the final achievement and the rapt return. No, it was a schooner that I was aboard of—a schooner whose masts raked devilishly as the leaping seas hissed along her low black gunwale. Many hairbrained youths started out on a mere cutter; but

I was prudent, and besides I had some inkling of the serious affairs that were ahead.

I have said I was already on board; and, indeed, on this occasion I was too hungry for adventure to linger over what would have been a special delight at a period of more leisure—the dangling about the harbour, the choosing your craft, selecting your shipmates, stowing your cargo, and fitting up your private cabin with everything you might want to put your hand on in any emergency whatever. I could not wait for that. Out beyond soundings the big seas were racing westward and calling me, albatrosses hovered motionless, expectant of a comrade, and a thousand islands held each of them a fresh adventure, stored up, hidden away, awaiting production, expressly saved for me. We were humming, close-hauled, down the Channel, spray in the eyes and the shrouds thrilling musically, in much less time than the average man would have taken to transfer his Gladstone bag and his rugs from the train to a sheltered place on the promenade-deck of the tame daily steamer.

So long as we were in pilotage I stuck manfully to the wheel. The undertaking was mine, and with it all its responsibilities, and there was some tricky steering to be done as we sped by headland and bay, ere we breasted the great seas outside and the land fell away behind us. But as soon as the Atlantic had opened out I began to feel that it would be rather nice to take tea by myself in my own cabin, and it therefore became necessary to invent a comrade or two, to take their turn at the wheel.

This was easy enough. A friend or two of my own age, from among the boys I knew; a friend or two from characters in the books I knew; and a friend or two from No-man's-land, where every fellow's a born sailor; and the crew was complete. I addressed them on the poop, divided them into watches, gave instructions I should be summoned on the first sign of pirates, whales, or Frenchmen, and retired below to a well-earned spell of relaxation.

That was the right sort of cabin that I stepped into, shutting the door behind me with a click. Of course, fire-arms were the first thing I looked for, and there they were, sure enough, in their racks, dozens of 'em—double-barrelled guns, and repeating-rifles, and long pistols, and shiny plated revolvers. I rang up the steward and ordered tea, with scones, and jam in its native pots—none of your finicking shallow glass dishes; and, when properly streaked with jam, and blown out with tea, I went through the armoury, clicked the rifles and revolvers, tested the edges of the cutlasses with my thumb, and filled the cartridge-belts chock-full. Everything was there, and of the best quality, just as if I had spent a whole fortnight knocking about Plymouth and ordering things. Clearly, if this cruise came to grief, it would not be for want of equipment.

Just as I was beginning on the lockers and the drawers, the watch reported icebergs on both bows—and, what was more to the point, coveys of Polar bears on the icebergs. I grasped a rifle or two, and hastened on deck. The spectacle was indeed magnificent—it generally is, with icebergs on both bows, and these were exceptionally enormous icebergs. But I hadn't come there to paint Academy pictures, so the captain's gig was in the water and manned almost ere the boatswain's whistle had ceased sounding, and we were pulling hard for the Polar bears—myself and the rifles in the stern-sheets.

I have rarely enjoyed better shooting than I got during that afternoon's tramp over the icebergs. Perhaps I was in specially good form; perhaps the bears "rose" well. Anyhow, the bag was a portentous one. In later days, on reading of the growing scarcity of Polar bears, my conscience has pricked me; but that afternoon I experienced no compunction. Nevertheless, when the huge pile of skins had been hoisted on board, and a stiff grog had been served out to the crew of the captain's gig, I ordered the schooner's head to be set due south. For icebergs were played out, for the moment, and it was getting to be time for something more tropical.

Tropical was a mild expression of what was to come, as was shortly proved. It was about three bells in the next day's forenoon watch when the look-out man first sighted the pirate brigantine. I disliked the looks of her from the first, and, after piping all hands to quarters, had the brass carronade on the fore-deck crammed with grape to the muzzle.

This proved a wise precaution. For the flagitious pirate craft, having crept up to us under the colours of the Swiss Republic, a state with which we were just then on the best possible terms, suddenly shook out the skull-and-cross-bones at her masthead, and let fly with round-shot at close quarters, knocking into pieces several of my crew, who could ill be spared. The sight of their disconnected limbs aroused my ire to its utmost height, and I let them have the contents of the brass carronade, with ghastly effect. Next moment the hulls of the two ships were grinding together, the cold steel flashed from its scabbard, and the death-grapple had begun.

In spite of the deadly work of my grape-gorged carronade, our foe still outnumbered us, I reckoned, by three to one. Honour forbade my fixing it at a lower figure—this was the minimum rate at which one dared to do business with pirates. They were stark veterans, too, every man seamed with ancient sabre-cuts, whereas my crew had many of them hardly attained the maturity which is the gift of ten long summers—and the whole thing was so sudden that I had no time to invent a reinforcement of riper years. It was not surprising, therefore, that my dauntless boarding-party, axe in hand and cutlass between teeth, fought their way to the pirates' deck only to be repulsed again and yet again, and that our planks were soon slippery with our own ungrudged and inexhaustible blood. At this critical point in the conflict, the bo'sun, grasping me by the arm, drew my attention to a magnificent British man-of-war, just hove to in the offing, while the signalman, his glass at his eye, reported that she was inquiring whether we wanted any assistance or preferred to go through with the little job ourselves.

This veiled attempt to share our laurels with us, courteously as it was worded, put me on my mettle. Wiping the blood out of my eyes, I ordered the signalman to reply instantly, with the half-dozen or so of flags that he had at his disposal, that much as we appreciated the valour of the regular service, and the delicacy of spirit that animated its commanders, still this was an orthodox case of young gentleman-adventurer versus the unshaved pirate, and Her Majesty's Marine had nothing to do but to form the usual admiring and applauding background. Then, rallying round me the remnant of my faithful crew, I selected a fresh cutlass (I had worn out three already) and plunged once more into the pleasing carnage.

The result was not long doubtful. Indeed, I could not allow it to be, as I was already getting somewhat bored with the pirate business, and was wanting to get on to something more southern and sensuous. All serious resistance came to an end as soon as I had reached the quarter-deck and cut down the pirate chief—a fine black-bearded fellow in his way, but hardly up to date in his parry-and-thrust business. Those whom our cutlasses had spared were marched out along their own plank, in the approved old fashion; and in tune the scuppers relieved the decks of the blood that made traffic temporarily impossible. And all the time the British-man-of-war admired and applauded in the offing.

As soon as we had got through with the necessary throat-cutting and swabbing-up all hands set to work to discover treasure; and soon the deck shone bravely with ingots and Mexican dollars and church plate. There were ropes of pearls, too, and big stacks of nougat; and rubies, and gold watches, and Turkish Delight in tubs. But I left these trifles to my crew, and continued the search alone. For by this time I had determined that there should be a Princess on board, carried off to be sold in captivity to the bold bad Moors, and now with beating heart awaiting her rescue by me, the Perseus of her dreams.

I came upon her at last in the big state-cabin in the stern; and she wore a holland pinafore over her Princess-clothes, and she had brown wavy hair, hanging down her back, just like—well, never mind, she had brown wavy hair. When gentle-folk meet, courtesies pass; and I will not weary other people with relating all the compliments and counter-compliments that we exchanged, all in the most approved manner. Occasions like this, when tongues wagged smoothly and speech flowed free, were always especially pleasing to me, who am naturally inclined to be tongue-tied with women. But at last ceremony was over, and we sat on the table and swung our legs and agreed to be fast friends. And I showed her my latest knife—one-bladed, horn-handled, terrific, hung round my neck with string; and she showed me the chiefest treasures the ship contained, hidden away in a most private and particular locker—a musical box with a glass top that let you see the works, and a railway train with real lines and a real tunnel, and a tin iron-clad that followed a magnet, and was ever so much handier in many respects than the real full-sized thing that still lay and applauded in the offing.

There was high feasting that night in my cabin. We invited the captain of the man-of-war—one could hardly do less, it seemed to me—and the Princess took one end of the table and I took the other, and the captain was very kind and nice, and told us fairy-stories, and asked us both to come and stay with him next Christmas, and promised we should have some hunting, on real ponies. When he left I gave him some ingots and things, and saw him into his boat; and then I went round the ship and addressed the crew in several set speeches, which moved them deeply, and with my own hands loaded up the carronade with grape-shot till it ran over at the mouth. This done, I retired into the cabin with the Princess, and locked the door. And first we started the musical box, taking turns to wind it up; and then we made toffee in the cabin-stove; and then we ran the train round and round the room, and through and through the tunnel; and lastly we swam the tin iron-clad in the bath, with the soap-dish for a pirate.

Next morning the air was rich with spices, porpoises rolled and gambolled round the bows, and the South Sea Islands lay full in view (they were the *real* South Sea Islands, of course—not the badly furnished journeymen-islands that are to be perceived on the map). As for the pirate brigantine and the man-of-war, I don't really know what became of them. They had played their part very well, for the time, but I wasn't going to bother to account for them, so I just let them evaporate quietly. The islands provided plenty of fresh occupation. For here were little bays of silvery sand, dotted with land-crabs; groves of palm-trees wherein monkeys frisked and pelted each other with cocoanuts; and caves, and sites for stockades, and hidden treasures significantly indicated by skulls, in riotous plenty; while birds and beasts of every colour and all latitudes made pleasing noises which excited the sporting instinct.

The islands lay conveniently close together, which necessitated careful steering as we threaded the devious and intricate channels that separated them. Of course no one else could be trusted at the wheel, so it is not surprising that for some time I quite forgot that there was such a thing as a Princess on board. This is too much the masculine way, whenever there's any real business doing. However, I remembered her as soon as the anchor was dropped, and I went below and consoled her, and we had breakfast together, and she was allowed to "pour out," which quite made up for everything. When breakfast was over we ordered out the captain's gig, and rowed all about the islands, and paddled, and explored, and hunted bisons and beetles and butterflies, and found everything we wanted. And

I gave her pink shells and tortoises and great milky pearls and little green lizards; and she gave me guinea-pigs, and coral to make into waistcoat-buttons; and tame sea-otters, and a real pirate's powder-horn. It was a prolific day and a long-lasting one, and weary were we with all our hunting and our getting and our gathering, when at last we clambered into the captain's gig and rowed back to a late tea.

The following day my conscience rose up and accused me. This was not what I had come out to do. These triflings with pearls and parrakeets, these al fresco luncheons of yams and bananas—there was no "making of history" about them. I resolved that without further dallying I would turn to and capture the French frigate, according to the original programme. So we upped anchor with the morning tide, and set all sail for San Salvador.

Of course I had no idea where San Salvador really was. I haven't now, for that matter. But it seemed a right-sounding sort of name for a place that was to have a bay that was to hold a French frigate that was to be cut out; so, as I said, we sailed for San Salvador, and made the bay about eight bells that evening, and saw the top-masts of the frigate over the headland that sheltered her. And forthwith there was summoned a Council of War.

It is a very serious matter, a Council of War. We had not held one hitherto, pirates and truck of that sort not calling for such solemn treatment. But in an affair that might almost be called international, it seemed well to proceed gravely and by regular steps. So we met in my cabin—the Princess, and the bo'sun, and a boy from the real-life lot, and a man from among the book-men, and a fellow from No-man's-land, and myself in the chair.

The bo'sun had taken part in so many cuttings-out during his past career that practically he did all the talking, and was the Council of War himself. It was to be an affair of boats, he explained. A boat's-crew would be told off to cut the cables, and two boats'-crews to climb stealthily on board and overpower the sleeping Frenchmen, and two more boats'-crews to haul the doomed vessel out of the bay. This made rather a demand on my limited resources as to crews; but I was prepared to stretch a point in a case like this, and I speedily brought my numbers up to the requisite efficiency.

The night was both moonless and starless—I had arranged all that—when the boats pushed off from the side of our vessel, and made their way toward the ship that, unfortunately for itself, had been singled out by Fate to carry me home in triumph. I was in excellent spirits, and, indeed, as I stepped over the side, a lawless idea crossed my mind, of discovering another Princess on board the frigate—a French one this time; I had heard that that sort was rather nice. But I abandoned the notion at once, recollecting that the heroes of all history had always been noted for their unswerving constancy.

The French captain was snug in bed when I clambered in through his cabin window and held a naked cutlass to his throat. Naturally he was surprised and considerably alarmed, till I discharged one of my set speeches at him, pointing out that my men already had his crew under hatchways, that his vessel was even then being towed out of harbour, and that, on his accepting the situation with a good grace, his person and private property would be treated with all the respect due to the representative of a great nation for which I entertained feelings of the profoundest admiration and regard and all that sort of thing. It was a beautiful speech. The Frenchman at once presented me with his parole, in the usual way, and, in a reply of some power and pathos, only begged that I would retire a moment while he put on his trousers. This I gracefully consented to do, and the incident ended.

Two of my boats were sunk by the fire from the forts on the shore, and several brave fellows were severely wounded in the hand-to-hand struggle with the French crew for the possession of the frigate. But the bo'sun's admirable strategy, and my own reckless gallantry in securing the French captain at the outset, had the fortunate result of keeping down the death-rate. It was all for the sake of the Princess that I had arranged so comparatively tame a victory. For myself, I rather liked a fair amount of blood-letting, red-hot shot, and flying splinters. But when you have girls about the place, they have got to be considered to a certain extent.

There was another supper-party that night, in my cabin, as soon as we had got well out to sea; and the French captain, who was the guest of the evening, was in the greatest possible form. We became sworn friends, and exchanged invitations to come and stay at each other's homes, and really it was quite difficult to induce him to take his leave. But at last he and his crew were bundled into their boats; and after I had pressed some pirate bullion upon them—delicately,

of course, but in a pleasant manner that admitted of no denial—
the gallant fellows quite broke down, and we parted, our bosoms
heaving with a full sense of each other's magnanimity and good
fellowship.

The next day, which was nearly all taken up with shifting our
quarters into the new frigate, so honourably and easily acquired,
was a very pleasant one, as everyone who has gone up in the world
and moved into a larger house will readily understand. At last I
had grim, black guns all along each side, instead of a rotten brass
carronade: at last I had a square-rigged ship, with real yards, and a
proper quarter-deck. In fact, now that I had soared as high as could
be hoped in a single voyage, it seemed about time to go home and
cut a dash and show off a bit. The worst of this ocean-theatre was, it
held no proper audience. It was hard, of course, to relinquish all the
adventures that still lay untouched in these Southern seas. Whaling,
for instance, had not yet been entered upon; the joys of exploration,
and strange inland cities innocent of the white man, still awaited me;
and the book of wrecks and rescues was not yet even opened. But
I had achieved a frigate and a Princess, and that was not so bad for
a beginning, and more than enough to show off with before those
dull unadventurous folk who continued on their mill-horse round
at home.

The voyage home was a record one, so far as mere speed was
concerned, and all adventures were scornfully left behind, as we
rattled along, for other adventurers who had still their laurels to
win. Hardly later than the noon of next day we dropped anchor
in Plymouth Sound, and heard the intoxicating clamour of bells,
the roar of artillery, and the hoarse cheers of an excited populace
surging down to the quays, that told us we were being appreciated at
something like our true merits. The Lord Mayor was waiting there to
receive us, and with him several Admirals of the Fleet, as we walked
down the lane of pushing, enthusiastic Devonians, the Princess and
I, and our war-worn, weather-beaten, spoil-laden crew. Everybody
was very nice about the French frigate, and the pirate booty, and
the scars still fresh on our young limbs; yet I think what I liked best
of all was, that they all pronounced the Princess to be a duck, and
a peerless, brown-haired darling, and a true mate for a hero, and of
the right Princess-breed.

The air was thick with invitations and with the smell of civic banquets in a forward stage; but I sternly waved all festivities aside. The coaches-and-four I had ordered immediately on arriving were blocking the whole of the High Street; the champing of bits and the pawing of gravel summoned us to take our seats and be off, to where the real performance awaited us, compared with which all this was but an interlude. I placed the Princess in the most highly gilded coach of the lot, and mounted to my place at her side; and the rest of the crew scrambled on board of the others as best they might. The whips cracked and the crowd scattered and cheered as we broke into a gallop for home. The noisy bells burst into a farewell peal—

Yes, that was undoubtedly the usual bell for school-room tea. And high time too, I thought, as I tumbled out of the bath, which was beginning to feel very hard to the projecting portions of my frame-work. As I trotted downstairs, hungrier even than usual, farewells floated up from the front door, and I heard the departing voices of our angular elderly visitors as they made their way down the walk. Man was still catching it, apparently—Man was getting it hot. And much Man cared! The seas were his, and their islands; he had his frigates for the taking, his pirates and their hoards for an unregarded cutlass-stroke or two; and there were Princesses in plenty waiting for him somewhere—Princesses of the right sort.

The Reluctant Dragon

Footprints in the snow have been unfailing provokers of sentiment ever since snow was first a white wonder in this drab-coloured world of ours. In a poetry-book presented to one of us by an aunt, there was a poem by one Wordsworth in which they stood out strongly with a picture all to themselves, too—but we didn't think very highly either of the poem or the sentiment. Footprints in the sand, now, were quite another matter, and we grasped Crusoe's attitude of mind much more easily than Wordsworth's. Excitement and mystery, curiosity and suspense—these were the only sentiments that tracks, whether in sand or in snow, were able to arouse in us.

We had awakened early that winter morning, puzzled at first by the added light that filled the room. Then, when the truth at last fully dawned on us and we knew that snow-balling was no longer a wistful dream, but a solid certainty waiting for us outside, it was a mere brute fight for the necessary clothes, and the lacing of boots seemed a clumsy invention, and the buttoning of coats an unduly tedious form of fastening, with all that snow going to waste at our very door.

When dinner-time came we had to be dragged in by the scruff of our necks. The short armistice over, the combat was resumed; but presently Charlotte and I, a little weary of contests and of missiles that ran shudderingly down inside one's clothes, forsook the trampled battle-field of the lawn and went exploring the blank virgin spaces of the white world that lay beyond. It stretched away unbroken on every side of us, this mysterious soft garment under which our familiar world had so suddenly hidden itself. Faint imprints showed where a casual bird had alighted, but of other traffic there was next to no sign; which made these strange tracks all the more puzzling.

We came across them first at the corner of the shrubbery, and pored over them long, our hands on our knees. Experienced trappers that we knew ourselves to be, it was annoying to be brought up suddenly by a beast we could not at once identify.

"Don't you know?" said Charlotte, rather scornfully. "Thought you knew all the beasts that ever was."

This put me on my mettle, and I hastily rattled off a string of animal names embracing both the arctic and the tropic zones, but without much real confidence.

"No," said Charlotte, on consideration; "they won't any of 'em quite do. Seems like something *lizardy*. Did you say a iguanodon? Might be that, p'raps. But that's not British, and we want a real British beast. *I* think it's a dragon!"

" 'Tisn't half big enough," I objected.

"Well, all dragons must be small to begin with," said Charlotte: "like everything else. P'raps this is a little dragon who's got lost. A little dragon would be rather nice to have. He might scratch and spit, but he couldn't *do* anything really. Let's track him down!"

So we set off into the wide snow-clad world, hand in hand, our hearts big with expectation—complacently confident that by a few smudgy traces in the snow we were in a fair way to capture a half-grown specimen of a fabulous beast.

We ran the monster across the paddock and along the hedge of the next field, and then he took to the road like any tame civilized tax-payer. Here his tracks became blended with and lost among more ordinary footprints, but imagination and a fixed idea will do a great deal, and we were sure we knew the direction a dragon would naturally take. The traces, too, kept reappearing at intervals—at least Charlotte maintained they did, and as it was her dragon I left the following of the slot to her and trotted along peacefully, feeling that it was an expedition anyhow and something was sure to come out of it.

Charlotte took me across another field or two, and through a copse, and into a fresh road; and I began to feel sure it was only her confounded pride that made her go on pretending to see dragon-tracks instead of owning she was entirely at fault, like a reasonable person. At last she dragged me excitedly through a gap in a hedge of an obviously private character; the waste, open world of field and hedgerow disappeared, and we found ourselves in a garden, well-kept, secluded, most undragon-haunted in appearance. Once inside, I knew where we were. This was the garden of my friend the circus-man, though I had never approached it before by a lawless gap, from this unfamiliar side. And here was the circus-man himself, placidly smoking a pipe as he strolled up and down the walks. I stepped up to him and asked him politely if he had lately seen a Beast.

"May I inquire," he said, with all civility, "what particular sort of a Beast you may happen to be looking for?"

"It's a *lizardy* sort of Beast," I explained. "Charlotte says it's a dragon, but she doesn't really know much about beasts."

The circus-man looked round about him slowly. "I don't *think*," he said, "that I've seen a dragon in these parts recently. But if I come across one I'll know it belongs to you, and I'll have him taken round to you at once."

"Thank you very much," said Charlotte, "but don't *trouble* about it, please, 'cos p'raps it isn't a dragon after all. Only I thought I saw his little footprints in the snow, and we followed 'em up, and they seemed to lead right in here, but maybe it's all a mistake, and thank you all the same."

"Oh, no trouble at all," said the circus-man, cheerfully. "I should be only too pleased. But of course, as you say, it *may* be a mistake. And it's getting dark, and he seems to have got away for the present, whatever he is. You'd better come in and have some tea. I'm quite alone, and we'll make a roaring fire, and I've got the biggest Book of Beasts you ever saw. It's got every beast in the world, and all of 'em coloured; and we'll try and find *your* beast in it!"

We were always ready for tea at any time, and especially when combined with beasts. There was marmalade, too, and apricot-jam, brought in expressly for us; and afterwards the beast-book was spread out, and, as the man had truly said, it contained every sort of beast that had ever been in the world.

The striking of six o'clock set the more prudent Charlotte nudging me, and we recalled ourselves with an effort from Beastland, and reluctantly stood up to go.

"Here, I'm coming along with you," said the circus-man. "I want another pipe, and a walk'll do me good. You needn't talk to me unless you like."

Our spirits rose to their wonted level again. The way had seemed so long, the outside world so dark and eerie, after the bright warm room and the highly-coloured beast-book. But a walk with a real Man—why, that was a treat in itself! We set off briskly, the Man in the middle. I looked up at him and wondered whether I should ever live to smoke a big pipe with that careless sort of majesty! But Charlotte, whose young mind was not set on tobacco as a possible goal, made herself heard from the other side.

"Now, then," she said, "tell us a story, please, won't you?"

The Man sighed heavily and looked about him. "I knew it," he groaned. "I *knew* I should have to tell a story. Oh, why did I leave my pleasant fireside? Well, I *will* tell you a story. Only let me think a minute."

So he thought a minute, and then he told us this story.

* * * * *

Long ago—might have been hundreds of years ago—in a cottage halfway between this village and yonder shoulder of the Downs up there, a shepherd lived with his wife and their little son. Now the shepherd spent his days—and at certain times of the year his nights too—up on the wide ocean-bosom of the Downs, with only the sun and the stars and the sheep for company, and the friendly chattering world of men and women far out of sight and hearing. But his little son, when he wasn't helping his father, and often when he was as well, spent much of his time buried in big volumes that he borrowed from the affable gentry and interested parsons of the country round about. And his parents were very fond of him, and rather proud of him too, though they didn't let on in his hearing, so he was left to go his own way and read as much as he liked; and instead of frequently getting a cuff on the side of the head, as might very well have happened to him, he was treated more or less as an equal by his parents, who sensibly thought it a very fair division of labour that they should supply the practical knowledge, and he the book-learning. They knew that book-learning often came in useful at a pinch, in spite of what their neighbours said. What the Boy chiefly dabbled in was natural history and fairy-tales, and he just took them as they came, in a sandwichy sort of way, without making any distinctions; and really his course of reading strikes one as rather sensible.

One evening the shepherd, who for some nights past had been disturbed and preoccupied, and off his usual mental balance, came home all of a tremble, and, sitting down at the table where his wife and son were peacefully employed, she with her seam, he in following out the adventures of the Giant with no Heart in his Body, exclaimed with much agitation:

"It's all up with me, Maria! Never no more can I go up on them there Downs, was it ever so!"

"Now don't you take on like that," said his wife, who was a *very* sensible woman: "but tell us all about it first, whatever it is as has given you this shake-up, and then me and you and the son here, between us, we ought to be able to get to the bottom of it!"

"It began some nights ago," said the shepherd. "You know that cave up there—I never liked it, somehow, and the sheep never liked it neither, and when sheep don't like a thing there's generally some reason for it. Well, for some time past there's been faint noises coming from that cave—noises like heavy sighings, with grunts mixed up in them; and sometimes a snoring, far away down—*real* snoring, yet somehow not *honest* snoring, like you and me o'nights, you know!"

"*I* know," remarked the Boy, quietly.

"Of course I was terrible frightened," the shepherd went on; "yet somehow I couldn't keep away. So this very evening, before I come down, I took a cast round by the cave, quietly. And there—O Lord! there I saw him at last, as plain as I see you!"

"Saw *who?*" said his wife, beginning to share in her husband's nervous terror.

"Why *him*, I'm a-telling you!" said the shepherd. "He was sticking half-way out of the cave, and seemed to be enjoying of the cool of the evening in a poetical sort of way. He was as big as four cart-horses, and all covered with shiny scales—deep-blue scales at the top of him, shading off to a tender sort o' green below. As he breathed, there was that sort of flicker over his nostrils that you see over our chalk roads on a baking windless day in summer. He had his chin on his paws, and I should say he was meditating about things. Oh, yes, a peaceable sort o' beast enough, and not ramping or carrying on or doing anything but what was quite right and proper. I admit all that. And yet, what am I to do? *Scales*, you know, and claws, and a tail for certain, though I didn't see that end of him—I ain't *used* to 'em, and I don't *hold* with 'em, and that's a fact!"

The Boy, who had apparently been absorbed in his book during his father's recital, now closed the volume, yawned, clasped his hands behind his head, and said sleepily:

"It's all right, father. Don't you worry. It's only a dragon."

"Only a dragon?" cried his father. "What do you mean, sitting there, you and your dragons? *Only* a dragon indeed! And what do *you* know about it?"

"'Cos it *is*, and 'cos I *do* know," replied the Boy, quietly. "Look here, father, you know we've each of us got our line. *You* know about sheep, and weather, and things; *I* know about dragons. I always said, you know, that that cave up there was a dragon-cave. I always said it must have belonged to a dragon sometime, and ought to belong to a dragon now, if rules count for anything. Well, now you tell me it *has* got a dragon, and so *that's* all right. I'm not half as much surprised as when you told me it *hadn't* got a dragon. Rules always come right if you wait quietly. Now, please, just leave this all to me. And I'll stroll up tomorrow morning—no, in the morning I can't, I've got a whole heap of things to do—well, perhaps in the evening, if I'm quite free, I'll go up and have a talk to him, and you'll find it'll be all right. Only, please, don't you go worrying round there without me. You don't understand 'em a bit, and they're very sensitive, you know!"

"He's quite right, father," said the sensible mother. "As he says, dragons is his line and not ours. He's wonderful knowing about book-beasts, as everyone allows. And to tell the truth, I'm not half happy in my own mind, thinking of that poor animal lying alone up there, without a bit o' hot supper or anyone to change the news with; and maybe we'll be able to do something for him; and if he ain't quite respectable our Boy'll find it out quick enough. He's got a pleasant sort o' way with him that makes everybody tell him everything."

Next day, after he'd had his tea, the Boy strolled up the chalky track that led to the summit of the Downs; and there, sure enough, he found the dragon, stretched lazily on the sward in front of his cave. The view from that point was a magnificent one. To the right and left, the bare and billowy leagues of Downs; in front, the vale, with its clustered homesteads, its threads of white roads running through orchards and well-tilled acreage, and, far away, a hint of grey old cities on the horizon. A cool breeze played over the surface of the grass and the silver shoulder of a large moon was showing above distant junipers. No wonder the dragon seemed in a peaceful and contented mood; indeed, as the Boy approached he could hear the beast purring with a happy regularity. "Well, we live and learn!" he said to himself. "None of my books ever told me that dragons purred!"

"Hullo, dragon!" said the Boy, quietly, when he had got up to him.

The dragon, on hearing the approaching footsteps, made the beginning of a courteous effort to rise. But when he saw it was a Boy, he set his eyebrows severely.

"Now don't you hit me," he said; "or bung stones, or squirt water, or anything. I won't have it, I tell you!"

"Not goin' to hit you," said the Boy wearily, dropping on the grass beside the beast: "and don't, for goodness' sake, keep on saying 'Don't'; I hear so much of it, and it's monotonous, and makes me tired. I've simply looked in to ask you how you were and all that sort of thing; but if I'm in the way I can easily clear out. I've lots of friends, and no one can say I'm in the habit of shoving myself in where I'm not wanted!"

"No, no, don't go off in a huff," said the dragon, hastily; "fact is—I'm as happy up here as the day's long; never without an occupation, dear fellow, never without an occupation! And yet, between ourselves, it *is* a trifle dull at times."

The Boy bit off a stalk of grass and chewed it. "Going to make a long stay here?" he asked, politely.

"Can't hardly say at present," replied the dragon. "It seems a nice place enough—but I've only been here a short time, and one must look about and reflect and consider before settling down. It's rather a serious thing, settling down. Besides—now I'm going to tell you something! You'd never guess it if you tried ever so!—fact is, I'm such a confoundedly lazy beggar!"

"You surprise me," said the Boy, civilly.

"It's the sad truth," the dragon went on, settling down between his paws and evidently delighted to have found a listener at last: "and I fancy that's really how I came to be here. You see all the other fellows were so active and *earnest* and all that sort of thing— always rampaging, and skirmishing, and scouring the desert sands, and pacing the margin of the sea, and chasing knights all over the place, and devouring damsels, and going on generally—whereas I liked to get my meals regular and then to prop my back against a bit of rock and snooze a bit, and wake up and think of things going on and how they kept going on just the same, you know! So when it happened I got fairly caught."

"When *what* happened, please?" asked the Boy.

"That's just what I don't precisely know," said the dragon. "I suppose the earth sneezed, or shook itself, or the bottom dropped out of something. Anyhow there was a shake and a roar and a general stramash, and I found myself miles away underground and wedged in as tight as tight. Well, thank goodness, my wants are few, and at any rate I had peace and quietness and wasn't always being asked to come along and *do* something. And I've got such an active mind—always occupied, I assure you! But time went on, and there was a certain sameness about the life, and at last I began to think it would be fun to work my way upstairs and see what you other fellows were doing. So I scratched and burrowed, and worked this way and that way and at last I came out through this cave here. And I like the country, and the view, and the people—what I've seen of 'em—and on the whole I feel inclined to settle down here."

"What's your mind always occupied about?" asked the Boy. "That's what I want to know."

The dragon coloured slightly and looked away. Presently he said bashfully:

"Did you ever—just for fun—try to make up poetry—verses, you know?"

"'Course I have," said the Boy. "Heaps of it. And some of it's quite good, I feel sure, only there's no one here cares about it. Mother's very kind and all that, when I read it to her, and so's father for that matter. But somehow they don't seem to—"

"Exactly," cried the dragon; "my own case exactly. They don't seem to, and you can't argue with 'em about it. Now you've got culture, you have, I could tell it on you at once, and I should just like your candid opinion about some little things I threw off lightly, when I was down there. I'm awfully pleased to have met you, and I'm hoping the other neighbours will be equally agreeable. There was a very nice old gentleman up here only last night, but he didn't seem to want to intrude."

"That was my father," said the boy, "and he *is* a nice old gentleman, and I'll introduce you someday if you like."

"Can't you two come up here and dine or something tomorrow?" asked the dragon eagerly. "Only, of course, if you've got nothing better to do," he added politely.

"Thanks awfully," said the Boy, "but we don't go out anywhere without my mother, and, to tell you the truth, I'm afraid she mightn't quite approve of you. You see there's no getting over the hard fact that you're a dragon, is there? And when you talk of settling down, and the neighbours, and so on, I can't help feeling that you don't quite realize your position. You're an enemy of the human race, you see!"

"Haven't got an enemy in the world," said the dragon, cheerfully. "Too lazy to make 'em, to begin with. And if I *do* read other fellows my poetry, I'm always ready to listen to theirs!"

"Oh, dear!" cried the Boy, "I wish you'd try and grasp the situation properly. When the other people find you out, they'll come after you with spears and swords and all sorts of things. You'll have to be exterminated, according to their way of looking at it! You're a scourge, and a pest, and a baneful monster!"

"Not a word of truth in it," said the dragon, wagging his head solemnly. "Character'll bear the strictest investigation. And now, there's a little sonnet-thing I was working on when you appeared on the scene—"

"Oh, if you *won't* be sensible," cried the Boy, getting up, "I'm going off home. No, I can't stop for sonnets; my mother's sitting up. I'll look you up tomorrow, sometime or other, and do for goodness' sake try and realize that you're a pestilential scourge, or you'll find yourself in a most awful fix. Good-night!"

The Boy found it an easy matter to set the mind of his parents at ease about his new friend. They had always left that branch to him, and they took his word without a murmur. The shepherd was formally introduced and many compliments and kind inquiries were exchanged. His wife, however, though expressing her willingness to do anything she could—to mend things, or set the cave to rights, or cook a little something when the dragon had been poring over sonnets and forgotten his meals, as male things *will* do, could not be brought to recognize him formally. The fact that he was a dragon and "they didn't know who he was" seemed to count for everything with her. She made no objection, however, to her little son spending his evenings with the dragon quietly, so long as he was home by nine o'clock: and many a pleasant night they had, sitting on the sward, while the dragon told stories of old, old times, when dragons were quite plentiful and the world was a livelier place than it is now, and life was full of thrills and jumps and surprises.

What the Boy had feared, however, soon came to pass. The most modest and retiring dragon in the world, if he's as big as four cart-horses and covered with blue scales, cannot keep altogether out of the public view. And so in the village tavern of nights the fact that a real live dragon sat brooding in the cave on the Downs was naturally a subject for talk. Though the villagers were extremely frightened, they were rather proud as well. It was a distinction to have a dragon of your own, and it was felt to be a feather in the cap of the village. Still, all were agreed that this sort of thing couldn't be allowed to go on. The dreadful beast must be exterminated, the country-side must be freed from this pest, this terror, this destroying scourge. The fact that not even a hen-roost was the worse for the dragon's arrival wasn't allowed to have anything to do with it. He was a dragon, and he couldn't deny it, and if he didn't choose to behave as such that was his own lookout. But in spite of much valiant talk no hero was found willing to take sword and spear and free the suffering village and win deathless fame; and each night's heated discussion always ended in nothing. Meanwhile the dragon, a happy Bohemian, lolled on the turf, enjoyed the sunsets, told antediluvian anecdotes to the Boy, and polished his old verses while meditating on fresh ones.

One day the Boy, on walking in to the village, found everything wearing a festal appearance which was not to be accounted for in the calendar. Carpets and gay-coloured stuffs were hung out of the windows, the church-bells clamoured noisily, the little street was flower-strewn, and the whole population jostled each other along either side of it, chattering, shoving, and ordering each other to stand back. The Boy saw a friend of his own age in the crowd and hailed.

"What's up?" he cried. "Is it the players, or bears, or a circus, or what?"

"It's all right," his friend hailed back. "He's a-coming."

"*Who's* a-coming?" demanded the Boy, thrusting into the throng.

"Why, St. George, of course," replied his friend. "He's heard tell of our dragon, and he's comin' on purpose to slay the deadly beast, and free us from his horrid yoke. O my! won't there be a jolly fight!"

Here was news indeed! The Boy felt that he ought to make quite sure for himself, and he wriggled himself in between the legs of his good-natured elders, abusing them all the time for their unmannerly habit of shoving. Once in the front rank, he breathlessly awaited the arrival.

Presently from the far-away end of the line came the sound of cheering. Next, the measured tramp of a great war-horse made his heart beat quicker, and then he found himself cheering with the rest, as, amidst welcoming shouts, shrill cries of women, uplifting of babies and waving of handkerchiefs, St. George paced slowly up the street. The Boy's heart stood still and he breathed with sobs, the beauty and the grace of the hero were so far beyond anything he had yet seen. His fluted armour was inlaid with gold, his plumed helmet hung at his saddle-bow, and his thick fair hair framed a face gracious and gentle beyond expression till you caught the sternness in his eyes. He drew rein in front of the little inn, and the villagers crowded round with greetings and thanks and voluble statements of their wrongs and grievances and oppressions. The Boy heard the grave gentle voice of the Saint, assuring them that all would be well now, and that he would stand by them and see them righted and free them from their foe; then he dismounted and passed through the doorway and the crowd poured in after him. But the Boy made off up the hill as fast as he could lay his legs to the ground.

"It's all up, dragon!" he shouted as soon as he was within sight of the beast. "He's coming! He's here now! You'll have to pull yourself together and *do* something at last!"

The dragon was licking his scales and rubbing them with a bit of house-flannel the Boy's mother had lent him, till he shone like a great turquoise.

"Don't be *violent*, Boy," he said without looking round. "Sit down and get your breath, and try and remember that the noun governs the verb, and then perhaps you'll be good enough to tell me *who's* coming?"

"That's right, take it coolly," said the Boy. "Hope you'll be half as cool when I've got through with my news. It's only St. George who's coming, that's all; he rode into the village half-an-hour ago. Of course you can lick him—a great big fellow like you! But I thought I'd warn you, 'cos he's sure to be round early, and he's got the longest, wickedest-looking spear you ever did see!" And the Boy got up and began to jump round in sheer delight at the prospect of the battle.

"O deary, deary me," moaned the dragon; "this is too awful. I won't see him, and that's flat. I don't want to know the fellow at all. I'm sure he's not nice. You must tell him to go away at once, please. Say he can write if he likes, but I can't give him an interview. I'm not seeing anybody at present."

"Now dragon, dragon," said the Boy imploringly, "don't be perverse and wrongheaded. You've *got* to fight him some time or other, you know, 'cos he's St. George and you're the dragon. Better get it over, and then we can go on with the sonnets. And you ought to consider other people a little, too. If it's been dull up here for you, think how dull it's been for me!"

"My dear little man," said the dragon solemnly, "just understand, once for all, that I can't fight and I won't fight. I've never fought in my life, and I'm not going to begin now, just to give you a Roman holiday. In old days I always let the other fellows—the *earnest* fellows—do all the fighting, and no doubt that's why I have the pleasure of being here now."

"But if you don't fight he'll cut your head off!" gasped the Boy, miserable at the prospect of losing both his fight and his friend.

"Oh, I think not," said the dragon in his lazy way. "You'll be able to arrange something. I've every confidence in you, you're such a *manager*. Just run down, there's a dear chap, and make it all right. I leave it entirely to you."

The Boy made his way back to the village in a state of great despondency. First of all, there wasn't going to be any fight; next, his dear and honoured friend the dragon hadn't shown up in quite such a heroic light as he would have liked; and lastly, whether the dragon was a hero at heart or not, it made no difference, for St. George would most undoubtedly cut his head off. "Arrange things indeed!" he said bitterly to himself. "The dragon treats the whole affair as if it was an invitation to tea and croquet."

The villagers were straggling homewards as he passed up the

street, all of them in the highest spirits, and gleefully discussing the splendid fight that was in store. The Boy pursued his way to the inn, and passed into the principal chamber, where St. George now sat alone, musing over the chances of the fight, and the sad stories of rapine and of wrong that had so lately been poured into his sympathetic ear.

"May I come in, St. George?" said the Boy politely, as he paused at the door. "I want to talk to you about this little matter of the dragon, if you're not tired of it by this time."

"Yes, come in, Boy," said the Saint kindly. "Another tale of misery and wrong, I fear me. Is it a kind parent, then, of whom the tyrant has bereft you? Or some tender sister or brother? Well, it shall soon be avenged."

"Nothing of the sort," said the Boy. "There's a misunderstanding somewhere, and I want to put it right. The fact is, this is a *good* dragon."

"Exactly," said St. George, smiling pleasantly, "I quite understand. A good *dragon*. Believe me, I do not in the least regret that he is an adversary worthy of my steel, and no feeble specimen of his noxious tribe."

"But he's *not* a noxious tribe," cried the Boy distressedly. "Oh dear, oh dear, how *stupid* men are when they get an idea into their heads! I tell you he's a *good* dragon, and a friend of mine, and tells me the most beautiful stories you ever heard, all about old times and when he was little. And he's been so kind to mother, and mother'd do anything for him. And father likes him too, though father doesn't hold with art and poetry much, and always falls asleep when the dragon starts talking about *style*. But the fact is, nobody can help liking him when once they know him. He's so engaging and so trustful, and as simple as a child!"

"Sit down, and draw your chair up," said St. George. "I like a fellow who sticks up for his friends, and I'm sure the dragon has his good points, if he's got a friend like you. But that's not the question. All this evening I've been listening, with grief and anguish unspeakable, to tales of murder, theft, and wrong; rather too highly coloured, perhaps, not always quite convincing, but forming in the main a most serious roll of crime. History teaches us that the greatest rascals often possess all the domestic virtues; and I fear that your cultivated friend, in spite of the qualities which have won (and rightly) your regard, has got to be speedily exterminated."

"Oh, you've been taking in all the yarns those fellows have been telling you," said the Boy impatiently. "Why, our villagers are the biggest story-tellers in all the country round. It's a known fact. You're a stranger in these parts, or else you'd have heard it already. All they want is a *fight*. They're the most awful beggars for getting up fights—it's meat and drink to them. Dogs, bulls, dragons— anything so long as it's a fight. Why, they've got a poor innocent badger in the stable behind here, at this moment. They were going to have some fun with him today, but they're saving him up now till *your* little affair's over. And I've no doubt they've been telling you what a hero you were, and how you were bound to win, in the cause of right and justice, and so on; but let me tell you, I came down the street just now, and they were betting six to four on the dragon freely!"

"Six to four on the dragon!" murmured St. George sadly, resting his cheek on his hand. "This is an evil world, and sometimes I begin to think that all the wickedness in it is not entirely bottled up inside the dragons. And yet—may not this wily beast have misled you as to his real character, in order that your good report of him may serve as a cloak for his evil deeds? Nay, may there not be, at this very moment, some hapless Princess immured within yonder gloomy cavern?"

The moment he had spoken, St. George was sorry for what he had said, the Boy looked so genuinely distressed.

"I assure you, St. George," he said earnestly, "there's nothing of the sort in the cave at all. The dragon's a real gentleman, every inch of him, and I may say that no one would be more shocked and grieved than he would, at hearing you talk in that—that *loose* way about matters on which he has very strong views!"

"Well, perhaps I've been over-credulous," said St. George. "Perhaps I've misjudged the animal. But what are we to do? Here are the dragon and I, almost face to face, each supposed to be thirsting for each other's blood. I don't see any way out of it, exactly. What do you suggest? Can't you arrange things, somehow?"

"That's just what the dragon said," replied the Boy, rather nettled. "Really, the way you two seem to leave everything to me—I suppose you couldn't be persuaded to go away quietly, could you?"

"Impossible, I fear," said the Saint. "Quite against the rules. *You* know that as well as I do."

"Well, then, look here," said the Boy, "it's early yet—would you mind strolling up with me and seeing the dragon and talking it over? It's not far, and any friend of mine will be most welcome."

"Well, it's *irregular*," said St. George, rising, "but really it seems about the most sensible thing to do. You're taking a lot of trouble on your friend's account," he added, good-naturedly, as they passed out through the door together. "But cheer up! Perhaps there won't have to be any fight after all."

"Oh, but I hope there will, though!" replied the little fellow, wistfully.

"I've brought a friend to see you, dragon," said the Boy, rather loud.

The dragon woke up with a start. "I was just—er—thinking about things," he said in his simple way. "Very pleased to make your acquaintance, sir. Charming weather we're having!"

"This is St. George," said the Boy, shortly. "St. George, let me introduce you to the dragon. We've come up to talk things over quietly, dragon, and now for goodness' sake do let us have a little straight common-sense, and come to some practical business-like arrangement, for I'm sick of views and theories of life and personal tendencies, and all that sort of thing. I may perhaps add that my mother's sitting up."

"So glad to meet you, St. George," began the dragon rather nervously, "because you've been a great traveller, I hear, and I've always been rather a stay-at-home. But I can show you many antiquities, many interesting features of our country-side, if you're stopping here any time—"

"I think," said St. George, in his frank, pleasant way, "that we'd really better take the advice of our young friend here, and try to come to some understanding, on a business footing, about this little affair of ours. Now don't you think that after all the simplest plan would be just to fight it out, according to the rules, and let the best man win? They're betting on you, I may tell you, down in the village, but I don't mind that!"

"Oh, yes, *do*, dragon," said the Boy, delightedly; "it'll save such a lot of bother!"

"My young friend, you shut up," said the dragon severely. "Believe me, St. George," he went on, "there's nobody in the world I'd sooner oblige than you and this young gentleman here. But the whole thing's nonsense, and conventionality, and popular thick-headedness. There's absolutely nothing to fight about, from beginning to end. And anyhow I'm not going to, so that settles it!"

"But supposing I make you?" said St. George, rather nettled.

"You can't," said the dragon, triumphantly. "I should only go into my cave and retire for a time down the hole I came up. You'd soon get heartily sick of sitting outside and waiting for me to come out and fight you. And as soon as you'd really gone away, why, I'd come up again gaily, for I tell you frankly, I like this place, and I'm going to stay here!"

St. George gazed for a while on the fair landscape around them. "But this would be a beautiful place for a fight," he began again persuasively. "These great bare rolling Downs for the arena—and me in my golden armour showing up against your big blue scaly coils! Think what a picture it would make!"

"Now you're trying to get at me through my artistic sensibilities," said the dragon. "But it won't work. Not but what it would make a very pretty picture, as you say," he added, wavering a little.

"We seem to be getting rather nearer to *business*," put in the Boy. "You must see, dragon, that there's got to be a fight of some sort, 'cos you can't want to have to go down that dirty old hole again and stop there till goodness knows when."

"It might be arranged," said St. George, thoughtfully. "I *must* spear you somewhere, of course, but I'm not bound to hurt you very much. There's such a lot of you that there must be a few *spare* places somewhere. Here, for instance, just behind your fore-leg. It couldn't hurt you much, just here!"

"Now you're tickling, George," said the dragon, coyly. "No, that place won't do at all. Even if it didn't hurt—and I'm sure it would, awfully—it would make me laugh, and that would spoil everything."

"Let's try somewhere else, then," said St. George, patiently. "Under your neck, for instance—all these folds of thick skin—if I speared you here you'd never even know I'd done it!"

"Yes, but are you sure you can hit off the right place?" asked the dragon, anxiously.

"Of course I am," said St. George, with confidence. "You leave that to me!"

"It's just because I've *got* to leave it to you that I'm asking," replied the dragon, rather testily. "No doubt you would deeply regret any error you might make in the hurry of the moment; but you wouldn't regret it half as much as I should! However, I suppose we've got to trust somebody, as we go through life, and your plan seems, on the whole, as good a one as any."

"Look here, dragon," interrupted the Boy, a little jealous on behalf of his friend, who seemed to be getting all the worst of the bargain: "I don't quite see where *you* come in! There's to be a fight, apparently, and you're to be licked; and what I want to know is, what are *you* going to get out of it?"

"St. George," said the dragon, "just tell him, please—what will happen after I'm vanquished in the deadly combat?"

"Well, according to the rules I suppose I shall lead you in triumph down to the market-place or whatever answers to it," said St. George.

"Precisely," said the dragon. "And then—"

"And then there'll be shoutings and speeches and things," continued St. George. "And I shall explain that you're converted, and see the error of your ways, and so on."

"Quite so," said the dragon. "And then—?"

"Oh, and then—" said St. George, "why, and then there will be the usual banquet, I suppose."

"Exactly," said the dragon; "and that's where *I* come in. Look here," he continued, addressing the Boy, "I'm bored to death up here, and no one really appreciates me. I'm going into Society, I am, through the kindly aid of our friend here, who's taking such a lot of trouble on my account; and you'll find I've got all the qualities to endear me to people who entertain! So now that's all settled, and if you don't mind—I'm an old-fashioned fellow—don't want to turn you out, but—"

"Remember, you'll have to do your proper share of the fighting, dragon!" said St. George, as he took the hint and rose to go; "I mean ramping, and breathing fire, and so on!"

"I can *ramp* all right," replied the dragon, confidently; "as to breathing fire, it's surprising how easily one gets out of practice, but I'll do the best I can. Good-night!"

They had descended the hill and were almost back in the village again, when St. George stopped short. "*Knew* I had forgotten something," he said. "There ought to be a Princess. Terror-stricken and chained to a rock, and all that sort of thing. Boy, can't you arrange a Princess?"

The Boy was in the middle of a tremendous yawn. "I'm tired to death," he wailed, "and I *can't* arrange a Princess, or anything more, at this time of night. And my mother's sitting up, and *do* stop asking me to arrange more things till tomorrow!"

* * * * *

Next morning the people began streaming up to the Downs at quite an early hour, in their Sunday clothes and carrying baskets with bottle-necks sticking out of them, everyone intent on securing good places for the combat. This was not exactly a simple matter, for of course it was quite possible that the dragon might win, and in that case even those who had put their money on him felt they could hardly expect him to deal with his backers on a different footing to the rest. Places were chosen, therefore, with circumspection and with a view to a speedy retreat in case of emergency; and the front rank was mostly composed of boys who had escaped from parental control and now sprawled and rolled about on the grass, regardless of the shrill threats and warnings discharged at them by their anxious mothers behind.

The Boy had secured a good front place, well up towards the cave, and was feeling as anxious as a stage-manager on a first night. Could the dragon be depended upon? He might change his mind and vote the whole performance rot; or else, seeing that the affair had been so hastily planned, without even a rehearsal, he might be too nervous to show up. The Boy looked narrowly at the cave, but it showed no sign of life or occupation. Could the dragon have made a moonlight flitting?

The higher portions of the ground were now black with sightseers, and presently a sound of cheering and a waving of handkerchiefs told that something was visible to them which the Boy, far up towards the dragon-end of the line as he was, could not yet see. A minute more and St. George's red plumes topped the hill, as the Saint rode slowly forth on the great level space which stretched up to the grim mouth of the cave. Very gallant and beautiful he looked, on his tall war-horse, his golden armour glancing in the sun, his great spear held erect, the little white pennon, crimson-crossed, fluttering at its point. He drew rein and remained motionless. The lines of spectators began to give back a little, nervously; and even the boys in front stopped pulling hair and cuffing each other, and leaned forward expectant.

"Now then, dragon!" muttered the Boy impatiently, fidgeting where he sat. He need not have distressed himself, had he only known. The dramatic possibilities of the thing had tickled the dragon immensely, and he had been up from an early hour, preparing for his first public appearance with as much heartiness as if the years had run backwards, and he had been again a little dragonlet, playing with his sisters on the floor of their mother's cave, at the game of saints-and-dragons, in which the dragon was bound to win.

A low muttering, mingled with snorts, now made itself heard; rising to a bellowing roar that seemed to fill the plain. Then a cloud of smoke obscured the mouth of the cave, and out of the midst of it the dragon himself, shining, sea-blue, magnificent, pranced splendidly forth; and everybody said, "Oo-oo-oo!" as if he had been a mighty rocket! His scales were glittering, his long spiky tail lashed his sides, his claws tore up the turf and sent it flying high over his back, and smoke and fire incessantly jetted from his angry nostrils. "Oh, well done, dragon!" cried the Boy, excitedly. "Didn't think he had it in him!" he added to himself.

St. George lowered his spear, bent his head, dug his heels into his horse's sides, and came thundering over the turf. The dragon charged with a roar and a squeal—a great blue whirling combination of coils and snorts and clashing jaws and spikes and fire.

"Missed!" yelled the crowd. There was a moment's entanglement of golden armour and blue-green coils, and spiky tail, and then the great horse, tearing at his bit, carried the Saint, his spear swung high in the air, almost up to the mouth of the cave.

The dragon sat down and barked viciously, while St. George with difficulty pulled his horse round into position.

"End of Round One!" thought the Boy. "How well they managed

it! But I hope the Saint won't get excited. I can trust the dragon all right. What a regular play-actor the fellow is!"

St. George had at last prevailed on his horse to stand steady, and was looking round him as he wiped his brow. Catching sight of the Boy, he smiled and nodded, and held up three fingers for an instant.

"It seems to be all planned out," said the Boy to himself. "Round Three is to be the finishing one, evidently. Wish it could have lasted a bit longer. Whatever's that old fool of a dragon up to now?"

The dragon was employing the interval in giving a ramping-performance for the benefit of the crowd. Ramping, it should be explained, consists in running round and round in a wide circle, and sending waves and ripples of movement along the whole length of your spine, from your pointed ears right down to the spike at the end of your long tail. When you are covered with blue scales, the effect is particularly pleasing; and the Boy recollected the dragon's recently expressed wish to become a social success.

St. George now gathered up his reins and began to move forward, dropping the point of his spear and settling himself firmly in the saddle.

"Time!" yelled everybody excitedly; and the dragon, leaving off his ramping sat up on end, and began to leap from one side to the other with huge ungainly bounds, whooping like a Red Indian. This naturally disconcerted the horse, who swerved violently, the Saint only just saving himself by the mane; and as they shot past the dragon delivered a vicious snap at the horse's tail which sent the poor beast careering madly far over the Downs, so that the language of the Saint, who had lost a stirrup, was fortunately inaudible to the general assemblage.

Round Two evoked audible evidence of friendly feeling towards the dragon. The spectators were not slow to appreciate a combatant who could hold his own so well and clearly wanted to show good sport; and many encouraging remarks reached the ears of our friend as he strutted to and fro, his chest thrust out and his tail in the air, hugely enjoying his new popularity.

St. George had dismounted and was tightening his girths, and telling his horse, with quite an Oriental flow of imagery, exactly what he thought of him, and his relations, and his conduct on the present occasion; so the Boy made his way down to the Saint's end of the line, and held his spear for him.

"It's been a jolly fight, St. George!" he said with a sigh. "Can't you let it last a bit longer?"

"Well, I think I'd better not," replied the Saint. "The fact is, your simple-minded old friend's getting conceited, now they've begun cheering him, and he'll forget all about the arrangement and take to playing the fool, and there's no telling where he would stop. I'll just finish him off this round."

He swung himself into the saddle and took his spear from the Boy. "Now don't you be afraid," he added kindly. "I've marked my spot exactly, and he's sure to give me all the assistance in his power, because he knows it's his only chance of being asked to the banquet!"

St. George now shortened his spear, bringing the butt well up under his arm; and, instead of galloping as before, trotted smartly towards the dragon, who crouched at his approach, flicking his tail till it cracked in the air like a great cart-whip. The Saint wheeled as he neared his opponent and circled warily round him, keeping his eye on the spare place; while the dragon, adopting similar tactics, paced with caution round the same circle, occasionally feinting with his head. So the two sparred for an opening, while the spectators maintained a breathless silence.

Though the round lasted for some minutes, the end was so swift that all the Boy saw was a lightning movement of the Saint's arm, and then a whirl and a confusion of spines, claws, tail, and flying bits of turf. The dust cleared away, the spectators whooped and ran in cheering, and the Boy made out that the dragon was down, pinned to the earth by the spear, while St. George had dismounted, and stood astride of him.

It all seemed so genuine that the Boy ran in breathlessly, hoping the dear old dragon wasn't really hurt. As he approached, the dragon lifted one large eyelid, winked solemnly, and collapsed again. He was held fast to earth by the neck, but the Saint had hit him in the spare place agreed upon, and it didn't even seem to tickle.

"Bain't you goin' to cut 'is 'ed orf, master?" asked one of the applauding crowd. He had backed the dragon, and naturally felt a trifle sore.

"Well, not today, I think," replied St. George, pleasantly. "You see, that can be done at any time. There's no hurry at all. I think we'll all go down to the village first, and have some refreshment, and then I'll give him a good talking-to, and you'll find he'll be a very different dragon!"

At that magic word *refreshment* the whole crowd formed up in procession and silently awaited the signal to start. The time for talking and cheering and betting was past, the hour for action had arrived. St. George, hauling on his spear with both hands, released the dragon, who rose and shook himself and ran his eye over his spikes and scales and things, to see that they were all in order. Then the Saint mounted and led off the procession, the dragon following meekly in the company of the Boy, while the thirsty spectators kept at a respectful interval behind.

There were great doings when they got down to the village again, and had formed up in front of the inn. After refreshment St. George made a speech, in which he informed his audience that he had removed their direful scourge, at a great deal of trouble and inconvenience to himself, and now they weren't to go about grumbling and fancying they'd got grievances, because they hadn't. And they shouldn't be so fond of fights, because next time they might have to do the fighting themselves, which would not be the same thing at all. And there was a certain badger in the inn stables which had got to be released at once, and he'd come and see it done himself. Then he told them that the dragon had been thinking over things, and saw that there were two sides to every question, and he wasn't going to do it any more, and if they were good perhaps he'd stay and settle down there. So they must make friends, and not be prejudiced; and go about fancying they knew everything there was to be known, because they didn't, not by a long way. And he warned them against the sin of romancing, and making up stories and fancying other people would believe them just because they were plausible and highly-coloured. Then he sat down, amidst much repentant cheering, and the dragon nudged the Boy in the ribs and whispered that he couldn't have done it better himself. Then everyone went off to get ready for the banquet.

Banquets are always pleasant things, consisting mostly, as they do, of eating and drinking; but the specially nice thing about a banquet is, that it comes when something's over, and there's nothing more to worry about, and tomorrow seems a long way off. St. George was happy because there had been a fight and he hadn't had to kill anybody; for he didn't really like killing, though he generally had to do it. The dragon was happy because there had been a fight, and so far from being hurt in it he had won popularity and a sure footing in society. The Boy was happy because there had been a fight, and in spite of it all his two friends were on the best of terms. And all the others were happy because there had been a fight, and—well, they didn't require any other reasons for their happiness. The dragon exerted himself to say the right thing to everybody, and proved the life and soul of the evening; while the Saint and the Boy, as they looked on, felt that they were only assisting at a feast of which the honour and the glory were entirely the dragon's. But they didn't mind that, being good fellows, and the dragon was not in the least proud or forgetful. On the contrary, every ten minutes or so he leant over towards the Boy and said impressively: "Look here! you will see me home afterwards, won't you?" And the Boy always nodded, though he had promised his mother not to be out late.

At last the banquet was over, the guests had dropped away with many good-nights and congratulations and invitations, and the dragon, who had seen the last of them off the premises, emerged into the street followed by the Boy, wiped his brow, sighed, sat down in the road and gazed at the stars. "Jolly night it's been!" he murmured. "Jolly stars! Jolly little place this! Think I shall just stop here. Don't feel like climbing up any beastly hill. Boy's promised to see me home. Boy had better do it then! No responsibility on my part. Responsibility all Boy's!" And his chin sank on his broad chest and he slumbered peacefully.

"Oh, get up, dragon," cried the Boy, piteously. "You know my mother's sitting up, and I'm so tired, and you made me promise to see you home, and I never knew what it meant or I wouldn't have done it!" And the Boy sat down in the road by the side of the sleeping dragon, and cried.

The door behind them opened, a stream of light illumined the road, and St. George, who had come out for a stroll in the cool night-air, caught sight of the two figures sitting there—the great motionless dragon and the tearful little Boy.

"What's the matter, Boy?" he inquired kindly, stepping to his side.

"Oh, it's this great lumbering *pig* of a dragon!" sobbed the Boy. "First he makes me promise to see him home, and then he says I'd better do it, and goes to sleep! Might as well try to see a *haystack* home! And I'm so tired, and mother's——" here he broke down again.

"Now don't take on," said St. George. "I'll stand by you, and we'll both see him home. Wake up, dragon!" he said sharply, shaking the beast by the elbow.

The dragon looked up sleepily. "What a night, George!" he murmured; "what a——"

"Now look here, dragon," said the Saint, firmly. "Here's this little fellow waiting to see you home, and you *know* he ought to have been in bed these two hours, and what his mother'll say *I* don't know, and anybody but a selfish pig would have *made* him go to bed long ago——"

"And he *shall* go to bed!" cried the dragon, starting up. "Poor little chap, only fancy his being up at this hour! It's a shame, that's what it is, and I don't think, St. George, you've been very considerate—but come along at once, and don't let us have any more arguing or shilly-shallying. You give me hold of your hand, Boy—thank you, George, an arm up the hill is just what I wanted!"

So they set off up the hill arm-in-arm, the Saint, the Dragon, and the Boy. The lights in the little village began to go out; but there were stars, and a late moon, as they climbed to the Downs together. And, as they turned the last corner and disappeared from view, snatches of an old song were borne back on the night-breeze. I can't be certain which of them was singing, but I *think* it was the Dragon!

"Here we are at your gate," said the man, abruptly, laying his hand on it. "Good-night. Cut along in sharp, or you'll catch it!"

Could it really be our own gate? Yes, there it was, sure enough, with the familiar marks on its bottom bar made by our feet when we swung on it.

"Oh, but wait a minute!" cried Charlotte. "I want to know a heap of things. Did the dragon really settle down? And did——"

"There isn't any more of that story," said the man, kindly but firmly. "At least, not tonight. Now be off! Good-bye!"

"Wonder if it's all true?" said Charlotte, as we hurried up the path. "Sounded dreadfully like nonsense, in parts!"

"P'raps it's true for all that," I replied encouragingly.

Charlotte bolted in like a rabbit, out of the cold and the dark; but I lingered a moment in the still, frosty air, for a backward glance at the silent white world without, ere I changed it for the land of firelight and cushions and laughter. It was the day for choir-practice, and carol-time was at hand, and a belated member was passing homewards down the road, singing as he went:

> *Then St. George: ee made rev'rence: in the stable so dim,*
> *Oo vanquished the dragon: so fearful and grim.*
> *So-o grim: and so-o fierce: that now may we say*
> *All peaceful is our wakin': on Chri-istmas Day!*

The singer receded, the carol died away. But I wondered, with my hand on the door-latch, whether that was the song, or something like it, that the dragon sang as he toddled contentedly up the hill.

A Departure

It is a very fine thing to be a real Prince. There are points about a Pirate Chief, and to succeed to the Captaincy of a Robber Band is a truly magnificent thing. But to be an Heir has also about it something extremely captivating. Not only a long-lost heir—an heir of the melodrama, strutting into your hitherto unsuspected kingdom at just the right moment, loaded up with the consciousness of unguessed merit and of rights so long feloniously withheld— but even to be a common humdrum domestic heir is a profession to which few would refuse to be apprenticed. To step from leading-strings and restrictions and one glass of port after dinner, into property and liberty and due appreciation, saved up, polished and varnished, dusted and laid in lavender, all expressly for you—why, even the Princedom and the Robber Captaincy, when their anxieties and responsibilities are considered, have hardly more to offer. And so it will continue to be a problem, to the youth in whom ambition struggles with a certain sensuous appreciation of life's side-dishes, whether the career he is called upon to select out of the glittering knick-knacks that strew the counter had better be that of an heir or an engine-driver.

In the case of eldest sons, this problem has a way of solving itself. In childhood, however, the actual heirship is apt to work on the principle of the "Borough-English" of our happier ancestors, and in most cases of inheritance it is the youngest that succeeds. Where the "res" is "angusta," and the weekly books are simply a series of stiff hurdles at each of which in succession the paternal legs falter with growing suspicion of their powers to clear the flight, it is in the affair of clothes that the right of succession tells, and "the hard heir strides about the land" in trousers long ago framed for fraternal limbs—*frondes novas et non sua poma*. A bitter thing indeed! Of those pretty silken threads that knit humanity together, high and low, past and present, none is tougher, more pervading, or more iridescent, than the honest, simple pleasure of new clothes. It tugs at the man as it tugs at the woman; the smirk of the well-fitted prince is no different from the smirk of the Sunday-clad peasant;

and the veins of the elders tingle with the same thrill that sets their fresh-frocked grandchildren skipping. Never trust people who pretend that they have no joy in their new clothes.

Let not our souls be wrung, however, at contemplation of the luckless urchin cut off by parental penury from the rapture of new clothes. Just as the heroes of his dreams are his immediate seniors, so his heroes' clothes share the glamour, and the reversion of them carries a high privilege—a special thing not sold by Swears and Wells. The sword of Galahad—and of many another hero—arrived on the scene already hoary with history, and the boy rather prefers his trousers to be legendary, famous, haloed by his hero's renown— even though the nap may have altogether vanished in the process.

But, putting clothes aside, there are other matters in which this reversed heirship comes into play. Take the case of Toys. It is hardly right or fitting—and in this the child quite acquiesces—that as he approaches the reverend period of nine or say ten years, he should still be the unabashed and proclaimed possessor of a hoop and a Noah's Ark. The child will quite see the reasonableness of this, and, the goal of his ambition being now a catapult, a pistol, or even a sword-stick, will be satisfied that the titular ownership should lapse to his juniors, so far below him in their kilted or petticoated incompetence. After all, the things are still there, and if relapses of spirit occur, on wet afternoons, one can still (nominally) borrow them and be happy on the floor as of old, without the reproach of being a habitual baby toy-caresser. Also one can pretend it's being done to amuse the younger ones.

None of us, therefore, grumbled when in the natural course of things the nominal ownership of the toys slipped down to Harold, and from him in turn devolved upon Charlotte. The toys were still there; they always had been there and always would be there, and when the nursery door was fast shut there were no Kings or Queens or First Estates in that small Republic on the floor. Charlotte, to be sure, chin-tilted, at last an owner of real estate, might patronize a little at times; but it was tacitly understood that her "title" was only a drawing-room one.

Why does a coming bereavement project no thin faint voice, no shadow of its woe, to warn its happy, heedless victims? Why cannot Olympians ever think it worth while to give some hint of the thunderbolts they are silently forging? And why, oh, why did it never enter any of our thick heads that the day would come when even Charlotte would be considered too matronly for toys? One's so-called education is hammered into one with rulers and with canes. Each fresh grammar or musical instrument, each new historical period or quaint arithmetical rule, is impressed on one by some painful physical prelude. Why does Time, the biggest Schoolmaster, alone neglect premonitory raps, at each stage of his curriculum, on our knuckles or our heads?

Uncle Thomas was at the bottom of it. This was not the first mine he had exploded under our bows. In his favourite pursuit of fads he had passed in turn from Psychical Research to the White Rose and thence to a Children's Hospital, and we were being daily inundated with leaflets headed by a woodcut depicting Little Annie (of Poplar) sitting up in her little white cot, surrounded by the toys of the nice, kind, rich children. The idea caught on with the Olympians, always open to sentiment of a treacly, woodcut order; and accordingly Charlotte, on entering one day dishevelled and panting, having been pursued by yelling Redskins up to the very threshold of our peaceful home, was curtly informed that her French lessons would begin on Monday, that she was henceforth to cease all pretence of being a trapper or a Redskin on utterly inadequate grounds, and moreover that the whole of her toys were at that moment being finally packed up in a box, for despatch to London, to gladden the lives and bring light into the eyes of London waifs and Poplar Annies.

Naturally enough, perhaps, we others received no official intimation of this grave cession of territory. We were not supposed to be interested. Harold had long ago been promoted to a knife—a recognized, birthday knife. As for me, it was known that I was already given over, heart and soul, to lawless abandoned catapults—catapults which were confiscated weekly for reasons of international complications, but with which Edward kept me steadily supplied, his school having a fine old tradition for excellence in their manufacture. Therefore no one was supposed to be really affected but Charlotte, and even she had already reached Miss Yonge, and should therefore have been more interested in prolific curates and harrowing deathbeds.

Notwithstanding, we all felt indignant, betrayed, and sullen to the verge of mutiny. Though for long we had affected to despise them, these toys, yet they had grown up with us, shared our joys and our sorrows, seen us at our worst, and become part of the accepted scheme of existence. As we gazed at untenanted shelves and empty, hatefully tidy corners, perhaps for the first time for long we began to do them a tardy justice.

There was old Leotard, for instance. Somehow he had come to be sadly neglected of late years—and yet how exactly he always responded to certain moods! He was an acrobat, this Leotard, who lived in a glass-fronted box. His loose-jointed limbs were cardboard, cardboard his slender trunk; and his hands eternally grasped the bar of a trapeze. You turned the box round swiftly five or six times; the wonderful unsolved machinery worked, and Leotard swung and leapt, backwards, forwards, now astride the bar, now flying free; iron-jointed, supple-sinewed, unceasingly novel in his invention of new, unguessable attitudes; while above, below, and around him, a richly-dressed audience, painted in skilful perspective of stalls, boxes, dress-circle, and gallery, watched the thrilling performance with a stolidity which seemed to mark them out as made in Germany. Hardly versatile enough, perhaps, this Leotard; unsympathetic, not a companion for all hours; nor would you have chosen him to take to bed with you. And yet, within his own limits, how fresh, how engrossing, how resourceful and inventive! Well, he was gone, it seemed—merely gone. Never specially cherished while he tarried with us, he had yet contrived to build himself a particular niche of his own. Sunrise and sunset, and the dinner-bell, and the sudden rainbow, and lessons, and Leotard, and the moon through the nursery windows—they were all part of the great order of things, and the displacement of any one item seemed to disorganize the whole machinery. The immediate point was, not that the world would continue to go round as of old, but that Leotard wouldn't.

Yonder corner, now swept and garnished, had been the stall wherein the spotty horse, at the close of each laborious day, was accustomed to doze peacefully the long night through. In days of old each of us in turn had been jerked thrillingly round the room on his precarious back, had dug our heels into his unyielding sides, and had scratched our hands on the tin tacks that secured his mane to his stiffly-curving neck. Later, with increasing stature, we came to overlook his merits as a beast of burden; but how frankly, how good-naturedly, he had recognized the new conditions, and adapted himself to them without a murmur! When the military spirit was abroad, who so ready to be a squadron of cavalry, a horde of Cossacks, or artillery pounding into position? He had even served with honour as a gun-boat, during a period when naval strategy was the only theme; and no false equine pride ever hindered him from taking the part of a roaring locomotive, earth-shaking, clangorous, annihilating time and space. Really it was no longer clear how life, with its manifold emergencies, was to be carried on at all without a fellow like the spotty horse, ready to step in at critical moments and take up just the part required of him.

In moments of mental depression, nothing is quite so consoling as the honest smell of a painted animal; and mechanically I turned towards the shelf that had been so long the Ararat of our weather-beaten Ark. The shelf was empty, the Ark had cast off moorings and sailed away to Poplar, and had taken with it its haunting smell, as well as that pleasant sense of disorder that the best conducted Ark is always able to impart. The sliding roof had rarely been known to close entirely. There was always a pair of giraffe-legs sticking out, or an elephant-trunk, taking from the stiffness of its outline, and reminding us that our motley crowd of friends inside were uncomfortably cramped for room and only too ready to leap in a cascade on the floor and browse and gallop, flutter and bellow and neigh, and be their natural selves again. I think that none of us ever really thought very much of Ham and Shem and Japhet. They were only there because they were in the story, but nobody really wanted them. The Ark was built for the animals, of course—animals with tails, and trunks, and horns, and at least three legs apiece, though some unfortunates had been unable to retain even that number. And in the animals were of course included the birds—the dove, for instance, grey with black wings, and the red-crested woodpecker—or was it a hoopoe?—and the insects, for there was a dear beetle, about the same size as the dove, that held its own with any of the mammalia.

Of the doll-department Charlotte had naturally been sole chief for a long time; if the staff were not in their places today, it was not I who had any official right to take notice. And yet one may have been member of a Club for many a year without ever exactly understanding the use and object of the other members, until one enters, some Christmas day or other holiday, and, surveying the deserted armchairs, the untenanted sofas, the barren hat-pegs, realizes, with depression, that those other fellows had their allotted functions, after all. Where was old Jerry? Where were Eugenie, Rosa, Sophy, Esmeralda? We had long drifted apart, it was true, we spoke but rarely; perhaps, absorbed in new ambitions, new achievements, I had even come to look down on these conservative, unprogressive members who were so clearly content to remain simply what they were. And now that their corners were unfilled, their chairs unoccupied—well, my eyes were opened and I wanted 'em back!

However, it was no business of mine. If grievances were the question, I hadn't a leg to stand upon. Though my catapults were officially confiscated, I knew the drawer in which they were incarcerated, and where the key of it was hidden, and I could make life a burden, if I chose, to every living thing within a square-mile radius, so long as the catapult was restored to its drawer in due and decent time. But I wondered how the others were taking it. The edict hit them more severely. They should have my moral countenance at any rate, if not more, in any protest or countermine they might be planning. And, indeed, something seemed possible, from the dogged, sullen air with which the two of them had trotted off in the direction of the raspberry-canes. Certain spots always had their insensible attraction for certain moods. In love, one sought the orchard. Weary of discipline, sick of convention, impassioned for the road, the mining-camp, the land across the border, one made for the big meadow. Mutinous, sulky, charged with plots and conspiracies, one always got behind the shelter of the raspberry-canes.

* * * * *

"You can come too if you like," said Harold, in a subdued sort of way, as soon as he was aware that I was sitting up in bed watching him. "We didn't think you'd care, 'cos you've got to catapults. But we're goin' to do what we've settled to do, so it's no good sayin' we hadn't ought and that sort of thing, 'cos we're goin' to!"

The day had passed in an ominous peacefulness. Charlotte and Harold had kept out of my way, as well as out of everybody else's, in a purposeful manner that ought to have bred suspicion. In the evening we had read books, or fitfully drawn ships and battles on fly-leaves, apart, in separate corners, void of conversation or criticism, oppressed by the lowering tidiness of the universe, till bedtime came, and disrobement, and prayers even more mechanical than usual, and lastly bed itself without so much as a giraffe under the pillow. Harold had grunted himself between the sheets with an ostentatious pretence of overpowering fatigue; but I noticed that he pulled his pillow forward and propped his head against the brass bars of his crib, and, as I was acquainted with most of his tricks and subterfuges, it was easy for me to gather that a painful wakefulness was his aim that night.

I had dozed off, however, and Harold was out and on his feet, poking under the bed for his shoes, when I sat up and grimly regarded him. Just as he said I could come if I liked, Charlotte slipped in, her face rigid and set. And then it was borne in upon me that I was not on in this scene. These youngsters had planned it all out, the piece was their own, and the mounting, and the cast. My sceptre had fallen, my rule had ceased. In this magic hour of the summer night laws went for nothing, codes were cancelled, and those who were most in touch with the moonlight and the warm June spirit and the topsy-turvydom that reigns when the clock strikes ten, were the true lords and lawmakers.

Humbly, almost timidly, I followed without a protest in the wake of these two remorseless, purposeful young persons, who were marching straight for the schoolroom. Here in the moonlight the grim big box stood visible—the box in which so large a portion of our past and our personality lay entombed, cold, swathed in paper, awaiting the carrier of the morning who should speed them forth to the strange, cold, distant Children's Hospital, where their little failings would all be misunderstood and no one would make allowances. A dreamy spectator, I stood idly by while Harold propped up the lid and the two plunged in their arms and probed and felt and grappled.

"Here's Rosa," said Harold, suddenly. "I know the feel of her hair. Will you have Rosa out?"

"Oh, give me Rosa!" cried Charlotte with a sort of gasp. And when Rosa had been dragged forth, quite unmoved apparently, placid as ever in her moonfaced contemplation of this comedy-world with its ups and downs, Charlotte retired with her to the window-seat, and there in the moonlight the two exchanged their private confidences, leaving Harold to his exploration alone.

"Here's something with sharp corners," said Harold, presently. "Must be Leotard, I think. Better let *him* go."

"Oh, yes, we can't save Leotard," assented Charlotte, limply.

Poor old Leotard! I said nothing, of course; I was not on in this piece. But, surely, had Leotard heard and rightly understood all that was going on above him, he must have sent up one feeble, strangled cry, one faint appeal to be rescued from unfamiliar little Annies and retained for an audience certain to appreciate and never unduly critical.

"Now I've got to the Noah's Ark," panted Harold, still groping blindly.

"Try and shove the lid back a bit," said Charlotte, "and pull out a dove or a zebra or a giraffe if there's one handy."

Harold toiled on with grunts and contortions, and presently produced in triumph a small grey elephant and a large beetle with a red stomach.

"They're jammed in too tight," he complained. "Can't get any more out. But as I came up I'm sure I felt Potiphar!" And down he dived again.

Potiphar was a finely modelled bull with a suede skin, rough and comfortable and warm in bed. He was my own special joy and pride, and I thrilled with honest emotion when Potiphar emerged to light once more, stout-necked and stalwart as ever.

"That'll have to do," said Charlotte, getting up. "We dursn't take any more, 'cos we'll be found out if we do. Make the box all right, and bring 'em along."

Harold rammed down the wads of paper and twists of straw he had disturbed, replaced the lid squarely and innocently, and picked up his small salvage; and we sneaked off for the window most generally in use for prison-breakings and nocturnal escapades. A few seconds later and we were hurrying silently in single file along the dark edge of the lawn.

Oh, the riot, the clamour, the crowding chorus, of all silent things that spoke by scent and colour and budding thrust and foison, that moonlit night of June! Under the laurel-shade all was still ghostly enough, brigand-haunted, crackling, whispering of night and all its possibilities of terror. But the open garden, when once we were in it—how it turned a glad new face to welcome us, glad as of old when the sunlight raked and searched it, new with the unfamiliar night-aspect that yet welcomed us as guests to a hall where the horns blew up to a new, strange banquet! Was this the same grass, could these be the same familiar flower-beds, alleys, clumps of verdure, patches of sward? At least this full white light that was flooding them was new, and accounted for all. It was Moonlight Land, and Past-Ten-o'clock Land, and we were in it and of it, and all its other denizens fully understood, and, tongue-free and awakened at last, responded and comprehended and knew. The other two, doubtless, hurrying forward full of their mission, noted little of all this. I, who was only a super, had leisure to take it all in, and, though the language and the message of the land were not all clear to me then, long afterwards I remembered and understood.

Under the farthest hedge, at the loose end of things, where the outer world began with the paddock, there was darkness once again—not the blackness that crouched so solidly under the crowding laurels, but a duskiness hung from far-spread arms of high-standing elms. There, where the small grave made a darker spot on the grey, I overtook them, only just in time to see Rosa laid stiffly out, her cherry cheeks pale in the moonlight, but her brave smile triumphant and undaunted as ever. It was a tiny grave and a shallow one, to hold so very much. Rosa once in, Potiphar, who had hitherto stood erect, stout-necked, through so many days and such various weather, must needs bow his head and lie down meekly on his side. The elephant and the beetle, equal now in a silent land where a vertebra and a red circulation counted for nothing, had to snuggle down where best they might, only a little less crowded than in their native Ark.

The earth was shovelled in and stamped down, and I was glad that no orisons were said and no speechifying took place. The whole thing was natural and right and self-explanatory, and needed no justifying or interpreting to our audience of stars and flowers.

The connection was not entirely broken now—one link remained between us and them. The Noah's Ark, with its cargo of sad-faced emigrants, might be hull down on the horizon, but two of its passengers had missed the boat and would henceforth be always near us; and, as we played above them, an elephant would understand, and a beetle would hear, and crawl again in spirit along a familiar floor. Henceforth the spotty horse would scour along far-distant plains and know the homesickness of alien stables; but Potiphar, though never again would he paw the arena when bull-fights were on the bill, was spared maltreatment by town-bred strangers, quite capable of mistaking him for a cow. Jerry and Esmeralda might shed their limbs and their stuffing, by slow or swift degrees, in uttermost parts and unguessed corners of the globe; but Rosa's book was finally closed, and no worse fate awaited her than natural dissolution almost within touch and hail of familiar faces and objects that had been friendly to her since first she opened her eyes on a world where she had never been treated as a stranger.

As we turned to go, the man in the moon, tangled in elm-boughs, caught my eye for a moment, and I thought that never had he looked so friendly. He was going to see after them, it was evident; for he was always there, more or less, and it was no trouble to him at all, and he would tell them how things were still going, up here, and throw in a story or two of his own whenever they seemed a trifle dull. It made the going away rather easier, to know one had left somebody behind on the spot; a good fellow, too, cheery, comforting, with a fund of anecdote; a man in whom one had every confidence.

Word Cloud Classics

Adventures of Huckleberry Finn

The Adventures of Sherlock Holmes

Aesop's Fables

The Age of Innocence

Alice's Adventures in Wonderland
and Through the Looking-Glass

Anna Karenina

Anne of Green Gables

The Art of War

The Autobiography of Benjamin
Franklin and Other Writings

The Awakening and Other Stories

The Beautiful and Damned
and Other Stories

Black Beauty

The Brothers Grimm 101 Fairy Tales

The Brothers Grimm Volume II:
110 Grimmer Fairy Tales

Bulfinch's Mythology:
Stories of Gods and Heroes

The Call of the Wild and Other Stories

A Christmas Carol and Other
Holiday Treasures

Classic Horror Tales

Classic Westerns: Zane Grey

Common Sense and Selected
Works of Thomas Paine

The Count of Monte Cristo

Crime and Punishment

Don Quixote

Dracula

Dubliners & A Portrait of the Artist
as a Young Man and Other Works

Emma

Frankenstein

Great Expectations

Hans Christian Andersen Tales

H. P. Lovecraft Cthulhu Mythos Tales

Inferno

The Inventions, Researches, and
Writings of Nikola Tesla

Jane Eyre

The Jungle Book

Lady Chatterley's Lover

Leaves of Grass

The Legend of Sleepy Hollow
and Other Tales

Word Cloud Classics

Les Misérables

Little Women

Madame Bovary

Mansfield Park

The Merry Adventures of Robin Hood

Moby-Dick

My Ántonia

Narrative of the Life of Frederick Douglass and Other Works

Northanger Abbey

Odyssey

Persuasion

Peter Pan

The Phantom of the Opera

The Picture of Dorian Gray

The Poetry of Emily Dickinson

Presidential Inaugural Addresses

Pride and Prejudice

The Prince and Other Writings

The Red Badge of Courage and Other Stories

The Romantic Poets

The Scarlet Letter

The Secret Garden

Selected Works of Alexander Hamilton

Sense and Sensibility

Shakespeare's Sonnets and Other Poems

Strange Case of Dr. Jekyll and Mr. Hyde & Other Stories

Tarzan of the Apes & The Return of Tarzan

The Three Musketeers

Treasure Island

12 Years a Slave

Twenty Thousand Leagues Under the Sea

Uncle Tom's Cabin, or Life Among the Lowly

The U.S. Constitution and Other Key American Writings

Walden and Civil Disobedience

The Wind in the Willows and Other Stories

The Wizard of Oz

Wuthering Heights